Praise for the
New York Times bestselling author
CHRISTINE WARREN

Heart of Stone

"The opening of Warren's hot new paranormal series is a snarky, creative, and steamy success that delights new and longtime fans alike." —*RT Book Reviews* (4 stars)

"The sexual attraction . . . is palpable." —*Publishers Weekly*

"Steamy scenes, mixed with an intriguing story line and a hearty helping of snarky humor." —*Reader to Reader*

"Rousing . . . [an] engaging urban fantasy."
—*Midwest Book Review*

"Fast-paced with characters you'll love, and even some you'll love to hate, *Heart of Stone* is another winner for author Christine Warren!" —*Romance Reviews*

Stone Cold Lover

"Soars with fun, witty characters and nonstop action."
—*Publishers Weekly*

"Fascinating, complex, and so well crafted . . . perfect for keeping fans . . . coming back for more."
—*RT Book Reviews* (4 stars)

Hard as a Rock

"Fiery, fierce, and fun." —*Publishers Weekly*

"Smoldering hot . . . the stakes are fatally high and the chemistry [is] simply blistering." —*RT Book Reviews*

Also by
Christine Warren

Hard to Handle
Hard as a Rock
Stone Cold Lover
Heart of Stone
Hungry Like a Wolf
Drive Me Wild
On the Prowl
Not Your Ordinary Faerie Tale
Black Magic Woman
Prince Charming Doesn't Live Here
Born to Be Wild
Big Bad Wolf
You're So Vein
One Bite with a Stranger
Walk on the Wild Side
Howl at the Moon
The Demon You Know
She's No Faerie Princess
Wolf at the Door

Anthologies

Huntress
No Rest for the Witches

Hard Breaker

Christine Warren

St. Martin's Paperbacks

This is a work of fiction. All of the characters, organizations, and events portrayed in this novel are either products of the author's imagination or are used fictitiously.

HARD BREAKER

Copyright © 2017 by Christine Warren.
Excerpt from *Baby, I'm Howling for You* copyright © 2017 by Christine Warren.

All rights reserved.

For information address St. Martin's Press, 175 Fifth Avenue, New York, NY 10010.

ISBN: 978-1-250-07739-4

Our books may be purchased in bulk for promotional, educational, or business use. Please contact your local bookseller or the Macmillan Corporate and Premium Sales Department at 1-800-221-7945, ext. 5442, or by e-mail at MacmillanSpecialMarkets@macmillan.com.

Printed in the United States of America

St. Martin's Paperbacks edition / November 2017

St. Martin's Paperbacks are published by St. Martin's Press, 175 Fifth Avenue, New York, NY 10010.

10 9 8 7 6 5 4 3 2 1

For my Girl,
because everything is different without her.
I miss you, Flopsy.

The Beginning

Once upon a time when the world was young and magic lived, a tenuous balance existed between the Light and the Darkness. The Light created and the Darkness destroyed. The Light illuminated and the Darkness obscured. The Light gave and the Darkness seized.

But in all things, the Darkness grew discontented. It sent its servants among the inhabitants of the earth to sway humanity into its thrall. It gathered power to itself, but the more it gained, the more it wanted.

It shaped itself into the form of Seven Demons, creatures of pure evil that existed only to feed on the souls of humanity. Glutted with strength, they would join together and devour the Light itself.

Humanity quaked. Against the powers of the Darkness, most had no defenses. Only those gifted with the ability to wield the energy of magic could affect the Darkness and its servants. These few joined together as Wardens, forming a Guild to stand against evil, but even they lacked the strength for victory. They needed a weapon of immense power, something that could only be granted by the Light itself. Joining their magic, they performed a spell of summoning and brought forth the Guardians.

Seven warriors answered the summoning, created by the Light to be its champions. Enormous, immortal figures, winged and powerful, descended from the skies. Each wielded a weapon in hand, but also possessed fangs and claws to tear apart their enemies. They became the Guardians of humanity and fought a long and bloody war against the Demons of the Darkness.

Blood spilled and the earth trembled, but at the end of the struggle, the Guardians of the Light prevailed. They tore the Seven Demons apart and cast them from the mortal plane into prisons prepared by the Wardens. Their duty finished, they stood among the humans as warriors without a war, inhuman, alien, and powerful. The Wardens of the Guild felt the Guardians had no place on the mortal plane and used their magic to send the immortal warriors into slumber. Encased in skins of stone, they slept through ages of men until once again, the Darkness threatened to break free into the world of humans.

The Guardians once again completed their task of ridding the human world of the threat from the Demons, and once again they were sent to slumber by the Wardens. They woke, they fought, and they slept. Time after time after time.

Eventually, the first Guardians lost any interest in protecting humanity. They had no connection to the people they defended, spent no time with them, and knew little of their characters or their customs. After several cycles, a time came when the Wardens summoned the Guardians to defend them from a new threat, but the Guardians did not wake. They failed to respond to the humans' need, and it looked as if the mortal world would fall to the Darkness.

The Guild despaired. Until one day, a woman of power—one who had magic of her own—appeared and ignored the Wardens' attempts to dismiss her. She knew the danger to humanity was great and that the Guardians represented the only hope for her people to survive. So she knelt at the feet of the statue of a Guardian and she prayed for him to awaken and defend her. The Wardens scoffed and berated her, but her pleas worked. The Guardian responded to her as if to a summons and woke from his magical slumber. He claimed the woman as his Warden and his mate and once again took up arms against the Darkness.

One by one, more women of power appeared and woke the Guardians, becoming their helpers and their mates. The supernatural warriors defeated the forces of Darkness, but once the threat was vanquished, they refused to return to sleep and be parted from their mates. Instead, they remained among the humans, giving up their immortality to live out their days with their partners. New Guardians were summoned, and the legends recorded that any who came after retained the right to find a human mate and to forfeit their position to remain at her side.

Prologue

Ivy turned, the covers tangled around her legs, but she didn't feel it. Or rather, it didn't register, her mind already occupied with a source of far greater discomfort. It echoed within her, loud, agonized, and dreadfully familiar.

I call thee forth, warrior of stone, to stand against the Enemy of All. Stir, and awaken.

Uncle George? In sleep, her brow furrowed and her head twisted on the pillow. She knew the voice but not the words. Mom's brother, confirmed eccentric. Black sheep in a family of decidedly gray ones. The one who spoke openly about magic and supernatural gifts and some endless, covert struggle against the forces of Darkness. As a child, Ivy had found his stories as chilling and exciting as the ones about the hook-handed killer, or the witch who appeared to steal your soul if you chanted her name three times into your mirror. She had never believed any of them, but she had sat and listened, wide-eyed and enthralled, to each and every one.

Dad, I just heard something. I think someone is out there.

Jamie's voice now, just as familiar. If Ivy had listened

intently to her uncle's stories, his son had hung on every word, learning them like holy gospel. Visits to and from the U.K. had never happened often enough, and Ivy had always looked wildly forward to the chance to reconnect and play with the cousin who had been a bare year older than herself. But while she had wanted to play ball or cops and robbers or intrepid jungle explorers, all Jamie wanted was to play at being Wardens and protecting the world from the demon invasion. Strangely enough, not games her friends in suburban New York had prepared her for. She always felt as if she had gotten the wrong script. She had played along, though, because Jamie was just that convincing.

And also because there wasn't much else to do at Uncle George's country house.

The familiarity bred by those long visits meant that even asleep, Ivy's subconscious had no trouble recognizing George's and Jamie's well-loved voices. Their tones, though . . . those made her frown in her sleep and twist again atop her rapidly warming mattress.

I need a few more minutes, boy. I have to complete the summoning. Once he wakes, we'll have nothing to fear.

Once who wakes? Ivy wanted to ask. What was going on? She could hear urgency and fear underlying her uncle's cool, British reserve, the same emotions that bubbled over in her cousin's words, but as usual, she could see nothing. Her talent never allowed her to put any images to what she heard. Clairaudience, the experts labeled it. Eavesdropping fit better. At least, Ivy thought so. Clairaudience sounded too scientific, as if she had some kind of radio receiver inside her head that she could tune to a certain frequency to pick up whatever sounds she wanted at any given time.

Wouldn't that have been convenient? But no, Ivy

hadn't gotten so lucky. Instead of that radio receiver, she had gotten the same sort of reception as the poor schmuck in that old joke whose tooth filling occasionally made opera broadcasts spill out whenever he opened his mouth. Ivy never got to choose what she could hear. It only came to her at the moments she least wanted to hear, moments filled with anger or fear or soul-wrenching grief. It had to be powered by emotion, and somehow the most powerful emotions always seemed to be the most painful ones.

Clairaudial empathy, someone had suggested as a label. Ivy just called it her curse.

She began to struggle against the choking grip of sleep. Her subconscious recognized the fear in her cousin's voice, the urgency in her uncle's. She might not know what the two of them were talking about inside her head, but she knew it was important, and she knew they felt as if they might be in danger. If she didn't wake up, she would be unable to help them.

Hell, she might not be able to help them anyway, but at least if she were awake, she might have a chance. Asleep, she only counted as so much dead weight.

Lethargy clung to her. Ivy fought hard, but somehow the unconsciousness seemed to fight back, holding her down like a hand in the face of a drowning victim. She even found herself struggling to breathe the same way, and it got harder to tell the difference between her relatives' fear and her own mounting panic.

Wake up, Ivy, she commanded herself. *They need you. Wake up and get them help. Do it. Now.*

Come forth, Guardian. Uncle George spoke with both authority and a new sense of urgency, a frantic sort of demand. It sounded almost like desperation.

A crash echoed in her mind, the kind of boom that

would have shaken the ground of the surrounding area. Ivy could almost swear she felt the vibrations.

Hurry up, Dad. We need to get out of here. They're coming.

I know. I'm trying. The spell isn't working, though. Something is wrong.

Another thundering crash, and Jamie swore. *We need to leave. We can try another night.*

No, we can't. If they find him here in this state, they can destroy him. He needs to waken, otherwise all we've done is lead the Order straight to him.

We don't have time.

We don't have a choice.

There was a moment of silence. Well, not so much silence as the absence of voices. The bone-rattling booms continued, like God's door knocker being plied by the devil himself.

Maybe we do. We can hide him.

How? her uncle demanded. He sounded confused and testy, like someone had presented him with a mug of tea without offering up a biscuit alongside. *He's a bit bloody hard to miss, don't you think?*

I found a spell, Jamie said. *In that book you dug up a few weeks ago. It's supposed to be undetectable, even to the* nocturnis. *I have it memorized. It's got to at least be worth a try.*

The next boom came louder than the others, if that was possible, and was accompanied by a sharp cracking sound, like wood splitting under the blade of an axe.

I don't think we have any choice, Jamie insisted. *We've run out of time.*

Another pause.

Do it.

Ivy heard a rush of air, like a deep inhalation, then the

sound of her cousin chanting something in a language she almost recognized. Not French, which she spoke a little, and not Latin, which she didn't, but something similar and just out of her reach.

She might not recognize the words, but she had no trouble with the cadence. Jamie spoke quickly, his voice low and urgent, full of power and will. She recognized it from all the times he had stayed up late into the night while her family visited him, after the adults thought them both tucked safely into bed. The wall between their rooms hadn't been thick enough to hide the fact that every spare moment not spent playing at being just like his father, Jamie had been studying so that one day he *would* be just like his father. He couldn't hide it from Ivy, though. Little pseudosisters could be better than spymasters when curiosity and twinges of jealousy spurred them forward.

You've done it, Uncle George cried, sounding almost as surprised as he did relieved. *Now we need to disappear, too. Come on.*

All at once, the booming and the cracking ceased and a deafening explosion reverberated in their place. It shook Ivy even in sleep, and though she still could see nothing, she could hear, mixed with the echo of the sonic wave, the patter of stone falling like rain, and dust whooshing along as if caught in the wake of a hurricane.

Then there was silence.

Terrible, black, empty, suffocating silence.

Ivy shot out of sleep, sitting up in a rush of motion, choking on the air she struggled to draw into protesting lungs. Her bedroom remained dark and still, but the sounds of collapsing rubble still filled her head. Her heart raced as if she had just run a marathon. A slick film of sweat coated her skin, making her thin cotton gown cling to her uncomfortably. She trembled from head to toe as the reality of what she had heard began to sink in.

"Jamie," she whispered into the night. "Uncle George. What have you done?"

With shaking hands, she fumbled for her phone and silently began to pray.

Chapter One

She had spent a week casing the joint, or at least that's how she liked to think of it. It calmed her nerves to view these things in terms of B-movie plots. Keeping the notion of danger mildly amusing instead of terrifying made it easier to do her job without ill-timed cases of the freak-outs.

It also made it easy to slip out the staff door at the rear of the pub at the proper time and return through the front five minutes later looking like an entirely different person. Her bag had been stashed in the alley behind the bins, well wrapped in plastic. She continued to hold out hope that one of these days she'd get to Scooby-Doo it and use a hole in a big old oak tree as her hiding place, but those were hard to come by in Croydon, South London. A girl had to work with what was available.

She wouldn't call her new appearance a disguise, exactly. More like camouflage. The secret wasn't to not be recognized (extremely unlikely given the total number of people she knew in this country had been cut in half a few months ago), it was to not stand out. Her natural coloring of bright red hair and glow-in-the-dark pale skin drew too many eyes, so she covered them up with something a little more common. Pancake makeup took care of the pallor, and to complete the picture, she had slathered on lipstick the approximate color of a double-decker bus and enough mascara and eyeliner to make a raccoon feel insecure. A wig sporting dark roots and brassy blond highlights covered up her own distinctive strands and presented just the right level of delinquent hair-color maintenance to make her convincing as a lapsed brunette.

Since clothes made the woman, she paid attention to those as well. Her tight skinny jeans disappeared into a pair of bulky, unstructured boots that looked like they belonged on either a moon landing or an unfortunate Inuit. Personally, she thought they were uglier than sin, but they possessed the twin virtues of an inexplicable claim to being "in" and flat soles. The suckers might be hideous, but at least they didn't hamper her movement.

Over the jeans—or, rather, above the jeans—she wore a midriff-skimming sweater in bright pink with a label that had absolutely no claim on reality. Topping it all, her anorak of shiny silver and faux-fur trim hung open, the better to display both the occasional flashes of belly her sweater revealed and the Burberry check scarf that hung around her neck. Another knockoff, of course, but it was the check that counted around here.

She looked as if she'd been born down the next street, meaning absolutely no one within a one-mile radius would bother looking at her twice. That was exactly how she wanted it.

Ivy pushed through the front door and into the Friday-night crowd, feeling a surge of nostalgia for the clouds of smoke that hadn't floated through the air of British pubs in decades. It would have lent things a certain Sherlock Holmesian air she would have appreciated. Instead, she had a clear view all the way from the tap to the back corner of the room. She could see exactly what she had come here for.

Pasting a casual smile on her face, Ivy began to weave her way through the crowd. She might be keeping her eye on the prize, but that didn't mean she wasn't keeping track of the bodies around her for more than the usual reason of not running into one of them and making a fool of herself. Situational awareness had become a hard-earned skill of hers since she'd gotten involved in her little side business here in London, and it had come in handy on more than one occasion.

Like now, when she tried to move past a knot of local lads cozied up to the bar.

She had made a mental note of them earlier, when she'd been lurking in her previous camouflaged incarnation, just as she'd made a mental note of the older couples occupying several tables, the group of ladies gathered for an obvious hen night, and the middle-aged men with their attention glued to the television in the corner that broadcast a seemingly nonstop schedule of football matches. Unlike those other groups, though, Ivy had made note of the lads because she knew they were the ones most likely to cause her trouble.

And now it appeared they didn't want to disappoint her. How sweet.

"Well, hello there, sweetheart. Buy you a drink?"

The young man closest to her reached out to pinch the fabric of her coat and tug her to a stop, all the while flashing her a crooked grin he probably practiced in his bathroom mirror, thinking it made him look rakish and charming. It might have even worked had the rest of him not screamed out "yob" at the top of its lungs. She couldn't go so far as to call him a chav (mostly due to fashion choice), but he bore the look of someone with an ASBO or five on his police record.

She replied with a studious avoidance of eye contact and a patently false, close-lipped smile. "Thanks, no. I'm meeting someone."

A couple of his mates snickered into their lagers, which of course did not help her escape attempt.

He tried another smile, but his eyes had narrowed. "Aw, don't be like that, love. Me name's Teddy. What's yours, eh?"

"Busy," Ivy said, revoking the smile and shrugging out of his grip.

She didn't wait for attempt number three, just plowed forward and refocused on her goal. Good thing, too, because said goal had taken on the slight grayish pallor of incipient panic. She needed to settle him down and get their plan back on track.

She also needed to ignore the mumbled curses and rather vile suggestions Teddy threw at her back as she left him to his friends. What a charmer, that one.

A few more strides and a couple of last-minute weaves brought her to the small table she'd been aiming for. The occupant stood at her approach, then had to reach out to steady the glasses resting on the wooden surface because he'd nearly knocked them over with the nervous energy of his movements. Ivy hid a wince behind a bright smile and reached up to peck the complete stranger right on the lips.

The things she did for duty.

Not that the stranger was physically repulsive, or anything. Frankly, he looked just like she'd expected—tall, a little gangly, with graying, light brown hair that had begun to recede just a bit above the temples, and tortoise-shell glasses that gave him the air of an insecure junior accountant. His name was Martin, she knew, and it suited him. He looked like a Martin. He also looked to be about thirty seconds away from puking on his own shoes. She needed to get him to calm the heck down before they could move on to step two of their prearranged plan.

"Hello, sweetie. Did you order me a drink?"

She kept her tone breezy and her voice just loud enough to be heard at the neighboring tables. Her accent sounded like a careful combination of RP and the Estuary accent. Think Judi Dench meets Russell Brand. It gave the careful impression that she was from London, was a member the working middle class, had a respectable position in an office somewhere local, but was looking to move up in the world. Amazing what the English could convey with no more than a couple of vowel sounds, wasn't it?

"Ta for that." She settled into her seat and tugged Martin down next to her. "Lord, what a week. I'm totally fagged. How was your day?"

For a moment, the man just stared at her, eyes wide and jaw slack. It took a stealthy kick to his shins beneath the table before he managed to stutter out a squeaky version of, "Oh, fine. Just fine, love. G-glad you're here."

Ivy smiled again and lifted her glass of ale, deliberately clicking the edge against his and meeting his gaze pointedly. "Me, too. Here's to our weekend, then."

"T-t-to our w-weekend." Martin didn't manage to force a smile, but at least he raised his pint and took a drink. Frankly, he looked like whisky would have done him better than beer at that moment. He all but radiated nervous energy, which just made her job more challenging. Lucky her.

"Come here, sweetie," she cooed, adopting a flirtatious expression. "I've missed you." She covered her hand with his, gave a squeeze, and leaned into him as if nuzzling playfully. Taking advantage of the appearance of intimacy, she hissed a few instructions into his ear. "Relax, Martin. Take a few deep breaths and remember the plan I e-mailed you. Did you memorize it?" Ivy waited for his jerky nod before she continued. "Good. Then everything is going to be fine. I have it under control, okay? I've done this a dozen times. The *nocturnis* are not going to get their hands on you, but you need to calm down and remember your part. I'll get you to the Guild. I promise."

There was a moment of silence while he digested her words, but after a shaky inhalation, Martin nodded and wrapped one arm around her in an only slightly awkward embrace. "Yes, sorry," he muttered. "This is all freaking me out, but I'll get a grip. Sorry."

Ivy picked up her beer again, but remained leaning against her companion, giving the impression of a couple in love out for a night together. In her experience, it was the kind of cover least likely to be questioned and easiest to fabricate on short notice. That was why she had so often relied on it since she'd begun her work smuggling Wardens in hiding along an improvised sort of Underground Railroad. The network had sprung up over the last year after it had become obvious that the latest strategy of the Order of Eternal Darkness was to eliminate the Guild of Wardens to thus ease the way for the return of their demonic masters to the realm of humanity.

Call her crazy, but Ivy figured that if a worthy cause had ever existed, then saving the earth from an apocalyptic war and enslavement by the forces of evil was it. She'd joined right up. You know, after she'd overheard her uncle and cousin becoming casualties of that war. Losing loved ones proved to be one hell of a motivator.

Martin was just the latest in the list of Wardens she had helped get out of England and to the relative safety of France, where their Guild had once been headquartered. The Guild itself had been destroyed by the Order, whose members were better known as *nocturnis,* but Ivy's research (more like half-blind poking around, really) had unearthed the existence of a resistance network dedicated to keeping any remaining Guild members safe and hidden from the Order. Contacts in the area around Paris had established a secret refuge, first gathering the few Wardens who had rushed to the city upon learning of the Guild headquarters' destruction by fiery magical attack. Then they began slowly taking in the more outlying members who had gone into hiding once it became clear their kind was being systematically hunted and eliminated by the servants of the Darkness.

Safety in numbers was the rallying cry, plus the Wardens had begun to realize that with more than three-quarters of their number dead and most of the rest reported missing, they needed to join together if they were going to come up with any way to stop the Order's plans to release the Seven Demons of Darkness from their magical prisons. That being their end goal, natch. Once freed, the Seven would be able to join together and bring Eternal Darkness to the human world, killing and enslaving all of existence, feeding off the souls and life-blood of humanity. Only one thing had ever successfully prevented that exact doom—the Guardians of the Light— and as far as anyone in the Guild could tell, those guys had gone completely MIA. No one had been able to figure out where they were, though Ivy's Paris contact assured her the search was the surviving Wardens' top priority.

Getting Martin to join in was adding one more soldier to the battle, and was the only way Ivy had found to cope with the deaths of her family. Some might call it revenge, and she was fine with that. As far as she was concerned, revenge was entirely justified. She didn't care if it was served cold, warm, or buffet style; she would have seconds, please.

Lifting her glass, Ivy sipped her malty beer and used

the opportunity to glance at the area immediately surrounding their table. The pub was doing a brisk trade typical of Friday evening as people stopped for a drink and a last chat with coworkers, settled in for a night spent downing pints and cheering the football, or met up with family and friends for a brief libation before moving on to the rest of their evening's entertainments. Exactly as Ivy and her companion appeared to be doing.

A pub provided the perfect setting for Ivy and an ideal launching point for her mission to meet with Martin, go over their arrangements, and then set off on the journey that would ultimately see him settled safely with the other surviving Wardens in France. The Friday-night crowd provided additional cover as it decreased the chances that anyone would find her and Martin any more interesting than the next white, heterosexual, working-class couple in the place. Blend in and move on. She used the motto so often, she ought to break down and cross-stitch that sucker on a pillowcase.

In her copious spare time.

No one appeared to be paying them any particular attention. Even good old Teddy had turned his back to their table, so Ivy let herself relax a little, though she kept her voice low as she spoke to Martin behind a casual smile.

"So, you got the information I e-mailed, and you memorized it, which means you ought to know basically what's going to happen," she said, leaning close like an adoring lover. "We have to stay here long enough to finish our drinks like any other couple. Blending in is the most important part of this whole operation, and the more you relax, the better you'll be at it. Got it?"

Martin took another long pull of his beer and nodded. The shaking in his hand appeared to be subsiding, so Ivy was going to call that a win.

"Good. A few more minutes here, and then we can leave. You're going to hold my hand, because that will look natural, but it will also insure that we don't get separated and that you keep up with me. You need to keep up. I'm as sure as I can be that nothing will go wrong, but if it does, we may need to move fast, and I can't be worried about losing you."

His Adam's apple bobbed, but he continued to meet her gaze, even though his eyes remained wide behind the lenses of his glasses. Poor guy. His life would have been a hell of a lot easier if he hadn't been born a Warden. He'd have made an excellent accountant. Or insurance actuary. Maybe a reference librarian. Something solitary and safe, with fewer soul-stealing demons to contend with.

"I'll do my best," he said, managing not to stutter through the brief statement. Ivy felt like cheering.

"That's exactly what you need to do. We'll have to walk to the tube station, which is about half a mile, but at this time of night, there ought to be enough people around to make anyone think twice about trying to waylay us. The tube will take us to King's Cross, and from there we duck into St. Pancras's and catch the Chunnel train to Coquelles. My contact will meet us there and take over getting you to Paris. Understand?"

"What? What do you mean? What contact?" Judging by his tone and expression, along with the way his grip tightened on her hand until she had to fight back a wince of discomfort, Martin did understand but wasn't very happy with what he'd just heard. Panic had once again reared its head. "You said you'd take me to safety. You, not some person I've never met. How am I supposed to trust a complete stranger?"

With her free hand, Ivy gave him a reassuring pat, then tried to pry his fingers from their death grip around hers. "Martin, I'm a complete stranger, remember? This is the first time you've ever set eyes on me."

"B-but we've talked. We've e-mailed and chatted online. We even spoke on the phone once, on the disposable mobile you told me to buy."

"Right, and I hope you have another one in your briefcase tonight, but that doesn't mean we aren't strangers. We are, but you trust me, and I promise you, you can trust my contacts in France. We've been working together for a long time, and you're far from the first person we've taken through this exact process. I can't take you all the way to Paris."

"Why not?"

Okay, now what Ivy had thought of as panic was just starting to sound like petulance. "Because," she said, striving for patience, and for the self-control not to yank her hand from under his, punishing grip or not, "you aren't the only person who needs my help. I told you there are other Wardens in hiding who want to get to safety. Helping them is my job, and I need to get them to this point the same way I got you here."

"But—"

"Besides, changing traveling companions is safer for you. This was all in the information I sent you. The stuff you said you read?"

Martin flushed, then gave a jerky nod. "Oh, right."

"There will be a change of clothes, new glasses, a new look waiting for you at the station. Paul will have his eye on us from the moment we arrive, but he won't make contact with you until we've split up at the loos. That's when you change. He'll be with you the minute you do, and I won't leave until I know you're safely in his hands. I promise."

"And how is that safer for me?" he asked, still suspicious.

"Because," she said, struggling for patience, "you go

from *you* traveling with *me* as half of a couple off for a romantic holiday weekend, to a different, single man meeting up with a mate for a casual holiday with your friend Paul. It's an extra layer of insurance in the unlikely event that someone were to track you that far."

"Has that ever happened? Being followed like that?"

"Never." Ivy lied with convincing ease. "And it won't happen this time, either."

Of all her proffered reassurances, that one seemed to have the greatest impact. She could see some of the tension melt from Martin's posture and gave a silent prayer of thanks. Dealing with nerves was to be expected, but real panic only put them both in danger.

Well, greater danger. It wasn't like this whole thing wasn't risky to begin with.

It still amazed her that for the most part, the general public continued to live in ignorance of the threat posed to them by the Order, and in spite of all the efforts of Ivy and the people like her, that threat only seemed to be growing. What had started with rumors of Order sects operating in Canada, the U.S., Eastern Europe, and South America had become newspaper headlines of bodies found with evidence of ritual slayings. Then there had been scattered terrorist attacks in places like Boston, Massachusetts, and Dublin, Ireland, ones where a handful of survivors babbled about devils and hooded cultists and were dismissed as crackpot liars or mentally ill.

By the time the natural disasters had surged in violence and frequency, Ivy and her brethren knew that global warming wasn't enough to account for the fact that some "earthquake" victims appeared to have been stabbed in the heart or had their throats slit before death. Not even modern science could explain why the "natural sinkholes" kept appearing in areas where legends and folklore had long whispered about portals to hell. The war had already started, even if the world at large had no idea, and humanity was in serious trouble.

In the last few months, Ivy had started to hear other rumors, though, ones even the people spreading them seemed reluctant to discuss in depth. Maybe because they sounded too good to be true. A few whispers had begun to say that some of the Guardians had woken.

Light above, she only wished that were true. According to the lore of the Wardens, thousands of years ago, the most powerful magic users in the Guild had joined together and summoned from the Light seven powerful, inhuman warriors to fight against the Demons of the Darkness. Appearing almost like medieval gargoyles, these creatures were immortal, almost entirely immune to magical attack, each as strong as a dozen of the strongest human athletes, and entirely dedicated to the battle against evil. They existed only to fight against the Demons and their servants, helping to imprison the Seven and keep them away from the human world throughout the past centuries. Then, when their task was complete, they were put to sleep in the form of stone statues that could only be woken again in time of need by the Wardens assigned as their personal aides.

Ivy had heard the story as a child. Her mother had come from a family of Wardens, her brother George and nephew James only the latest in a long line that had included her father and grandfather and his father before that. Even though removed from the business of the Guild itself, Dorothy Fitzroy Beckett possessed a great deal of pride in her family's legacy and her brother's place in it. She'd shared a lot of knowledge with her daughter in the form of family stories, and Ivy had learned a lot more since she'd first looked into Uncle George's and his son's deaths.

She knew all about the Guardians, including the fact

that the records of their whereabouts had been destroyed—along with everything else in the Guild's records—at the library in their headquarters. No one knew where they were, and the attempts to locate them that Ivy's contacts in Paris had been making had so far turned up next to nothing. Which sucked, when you figured that without them, humanity had next to no chance of stopping the Order from unleashing the Seven on an unsuspecting world. In fact, according to Ivy's main informant, the surviving Wardens felt certain that at least three of the Seven had already been freed from their prisons. The presence of those Demons in the mortal realm offered the true explanation for the ritual slayings, the terrorist attacks, and the flurry of (un)natural disasters.

Still, even if humanity was screwed, that didn't mean they would stop fighting. Ivy certainly wouldn't, and getting Martin to safety meant one more Warden working to find the Guardians and wake them before it was too late.

Draining her half-pint glass, Ivy set it on the table with a click and turned to look at her companion. "Time to get moving. Are you ready?"

For half a second, she thought he might say no. Either that or pass out. But then Martin grabbed his beer, chugged it down like an American frat boy, and gave a shaky nod. "Let's go, then."

Chapter Two

Ivy felt a surge of satisfaction. Well, adrenaline, really, but whatever.

"Perfect." She got to her feet and pitched her voice back to where it could just be overheard—significantly louder, but still natural. Also, a bit wheedling. "Let's get out of here, Marty. You promised me dinner in a proper restaurant, not a pub, and I'm abso famished."

Martin rose awkwardly, sending their glasses to wobbling again. "Lead on, then, darling. Wherever you like."

She forced a giggle. She hated to giggle. "Oh, you're such a pudding. But now I've got to decide. Hm, Judy told me about this café . . ."

Her mouth continued to babble, spewing nonsense she pulled off the top of her head as she led the way through the crowd—steering well clear of Teddy and his mates—and out the front door. Turning onto the pavement, she kept up the patter until they had stepped well away from the pub en route to the tube station. Even then, though she let the inane drivel dry up, she continued to clasp Martin's hand in hers and lean into him. They hadn't been the only ones to leave the pub and the streets continued to bustle with both vehicular and pedestrian traffic. It was important to keep up appearances all the way through this journey.

"Okay, stage two," she said softly as they strode toward the Underground station. "I have a bag at Left Luggage in King's Cross that we'll need to pick up. It has more information you'll need to look over for your time with Paul, some snacks, and cash and new identification for you hidden in the lining. I'll show you where. We're on the last train tonight, but we should have plenty of time to make it, so don't worry about that."

He nodded, but his gaze was glued to the pavement in front of them. Poor guy really didn't have the right temperament for all this cloak-and-dagger stuff. But then again, she hadn't thought she did, either, and look at her now—practically an expert, and armed on top of it.

Under her anorak and tight jeans, a custom-made dagger rode in a sheath at the small of her back. And oddly enough, she knew how to use it. Over the last several months, she hadn't had much choice but to learn, until these days, it felt so comfortable, she almost forgot it was there.

Until moments like this, that is, when the hair on the back of her neck began to stand up and her senses put her on high alert.

"Bollocks," she muttered. Faking another giggle, she turned playfully into Martin's side and pretended to bury her face in his shoulder. In reality, she used the opportunity to take a look at the area behind them. She had felt confident that there had been no *nocturnis* in the pub with them who might try to follow, but she should have paid a bit more attention to Teddy and his band of happy hooligans. Three of them had exited the bar after Ivy and Martin and now trailed sixty or seventy feet behind them.

Normally, Ivy would have considered such an event no more than a slight bother, but something about their posture niggled at the back of her mind. The aggression she would have expected, but for some reason their stance struck her as more menacing than it ought to be.

Damn it, they didn't have time for this shit. Or even if they did, Ivy just didn't have the patience. Even worse, she knew they were coming up on the narrow cross street they would have to traverse to get to the tube. She'd researched the route. The cross street was largely home to a few small businesses that would have closed down by six o'clock, a couple of daytime shops, at least one vacant building, and a church that had been abandoned a few years ago due to lack of funds available to repair a roof with more holes than tiles remaining. It was a quiet block, and quiet meant fewer people, which meant more opportunity for Teddy et al. to try something stupid.

"What's wrong?" Martin asked nervously as she turned back and casually picked up the pace of their walk. "What's the matter? Is it *nocturnis*? Have they found me?"

The last question emerged on a squeak, and Ivy winced. She laughed loudly to cover up his blunder. "Oh, you!" she cried, then lowered her voice. "No, Martin. And you need to stay calm. How about you tell me more about yourself? What's your main talent? I don't think you told me that."

By talent, she was referring to the magical ability that made up the most basic requirement of becoming a Warden. All members of the Guild needed to possess a talent—demonstrating the ability to wield magic—in order to be considered for admission. With luck, Martin's would have some utility in a fight.

"What? Talent? Oh, er, I'm a dowser. Water dowser. Why?"

Oh, yeah, because a nice, deep aquifer was just what they needed right now.

"No reason," she gritted out, fingers itching for the hilt of her knife. "No reason at all."

Which was when she glanced over her shoulder and saw a dark shadow coalesce around Teddy and his friends. A shadow that swirled and twisted and then seemed to disappear. *Inside* the three men.

Shit.

"What is it? What's wrong."

There went the panic again, creeping back into Martin's voice at the least opportune of moments. Impatient, Ivy shook her head and urged him to walk a little faster. Not that it was likely to do them much good. "Nothing. Let's just concentrate on getting to the station, shall we?"

She could hear her accent beginning to fray at the edges, her natural American pronunciation creeping in here and there, but right now that counted as the least of their worries. Much higher on the list was the fact that they were being followed down a now deserted street by three large, loutish men who hadn't liked her to begin with and who now appeared to have fallen under demonic influence if not outright possession.

You know, one of these days one of her plans was going to have to go utterly smoothly, right? Just the law of large numbers made it inevitable, didn't it? Well, today would have been a really good day for that to happen.

Instinct had her increasing her pace yet again until she found herself half a step from jogging down the pavement, tugging Martin along by her side.

"Hang on, then," he protested, pulling against her grip and trying to actually slow her pace. The idiot. "If nothing's wrong, why are you suddenly running?"

"I think that's down to us, mate," a voice snarled, closer

behind them than it should have been. Their pursuers had moved fast, faster than normal.

Faster than was natural.

An instant later, something hit Ivy from the side, hard. The impact sent her staggering into the alley that opened up between two buildings at the side of the street. She stumbled into heavy darkness, away from the abandoned Gothic church across the way, away from the sight of anyone else who might wander onto the nearby pavement. To her credit, though, she managed to maintain her grip on Martin in spite of that, so she pulled him into the shadows beside her.

Perfect. Now they could be in deep shit together.

The hit had come as a surprise, but the three shapes rapidly closing in behind her, driving her and Martin deeper into the alley, did not. Ivy's hand had moved at the first moment of contact with her attacker, fingers closing around the hilt of her dagger and tugging it out of concealment in a smooth, practiced motion. Now, she held it in front of her as she used her grip on her companion to swing him out of the way behind her, placing him between her and the brick building wall.

"Ooh, you've brought along a toy, have you?" Teddy asked, grinning as he stalked forward, herding them away from the street and the potential of being seen by passersby. "Want to play, then, do you, luvie? I like a good game now and then."

Ivy flicked her gaze among the three looming figures. She recognized all of them from the group gathered around the bar earlier, the ones who had witnessed Teddy hitting on her and her subsequent rejection of him. They had laughed at the time and gone right back to drinking, already half-pissed when the whole thing began. Was it too much for her to hope that she had been mistaken? That this was just a garden-variety assault and maybe potential rape fueled by alcohol and wounded machismo? Because frankly, that would be a relief compared to the alternative.

"Yeh, we like to play," the second lad hissed as he stepped forward until Ivy could see his face in the dim light of the alleyway. "We especially like to play with his sort." He bared his teeth, and his eyes lit up with malice.

And Ivy didn't mean that metaphorically. His eyes actually lit up. As in, started glowing. With a sick, rusty-red light that reminded her of old blood and dried scabs. Very attractive.

And very much indicative of demonic influence.

Yay. She'd been right. It wasn't really her these three were after. They wanted Martin. They wanted the Warden.

Well, they weren't going to get him. Not until they got past her.

"I'm ready to go, boys." She took a step forward and flashed a toothy smile of her own. "And you know the rules. White makes the first move."

Ivy struck with a feint toward Teddy, who stood closest to her, directly ahead. When instinct had him leaping back out of the way of her blade, she spun backward to her left and landed a heel-first kick directly to the sternum of hissy boy. He grunted and stumbled back in surprise, but bachelor number three was already on the move. He closed in on Ivy from the left and grabbed her around her upper body, effectively pinning her biceps to her sides. She'd been expecting the move and countered by thrusting the dagger in a short, upward dig that buried it deep in number three's thigh.

"Go, Martin!" she shouted above Three's scream. "Get to the station! Lost Luggage under your name! *Now!*"

All of her attackers howled in protest. Three's cry was

still tinged with pain. It gave her a warm surge of satisfaction, even though it rendered her nearly deaf in her left
ear, the one closest to his mouth. Jerking the knife back,
she freed it from the man's leg and went limp in his grip,
relaxing her muscles until she slid straight out of his arms
to the floor of the alley.

Even as she hit the cobbles, she was already moving.
She braced one hand, shifted her weight, and swung one
leg around, aiming a heavy kick at the knee of the grabby
Three's wounded leg. He crumpled with a heavy grunt.

Teddy and number two rushed in to take his place,
converging on Ivy before she could manage a glimpse to
see if Martin had followed her directions. If he hadn't,
he was either dumber than he looked, or part possum and
his nervous system had shut down from fear. Neither option would keep him alive, though, and as skilled as she
had become in hand-to-hand combat after her years of
self-defense classes back in New York and her training
since taking on her rescue work in England, one human
woman against three demonically influenced men didn't
offer her very good odds.

Chances were she wouldn't leave this alley under her
own power. Hell, she'd be lucky if she didn't leave it in a
coroner's van. Which meant Martin had better be halfway down the steps to the tube already.

She ducked away from a swipe of Teddy's outstretched
hand, trying not to get distracted by the way the skin of
his fingertips had split to allow the emergence of glistening black claws that dripped some sort of dark, stinking
fluid. The smell of decayed flesh and filthy swamp water
suddenly filled the alley, and Ivy had to fight back the
urge to gag.

Oh, yeah. She'd say this officially went beyond the
realm of demonic influence. Hell, this went beyond
possession. Somehow, demons had not just taken over

these men's bodies, they had used the energy of the human bodies to allow them to fully manifest into the human world.

In case anyone wondered, that was a really, *really* bad thing. Something Ivy wouldn't have thought possible six months ago.

But then again, six months ago, the world hadn't quite started coming to an end yet. Today, anything was possible.

With that cheery thought filling her mind, she swung her dagger in a wide arc that managed to catch opponent number two in the side, opening up a wound that audibly sizzled and began to ooze something much darker and slimier than blood. It didn't smell like blood, either. The ichor reeked of the same foulness that hung around the venom dripping from Teddy's claws.

Seriously, it was becoming a real challenge not to puke. What she wouldn't give for a nice, stiff breeze right about then to dissipate some of the stink.

Two—Thing Two, Ivy decided to call him—hissed, his corrupt red gaze flicking between her and her blade with manic hatred. It made her smile in spite of the nausea.

"What's the matter, pumpkin?" she taunted him. "Aren't you a fan of blessed and consecrated silver? Me, I just adore the stuff."

She demonstrated those feelings with another quick slash of her arm, a motion that sliced through the jacket and shirt Teddy wore and into the flesh of his shoulder. She wasn't particularly aiming for the brachial plexus nerve or a major artery, but she wasn't going to cry if he started to bleed out or lost the use of his arm.

He screamed, but Ivy just continued her stroke and caught Thing Two across the cheek, just millimeters away from his left eye. Hm, close call, that. What a shame.

"Bitch!" the demon howled.

Ivy blew him a kiss. "Aw, love you, too, snookums."

Her mother had always told her that her smart mouth would get her into trouble one day. Somehow Ivy didn't think this particular trouble was what she'd had in mind. You know, the whole "ripped apart by demons in a deserted alley" thing. Dorothy probably hadn't seen that one coming.

One would hope.

By now, Thing Three was back on his feet, and Ivy knew she was seriously fucked. Three against one. Three *demons* against one, with no backup on the way. Working alone was one of the keys to protecting the Wardens people like her assisted. Now, it looked like she was going to die alone.

"Sorry, Uncle George," she muttered, putting her back to the alley wall and keeping her gaze on the man-shaped creatures in front of her. They had realized her predicament just as clearly as she had, and now they were toying with her, watching her with evil, hungry gazes. Not the kind of hunger that would scare most women alone in an alley, but the kind of hunger that scared American turkeys in the middle of November.

"Sorry, Jamie," Ivy added. "But on the bright side, looks like I'll be seeing you both again soon."

Thing Two snapped its jaws at her, jaws that it then unhinged to make room for the second row of pointed teeth that appeared to be growing behind the first, human set.

"Very, very soon."

Holding her dagger in front of her and carefully balancing her weight on the balls of her feet, Ivy prepared to die fighting.

Oddly enough, that's not what happened.

One minute, she stared down the face of the Grim

Reaper and the next, reality went sideways. Instead of the front of three demons clearly prepared to feast on her living flesh, she felt a rush of cool air, heard a pavement-shaking roar, and found herself staring into a wide barrier the color of dark, aged granite.

She blinked, then shook her head and blinked again. The view didn't change. Gradually her brain caught up with her corneas, and she realized that what had looked like a barrier of solid stone was actually a pair of wings. Huge wings, each easily twelve or thirteen feet from base to tip, leathery and membranous like a bat's.

And they were attached to the broadest, most muscular back she had ever seen. A back that could only conceivably belong to one of two things:

A dragon.

Or a Guardian.

Chapter Three

The first rush of breath filled his lungs and went to his head like the strongest liquor, making Baen momentarily dizzy with the intoxicating sensation of awareness. He hadn't felt anything like it in three hundred years.

Fast on the heels of that first inhalation, his living senses came shrieking back to life. The muffled impressions that had been all he could perceive during the long ages of sleep went instantly sharp, as if a hand had passed across the glass of a window and wiped away the fog of steam that obscured the view. He could hear, see, touch, and smell the world around him again, even taste the dust and rot of stale air in the abandoned place that surrounded him. He breathed it in and along with it came a trace of something fresh and sweet and entirely out of place. Something that reminded him of . . .

Orange rinds.

"What's the matter, pumpkin?" A woman's voice cut through the lingering traces of sleep, sharp with taunting sarcasm. "Aren't you a fan of blessed and consecrated silver? Me, I just adore the stuff."

So did Baen, come to think of it, but that wasn't important at the moment. The woman was in danger, the kind of danger he had been born to expunge from existence. Nothing else needed to be fought with a weapon dedicated to the Light.

He was moving before his mind even finished registering her scent, let alone her words. Talons bit into heavy stone as he launched himself from his sleeping place nestled just beneath the apex of the church's peaked and leaky roof. He dove down across the space of a deserted street, savoring for an instant the sensation of his wings spreading to catch his weight as they helped him land in an agile, predatory crouch. He had soared into a narrow alley between the orange-scented female and three demon-infested male humans who threatened her.

All four of them made noises of shock, the demons at a higher pitch than the woman at his back, Baen noted with grim satisfaction. He also noticed the way the demons' first instinct was to back warily away from him, and he curled his lip at their cowardice. These were lesser creatures of the Darkness, the kind he had battled and destroyed countless times over the centuries. They existed as mere thralls to the Seven, the scourge he truly existed to face. These offered him little real challenge.

"Back. Away," he growled, his long unused voice low and rough like the snarl of a huge animal, which was what he was. At least part of him. He knew it, and he used it to his advantage.

He drew back his lips to expose the glinting length of razor-sharp fangs and let his long, curved talons click against the stone of the cobbles like the warning rattle of a snake about to strike. A small shift of heavy muscle balanced him perfectly for combat, and the leathery skin of his wings rustled as they quivered like the flicking tail of an angry lion. Everything about him conveyed menace and power barely leashed.

After all this time imprisoned in sleep, he really, really wanted to unleash it.

The tallest of the demon males gave him the opportunity.

It launched itself forward in a desperate surge, claws protruding from bloody stumps where human fingers used to be. It raked them at his face, aiming for his eyes, but Guardian skin in its natural form was almost as hard as the stone it resembled. The weapons failed to penetrate, but the attack had brought the creature too close. It survived for less than ten more seconds.

Baen's own claws were just as sharp as the demon's, but the human body hosting the foul creature was infinitely more fragile. A hard thrust ripped through mortal flesh, broke bones, and allowed his fingers to close around the heart that maintained the vessel's function. He ripped it out in a smooth, savage motion and watched the body collapse like a rag doll that had lost its stuffing.

Immediately, he heard noises like someone vomiting coming from several feet farther down the alley, but he had no time to admonish the woman for moving from the protection of his back. He would just have to keep the demons too busy to turn on her.

The two remaining creatures flew at him together, probably hoping to confuse him with simultaneous attacks. Did they think he had been summoned yesterday?

He let them come, stretching his arms out to catch them in his huge hands and then using their own momentum to add to the force as he slammed them together. It didn't really do them much damage, but it brought Baen a significant amount of satisfaction.

It also distracted them momentarily. Lower demons like these were basically stupid, animalistic creatures who operated on the basest levels of instinct. Whatever threatened them or caused them pain, they would turn on, despite what their original mission might have been. And that was exactly what happened. They wasted valuable seconds swiping at each other following their collision, giving Baen the opportunity to alter his grip on them and quickly twist his wrists, breaking their necks with nearly simultaneous cracking sounds.

More vomiting, and he turned his head to sweep his gaze around the alley in the direction from which the sound came. To his surprise, his eyes spied not a female form but another male one, this one doubled over as it emptied the contents of its stomach onto the floor of the alley.

"Guardian."

The feminine voice came from behind him, right where he had thought the woman had been. Apparently, she had not moved as he had assumed during his brief altercation, but had remained in place while he dispatched her attackers.

He looked back toward the vomiting male and frowned. He had never seen a demon overcome by human sickness before, but he would not tolerate even a potential threat to the woman.

Baen did not waste time analyzing that unfamiliar surge of protective instinct, but instead turned to dispatch this last little problem.

"Guardian, wait."

The woman stepped forward and reached out, her fingertips just brushing the edge of one wing. The jolt of energy that surged through him at the brief contact nearly made him rock back on his heels. He had experienced nothing like it in all his long centuries of existence.

"He's not possessed," the woman explained when he turned to look at her. "He's human. Actually he's a Warden. I was trying to get him someplace safe when the demons attacked us."

Her voice both surprised and intrigued him. He would have expected something lighter and sweeter to come from this small, slender creature, something to match her citrusy scent. Instead, she sounded more like vanilla or clove, dark and rich. He looked closer, his keen vision having no trouble picking her out in the dark.

"A Warden?"

His voice rumbled between them, naturally deep and roughened from disuse. Another human might have found it menacing, but this female did not so much as flinch.

"Yes. Is he yours?"

"Mine?"

"His?"

The last question, uttered in an indefinable style somewhere between a squeak and a groan drew both Baen's and the woman's attention to the male figure still hunched over a puddle of vomit farther down the alley. His expression still looked somewhat queasy, if you asked Baen.

"Did you summon him, Martin?" the female demanded, frowning at the other human. "You didn't tell me you were personal Warden to a Guardian! Don't you think that's the kind of information you should have shared?"

"But I'm not! I swear," Martin protested. "No one in my family has ever been assigned to a Guardian. Not in our entire history. I've no idea how to do a proper summoning."

Baen pushed away his initial surprise to examine the situation. He felt no particular connection to the scrawny male called Martin, and he certainly hadn't been introduced to him at the end of his last Warden's life. In fact, the last time he had been introduced to a new Warden had been a very long time ago indeed, if his instincts were correct.

"What is your full name?" he demanded of the human, just to be certain.

"P-P-Pickering," the man stammered. "M-Martin Louis Pickering. Why?"

Baen ignored the question and looked back at the woman. "My last Warden was from the house of Beauclerk. Henry Fitzallen Beauclerk."

She made a face indicating a good deal of displeasure. "Damn. It would have made things a hell of a lot simpler."

Martin finally straightened up from his bent-over position. The hands he had braced on his thighs during his bout of sickness trembled visibly until he pressed them to his stomach. The obvious sign of fear, or at least intense discomfort, inspired no sympathy in Baen. It only served to highlight the human's weakness, and weakness was something all Guardians disdained.

"W-why are we still standing around here?" Martin asked. "What if more of those things show up?"

Baen curled his lip. "An army of 'those things' could show up and prove no more of a challenge than the three I have already dispatched."

"So you're really one of them, then? A G-Guardian?"

The human's stutter was beginning to irritate Baen. He scowled. "Obviously."

Martin turned to the female and thrust a pointed finger in Baen's direction. "Then I want him to take me to Paris. He can protect me a lot better than you can."

The woman nodded, her expression serious. "You're right. He can. Besides, I'm all on my own here. The only contacts I have are anonymous and in hiding." She turned her attention to Baen. "But I know there are Wardens in France, a good number of them. I made sure some of them got there. They need to know about you as soon as possible. You have to go to Paris with Martin. The Guild has been searching for the Guardians for a very long time."

That news made Baen frown. The Guild had to search for his kind? They were supposed to know exactly where he and his brethren slept at all times. After all, they were the ones who put them to sleep, and the Guild members were nothing if not meticulous recordkeepers.

Something must be very, very wrong.

At the moment, however, Baen had one very particular reason for not liking the citrus-scented female's suggestion that he leave her side and escort Martin to the Guild headquarters.

"I cannot travel to Paris with this male," he said, folding his wings and crossing his arms over his chest.

"Why not?" Martin asked, his tone petulant. It only added to Baen's disdain for him.

"Why not?" the female echoed, looking unintimidated by his size or determined stance.

"Because Martin is not my Warden," Baen informed her, his eyes narrowing as certainty and satisfaction filled him. "You are."

Chapter Four

The words hit Ivy harder than the Guardian had hit the demons. She felt it right in the solar plexus, knocking the wind out of her faster than a roundhouse kick to the diaphragm.

Her? Personal Warden to one of the seven Guardians of the Light? But she wasn't a member of the Guild.

Hell, she wasn't even a Warden!

Her head shook almost of its own volition. "That's impossible."

"It is truth."

"But you told me you weren't from the Guild," Martin protested. When had his voice become so nasal and annoying? she wondered. Had it always sounded like that? "You said you weren't a Warden."

Ivy stamped back her irritation. Her shock felt like more than enough to deal with at the moment. "I'm not." She blinked up at the Guardian and said with more force, "I'm not a Warden."

For a creature made of stone, the enormous male had no trouble conveying his thoughts through his expression. One heavy brow lifted at the corner, a clear indication of skepticism. And amusement at her expense.

"You think this is something a Guardian would mistake?"

"Yes. I mean, no. I mean—" She broke off and shook her head. Maybe some sense would fall back in. "I'm not saying you're not the expert on Guardians and Wardens here. I'm just saying that I think you should . . . reexamine your impressions. I can't be your Warden, because I'm not *a* Warden. I'm not a member of the Guild. I was never even tested. I'm female."

The arched brow fell, joined quickly by its mate. "What significance does your gender play in your role as a Warden? You have talent. You can use magic. What else is required?"

"Um, training, for one?" Ivy offered. She shook her head. "Besides, I can't use magic. I've never performed a spell in my life."

His gaze, black and intense and lit with inner flames, bored into her. "But you do have talent."

"If that's what you want to call it," she muttered, looking away.

This conversation was getting way out of hand. It was bad enough that her impeccably planned mission to get Martin to safety in France had just gone sideways, but to add a demon attack on top of that was enough to throw any girl off her game. Then sprinkle in the sudden appearance of one of the seven missing Guardians, and it was a wonder she could still speak. She did not have the bandwidth to deal with the ludicrous assertion that she was supposedly now not just a Warden, but the personal Warden to said Guardian.

She had it hard enough processing just the mysteriously appearing Guardian part. After all, how many girls got rescued from a demonic attack by a seven-foottall gargoyle with superstrength?

Um, one, apparently. Lucky her?

Oh, it's not like she didn't feel grateful that she was still breathing rather than decorating the digestive tracts of three creatures of the Darkness. She preferred life to death by a fairly significant margin, but that didn't mean she didn't deserve a few minutes to get a grip on the situation. For Pete's sake, she had barely had time to get a good look at the Guardian, and now he was trying to tell her she had been ordained by Fate as his magical P.A.? Did he think her degree came from Hogwarts? Because that would be a hell of a shock to her parents and the student loan people who had sent all that money to SUNY instead.

Not, of course, that getting a good look at him helped.

The alley boasted pretty poor lighting, but after all this time, her eyes had adjusted well enough to make out the basics of the Guardian's physique. He looked as if Smaug the dragon and a male model had managed to conceive a love child. Only, you know, hotter.

His height wasn't the only reason the Guardian gave the impression of blocking out the streetlights with his size. His shoulders looked like they'd have trouble squeezing through a standard doorway—a standard *American* doorway. In fact, it wouldn't surprise her if he had to twist sideways to make it. And every inch of the man rippled with muscle, the dense, heavy kind that should have made him look slow and lumbering. Instead, it just made him look deadly, like he could crush a Volkswagen microbus the way normal men could crush a beer can.

No way could he be mistaken for normal, or even human. Sure, he wore the same basic shape—one head, two arms, two legs—but the gigantic dragon wings protruding from his back offered the first little clue. Then there were the horns that swept back from just above his temples and curved gracefully into skyward points. Deadly points. They made the Minotaur look like a poncy git.

Hell, compared to the Guardian, entire mythological pantheons looked like poncy gits. Including the ones that demanded human sacrifice.

I can think of one or two things I'd like to sacrifice to him, a voice inside her purred. Ivy nearly jumped out of her skin. WTF? Where had that thought come from? Since when was she the kind of girl who dropped her panties at the first sight of some hard biceps and a visible six-pack?

Try eight-pack. Rrawr!

Down, girl!

Ivy pinched herself discreetly. Now was not the time to get distracted. Not even by her own libido. Maybe she should focus on something like those three-inch-long claws of his. Those did not look like the sort of things she wanted anywhere near her tender bits.

Luckily for her, a sound leaked into the alley and offered the best distraction she could have hoped for. "Do you hear that?"

"Hear what?" Martin asked. As if he were still part of the conversation.

The Guardian just stared at her. "I hear many things."

He probably did, too. Guardians were known for their keen senses—vision, hearing, and smell all said to be dozens of times more acute than the average human's. He could probably hear automobiles rumbling down nearby streets, hear the noisy crowd gathered at the pub they had been at earlier, even hear a baby crying in a flat a couple of streets away. But even if he could hear all of it, there was only one sound that mattered to Ivy just then.

"The siren. Do you hear a siren?"

His head pulled back a bit and a look of confusion

settled over his handsome, mostly human face. "Singing? Here?"

Now it was her turn to look at him as if he'd just switched to speaking a foreign language. It took a second before her brain processed the confusion over words with more than one meaning. Honestly, though, did he think she had really started babbling about mermaids in modern London? Especially at a time like this.

"Not that kind of siren. Police sirens."

His expression cleared. "Ah, mechanical devices that produce audible warning signals. Yes. One has been drawing closer for a couple of minutes."

"Thank God!" Martin cried.

Ivy wanted to smack him. " 'Thank God'?" she repeated. "Are you insane? We're standing in an alley with three dead bodies and a damned gargoyle. Do you think the police are coming to help you, Martin? Don't be an idiot. We need to get out of here before we wind up in jail on suspicion of murder."

The Warden got a stubborn look on his face that made Ivy's own heart sink. "Maybe jail is the safest place for me at the moment. Did you ever think of that? There's no way to make the last train across the Channel at this rate, and you've already shown me what kind of protection you can offer me. If the Guardian isn't going to keep me safe, maybe the police will."

"Don't be an idiot. First, the police are not going to be in the right frame of mind to listen when you tell them you didn't just kill the three people lying at your feet with various fatal injuries. And second, the Darkness just got to you—almost killed you—by possessing three random dudes we ran into in a pub in Croydon. What the hell makes you think it can't get you by possessing someone at the local police station? Glass-half-full optimism?"

She saw her words hit him, saw him digest them like

a bit of leftover curry that might or might not have gone off during its time in the fridge. At any other time, she might have felt a stirring of sympathy for the man. He was in danger, after all. He had been forced into hiding by circumstances that were no fault of his own, and when someone had finally appeared offering to get him to safety, had promised him they had almost reached it, the rug had been pulled out from under him again and safety now likely appeared to be farther out of reach than ever before. She'd probably be feeling a bit sullen about the whole thing, too, if she were in his shoes.

But she wasn't. She still wore these stupid, fashion-victim boots, and she'd be damned if she'd wear them in her very first mug shot, whether they'd be out of frame or not.

"The source of the siren is coming closer," the Guardian informed them helpfully. "I estimate it will reach us in fewer than four minutes."

Ivy cursed. "Martin, we have to go. Now. I promise that I will find a way to keep you safe in the long term, but from right now, all three of us need to get moving. Together. Let the Guardian protect you for now. Just until we get somewhere that won't land us in a cell. All right?"

"Three minutes."

She shot the Guardian a withering glare. What was he? Her frickin' alarm clock?

Martin dithered for another few seconds (this was worse than having to pee in the middle of an urban traffic jam) before he finally gave a brief nod. "Fine. Where do we go?"

"I know someplace we can hole up, out of the way and where no one will be looking for either of us. Any of us," she corrected, looking at the Guardian, "but first we have to get away from here without being seen. I think the back of this alley connects to the mews at the back of a row of town houses on the next block. If we can sneak through there, we might be able to blend in with the crowd on the high street, but I'm not sure our new friend here is really blendable."

"We don't have time," the Guardian said. "The police will reach us before we are out of range of their hearing. Besides, I have a better idea."

"Really? What's that?"

"Hang on."

She would have demanded clarification—probably in a rather snippy tone of voice, if she were honest—but in the space of the next heartbeat, she was too busy biting back a shriek of surprise to bother. The Guardian had grabbed her around the waist, wrapped his other arm around Martin's skinny frame, and launched himself into the night sky.

Cold air rushed over her, past her, as the Guardian carried them over the tops of the buildings surrounding the alley, seemingly unconcerned by the weight of his twin passengers, let alone by the distance between the three of them and the very, extremely, hazardously hard ground below them.

"Are you insane?" Ivy hissed after her brain and mouth started working again. She felt a little embarrassed about how long that actually took—long enough for the Guardian to skim across at least three blocks' worth of rooftops. "You can't just fly us off into the sunset, Gibraltar. What the hell are you thinking?"

"I am called Baen," he informed her, "and the sun clearly set a significant time ago."

"It was a figure of speech. I meant that before you grab people and remove them from a given location, it's generally a good idea to obtain their consent. Right, Martin?"

"The male is unconscious. I do not believe he possesses a liking for heights."

Ivy wasn't exactly wild about them either, but she wasn't about to faint. While she knew she was being uncharitable, she couldn't stop her brain from labeling the passed-out Warden with a scoffing, mental "Wuss."

She also couldn't stop herself from using his state to bolster her argument. "Really? Maybe he just objects to being kidnapped by an airborne bully. Or he would have preferred to have a bloody destination in mind. Were you planning to just fly around the skies above London until you caused a city-wide UFO panic?"

The Guardian didn't bother to answer. Instead he touched down on the roof of a building with surprising lightness for his massive frame. Then he set Ivy carefully onto her feet and lowered Martin to slump against a chimney stack. When he straightened, he fixed her with that burning black gaze of his, one that didn't match his bland expression.

"You expressed urgency in removing ourselves from the alley before the human authorities discovered us there. As the arrival of the police became imminent, it seemed prudent to ensure our anonymity. Forgive me for pointing it out, but you and the male could not have moved with sufficient speed to avoid capture and questioning by the police. I merely acted in accordance with your wishes and with the best interests of all of us in mind."

It was the politest version of "go to hell" Ivy had ever had directed her way.

No, that wasn't fair, she told herself and forced her hands to unclench from the fists she hadn't realized she had made. Nothing in his tone or his posture indicated he felt any hostility over her reaction. Her overreaction.

He had merely offered an explanation to counter her anger. Her fairly inappropriate anger.

Okay, Ivy. Time to step back and take a deep breath here. Then get a grip. The middle of a sticky situation is not the time to get distracted by emotion and bogged down in things that don't matter. It's the time to figure a way out of it. So, get busy.

Her inner voice was right. Closing her eyes, she took stock of her racing heartbeat, her trembling fingers, and the knot that had formed in the pit of her stomach—all signs of an adrenaline overdose. She had let the stress-induced hormone take over her thinking, and she knew from experience that reactions like that didn't do anyone any good. She needed to get rational quick and switch to plan B.

One more deep breath, and she opened her eyes to meet the Guardian's—Baen, he had said his name was—curious gaze.

"You're right. Sorry," she said, resetting her shoulders and subtly shaking some of the tension from her arms. "Getting out of there was the most important thing. Now we just need to regroup and figure out where to go from here."

His expression hardened, suddenly looking a lot more like real carved granite. "My mind is still sorting through the return of my memories, but already I know that the Darkness is stirring and that this threat is larger than any my kind has faced in many centuries. We must contact the Guild and warn them, and then we must locate my brothers and root out whatever plan the Order has put into action this time."

Man, if he only knew the half of it . . .

"Yeah, about that," Ivy began.

Beside them, Martin stirred and gave a low moan.

Damn it. First things first.

"Warden?" Baen prompted, ignoring the waking man.

"My name is Ivy," she told him. "You might as well use it. As for everything else, I'll fill you in with as much as I know, but first we need to get someplace more secure than some random London rooftop. Those demons before pretty much came out of nowhere. I'd been watching, and until they appeared, the coast was looking clear, which means more could do the same thing and pop up any minute."

"Do you have a suggestion?"

Ivy started to shake her head, and then hesitated. She already knew that getting to France tonight was out of the question, but taking Martin and the Guardian back to her uncle's house in Little Naughton didn't feel like an option. First off, in the little village, their presence would stand out like a plague sore, and secondly, everyone there knew who she was. She really had thought tonight's mission was operating completely under the radar of the Order, but after the demon attack, she could no longer be so sure. Maybe she'd been identified, and if so, that also ruled out where she'd been staying in London—her cousin Jamie's flat in Marylebone.

Another option occurred to her, though, one that might be safe for the simple reason that the worst had already happened there.

"Yeah, I do," she finally said with a nod. "There's a flat in Camden. I think we'd be fairly safe there. You know, all things considered. I'd say we can take the tube, but . . ." She ran her gaze over his hulking, horned, winged, clawed, generally inhuman form. "Ah . . . I'm not sure you wouldn't cause a riot."

Baen followed her glance. "You refer to my appearance standing out among the humans in a public place."

"Maybe a little." She held up her thumb and finger half an inch apart.

"This may be true, but I believe your kind would be equally curious about the reason why even a fellow human would be transporting an unconscious man on your transport system."

Ivy glanced at Martin, who had slipped back into oblivion. Maybe Baen had a point.

"Besides, I can take us to our destination much faster and with little chance of being seen. You will simply guide me where I need to go."

Her expression turned sour. "You mean you want to fly us over half of London like a low-budget airline. The kind that doesn't even have seats on the planes. Or, you know, planes."

"You doubt your safety with me?"

The Guardian looked so insulted that Ivy had to bite back a laugh. Apparently, the legends about his kind's sense of honor had not been exaggerated. If anything, it sounded like Uncle George's stories might have underplayed the situation.

"No. Of course not. But humans don't just—" She broke off when she saw his expression turn stonier and stonier. He was really good at that. Quelle shocker. "You know what? Fine. We'll play Stork-and-Baby-Delivery. Just don't head for the stratosphere, okay? Try and keep the fall survivable for me."

"I would not drop you." He snarled. "And to avoid being seen, we must stay above the city lights. Or are you no longer concerned with UFO sightings?"

"Fine. I'll keep my eyes closed." She gritted the words out from between clenched teeth, wondering if it was better to punch the Guardian now so that he didn't drop her from surprise when she decked him mid-flight. It wasn't like she could hurt him, not with her best moves. She could pack every ounce of power she had into a kick right to his face and it would probably feel to him like a fly had landed on his nose.

Stony bastard.

Baen nodded and turned away as if that settled everything, so he didn't see the glare she aimed at him. He simply scooped Martin up into one brawny arm and then turned back to her with an air of expectancy.

Ivy stepped close and let him lift her as well. Unlike Martin, though, she made sure to wrap her arms around Baen's neck in a good grip of her own. She had no intention of falling, no matter how secure he thought his grasp was.

She also had no intention of noticing the way his hard muscles and ripped body felt pressed so close against her own.

Bloody hormones.

"Just be careful, big guy," she told him, resisting the urge to wrap her legs around his hips for good measure. You know, to get a better hold. Against falling. Really.

"Do not worry, human. It has been centuries since I killed an innocent human. Technically."

Ivy bit back a scream as the Guardian launched himself into the sky with the speed of a bullet.

Jerk.

Chapter Five

Baen touched down on the rooftop indicated by his Warden and set her gently beside him. She had ceased to tremble with nerves some minutes ago and had even sounded delighted with her view of the city when she finally opened her eyes to identify their destination.

Before that, she had remained silent during their brief trip, which had given him his first chance to wonder at their situation. Something felt very off. It had little to do with Ivy or Martin themselves, but rather the circumstances bringing all three of them together. He could tell that Martin was indeed a Warden, as he possessed a definite signature of magical ability, faint though it was, and he bore every indication of being trained by the Guild; but Baen did not understand why Ivy insisted that she was not a Warden as well.

Her power easily eclipsed Martin's, and she had been the one in charge when he found them in the alley. That had been obvious. While Martin had retreated to the back of the alley in the face of the demonic attack and contributed to the fight by losing hold of his last meal, Ivy had fought their attackers head-on, with every ounce of strength and determination she possessed. Only one of those reactions suited the position of Warden in Baen's mind. The other spoke too loudly of cowardice and ill preparation for a dangerous situation.

Of everything, the danger was the part of the picture of which Baen felt most certain. He had woken into a cloud of Darkness. He could feel it polluting the atmosphere of the human world, and he knew the threat posed by the Order was stronger than he had ever before experienced. He only wished he had woken sooner. As it was, he would need to get himself up to speed as quickly as possible, and he would need the help of both these Wardens to manage that.

"Is he still passed out?" Ivy asked, her voice tipping him out of his own thoughts.

"Again more than 'still,'" Baen answered, glancing down at Martin's limp form. He stirred once, then immediately passed out again. "I do not think he enjoys heights."

"Gee, I wonder why. Could it have something to do with the fear of falling from them and landing on a nice, hard patch of concrete? Why would something like that bother a person?"

"I may not be human, but I recognize the normal human responses to stress. You use sarcasm in order to express your feelings of irritation. Does this make you feel better?" he asked, curious.

She just glared at him. "Come on. Let's get inside. Can you manage Martin?"

In answer, Baen merely shifted the Warden to a one-armed grip and gestured for Ivy to lead the way. She shook her head.

"We need to go down the fire escape on the outside of the building, and it's still early enough that in this neighborhood, there's a decent chance of being seen," she informed him. "I don't suppose you can do anything to, uh, stand out a little less, is there? I mean, you can't, like, fold the wings up any smaller, can you?"

"Ah, you wish to be cautious and to 'blend in' to the area?" He thought she might have rolled her eyes before nodding in reply, but the gesture was quick. He thought it best not to waste time in an argument—not when he planned to spend much of the remaining night requiring her to answer his questions—so he ignored it.

He set Martin down at his feet, then stepped back to give himself a little room. With a quick thought and a mental rearrangement of his inherent magic, Baen reshaped himself into a small, human-seeming version of himself. His features retained their same basic shape, but smoothed out the most drastic lines and angles. His horns shrank down and disappeared, his wings melted away into his muscles, his claws retracted into human fingernails, and his skin thinned and turned a shade of light tan that looked drastically different from its natural gray tone. He shrank several inches, both in height and in breadth, now standing only a few inches over six feet with a proportional reduction in his musculature.

He even used the information in his communal knowledge bank to generate for himself a suitably human set of clothing, consisting of worn denim jeans, a dark-colored shirt, and a pair of sturdy boots. After a quick look at his human companions, he added a jacket over the top in concession to the air he guessed their species might consider chilly.

"Is this better?" he asked Ivy.

For a moment, she simply stared at him, her eyes wide and her lips slightly parted. She looked almost stupefied.

"Warden?" he prompted after a moment. Then, when she didn't respond, "Ivy?"

She jumped. "Huh? What? Oh. Oh, uh, yeah," she mumbled, turning away and shoving her hands into her pockets. "Yeah, that's fine. Thanks. The, uh, the stairs are this way."

Ivy crossed to the rear corner of the roof where a set of curved safety rails stood up over the top of the wall. Using both arms this time, Baen lifted Martin and followed, carefully descending the ladder to a small landing where the system changed to a set of steep iron stairs. At the bottom, the female drew a heavy set of keys from her pocket and unlocked a door painted a bright but chipping shade of blue.

"In here," she said, stepping over the threshold into an unlit kitchen. Baen crossed behind her and deposited his unconscious passenger in a straight-backed chair, even as the flick of a switch illuminated the room around them. Martin shifted and moaned, but neither of them paid him any attention.

"Do you live here?" Baen asked, looking around the cramped space. He couldn't picture her easily in these surroundings. The cabinets had been painted white, but looked more gray than anything else. Dingy. The cheap material of the countertop had chipped along the edges, and while the place looked tidy—no dirty dishes or used pots and pans piled up—dust covered most of the surfaces and an air of unkempt neglect hung over it.

It came from more than the dust and the smudged windows, too. He noticed no personal touches in the space, no plants on the windowsill, no pictures on the walls. Not even a whimsical canister to enliven the stark anonymity of the place. It didn't suit the citrus-scented Warden called Ivy in the least.

"No. Wouldn't want to be tracked there," she said, turning to grab a dented teakettle off the stove. She rinsed it inside and out before filling it with clean water and setting it back on the burner she quickly lit. "Or take the chance of someone waiting for us there, either. This place belonged to another Warden. I figured it was probably safe because he's already dead. No reason for the Order to come back and kill him again."

"Dead? And you believe the *nocturnis* bear the responsibility." The news did not shock Baen, but it did renew his determination to get a firm handle on the current situation. Certainly the Guild of Wardens and the Order of Eternal Darkness had been at odds for millennia, but rarely did they manage to slaughter each other without bringing about swift and decisive conflicts that restored the balance between them.

Ivy shot him a sour look before she began opening and closing cupboards. Her intent became clear when she paused and pulled down several heavy mugs and a squat brown teapot. "Of course they do. For this guy, and for all the others."

Baen felt a growl rise in his chest. Reflex and instinct. Guardians existed to protect humanity, after all, and for all their magical talents, Wardens were still human beings. "What others?"

The female opened her mouth, and judging by her expression, her intended response would have been sharp, but she caught herself before she uttered it. Her lips pressed together, and she took time for a deep breath.

"Sorry," she said. "You have just woken, and I shouldn't expect you to know everything that's going on. It's just, now that you are awake, and we finally have a Guardian on our side again, it's really hard not to expect you to just snap your fingers—or maybe flap your wings—and put everything back to normal again. But I suppose it's too late for just one of you to be able to do that now. So, I'm sorry."

Baen dismissed her apology. It was unimportant, and he had been unoffended. "Explain to me what you mean. What is not normal? And what do you mean that you 'fi-

nally have a Guardian on your side again'? My kind do
not turn from humanity, let alone from the Wardens."

"She means we've been up shit creek while you lot
have been catching up on your beauty sleep."

Martin's voice made them both turn and note with surprise that the cowardly Warden had finally regained his
senses and now sat slightly less slumped in his chair. He
looked no happier than he did in the alley where the demon attack had occurred, but at least he could move
under his own power again. That was helpful.

"The Order has wiped the Guild off the bloody map,"
Martin continued bitterly. "The Light knows how many
of us are left, but it's sure as hell not enough for us to stop
whatever those bastards have planned. And I think we
can all hazard a guess as to what they've got planned."

The Order only ever had one plan—to free the Seven
from their prisons and allow them to unite to devour the
human world with their evil. It was all very straightforward, really. Demonic and thoroughly malevolent, but
straightforward. It was why the Guardians existed.

One problem at a time, though. What had the cowardly Warden meant about the Guild being wiped out?

When he asked, Ivy answered.

"He's right. We don't really know how many Wardens
are left," she said, "but we do know that a great, great
many of them are dead and most of the rest are still missing. That's why I was trying to get Martin to France.
We're trying to send all the survivors we can find to
somewhere near Paris. We have a kind of Underground
Railroad set up to move them there undetected. I take
care of the ones who come through London and get them
across the Channel, and my contact there picks them up
for the last leg of the trip, delivering them to another contact who operates out of the city. The Guild hall itself is
gone, of course, but they've set up a kind of safe house

that they're turning into a new temporary headquarters. Only the people there know exactly what's going on. We try to limit contact between stages of the trip so that if one operative is discovered he or she can't tell the Order too much about anyone else."

Her mouth quirked in a wry grin. "It's kind of like living in a spy movie, actually. I have a code name and everything. My contact in Coquelles knows me as Holly. Totally surreal."

"No wonder your accent is gone," Martin said, eyeing her suspiciously. "You had it down really well, but now you sound American."

"I am," she said. "Half anyway. My mum is English, and I was actually born in Oxford, but my dad is American and I grew up there."

"So why aren't you operating in America? Why come to London?"

Ivy turned away then and opened another cabinet to pull out a brightly colored paper box. From it, she pulled out a few tea bags and dropped them into the pot. "Long story. Now's not the time."

"Right," Martin agreed. "Now's the time to figure out how the bloody hell those demons found me and how I'm supposed to get to France if they're still looking for me."

Baen aimed a glare at the male, feeling a faint stirring of regret that his features in this form didn't hold the same powers of intimidation that they did in his natural state. He'd like to scare some sense into the selfish coward. "No, now is the time for us to get a firm grasp on the situation and to decide on our next move."

"Which should be getting me to France," the Warden insisted. "You heard her. The Order is trying to kill me—to kill everyone in the Guild. If they do manage to wipe all of us out, humanity is doomed. Who's going to save them if there's no one left to summon the Guardians, eh?"

Baen stepped forward and curled his lip, wishing there were a fang there for him to flash. "I do not recall you summoning anyone, human, so perhaps one more lost Warden will not make such a very big impact."

"Hey, settle down." Ivy moved to stand between the Warden and Baen looming over him. "The last thing we need here is arguing among ourselves. Everybody take a deep breath and get a grip."

The kettle chose just that moment to whistle, the sound making Martin jump visibly. Baen felt a surge of dark satisfaction.

"Guardian, you should sit," she instructed. "There." She pointed to the chair at the small dinette that held the position farthest from Martin. The distance would not slow down an angry Guardian, but it might offer the human a false sense of security. "I think we could all use some tea."

"I could use more information." Reluctantly, Baen took the seat the female indicated, settling his large frame onto the spindly wooden frame with caution. "To begin with, what has happened to the Guild of Wardens?"

"How much time have you got?" Martin scoffed.

Ivy sent him a narrow look. "I doubt there's any milk in the fridge, Martin, but why don't you look for some sugar?"

If Baen read the subtext properly—never a Guardian's strong suit, mind you; his kind tended to find human behavior baffling—he detected a definite note of "and if you tell me you take it black I'll pour it down your trousers" in the request. Perhaps the human male did, too, because he rose to examine the counters and cupboards.

"I told you I'm not a member of the Guild," Ivy said, "so I wasn't aware of any problem at all until about eight months ago. That's when my uncle and cousin were killed."

He watched her fiddle with the teapot, lifting the lid to check the color of the brew before pouring three mugs of the hot liquid. Baen had no desire to drink tea, but even less to interrupt the female's story, so he said nothing.

"They were both members of the Guild," she continued. "Uncle George was my mother's older brother, and Jamie—James—was his son. His only child. Mum's family have been in the Guild for generations. The Fitzroys. I grew up knowing about the existence of magic and the basics behind the Guild and the Order. I heard all the stories and everything, but we moved back to the States when I was only three, and since neither of my parents was a Warden I was well out of it for most of my life. I mean, we visited Uncle George every year, but demon hunting really never featured as a topic during family reunions."

Baen should hope not. The Guild and the Guardians existed so that the rest of humanity did not have to concern themselves with the activities of the Order or the Demons they served. That should apply especially to human children, as Ivy had been.

"I knew Uncle George was a Warden, though, and I knew Jamie trained as one, too. We all sent him congratulations and gifts when he was inducted into the Guild, but that's as much thought as I really gave it. I guess like most people, I took for granted that we weren't in any real danger from the Darkness, because if we were, then the Wardens and the Guardians were there to deal with the threat."

"That is how it's supposed to work." Martin set a small bowl on the table and immediately transferred three spoonfuls of white crystals from it into his teacup. "Most Wardens don't expect to get involved in anything too messy. That's why each Guardian has a personal Warden and why some Wardens specialize in battle magic and such things. Me, I was always much more the academic sort. I did research, spell testing, that kind of thing."

Of that, Baen had no doubt. He could never imagine the timid male willingly facing off against a threat, even one as minor as a single *nocturni*. Put him up against a demon, and Martin would run screaming.

Or puking, as he had demonstrated in the alley earlier.

"Yes, well, it only works like that when the Guild has enough members," Ivy said, shaking her head when the other human nudged the sugar bowl her way. "I didn't know it until Uncle George was already gone, but several years ago, the Order began to . . . to pick off Wardens. I guess that's the only way to describe it. They started with the most isolated ones, the ones least likely to be missed, and just made them disappear. They killed them."

She paused to sip her tea before continuing. "No one registered it was a pattern until they started disappearing faster than the Guild could induct and train replacements. And still, it stayed quiet except in the immediate community of Wardens. It's not the sort of thing they'd want to advertise, you know? Plus, outside of the Guild, who even knows they exist? Besides the *nocturnis,* of course. But not talking about it only made it easier for the Order to get to them, because they weren't really expecting trouble. Then they hit the Guild headquarters directly. Not only did they take out almost a hundred Wardens in one shot, they destroyed the archives as well. It threw everything into chaos. The head council was wiped out; the rosters were gone. Honestly, had it never occurred to anyone that an electronic backup might be an idea worth considering? But anyway, no one even had access to records to tell them which Wardens were left or where to find them. At that point, the ones who were still alive went into hiding for their own protection."

Baen tried to imagine the situation. It would have been chaos, indeed. The Guild had always clung to the traditions laid down during its long history, distrusting technology because they claimed it interfered with their magical abilities. He didn't know if that was true or not. Guardians were magical beings, made of magic, but they could not utilize it in the way the Wardens did. A Guardian could never cast a spell. It might appear to be magic when he altered his form to appear human, but that was simply an alternate state of being as natural to him as his winged form. It had no effect on technology, and technology could not affect it.

Ivy grimaced, pulling his attention back to her story. "Maybe if Uncle George and Jamie had hidden, they'd still be alive, but they had realized what was happening. The Order had gone after the Guild to weaken it, but especially to prevent them from summoning the Guardians. We think the *nocturnis* have been trying to locate you guys as urgently as we have, only they want to get to you so that they can destroy you while you're vulnerable."

It was a sensible plan, though entirely lacking in honor. A Guardian possessed very few physical vulnerabilities. They were almost entirely immune to magic, supernaturally strong, and fiercely effective in battle. In their natural forms, their skin acted as armor superior to anything mankind had ever invented, and even when disguised as human, they remained stronger, faster, and harder to injure than any mortal. They also healed from wounds with amazing speed. An active Guardian was nearly impossible to kill.

However, when in their sleeping state, in the grip of magical slumber, a Guardian was very much like the stone statue he resembled. He weathered like stone in the elements—though that damage would disappear upon waking—and he could be smashed like stone with sufficient force. Being dropped from a great height, for example, would destroy a Guardian, as would explosives, or anything else that could generate massive concussive force.

Baen frowned. "I am confused by this. Yes, the *nocturnis* could attempt to destroy me and my brothers while we slept, but when one Guardian falls, another is immediately summoned. What good would it do the servants of the Darkness to break our sleeping forms when we would simply be replaced by another of equal ferocity?"

"The Guild has already discovered that's not quite the way it works," Ivy said, her expression grim. "An active Guardian who falls is immediately replaced, but if one of you is destroyed while you're asleep, you don't get a replacement until you're called for. Until he's called for. Whatever. A Guardian doesn't just appear. A summoning still has to take place. So if the Order could thin out the Guild, destroy the Guardians while they're in their statue forms, and not have enough Wardens left to perform summonings—"

"They could potentially strike before we could rise to stop them," Baen finished, his voice degenerating into a snarl as the intention behind the *nocturnis'* scheme became clear. "They could perhaps even manage to free one of the Seven from its prison without anything to stand in their way."

"One?" Martin scoffed. The sound held a note of hysteria. "We'd be lucky if it were just one."

"What do you mean?"

He'd risen halfway out of his chair before Ivy's outstretched hand brushed against his arm and stopped him in his tracks. He didn't know why.

"He means that we think that's already happened," she told him, a soft push urging him back into his seat. He fixed his gaze on her, and found her misty-gray eyes already watching him, their expression troubled but determined. "In fact, we think it's happened more than once."

The news made sparks of rage light in Baen's chest. The urge to fly at something, to fight, to destroy, filled his veins with heat and burned behind his eyes. How had this been allowed to happen? Where were his brothers while this scourge of Darkness invaded the human world? Surely, in the face of such a serious threat, they could have woken without their Wardens' ritual summonings.

"My contact in France says the group in Paris think there may be three of the Seven already here. And the Order won't stop until they have freed them all."

Chapter Six

For a minute there, Ivy thought she might be trapped in a cartoon, because it certainly looked as if Baen's head was about to explode all over the dead Warden's kitchen. The news of the Order's recent activities clearly did not sit well with the Guardian.

Imagine that—a warrior all bent out of shape over the idea that his enemies were on the verge of routing his side before he'd ever gotten a chance to take the field. Who'da thunk?

"I must make contact with my brothers. Immediately."

It took a minute for Ivy to figure out what Baen had said. She had to translate the words into English from the barely intelligible, animalistic snarl in which he'd actually uttered them.

"The other Guardians? Good luck." She shook her head. "Do you think that every remaining member of the Guild hasn't been searching for them from the first moment they realized what was going on? You guys are MIA. You were stationed in cities all over the world, from what anyone can remember, but only the archives recorded exactly where. And we're pretty sure that your personal Wardens were the first ones the Order got rid of, making finding you next to impossible. Let alone summoning you."

He locked that blazing gaze on her, the flames that had previously flickered in the black depths now roaring like an inferno, almost obscuring the dark. "I am here now. I also do not believe that none of my brothers would not have already woken in the face of such a grave threat."

"Oh, yeah? Well, where are they, then?" Martin asked. He looked both belligerent and downtrodden, an odd combination, but each emotion suited what Ivy had seen of his character. He had shown himself to be both a wuss and a whiner. "If the Guardians are among us, they're bloody well taking their time in sorting this mess out."

As much as Ivy hated to agree with the man, he did have a point. "The remaining Guild in Paris have had no contact from any of you. Wouldn't that be the first thing you did if you were summoned? Get in touch with other Wardens?"

"Were we summoned?" Baen countered. "Did either of you perform that ritual to waken me from my sleep?"

The question struck Ivy for the first time. In the face of the demonic attack, she had not stopped to think about where the Guardian had come from, let alone how he had gotten there. She had been too grateful for his rescue to worry about the hows and whys. But now that she thought about it, it made no sense. At least, not according to all the stories and legends her family had told her over the years.

The Guardians had not been created by the Guild. As far as anyone could tell, they had been created by the Light itself, but they had first been summoned by the Wardens in order to battle the Demons of the Darkness. When the enemy had been defeated, the Wardens had then placed them in a form of magical slumber until they might again be needed to defend humanity. So, in a way, the appearance and withdrawal of the stone warriors had always been under the control of the members of the Guild.

Personally, the idea had always struck Ivy as unfair, almost a form of slavery. Instead of allowing the Guardians to live in the world they defended, the Wardens kept them on a sort of magical leash, only allowing them brief periods of freedom during which they were expected to fight to save a population of beings to whom they had no real connection, either physical or emotional. Clearly, the Guardians were not human, but a separate species altogether, and since they did not live among humans, they had no chance to form any kind of emotional attachment to them. The Guild treated them like junkyard dogs in a way, isolating and ostracizing them, while still expecting loyalty and protection in the face of danger.

Talk about getting the short end of the stick. From what Ivy could tell, the Guardians got that short end poked right in their eyes.

Baen made a good point, though. Neither she nor Martin had performed the summoning spell that was supposedly required to draw a Guardian from sleep. She doubted either of them would have known how to go about it, even if they had wanted to. So, why was Baen not still sleeping atop that abandoned Gothic church in Croydon? His appearance and timely rescue should never have happened. It should have been impossible.

"No," she finally said in answer to his question. "We didn't wake you. Not deliberately, anyway. How did that happen? Has it ever happened before? Is there supposed to be some other way to wake a Guardian than using the Guild's spell?"

She looked from Baen to Martin, but the Warden was shaking his head. "Not that I know of. Only personal Wardens are taught the spell to begin with, but according to the Guild, you have to perform it, and perform it properly, in order to wake one up."

"Then you shouldn't be here." She looked at Baen, now truly confused.

"Yet here I am." He spread his arms to indicate his presence. As if someone his size could be overlooked.

"So you think that if you woke without a direct summons from a Warden, others like you might have done the same thing?"

"Why not?"

Martin made a face. "Perhaps because it should have been impossible the first time, so the odds against it happening a second, let alone a third or a seventh, rank somewhere in the range of astronomical. Trust me, Wardens don't have that kind of luck. Not these days."

Ivy had to stifle the urge to slap the man. She'd had just about enough of his whinging. She ignored him and instead thought about the possibility for the first time.

"If any other Guardians have woken, my contacts haven't mentioned it," she said. "I don't think that's the kind of thing they would have kept to themselves, either. Not only could everyone on our side use the morale boost that kind of news would have given us, but I'm pretty sure that putting the word out would make the best use of the network when it came to finding more of you. And I know the Guild has been looking. It's the main task everyone we've gotten to safety has been put to work on. The survivors know perfectly well that without the Guardians, the world is pretty much screwed."

"We're screwed anyway."

"My God, would you shut up?" Ivy rounded on Martin with a furious glare. "You are not helping, you whiny bastard. If you can't contribute anything positive to the conversation, you can feel free to leave."

The man went white. "Y-you're kicking me out?

But—but what if there are more demons out there? Or *nocturnis*?"

She rolled her eyes. "I meant you could leave the room." As appealing as the idea of washing her hands of the Warden was, her conscience wouldn't let her throw him to the wolves. More's the pity. "There's an entire empty house here, including three bedrooms upstairs. Why don't you go and try to get some sleep, or something?"

His expression of panic faded, and his features settled back into their lines of discontent. "Fine. I know when I'm not wanted."

Ivy and Baen watched him shove away from the table and stalk out of the kitchen. A moment later, his footsteps sounded on the stairs to the second floor.

"Clearly, he does not," Baen rumbled, "or he would have made himself scarce some time ago."

Ivy snorted, but she actually felt some of the tension leave her muscles without Martin around to throw in his two cents. "I'm sure he's just reacting badly to the fear and stress. He can't be that bad normally, right?"

Baen looked doubtful, but said nothing.

She refocused on the interrupted conversation. "Anyway, I am pretty certain that if there are other Guardians currently awake and moving around, the contacts I have in France aren't aware of it. Neither are the ones in Scotland, Spain, or the Channel Islands. So how could we find out either way?"

The Guardian eyed her for a moment. He must have calmed down a bit from the shock of her news, because his eyes no longer looked the same as they had in his gargoylelike form. Now, they appeared entirely human, though she didn't think she had ever seen a brown so deep before. Only a ring of dark amber around his pupils kept the iris from blending entirely into the black.

"It would be helpful if you had received the proper training," he said after a moment.

"Training?" It took a moment for her to catch on. "You mean Guild training? I told you, I'm not a Warden."

"And I told you, you are mine."

The words sent a jolt through her, one that had very little to do with the shock of being called a Warden. Butterflies jigged in her belly, and an inappropriate flush of heat filled her.

"My Warden," he added a moment later. His gaze had heated, though. At least, she thought it had. The amber around his pupils suddenly bore a stark resemblance to the fire that burned behind his gargoyle's black eyes.

Or was she imagining things? Could she really be attracted to a creature who wasn't even human? No matter how well he pretended. Something about it seemed . . . inappropriate.

In fact, when she thought about it, even his human form was out of her league. He could have passed for an actor, or a male model, with his perfect, chiseled features and athlete's body. Take his shirt off and point a camera at him, and he'd look perfectly at home on the set of a blockbuster superhero action movie. She, on the other hand, looked entirely average. Her coloring might be striking, and she had gotten to be in very good shape while working to save Wardens from the Order, but her features were nothing special. Her nose was a shade too big for her face, her mouth a shade too small. It had a nice enough shape, but her lips weren't plump, and her front teeth overlapped just a bit when she smiled. She also had freckles. Lots of freckles. In an age of airbrushed skin perfection, she stood out like polka-dotted cotton in a sea of peach-toned silk.

Besides, they each had more important things to worry

about than whether or not they found the other attractive. Things like . . . hm, the end of the world, maybe?

Ivy cleared her throat and tried to focus back on the conversation. "Right. Your Warden. I'm still not sure I believe that. It doesn't make any sense. Not only don't I have any training at serving a Guardian, I don't have any training at all. I have no official association with the Guild whatsoever. Never inducted, never tested, never met anyone who was a member, outside of Jamie and Uncle George. Not until all this started happening. I don't see how it's possible that I could be a Warden and somehow just get overlooked for twenty-six years."

"The Guardians have never concerned ourselves with the inner workings of the Guild," Baen dismissed. "I cannot say why they would not have brought you into the fold, but it is clear that you were meant to be there. You have magic, much stronger magic than the male Warden, not to mention a character better suited for defending against the machinations of the Order than that weakling."

That sort of praise could go to a girl's head if she let it, but the reference to her "magic" helped her stay grounded. She didn't find anything particularly magical in the ability to listen helplessly while terrible things happened to other people. It didn't do anyone any good, and it only made her feel like a failure. There had been plenty of times during her life when she'd considered it a hell of a long way from a blessing. The ability to cast a spell or even physically manipulate energy, those would have been useful. Maybe with a talent like that, she could have actually helped someone. That would have counted as magic.

"I don't have any magic," she said, her tone dismissive to match her feelings. "You're seeing something that isn't there."

"I do not think so. Do you not possess abilities that other humans do not?"

"That's not magic. Some people have certain psychic talents in this world. It makes us freaks, but it doesn't make us Wardens."

"Your answer is yes, then," he said, looking smug. "You do have abilities."

"Ability," she corrected. She still felt loath to admit it, especially when he seemed to view it as something positive. "And not a very useful one at that."

"What is it?"

Ivy grimaced. He would have to make her get into specifics. "I hear things sometimes," she admitted reluctantly. "Things that are happening in other places. I don't see them, or anything. They aren't like visions. There's no vision involved at all, and I only hear them while they're happening. Simultaneously. I don't get to listen in ahead of time and warn anybody, because they're not predictions. They don't do anyone any good at all. Least of all me."

"And you do not consider this magical?"

"How is it magic to know when someone is frightened or furious or heartbroken or in pain and not be able to do anything about it?" The memory of lying in the dark, listening while something tore her uncle and cousin into pieces came flooding back and she had to swallow hard against both the grief and the sickness it inspired. Sometimes she believed she would still be hearing those noises when she was a little old lady in a rocking chair. They hadn't strayed far from her mind since the moment she first heard them.

"How is it not?" Baen asked. "You seem to have a mistaken impression as to what magic is. Perhaps this comes from your lack of training from the Guild. In any event, magic is merely the deliberate use of energy to accomplish things that may or may not be accomplished otherwise."

"Yeah, and like I said, my ability has never accomplished doodly-squat."

"Do not be obtuse. Hearing those events is the accomplishment. That is how your mind has been manipulating energy for years now. The fact that it has been doing so with no conscious effort on your part merely speaks to your innate power. Of course you have been unable to make use of your abilities; you have never been instructed in how to do so. But clearly the ability to manipulate energy is within you. You just need to learn how to channel your own instincts."

Huh?

Ivy had to look down at her feet to make sure they still had contact with the floor. She felt as if she'd just been bowled over like a ninepin. If the Guardian was right, the entire world was about to tilt on its access. Everything she had ever believed would go up in smoke, because it meant that she might actually have to take him seriously about her potential to become a Warden.

And that stirred up a bunch more questions, ones it actually hurt her to think about. If Ivy had always been meant to be a Warden, why had the Guild never made contact with her. Why had her own family not told her? Had Uncle George never seen it? That seemed impossible, given he had known her for twenty-five years and Baen had spotted it in less than that number of minutes.

Or even worse, had her uncle known and deliberately kept the information from her? That thought hit like a fist to the solar plexus; it knocked the wind from her. He had known, her whole family had known, how badly some of her "episodes" affected her. There had been times when the sounds of someone else's grief or agony had literally knocked her to the floor with empathic backlash, times when she had sobbed her eyes out at her inability to help or even comfort those whose tragedies she overheard. Uncle George had seen at least one event with his own eyes, and he had never told her that a little bit of training might not only make it easier to bear, but might actually give her the power to take action.

How could he have done that to her?

Shaking, Ivy pushed out of her chair and began to pace the narrow kitchen floor. "That's—I don't—I'm not sure I believe that." She finally got the words out, but it took some pushing and stuttering and headshaking along the way. "I'm not sure I want to believe that."

"Does that matter? Truth is. It exists separately from belief and independent of it."

"Yeah, can we not get all deep and philosophical right now? I think I've got more than enough on my plate at the moment without having to contemplate the nature of reality."

He fell cooperatively silent, but she could still feel his gaze on her as she moved back and forth across the tile. Part of her wondered whether he could see inside her with that burning stare of his, but she dismissed the thought. Not only did it make her stomach do weird flips, but since he hadn't run away screaming, it seemed unlikely. No one seeing the mess of turmoil and exhaustion under her controlled exterior would have wanted to stick around, let alone think she could be of any use to anyone.

And right there Ivy realized her fatal mistake—she had allowed herself to think the word "exhaustion," and like a Pavlovian response, acknowledging the existence of the weight of her own tiredness brought it crashing down on top of her head. How long had it been since she had gotten some sleep? Not last night, not with planning this evening's adventure down to the last cocked-up detail.

What time was it, anyway?

She searched the room until she spotted the display on the microwave oven. It was just after midnight. Not horribly late in the grand scheme of things, but to Ivy it felt like the wee hours of the morning. She rubbed her eyes and tried to focus. What had she been saying?

"Right. Magic, Wardens, talents. Me," she muttered, mostly to herself. "Let's just set that aside for the moment and focus on priorities. What's priority number one at this moment, given the circumstances we're in?"

Baen replied as if she had directed the question to him. "We must locate the rest of my brethren. If any of the Seven already move among the mortals of this realm as you believe, then all of us may be required to ensure we can banish them once more."

"And now we're just repeating the same conversation," she snapped. "I already told you, if any other Guardian is awake, I haven't heard of it, and neither has anyone I know. So what do you suggest we do to find them? Start knocking on doors? I'll take the house on the left, you try the one on the right?"

"Once again you use sarcasm to express a negative reaction. I must assume this is the case, because such an action would be futile and waste precious time."

Ivy stopped pacing and faced him, crossing her arms over her chest and glaring at him through eyes she had to imagine were narrow and bloodshot by now. "You have a better suggestion, then? Brilliant. Let's hear it."

This time he ignored the sting of sarcasm in her voice and simply answered her challenge. "First, you must alert the Guild's survivors of my presence. This will give them renewed faith in our presence and inspire their continued search."

"Yeah, obviously the Guild needs to know," she grumbled. "I wasn't planning to keep you a secret from them. But that still doesn't get us any closer to the other Guardians."

"Second," Baen continued, as if she had not interrupted, "you must indicate my presence in London in a public forum. Guardians monitor such things whenever we are able so that we can connect to face threats requiring greater strength than a single one of us can muster."

Announce it in a public forum? What did he expect her to do? she wondered. Produce a television commercial? Stand in the middle of Piccadilly Circus and hand out flyers? "Sorry, but we're all out of town criers at the moment. Do you think smoke signals would work in a pinch? And yes, I'm being sarcastic," she snapped as soon as she saw his mouth open. "Sue me. It's how I react to stress."

"I can see that," he said, his deep voice even but somehow tinged with amusement. At her expense, of course. "But I did not intend to suggest such primitive methods. We must reach the greatest possible audience in the smallest possible time. The situation is urgent. You must use your electronic machines to speak with people all over the world in the same instant."

She blinked, her brows furrowing as she tried to translate his archaic speech to modern technology. "Electronic machines? You mean computers? You want me to spread you all over the Internet?"

"Yes, the Internet. Forgive me. While I may know the concepts, sometime it takes longer to process the language of what I receive when it comes to new knowledge."

"What are you talking about? What knowledge that you receive? And if you've been asleep for a few hundred years, what do you know about computers and the Internet?"

"I know of their existence," he said firmly. "A Guardian's slumber is not like that of a human. We retain a certain awareness even as we sleep. In addition, we share our knowledge among ourselves. When one Guardian learns of a significant change in the world, he adds it to the understanding of all of us. It is a trick we use to compensate for the passage of time between our wakings."

Okay, that sounded pretty cool. Ivy imagined it would go a long way to coping with the twenty-first century after falling asleep in the seventeenth if you could just download a summary of everything that had changed in that time from a sort of hive mind.

Not that she was comparing the Guardians to bees, mind you. Or, you know, the Borg.

Then the true implications of his revelation hit her. "Wait. But computers have only been in everyday use for the last thirty or forty years, and the Internet for, like, twenty. So that would mean a Guardian would *have* to have been awake during that time for you to know about all that. Right?"

Baen nodded. "Exactly. Therefore, at least one of my brethren is out there now, waiting to be found. Someone will be aware of it and will be attempting to make contact just as I am. We merely need to achieve an intersection of those attempts."

"Still easier said than done," Ivy warned, but at least she could see the possibility now. "I guess it's worth a try, though. Come on."

Chapter Seven

She turned to stride out of the kitchen, the scrape of chair legs across tile telling her the Guardian had obeyed her summons (no pun intended). He followed her down the short hall to the town house's front room where a desk in the corner supported a small desktop computer. Ivy settled herself into the chair in front of it and booted up the system. When she glanced over at Baen, she found him examining the surroundings with a slight frown.

"What's wrong?"

He looked back at her. "You said that the human who lived here was a Warden, but that he is among those who were killed by the Order?"

"Yes. So?"

"I did not think that a dwelling of this sort would remain untouched after its owner's death. Should someone else not be living here now? Do we not run the risk of discovery by remaining here?"

"Oh, that. Yeah, that's why I chose this place," she said, only half paying attention to the questions. She was relieved to see Adam Harris had not bothered to put a password on his desktop. "Normally, you'd be right, but this guy's disappearance was one of the first things I

looked into when I got to England and got involved in
the missing Wardens. Harris—the owner of this place—
had no next of kin and he was a bit of a recluse. He
worked from home, paid all of his bills by electronic
transfer from his bank, and he was only in his late thirties. I guess he hadn't seen the need to write a will yet,
so no one was set up to inherit the house. As long as the
money in his accounts holds out, no one is going to turn
off the power or come looking into buying the building."

She pulled up an Internet search engine and directed
it to her online mail server, the one she used for her work
with the Warden relocation network. "We won't be staying past morning, so for now, we're fine."

If by fine, she meant exhausted, strung out, and
running on pure adrenaline, which at the moment she
was. But they were at least safe from immediate discovery. Baen merely grunted, which she decided to take for
an indication that he trusted her.

Hey, it had been a long day. She was ready to take
what she could get.

Her fingers stumbled a little over the keyboard as she
first sent a message to Paris. She'd already sent Paul a
brief coded text message (little more than one word) to
let him know Martin wouldn't arrive. Later, she'd get
him a more detailed summary of what had happened.
But for now, she wanted to go straight to the person who
had the most immediate contact with the Wardens' safe
house—the contact she knew as Asile, the French word
for "asylum."

The delete key got a hefty workout, but after a couple
of minutes, she had drafted a carefully worded, deliberately obscure message that should alert Asile that a
Guardian had surfaced in London and wanted to join up
against the Darkness. That would take care of getting
word out to the assembled Wardens in Paris. Now the

question was where to make a similar announcement on the Net that would attract the attention of the right parties (namely, other awoken Guardians) without bringing the collective might of the Order down on their heads.

No pressure or anything.

"You know, it would be a heck of a lot easier to make this brilliant idea of yours work if I knew more about computers," she grumbled, scowling at the monitor while she chewed on her thumbnail. "I'm a technical writer, not a hacker. Or a criminal mastermind. I don't troll the Dark Net looking to score plutonium so I can make my own nukes. I don't even know how to get to the Dark Net."

Baen had given up prowling about the room and had come to stand behind her chair. Because looming was always the way to make someone more comfortable. "I do not know what you refer to, but I believe there are places in this electronic world where humans post advertisements for others they wish to meet or for things they wish to acquire. Are there not?"

She rolled her eyes. "You want me to set up a profile for you on LuvMatch dot com? I'm not sure you're going to wind up with exactly the sort of response you're looking for with that tactic."

Her fingers froze over the keys and her eyes narrowed as his words really sank in. "Oh, holy crap," she muttered to herself as she began typing furiously. "It can't possibly be that obvious, can it? There's no way."

A Web site popped up on the monitor, blocks of columned text with the occasional bold heading. It was Spartan and inelegant and ridiculously familiar.

"What is this?" Baen leaned over her shoulder to peer at the screen.

Ivy snorted out a laugh. "Welcome to Craigslist, Guardian. If you want people all over the world to see what you have to offer, this is the place to show it to them. Shall we see if anyone's out there waiting to snap you up?"

She had her head tilted back so she could see his face, a slightly goofy smile born of a mix of exhaustion and elation curving her lips when he looked down. Maybe it was because of seeing his features upside down, or maybe it was a hallucination born from lack of sleep, but for a moment, Ivy could have sworn the fire flared back into his gaze as he studied her features. Her smile faded, and she told herself that it was only in her imagination that the flames brightened as he watched her lips move into a more uncertain expression.

"Absolutely," he finally rumbled, his voice quiet. Something about the deep, gravelly pitch rattled her, rolling around low in her belly. The sensation bore a vague resemblance to her earlier butterflies, except this one was accompanied by a surge of warmth that raced in the opposite direction from her blushing cheeks.

"What shall we say?"

Ivy jerked her head forward and fixed her wide-eyed gaze on the computer monitor. A jolt of adrenaline temporarily wiped away the strain of fatigue. "Uh, um, what about something like this?"

Her fingers flew as she composed a posting that said nothing specific, yet would be read by someone familiar with the Guild and the Guardians as highly significant. It helped that she had just written something very similar to Asile, and she borrowed heavily from that message.

Baen leaned closer as he read the draft, his chest brushing up against her shoulder in a move that made her wonder if it was entirely accidental. Either way, it made her fight hard against a shiver of awareness. In the back of her mind, she realized that she had expected him to be cold for some reason, maybe because of the stone he resembled in his natural form, but she'd been wrong. The Guardian radiated heat, a heat she wanted to lean into and absorb through direct skin-to-skin contact.

Down, girl.

Oh, bollocks. She was losing her bloody mind here. She needed to get a grip.

Ivy cleared her throat and tried to subtly scoot herself out of accidental touching range. Because that was all it could be, she assured herself—entirely accidental. "So, uh, what do you think? Will this work?"

"There is only one way to know for certain," Baen said, straightening. "Allow others to read this message and hope that among them, we can find my brothers."

"Okay, then." Ivy clicked the button to post the ad and let out a sigh. The act seemed to drain the last of her energy, and she almost swayed on her feet when she stood up from the desk chair. "Now all we can do is wait, and I plan to wait while I'm unconscious. I really, really, really need to get some sleep."

She felt the Guardian rake his gaze over her, taking in her red and swollen eyes, her pale skin, and the subtle tremor in her arms and legs. "You have allowed yourself to become too exhausted," he growled. "This is unacceptable. Where do you plan to rest this night?"

"Uh, duh. Of course I'm exhausted." She glared at him. "In case you didn't notice, there were a lot of things I had to get done tonight. Did I hallucinate that you watched me do most of them? And where the heck do you think I'm sleeping? Like I told Martin, there are three bedrooms upstairs. I'm kind of assuming he's only using one of them. I'll take the second, and you can use the third."

Before she had more than the first few words out, Baen had reached out and swept her off her feet. Literally. It wasn't terribly romantic, given he had just scolded her for something she hadn't been able to avoid and she was in the process of chewing him out over that, but it happened nonetheless. When she mentioned the bedroom situation, he turned toward the hall and the stairs to the second floor. Carrying her. Like a toddler having a tantrum over nap time.

Bad analogy, though, because Ivy wanted nothing more just then than a soft mattress and her warm blankie. Automatically she took a deep breath, gearing herself up to protest being manhandled, when a voice in her head demanded to know what was wrong with her. The Guardian wasn't hurting her, and him carrying her would save her from expending energy she didn't have to drag her drooping behind up a flight of stairs and down another hall to the place where she could finally get some sleep. Why shouldn't she let him?

"I have no need of more sleep," Baen said. The words vibrated from his chest in a way she could actually feel as he cradled her against him. It felt almost like the purring of a really gigantic cat. She kind of liked it. "I have had my fill over the past few centuries. I will keep watch while you and the other Warden rest."

Ivy didn't realize her eyes had closed until they flew open at the feel of being set down on a bed and covered with a thick duvet. She had missed most of the trip, her body giving out on her with the need to sleep. Now, the Guardian leaned over her, his face only inches from hers. Without her permission, her hand lifted from beneath the heavy cover and reached up to press her palm against his cheek. His skin felt at once both smooth and rough, like polished marble warmed by the sun and rough granite weathered by wind and rain.

Or maybe that was just evening stubble. Whatever. Either way, it made her fingertips tingle.

Somewhere in the back of her mind, a tiny little chirping tried to tell her to stop! Back away! Run for her life! Avoid all entanglements! But Ivy was too tired to listen. Her eyes drifted shut again, and her lips curved in a small smile.

"G'night, Guardian."

She slurred the words, already half asleep. But that didn't prevent her from feeling the very distinct pressure of warm male lips pressed to hers for a lingering moment.

"Good night, little Warden." The deep, familiar voice caressed her as she drifted into oblivion. "Rest well. And dream of me."

As tempted as he was to remain at her side and watch her sleep, Baen rose from his seat on the side of Ivy's bed and forced himself to leave the room. The sight of her warm and relaxed in slumber tempted him on a level he had never before experienced, and that in itself was something that called for careful consideration.

A Guardian was not supposed to form an attachment to any particular human. His kind existed in order to protect humanity as a whole, not to single out individuals for special favor. Never before in his long centuries of existence had he even considered anything different, but meeting the small female named Ivy had turned his entire world on its head.

He padded down the stairs to the ground floor, his steps naturally silent even in his human guise, which had begun to chafe and bind like a set of clothes one size too small. He itched to return to his natural form, but such a confined space would barely accommodate his body, let alone his massive wings, so he would have to tough it out for a while longer.

Might as well take advantage, he thought, and threw

himself down backward onto the sofa in the modest living room. Couldn't do that while wearing his wings.

Baen stared up at the ceiling and tried to sort through the huge amount of information that had crashed down upon him since his waking. The fact that Ivy kept intruding into his thoughts didn't help, but it did add to the evidence that had begun to pile up to indicate that this waking would turn out to be something very different from the ones in his past. Something strange was afoot here.

It all had begun with the manner of his waking. He had been correct in thinking that neither Ivy nor the cowardly Warden, Martin, had intentionally summoned him from slumber. That counted as oddity number one. Like them, he had always believed that nothing else could penetrate the magical sleep that held the Guardians in stasis between the times when their aid was needed to battle against the Demons of the Darkness. All the legends indicated this.

Well, all except one.

Baen stacked his hands behind his head and let his mind settle on that particular legend. He had never paid that one much attention in the past. After all, it had all happened so long ago, back at the very origins of his kind, that most Guardians, himself included, tended to dismiss it as folklore. A pretty tale, romantic and sweet, but not at all applicable to the Guardians who existed in Baen's time.

The Guardians and the Maidens, the tale was called, during those few times when anyone bothered to mention it. According to the story, after the Guild had initially summoned the first seven Guardians and those warriors had completed their task by ridding the human world of the threat from the Demons, they had been sent into their first slumber by the Wardens. That had been fine, but after they woke to battle the next threat, they received the same treatment, and the same after that.

And the same after that.

After a time, the first Guardians had lost any interest in protecting humanity. They had no connection to the people they defended, spent no time with them, knew little of their characters or their customs. Eventually, a time came when the Wardens summoned the Guardians to defend them from a new threat, but the Guardians did not wake. They failed to respond to the humans' need, and it looked as if the mortal world would fall to the Darkness.

The Guild had despaired. Until one day, a woman of power—one who had magic of her own—appeared and ignored the Wardens' attempts to dismiss her. She knew the danger to humanity was great and that the Guardians represented the only hope for her people to survive. So she knelt at the foot of the statue of a Guardian and she prayed for him to awaken and defend her. The Wardens scoffed and berated her, but her pleas worked. The Guardian responded to her as if to a summons and woke from his magical slumber. He claimed the woman as his Warden and his mate and once again took up arms against the Darkness.

One by one, more women of power appeared and woke the Guardians, becoming their helpers and their mates. The supernatural warriors defeated the forces of Darkness, but once the threat was vanquished, they refused to return to sleep and be parted from their mates. Instead, they remained among the humans, giving up their immortality to live out their days with their partners. New Guardians were summoned, and the legends recorded that any who came after retained the right to find a human mate and forfeit their position to remain at her side.

Among the Guardians who came after them, the story took on the status of a fairy tale—something to be told and retold, passed down across generations, but unlikely to ever actually happen. Baen had never even considered the possibility.

Until he had smelled the sharp, sweet tang of citrus and seen a tiny human female take a stand against three minor demons and fight like a Valkyrie, despite the near inevitability of defeat. She had captured his attention, to be certain. Ivy fascinated him, and he found that implication . . . disturbing.

His mind skittered away from the M-word. He had no proof of the legend of the Maidens, and he had certainly never wasted his time contemplating the repercussions of its veracity. He couldn't afford to waste time now, either. Instead of worrying about his reaction to Ivy—strong and unexpected though it might be—he should worry over how exactly he had woken from his sleep.

Clearly there had been no summoning, and he harbored no illusions that Ivy had paused in that alley while cornered by three demons to pray for the intervention of a Guardian. There had to be something else behind his waking, a sort of magic he had never before encountered.

He made a sound of disgust and shifted his position on the battered sofa. He lifted his feet to balance his lower legs on the arm of the piece of furniture to compensate for it being too short to encompass his entire frame. Yet another inconvenience of the human realm. Even in his disguise, this place was not designed to accommodate him.

Perhaps Ivy was, though.

Groaning, he cursed his thoughts for drifting even as her image appeared in his mind's eye. He wished he had seen her in sunlight instead of the dark alley and then the dim, artificial lights inside this dwelling. As keen as his night vision might be for shapes and details, it could not show him the true color of her pale skin or long, straight hair. Those things could only be appreciated in the day, and morning still had hours before its arrival.

Until then, he would just have to experience frustration. It built within him, only accentuated by the memory of that single, chaste kiss.

He shouldn't have done it. Baen knew perfectly well it had been a mistake, knew it even before it happened, but he had been helpless to resist. She had felt so tempting in his arms, small and delicate and soft in spite of her obvious strength. The excuse of carrying her up the stairs had not lasted long enough, and he had placed her on the narrow bed with great reluctance. His instincts had urged him to hold on to her, or better yet, to stretch out beside her and cradle her close while she slept.

When he thought of it in those terms, a brief kiss seemed like a reasonable consolation prize.

Perhaps it would count as such if it didn't haunt him now, the feeling of her soft lips, her sleepy warmth, the faint taste of flowery hops and sweet malt mingling with bitter tea on her lips. Her scent had filled his head, bright and mouthwatering, and now he could not get it out of his mind.

It was a good thing a Guardian needed so little sleep during his brief periods of wakefulness, Baen reflected, glowering up at the ceiling, because at the moment, he could not have rested had the fate of humanity depended upon it. His mind was too full of Ivy.

And Ivy's bed was too empty of him.

Chapter Eight

A heavy knock rattled the front door at barely half past nine the next morning.

In the kitchen, Martin gave a sharp squeak and jumped so hard, he sloshed a full cup of tea out over his hand. Then he squeaked again at the pain of the scalding liquid. Ivy turned to glance at Baen, also surprised but hardly ready to panic.

"No one should know we're here," she said even as she pushed out of her chair and set down her half-eaten slice of toast. "Hopefully, it's just kids working for some fundraiser or other."

"At this time of morning? On a school day?" Martin shook his head and darted a glance at the back door. "We should run."

"We should keep calm," Baen said, and followed Ivy into the hall.

Another knock sounded, even louder than the last.

"That does *not* sound like kids," Martin hissed from behind them. "For God's sake, don't open it!"

Ivy ignored him. Not that she yanked the panel wide and invited in every stranger and demon passing in the street, but she stood on her toes to peek out the judas hole. The distorted image of two people, a man and a woman, looked calmly back at her.

She settled back on her heels and turned to look at Baen.

It was an action she had so far avoided this morning. Waking up alone in a strange bed, in a strange house, had been one thing, but then the memories of her failed attempt to get Martin to France had flooded back, followed by the attack by the demons, followed by the appearance of the Guardian.

Followed by that Kiss.

It earned that capital letter.

Not because it was the best kiss she had ever received, or the hottest, or even the most unexpected. It got the big K because it had shaken her down to her pink-polished toenails, even though she couldn't be entirely sure she hadn't imagined it.

She couldn't have, right? Ivy wasn't the sort of girl who went around imagining that men had kissed her when they really hadn't, not even when she found them ridiculously attractive and they carried her to bed when she nearly passed out from exhaustion. She didn't. Honest.

Which could only mean that Baen had kissed her.

Why?

A third knock made her jump, which made her cheeks turn the approximate color of ripe pomegranate. She knew from experience that the shade was oh so becoming on her, especially now, since she had removed her wig and makeup as soon as she had woken up that morning. If past experience was any indicator, she probably looked like the illegitimate offspring of Bozo the Clown and the Great Pumpkin.

"Two people," she managed to spit out, shifting her gaze to somewhere over Baen's left ear. "I don't recognize them, but they look pretty normal."

He maintained the same stony expression he'd worn all morning. The one that had made her start questioning the reality of the Kiss. "I detect no energy of the Darkness, but you will step back while I ascertain their identities."

Her red cheeks and embarrassment left Ivy incapable of offering up a protest at the overprotective order. At least, that's what she told herself. It sounded better than admitting to herself that she leaped to obey his commands like some meek little miss.

Baen slid back the bolt from its latch, then opened the main lock to pull the door ajar a bare few inches. He didn't bother to offer a greeting, just gazed out at the figures on the stoop like a bouncer at the door to a club.

From her vantage point behind him, Ivy couldn't see anything more than she had spied out the peephole. She recalled a woman of average height with an athletic figure and dark hair, as well as a tall, wiry man with a swimmer's build and hair that fell in tousled waves. Like she had told Baen, they had looked normal to her.

Then she heard the woman speak and "normal" morphed into a relative thing.

"Thank the Light, it is you. We had feared the message was a mistake, or even a trap. Welcome back, brother. It is very good to see you."

Brother?

Startled, Ivy stepped to the side and tried to scoot around Baen's imposing form to get a better look at their visitors. His arm shot out to block her path and keep her from moving past his side. She looked up at him, back to the dark-haired woman, then back to Baen.

"What's going on?" she demanded. "I thought 'brother' was what you guys called each other. What gives?"

The woman turned her gaze to Ivy and her brow furrowed. "Are you his Warden, female?"

"Female?" Ivy repeated with a snort. "Well, I suppose that's more original than plain ol' 'bitch.' Who the hell are you? And what do you mean, am I his Warden?"

The man on the steps inched forward and placed his hand on his companion's shoulder, giving it a squeeze. "Sorry. Ash didn't mean to sound insulting. She hasn't quite gotten the hang of the local vernacular, if you take my meaning."

He had a lyrical Irish accent, nothing too thick, just enough to complement his relaxed air. An air that was completely lacking in his female friend.

He extended his free hand and offered it to them with a smile. "My name is Michael Drummond, and this is my partner, Ash. We saw the ad you posted on Craigslist last night and came over on the first plane. May we come in?"

Baen ignored Michael's outstretched hand, but Ivy shook it reflexively.

"The ad?" she repeated, casting the Guardian beside her a sideways glance full of questions. He didn't so much as twitch. "What ad are you referring to? Specifically."

"The one that said a Guardian had woken here in London and was seeking others of his kind," Ash said bluntly. "Others like me."

"Like you?" She couldn't help it. Ivy glanced from the brunette woman in front of her to the hulking male mountain by her side and back again. Several times. She somehow failed to see the resemblance. "Are you trying to tell us that you're a Guardian?"

Her incredulous tone might not have been all that polite, but she just couldn't help it. There was no such thing as a female Guardian.

Was there?

"What do you know of Guardians, female?" Baen finally asked, his voice emerging as a low, menacing growl.

"Clearly it cannot be much if you do not understand that they are warriors, not nursemaids."

"Oh, feck," Michael hissed, visibly wincing as he took two large steps to the side, until he nearly fell off the steps. He shot Ivy a wry glance. "You might want to back up there a bit. He's going to be sorry he said that."

It didn't take Ivy long to understand what he meant.

The woman called Ash didn't even bother to reply to Baen's insulting words or his sneering expression. Instead, she simply stepped forward into the shadows of the threshold and reached out with an arm that was suddenly gray and muscular and tipped with lethally sharp claws. She snapped her fingers closed around the Guardian's throat—the *other* Guardian's throat, Ivy suddenly understood—and bared a set of long, intimidating fangs.

"Would you care to rephrase that, brother?" Ash spit out, her own growl more than a match for Baen's. "Or should I rip out your throat and let the Guardian who takes your place offer his apology in your stead?"

Baen remained silent, and Ivy shot frantic glances around the assembly, waiting for someone to do something sensible. When her gaze lit on Michael, he just shrugged as if to indicate he had tried to warn them.

Wondering where she had left her sanity, Ivy stepped forward, insinuating her much smaller frame between the two snarling Guardians. "Wow, way to get the family reunion off to an exciting start." She tried to offer Ash a smile, but she had the feeling it looked more like a pained grimace. "I apologize for Baen. He's been a little grumpy this morning. We had kind of a rough night. Do you think you could let him go now? I mean, yes, that was a lousy thing for him to say, but you kind of took us by surprise. We weren't even sure anyone would see that Craigslist ad, let alone respond this quickly. Please?" she added when Ash didn't move. "I think we should all sit down inside and talk. Okay?"

It took another several heartbeats—admittedly, racing ones—before Ash released her grip and swept past Baen into the front hall. "Fine, but we must talk quickly. It is important that we all begin our journey as soon as possible."

"Journey? What journey?" Baen demanded, grudgingly responding to Ivy's nudge and moving to allow their visitors inside.

"To Paris," Michael said. "My sister said that we all need to get to Paris as soon as possible."

"Your sister said."

Ivy could hear the skepticism and frustration vibrating through Baen's flat tone and instinctively reached out to lay a hand on his arm. "No offense, but I think we're going to need a little more information than that before we pack up and take your word for it, Michael."

"Drum. Only my mother calls me Michael."

"As I said, we must talk quickly." Ash glared at her partner. "The basic information you require is this. Five of the Guardians have woken before you. The other four are in North America. We have all made contact and have been working together to battle the worst of the threats from the Darkness, but in the past weeks, the situation has escalated to the point that we can no longer be everywhere that our presence is required. Among us, we have been able to confirm the escape of at least five of the Seven into the human realm."

Ivy felt the muscle under her hand jump and saw Baen stiffen until he should have been shaking with the tension.

"Five?" he repeated, sounding incredulous. "By the Light, how has such a thing been allowed to happen?"

"The Guild has been compromised. The Order

launched a covert war against them some time ago, and they have managed to murder more than half of the existing Wardens over the past two to three years."

Ivy nodded to Ash. "I already explained about the Guild, about the headquarters being destroyed, and about the survivors going into hiding. Baen is aware of all that."

The female Guardian switched her focus to Ivy. "Then you are his Warden."

"No."

"Yes."

Baen spoke over her denial, fixing her with a glare.

She sighed and tried to explain. "I'm not a member of the Guild. Baen seems to think that I must be his Warden. Although I have Wardens in my family—had them," she clarified, "—I was never recruited. I never took the Guild's entrance exam, never had any contact from them, and have absolutely no training. I wouldn't know how to cast a spell if you tattooed it on the back of my hand."

"Welcome to the club." Michael's dry tone caught her attention and she looked to see him sporting a crooked smile. "You'll get your membership pin and personalized jacket in your welcome packet by post."

"I can't be a Warden."

"You may protest all you like, but I will warn you that it changed nothing for the five new Wardens before you," Ash told her bluntly. Ivy was beginning to think Ash did everything bluntly. "Each Guardian who has woken in the past months has claimed a Warden with no previous training or connection to the Guild. I believe the human expression would say they had 'on-the-job training.'"

Ivy glanced at Baen, then back to their two visitors. Neither of them appeared to be joking about any of this. Hello, brain overload.

"So, you're really serious? You really think I'm some kind of latent Warden, even though I've been working with surviving Wardens in hiding for the past eight months or more and not one of them has ever said anything to indicate I might be one of them? How is it that more than a dozen Guild members spent all that time with me, and that idea was never even tossed onto the front step, let alone had the cat wander anywhere near it?"

Ash raised an eyebrow. "How many of those Wardens you worked with were male?"

"All of them." Duh. Ivy left the "duh" to be implied. What sort of question was that, anyway? Wardens were always male. She had never even heard of a female Guild member.

When Ash said nothing more, Ivy started to get irritated. She was about to snap something quite rude when Michael—when *Drum*—stepped in.

"You'd get a much longer and more passionate explanation on this subject from Wynn," he said with another of those crooked smiles. "She's in America. Chicago, to be precise, with her Guardian, Knox. By now she's probably formed the International Wardens' Committee to Combat Gender Discrimination. It's a bit of a pet subject of hers, and she'd be happy to tell you I'm the only new Warden who turned out to be male, just like Ash is the only Guardian—ever, as it happens—who turned out to be female. All the other new recruits are ladies, just like yourself."

"Which means that the Guild will be faced with some very harsh truths about its practice of excluding females, once it re-forms," Ash said. "But in the meantime, all the previously existing members remain male, and they remain oblivious to the idea that females could possibly number among their kind."

"Sexism?" Ivy's mind reeled and she felt like laughing.

"You're telling me the explanation is good old-fashioned male chauvinism? Seriously?"

Ash shrugged. "If the pig foot fits . . ."

"Then I'm really a Warden? Baen's Warden?"

"I informed you thusly."

Ivy spun on Baen and stared at him, wide-eyed and slack-jawed. Literally. For the first time in her life, she truly got that expression. "You did *not* just tell me you told me so."

Drum almost tripped over himself stepping into the fray. "Ah, my friends, that's really not the issue of the moment, now is it? The important point to remember is that the Guild as such doesn't really exist anymore, so we can't rely on getting assistance from a large force of Wardens against the Order, let alone the Seven. That makes it even more important than ever that we all work together on this, all six of the Guardians who've woken, along with their Wardens. If we don't, we might as well start dabbing vinegar behind our ears so we're ready when the Demons come to gobble us down like hot chips."

"Then your sister has also proven to be a Warden to one of my brothers." Baen glanced at Ash, frowned, then grudgingly corrected himself. "Siblings."

Ash bared her teeth at him. Wow, they really did act just like family.

"No," Drum said. "But she has the Sight. Maeve can see events before they happen, and she's had a vision that says we all need to be in Paris for whatever's coming at us. If we're not . . ." He shook his head. "She wouldn't even tell me what she saw happening if we're not there, but when she first came out of the vision she spent twenty minutes bent over the toilet, heaving up her guts. I figure that's a pretty fair indication we might want to avoid that alternative."

"We have already discussed this with the others, and they agree that a major strike by the Order in Paris would be logical," Ash said. "It is the traditional stronghold of the Guild, and we speculate that any who survived the destruction of the headquarters might not have scattered far from the city. There is also a strong possibility that Wardens who received news of the attack there might have been drawn back in hopes of lending assistance, or even on the slim chance of finding that the news had been false and the Guild still stood."

Ivy nodded. "You're right on both counts. Both those things did happen. Survivors did remain in Paris, and more returned right after the fire. They were the ones who established the network to gather up the Wardens who went into hiding and get them to safety. I've been working with them since I got to England." She briefly related the story of her uncle's death and how it had drawn her to England and spurred her mission to save any surviving Guild members. "We try to remain anonymous, even to each other, though, so I can't tell you exactly how to find Asile. I can let him know about you, though, next time I hear from him. I sent a message last night, about Baen, so he should contact me soon."

"That's fantastic news." Drum glanced at Ash and squeezed her hand. "Better than we had hoped for, in fact. We were starting to fear that we weren't going to find any surviving members of the Guild. The others have been searching for a while now, with no luck."

"They're kind of a wary bunch at this point," Ivy said. "We've worked out ways to get through to them, but mostly we've had to let them come to us. Anyone who's actively seeking them out is looked at with a lot of suspicion in case they turn out to be *nocturni*. The Order hasn't given up on finding and killing all the Wardens they missed in their earlier strikes."

"We never believed they had."

"Knowing the survivors have gathered in the city makes it that much more important that we make our way to Paris as well," Ash said. "We will contact the others and confirm that a sixth Guardian has woken and urge them all to make their way to us immediately. If what Maeve has seen is correct—and she is never wrong— our most important battle will be fought in that place. We must gather all of our numbers and prepare ourselves for war against the Darkness."

Oh, goodie. Didn't that sound like fun times?

"You should return with us to Dublin," the female Guardian continued. "This dwelling is not warded. It cannot remain safe from the *nocturnis* for long. Our home is much more secure and several of the others have been there before. They will have no trouble locating us so that we may organize our approach to Paris."

"Whoa, hold on a minute." Ivy threw on the brakes with a palms-out gesture. "Why should we go to Dublin? Last time I checked, that was in the opposite direction from Paris. Besides, I still have stuff to do here. I need to contact Asile, I need to deal with the guy in the kitchen, and most importantly, I need a while to digest what's going on here. You can't just pour this stuff down my throat and expect me to swallow it, no problem. I am not nineteen years old, and this is no beer funnel. It's going to take a little getting used to."

"You can think and pack at the same time," Baen growled at her. "I also dislike plans made by others on my behalf, but if these two are correct, then it is a sensible course of action."

"Wait a second," Drum interrupted. "What guy in the kitchen? What are you talking about?"

Ivy wished she had a CliffsNotes summary of the past eighteen hours so she could just hand the newcomers a copy and not have to keep filling in the blanks for them. "Martin. He's the Warden I was trying to get to France last night when demons attacked us and Baen woke up to rescue us. It's kind of a long story. Can we talk about it later and settle this trip to Dublin thing first?"

No one answered her, probably because the question hadn't been directed at Baen, and he was the only one left standing in the hallway after their visitors both spun on their heels and sprinted toward the back of the house. Confused, Ivy sent her Guardian a questioning glance and then hurried after them.

"Hey, what's going on?" she called out before she even reached the door to the kitchen. When she pushed it open, she found Drum leaning against the counter and cursing as she gazed out the window. Ash stood on the open threshold of the back entrance with her skin turning stony gray. Fangs already flashed behind lips curled into a snarl.

Martin was nowhere to be seen.

"What happened?" Ivy demanded. "Where's Martin? Did you scare him off? He's kind of jumpy at the best of times."

Ash growled something in a language Ivy didn't recognize. Presumably a dead one. If it hadn't been dead before, it might very well have keeled over the second it got a glimpse of the fury on the female Guardian's face.

Drum shoved away from the window. He didn't look much happier than his partner, but at least he didn't appear ready to disembowel whoever happened to be standing closest to him.

"You're seeing what we saw," he said, shaking his head. "We ran in to find the room empty and the back door hanging wide."

"Did he run away? That's just stupid. He saw what happened when those demons attacked last night. He wouldn't last three seconds alone if another one found him."

"Oh, he has been found." Ash finally managed to speak. Her voice was tight and hoarse with rage, but intelligible. Mostly. "He has been found by the *nocturnis*."

"As if that is any better." Baen's temper appeared to be fraying even as Ash struggled to get a grip on hers.

"What? How can you know that? Who's to say he didn't just lose his mind and decide to strike off on his own? He was pretty freaked out when you guys rang the bell. He immediately decided *you* were the Order and you were after him."

Baen's nostrils flared as he drew in a deep breath. "No, it was *nocturnis*. You can smell them."

"Um, actually, no I can't."

"I can," Ash agreed. "Like the inside of a slaughterhouse. Blood and offal and Darkness. They were here, and your friend left with them."

"They took him? I let him get kidnapped right under my damned nose? Great. Like the plan exploding last night wasn't bad enough. I have never lost a Warden before."

"I doubt you lost this one, either. I believe he wandered off all on his own."

"What?"

Drum swept his hand around the room in an encompassing gesture. "Look around. There are no signs of struggle. Nothing broken, no blood. Not so much as a spilled cup or an overturned chair. If someone did take the Warden out of here against his will, he didn't put up much of a fight."

"Or any fight at all," Baen agreed. He moved to where

Ash stood in the doorway they had all come in through the night before. He crouched and peered at the floor and the cobbles in the drive behind the building. "No drag marks, no scuffs. No indications anyone carried something as heavy as a body. It appears that anyone who entered the kitchen left again under their own power, walking calmly."

"So what are you saying?" Ivy demanded. "Are you trying to tell me that Martin wasn't a Warden after all? That he was some kind of imposter?"

"Not necessarily an imposter, but perhaps one with divided loyalties. Some of us have suspected that the Guild headquarters could not have been destroyed unless a member or members had aided in the planning and execution," Ash said. "Some of the most powerful wards and magical protections in the world guarded that place, and yet it burned to the ground, killing dozens of high-level Wardens with formidable powers of defense at their disposal. Infiltration by those under the influence of the Order seems the only logical explanation."

Ivy snorted. "I don't see it's logical to assume that anyone could possibly turn to the Darkness after having seen and learned what it's capable of, let alone what it wants to achieve. What kind of person learns that there's something out there that wants to destroy the world and enslave and consume humanity and says, 'Hey, sign me up'? It's ridiculous."

"It is about power," Baen said. "It is something that has corrupted more than one devout human throughout the ages. From wise men to fools, your race seems to be vulnerable to the temptation posed by promises of power over others."

"Gee, thanks. Nice to know you think so highly of us."

Ash shrugged. "You did ask."

When would Ivy finally learn not to go looking for answers she knew she wouldn't like? Not today, apparently.

"So what do we do now?" Even if she didn't like the answer to that question either, it was still important to know, and she damned sure had no idea of her own. "Do we go after him? Even if he doesn't want to be rescued, which we don't know for certain."

"It seems most likely he left willingly." Drum at least tried to sound apologetic about it. He appeared to possess the only ounce of diplomacy left in the room. "When whoever came here to fetch him, he didn't cry out for help, and he didn't struggle. That sort of points toward him leaving voluntarily. But either way, we have no way of knowing where he's gone, and I'm afraid we don't have the time to mount a large-scale search. Maeve's vision was urgent. We need to get all the Guardians we have to Paris as soon as possible."

"We had hoped to have all seven of us together before we reached this point," Ash said, her stern expression drawing into a frown, "but finding our sixth is better than having only five."

"I am overwhelmed by your effusive welcome, sister," Baen said, and Ivy found herself holding her breath waiting for Ash to fly at him again. This time, she felt pretty confident blood would be shed.

Instead, the female Guardian must have caught the teasing note in Baen's voice because she merely kicked him in the thigh with a desultory motion. "I have no doubt I could overwhelm you with both wings pinned to my back," she said, "but as my Warden has already indicated, we all have better things to do."

"Aaaannnnd now the world has stopped making sense," Ivy muttered to herself. "But never let it be said I can't play along." She raised her voice and glared at the room at large, unsure who was irritating her the most at the moment. "You all want to go to Dublin, we'll go to Dublin, but I need a few minutes to pack my passport and my toothbrush. The oncoming apocalypse is no reason to neglect dental hygiene. Or spend seventeen hours getting searched and interrogated by airport and national security forces."

No one responded to her sarcastic tone, but she saw Drum's lips twitch before he covered them and coughed into his palm. Baen simply nodded.

"You should also check for a message from your French contact. Perhaps he can offer more information about the situation into which we will be arriving."

Ivy felt a twitch at the corner of her eye. "Thanks."

She spun on her heel and stalked out of the kitchen. If she didn't get thirty seconds to herself right then, she felt positive a brain aneurysm would feature prominently in her immediate future.

Luckily, none of the others followed. She assumed they remained in the room to bond over the best way to behead a *nocturni,* or maybe which spells best simulated gallows hangings. How the hell should she know? She only cared that they stayed where they were and gave her some breathing room.

What the hell was happening?

The question rattled around in her brain like a pinball while she sank onto the desk chair in the little front room and waited for the computer to boot up. She had thought the change in her life from being a carefree New York technical writer—whose biggest problem was how to translate High Geek into a form of English understandable to the average person with an eighth-grade education—to becoming an undercover vigilante working to smuggle Wardens between nations had felt surreal. Ha! The last eighteen hours had taken her from the foundational concepts of Freud's psychology to the middle of a Max Ernst painting without passing go, let alone collecting two hundred bloody dollars. Her mind wasn't just reeling; she had to wonder if her grip on reality was slipping.

After all, here she was with the Warden she had been trying to save apparently run off to join the enemy, while in the other room, two creatures of legend and an Irishman who supposedly had magical powers were probably sipping tea and chatting like old friends. And she was about to leave with them to visit foreign countries and save the universe from the ultimate evil.

Put that way, she should stop wondering about her sanity. Clearly, that cat was already out of the bag and galloping away on the back of the horse who'd gotten out through the barn door she hadn't closed. And any other animalian metaphors she could possible come up with.

Well, if she were to look on the bright side, maybe she could use her obvious descent into mental illness to explain away her nagging attraction to Baen. Only a lunatic developed the hots for a shapeshifting gargoyle she'd only met a few hours ago, right?

It had to be the hots—basic chemistry, elemental sexual attraction. The product of going too long without a date, let alone sex or anything even remotely resembling a romantic relationship. If she could just dismiss it as that, Ivy could almost forgive herself for those pesky little feelings. After all, when he wasn't seven feet tall and made of stone, Baen was gorgeous. Like drop-dead-sexy, male-model, movie-star gorgeous. He had that rugged, masculine face that kept him from looking prettier than she did, and his body could make her grandmother sit up and fan herself. And granny had been dead for twenty years. It was no wonder Ivy found him physically attractive. No one could blame her for that.

But could they blame her for the something else she felt when he got close to her?

She tried to shove the thought away, but it kept creeping back and poking at her, like a fingertip to the rib cage. Jamie used to do that to try and rile her at the dinner table during family visits. It had always worked when she was a kid, and damn it, but it was working now.

The problem was that she didn't know precisely what that something was that she felt whenever Baen was near her. Sure, the zip of attraction was there, but it felt like something else simmered in the background along with it, she just couldn't figure out what to call it.

Affinity, maybe?

No, that was a weak word. Hell, she had affinity for cheese and onion crisps and a nice glass of milk. It didn't describe her reaction to the Guardian. She just always seemed *aware* of him when he was close, like she could reach out with her eyes closed and point out exactly where he stood and what expression he wore and how he was carrying himself in that moment. Like she knew him on a level she didn't think she had ever known anyone, not friends, not lovers, not even family. And she couldn't figure out how that could happen.

Ivy hated not being able to figure things out. She explained things for a living, for God's sake; she had to be pretty good at understanding concepts and breaking them down into easy-to-comprehend language. If she couldn't she didn't get paid. Yet here she was, entirely baffled by one man—sort of—with a strange effect on her. If she could, she would have fired herself over this.

"Well? Do you have news from France?"

Baen's voice made her jump half out of her chair and

land back on her butt with a jolt. She felt her face flushing lobster red and tried to hide it by keeping her head turned toward the computer. Stupid fair skin.

"Uh, I don't know yet," she said, fiddling with the mouse. "This is an old system, so it takes a while to boot up. Here we go. Now I can check."

She felt him step up behind her and tried not to go all tense and idiotic, but when his hands rested on the back of her chair, knuckles accidentally brushing her shoulder blades, she had to fight to force her shoulders down from around her ears.

She also had to fight to remember what she'd been doing. The Guardian's presence really did scramble her brain.

Her e-mail server's Web page popped up in response to her earlier command, and thankfully pointed her in the correct direction. Message. France. Asile. Right. She could do this. Honest.

A couple of clicks, and the brief lines appeared in the e-mail window. There was no salutation, no idle questions about the weather or her health. There were less than two dozen words, brief, stark, and to the point.

If sincere, bring your new friend immediately. Meet tomorrow 6 P.M. Louvre pyramid, north side. Will wear blue, yellow flower. Secrecy vital.

It was signed "Asile."

Ivy frowned at the screen, an uncertain feeling tightening in her belly. "That sounds . . . urgent. And kind of alarming."

"How well do you know this person?"

Ivy swiveled her chair to see Ash and Drum enter from the hall, both looking serious. Not that Ash didn't always look serious, but Drum usually appeared more relaxed. "We've been working together since I first got to England and got involved with moving the Wardens. Asile basically runs the network, and he set up the safe house in Paris and oversees that, too. Why?"

"But you have not actually met," Ash prompted.

"No. He's in Paris and I'm here. Why?" Her mind flashed to their conversation over Martin, and she scowled. "Don't tell me you're trying to imply that Asile is another traitor? For God's sake, he's gotten dozens and dozens of Wardens away from the Order; he doesn't work for them!"

"How do you know? Have you maintained contact with the Wardens once they arrived in Paris?"

Ivy froze, her throat tightening. "Well, no. But that wouldn't be safe. Too much chance of me being identified, or communication being intercepted and leading the Order to me or to them. But I get word when they get to the safe house to let me know everything went smoothly."

"Word from Asile."

"Who else?" Ivy snapped.

"Then you cannot be absolutely certain that the Wardens are safe," Ash said, her expression hard. "You cannot be certain that this safe house even exists, let alone that it is where the Wardens go after you leave them in France. You have no proof that this contact of yours does not collect them from you and pass them straight into the hands of the *nocturnis*."

Bile welled in Ivy's throat. Reflexively, she pressed her fingers to her mouth and swallowed hard. It took a few deep breaths before she could manage to speak again. "You think I've actually been helping the Order all this time? That I've been handing survivors over to their deaths. Is that what you're telling me? That I'm an accomplice to murder? Am I?"

Drum stepped forward then, laying a hand on Ash's shoulder when she would have spoken again. "No one is accusing you of being on the side of the Darkness, Ivy. We all know you've been doing what you thought you needed to do to save the Wardens. Ash is just worried that you could have been lied to. These days, it's hard to know who to trust."

Ivy knew the man was only trying to make her feel better, but he wasn't. She wanted to vomit. The very idea that she had been sending Wardens to their deaths when she had wanted so desperately to save them from the same fate that had taken her uncle and cousin felt like a punch to the heart. A Guardian's punch, since it packed an inhuman amount of force. How was she supposed to live with it if that turned out to be the truth?

Her hands shook as she struggled to keep control. Spewing her breakfast all over the shoes of the assembled company wasn't going to do anyone any good, and she had the definite feeling that it wasn't going to make her feel any better, anyway. She wasn't sure anything could make her feel better.

"So what do I do, then?" she asked, her throat so tight she had to force the words through it. "Do I not reply? Do we not go to France? What happens now? Asile has a whole network of people like me all over the world. We can't just let him keep collecting Wardens for the Order. We can't let those people keep dying."

Baen crouched down beside her chair and took Ivy's hands in his. "Calm yourself, little human. We have no proof that your contact is involved with the *nocturnis*. Ash merely speculates on one possibility out of many. Don't you?" He turned his head to glare at the other Guardian.

Ash shrugged. "We have no proof that my speculation is incorrect, either."

"Not helping, love," Drum murmured.

Ivy looked at Baen. Somehow his dark gaze made her feel steadier. Stronger. She drew in a shaking breath. "So what do we do?" she repeated, asking just him this time. He was the one she trusted, even as short of a time as she had known him.

"I think we must go to France," he said, squeezing her hands. "We may discover that Ash suffers from paranoia where your contact is concerned. If that is true, he can take us to the other Wardens and we may begin to plan a way in which we may strike back against the Darkness."

"But what if she's right about Asile?"

Baen's mouth firmed and his eyes bled back into the fiery darkness of his natural form. "If she is right, then I will kill him, and I will destroy any who have assisted him in strengthening the Order. The Wardens will be avenged."

"*We* will destroy them, brother," Ash corrected. "You should not go to Paris alone. If my worst fears are confirmed, there must be an entire sect of *nocturnis* in the city. They would need numbers in order to operate such a highly organized system."

Drum reached into his pocket and pulled out his mobile phone. "If we're not going back to Dublin first, I need to contact the others and tell them the new plan. Should they just head straight to Paris and meet us there?"

Ivy listened to the others debate strategy for a few seconds before a pinging sound from the computer drew her attention back to the monitor. A new window had opened on the screen. It looked like a news bulletin. Harris must have set up some sort of alert system to notify him whenever certain headlines appeared on designated Internet sites. This one came from a major international news outlet. As she scanned it, her eyes got wider and wider.

"Um, guys."

They continued debating behind her back.

"Guys!"

This time, at least Baen turned to look at her. "What is it?"

"This." She pointed at the news blurb. "There's been a major bombing in Belfast. They're calling it the biggest terrorist attack in more than twenty-five years."

"That's unexpected," Drum said, frowning and moving closer to read the article for himself. "The Troubles have calmed down quite a lot. They still have incidents in the North, but nothing on this scale. They're right about that. Not in years and years."

Ivy moved her finger down to the bottom of the story. "The authorities are claiming the explosives were accompanied by some sort of nerve-gas release that caused hallucinations in many of the witnesses, who claimed to have seen hooded figures and demons in the chaos."

Drum swore, creatively enough that Ivy actually learned a few things. "We need to get there fast and find out what's happened. We know the *nocturnis* have been actively searching for an opportunity to release the last of the Seven, and we can't let that happen."

"What about Paris? And if anyone says we'll always have it, I will hurt them." Ivy glared at the others.

Drum snorted, but the Guardians just looked confused.

"We must not fail to meet your contact," Ash said. "If I am wrong and he is honest, to do so might frighten him into hiding and lose us access to the surviving Guild members. And if he is corrupt, it might show him that we are aware of his betrayal, which would also send him running. We can afford neither outcome."

"Then Ivy and I shall go to Paris as planned, while you and your Warden head for Belfast." Baen outlined the plan in firm tones. "We shall investigate both situations."

"You know, there's a chance this thing in Belfast is only a distraction," Drum said. "A few months ago, the Order did something similar. They staged an attack in Boston to distract from their true target in Dublin. That plan resulted in the escape of the fourth Demon."

Ash nodded. "It could also be a trap, an attempt to lure us into a vulnerable position. The Order knows that a Guardian has been in Ireland after the incident in the cave, but can we afford to assume that either possibility is the truth? If this strike is indeed intended to bring another of the Seven to this plane, we have no choice but to prevent it."

"Then we're caught between a rock and a hard place." Ivy grimaced.

"Not necessarily," Ash said. "We have allies to call upon. Drum, you will contact the others. Have Ella, Kees, Fil, and Spar meet us in Belfast. Wynn, Knox, Dag, and Kylie can head straight for Paris. None of us will be without backup, as the humans say."

Baen nodded. "A sound plan. We should all leave immediately."

Ivy turned back to the keyboard and started typing. "I'll confirm the meeting with Asile." *And cross my fingers that he's not an evil fuck,* she added to herself. "But I still need to go back to my flat to get my passport and a couple of other things. We can still be on the road within an hour or two."

Well, that would have been true. You know, if a loud crash from the direction of the kitchen hadn't preceded a flood of black-clad figures racing toward them with magic, weapons, and evil leading the way.

Bloody hell.

Chapter Nine

Baen heard the kitchen door crash open an instant before the stench of Darkness hit him. It never changed. No matter the time or the place, evil always carried the same smell—old blood, rotten meat, sickness, and corruption. Sweet and sickly and stomach turning, it made the attack of the *nocturnis* immediately identifiable.

It also meant that Baen and Ash were ready for them by the time they rushed through the door of the front room. They each moved forward to place themselves between the entrance and the humans, knowing Drum and Ivy to be much more vulnerable to both magical and physical attack than the Guardians themselves.

The *nocturnis* knew it too, and it quickly became clear that the enemy had planned this attack carefully. More than half a dozen black-clad figures swarmed into the tight space while two more hung back in the hall just outside the entrance. The one on the left raised his hand and let loose a foul stream of demonic chanting before pushing his palm forward and sending a rusty red ball of corrupt energy shooting toward Ivy's head.

The female instinctively raised her hands to defend herself, but the gesture was futile in the face of the magical attack. Baen roared his outrage and tried to move toward her, to knock her out of the way, but he found himself hemmed in by four *nocturnis* armed with heavy blades and obvious training in their use. They slashed at him, coordinating their attacks to distract and occupy him, to keep him from rushing to the defense of the humans. He could see Ash facing the same problems a few feet away, but Drum took action.

The male human stood too far away from Ivy to physically rescue her, but he, at least, had clearly gotten the sort of Warden's training that Ivy had been denied. He shouted a few words of his own and threw a wave of energy at the woman that knocked her off her feet, sending her stumbling hard against the nearest wall even as the angry red pulse of the *nocturni's* spell flashed by close enough to ruffle her hair.

She cried out, a combination of fear, surprise, and outrage, and Drum's shouted, "Sorry!" only added to the chaos in the room. The *nocturni* caster shrieked in outrage, and flung a second spell, this one clearly aimed at Drum.

The male Warden was ready for it. He mumbled a few words and raised a narrow wall of energy that deflected the sorcerer's dark lightning bolt, dissolving it into a shower of dirty sparks that rained onto the floor in a fall of ashes. Though he could clearly defend himself, Ash equally clearly disliked that he had to. She roared out her feelings and, with one blow, sent two of her attackers flying back so she could rush to her Warden's side.

Drum dismissed her with a crooked grin. "I'm fine, darlin'. Watch your own back this time."

Baen saw his sister's lips move in grumbled displeasure, but she clearly trusted her partner's judgment, because she turned from him and focused once again on the armed *nocturnis*. He wanted to mirror her move by flying to Ivy's aid, but Drum beat him to it. The human knelt at Ivy's side as she slumped, clearly stunned, at the base of a wall of bookshelves. He checked her responses and clearly got some kind of positive indication, because he shouted, "She's all right!"

Relief surged through Baen, but he didn't allow himself to relax. Instead he forced himself to focus back on the battle. As he turned to resume his struggle against the armed *nocturnis* surrounding him, he saw the second sorcerer in the hall focusing on Ivy with manic intensity. Beneath the hooded cowl, pale lips moved quickly, but Baen couldn't make out the words. He didn't really need to. Even as the magic user lifted his hands to release the magic he had gathered, Baen shifted, letting his natural form out in a burst of power.

There wasn't really enough room in the cramped space for a creature his size, but he didn't care. His wings fluttered, spreading just enough to form a barrier between the sorcerer and Ivy's crumpled form. The spell intended to hit her bounced off the leathery membrane instead, making the *nocturnis* hiss in frustration.

The attackers gathered around Baen echoed that sentiment, now realizing their weapons had been rendered all but useless against the tough, stone hide of a Guardian's natural skin. They must have been counting on the tight space to inhibit him and Ash from shifting, thus trapping them in their more vulnerable human skins, because the weapons they carried held no trace of magic about them. They had no chance of causing their opponents serious injury.

"Baen!"

Drum's voice had Baen's head whipping around to see the human leaning over Ivy with a worried expression.

"Something's going on with your girl," the man said. "She seemed fine for a few seconds, but then her eyes glazed over, and she went totally out of it. Does she have seizures?"

Baen did not know, but the thought distracted him long enough to allow his attackers to regroup and launch a coordinated offensive that kept him too busy to answer for several seconds. Before he could open his mouth, though, he heard her voice, weak but determined.

"Sorry," she groaned. "It wasn't a seizure. I heard something."

Baen recalled what the woman had told him of her power and felt a wave of cold run through him like a warning.

"There are more outside. Close by. They were doing some kind of ritual. I think they were summoning something."

It only gave them a few seconds of warning, but that was long enough for Baen and Ash to exchange glances and for Drum to utter something profoundly filthy. Before the syllables had even faded from the air, an overwhelming stench drifted in from the hall an instant before the form of a demon appeared in the dwelling's small hall.

The evil creature filled the space, blocking out everything else, absorbing light and energy like a black hole of malevolence. Shadows and flame swirled around it, not the clean, orange flame of real fire, but something darker, sickly and polluted. That alone betrayed its identity. This was an *ukobahk,* a servant of the Seven and among the most powerful of the minor orders of demons. To know that the Order had gained the ability to bring one here at their command offered disquieting proof of their accumulated power.

It wore the hideous, unnatural shape of a gorilla crossed with a bull and was formed entirely out of corrupted flame. Huge horns adorned its flattened, bovine head, and when it opened its mouth, fire and lavalike streams of molten rock disgorged like vomit. Its freakishly long arms and crouched posture left its huge, curved claws dragging on the ground behind it, carving furrows in the old wooden floors. It glared at Baen with eyes lacking in intelligence but glinting with primal hate. It recognized its ancestral nemesis and it seethed.

Baen launched himself forward. The broad sweep of his wings knocked aside the villains in his path, but he took no notice. The *ukobahk* leaped to meet him and demon and Guardian clashed together in a thunderous clap of fire and stone.

Claw and fang slashed and tore and bellows of pain and rage filled the air. The sounds of battle drowned out almost everything else, but Baen could just faintly make out the sharp tone of Ash's words ordering Drum to keep the other human safe. A moment later, the corner of the room where he had last seen Ivy lit up with a bright, pure light and Baen felt something inside him relax. Knowing his Warden would be looked after sent renewed energy and determination coursing through him, and he beat back the demon's advance with heavy blows from his clenched, granite-hard fists.

The beast met him blow for blow, the impact of its hits occasionally sending up a shower of sparks that scattered into the room around him. Most smoldered only a second before extinguishing themselves, but inevitably a whiff of smoke told Baen that one had settled in something like paper or fabric and begun to burn.

Cursing, the Guardian pivoted to the side, carving out the split second he needed to summon his bardiche from the ether and swing the long, curved blade into motion. Mounted in two places at one end of the four-foot banded shaft, the razor-sharp axe blade swept back so dramatically it almost formed a crescent moon, with the bottom point secured to the handle and the top extending free to a lethally honed tip. Baen kept both edges of that end sharpened to allow thrusting and hooking slices, as well as the natural swings and hacks of combat axemanship.

One such backhanded slice caught the *ukobahk* across its abdomen, sending a spill of lava to pool on the floorboards. A second fire broke out there and Baen started to see smoke fill the room as flames began to lick at the corners of his vision. He and Ash needed to get the humans out of there. If the *nocturnis* and their pet demon didn't kill them, the inferno surely would.

A quick glance around showed him that while he had faced off against the fire demon, Ash had taken care of the armed *nocturnis*. Slain or unconscious, they littered the floor, the last one falling under a powerful blow from her weapon. As soon as that opponent began to crumple, she flew to her partner's side, crouching next to him. She threw one glance back at Baen, her expression fierce.

"I will get them out. You slay the *ukobahk*."

Gladly.

He turned back to the demon and adjusted his double-handed grip on the bardiche. The creature roared, shaking its head and tearing through the plaster around the doorway with its broadly set horns. The show of aggression didn't impress Baen. He flashed it a mouthful of fang and then sprang.

His blade swung before him, cleaving through the thick smoke and then the burning shape of the monster's flesh. One stroke severed clean through its neck, and its head rolled off one shoulder to bounce at his feet.

Immediately, the thing's flame went out, like a snuffed candle. The shape it had maintained on this plane ceased to hold together. It imploded on itself in a shower of charcoal and ash, leaving nothing behind but a sooty pile on the hallway floor.

Baen threw back his head and howled in victory. His foe lay vanquished on the field. Now was the time to celebrate his warrior's prowess.

Except for the matter of the burning house and his wounded Warden.

He spun back to locate the others, but all he found was the open window nearby. Ash had spirited them outside and hopefully out of danger.

Sending his weapon away with a thought, Baen forced himself to breathe deeply in order to bring on another shift. His human skin felt especially tight after the heat of battle, but if he needed to go out onto the humans' streets, it would not do to wear his natural form.

Also, there was no way he would have gotten his wings out that stingy window opening. As it was, he nearly scraped the skin off his back on his way through. Stupid puny human architecture.

He used his senses to pick up the trail of Guardian and Wardens, jogging after the faint traces of citrus and white stone in the air. A few minutes later, he found them clustered around a bench in a small green square a few streets from the house. Immediately, he pushed forward to kneel at Ivy's side.

She half lay, slumped against the back of the bench, while Ash paced behind her and Drum sat close, holding on to one of her small, pale hands as he peered into her bloodshot eyes. Baen couldn't suppress his growl.

Instantly Drum dropped her hand and eased back, his mouth quirking. "She hit that wall pretty hard, and then the . . . well, whatever you want to call it . . . what she heard. That seems to have taken some of her energy," he said. "But her pulse is strong and steady, and I don't see any evidence of a concussion. I'm not a doctor, but I know basic first aid and what to look out for. I think she'll be fine."

Knowing that the Irishman had merely been looking after Ivy's health should have made Baen feel better, but he still found himself giving in to the urge to insinuate himself between them. He gathered both her hands in his and squeezed gently.

"Are you all right, little one?" he asked. "Were you hurt? Do you require medical attention?"

She shook her head, wincing a little and pressing her fingers to her temple at the motion. "What I need is a stiff shot of bourbon and some intensive psychotherapy," she muttered. "Did I really just see a bloody demon? Is that what that thing was? Was that one of the Seven?"

Ash snorted. "If it had been, more than a single house would have been destroyed, and we would likely not all be standing here now. That was a mere minion. Pray you never have to come face-to-face with one of its masters."

"Yeah, I think that ship has sailed." Ivy grimaced. "Or did the plans to go to Paris and help stop them from taking over the world change while I was semiconscious?"

"It just got a bit more pressing, I think." Drum stood and circled around the bench to sling one arm around Ash's shoulder. He pulled her against him, and pressed a kiss to her forehead. "Your friend from last night must have alerted the Order to a new Guardian being woken. That's the first fire demon we've seen. Before this, they seemed to be relying mostly on *hhissihh* and ghouls. You've prompted them to up their game." He nodded at Baen.

The Guardian snarled. "I would have preferred the element of surprise."

"That no longer appears to be a tool in our arsenal," Ash said, her mouth tight and expression hard. "We must now hurry to gather our forces. We definitely cannot afford to spend time combing the globe for our last sleeping brother. But this attack does offer us some valuable information."

"Such as?"

"It makes clear that the man you dealt with last night is indeed a traitor to the Guild," the female Guardian said. "Where there was one, there will be more, which removes the last doubt regarding complicity from within the Guild before the purge of the Wardens began. But more importantly, it tells us that the Order will know for certain the information you had on the gathering of Wardens in France. They will know that the survivors have banded together there."

"And they'll go after them," Ivy declared. She squeezed her eyes shut and let out a few curses Baen would never have predicted she might use. Not unless she had a past in the merchant marines that she had failed to tell him about. "We need to get to Paris, like, yesterday. We need to warn them the Order will be coming for them."

"If they're not idiots, they already know that," Drum said. "But we can warn them that they'll be coming soon, and probably in pretty decent numbers."

Ivy turned to meet Baen's gaze, her own gone cloudy with a mix of emotions so complex, she couldn't begin to name them all. "We should leave now. Right now. Maybe we can find a boat to sneak us into France via an unmonitored beach. I don't even want to take the time to go find my passport."

Baen shook his head. He offered a squeeze of reassurance to her trembling fingers. "Any attempt to travel covertly requires either careful planning or the cover of darkness. We might not have time for the first, but I believe we have no choice but to wait for the second. We cannot leave for France before nightfall. There will be time to retrieve your passport, but you won't need it. We will fly to Paris."

"If we fly, I'm definitely going to need a passport, and so are you. There's no other way to get on a plane these days. Can you, you know, magic something up?"

Baen quirked a brow at her. "Who said anything about planes?"

Chapter Ten

Ivy was still arguing with him two hours later. A quick hop across London was one thing, and it had still nearly given her a heart attack. No way was she willing to cross the English frickin' Channel with nothing between her and the icy-cold-water-slash-certain-death thing but Mr. Grabbyhands's overinflated ego. Uh-uh. No way. Not. Happening.

Ever.

As it turned out, Baen appeared to suffer from the same sort of situational deafness around the word "no" that the average basset hound suffered around the word "come." Maybe she should try tossing kibble at him, see if that helped encourage the proper responses. They had hours to kill before dark, when the Guardian apparently planned to scoop her up in his arms and carry her like a sack of potatoes across the rough seas and rocky shores separating England from France. Plenty of time to run down to the market and pick up a few Milk-Bones for the occasion.

At the moment, Baen was looking entirely too at home sprawled across seven-eighths of her sofa while she paced back and forth around the flat, ostensibly packing a few essentials for their trip, but really trying to figure out if there was anything here in Cousin Jamie's home that qualified as large and heavy enough to knock some sense into that supernaturally thick skull.

She doubted it. Personally, she was coming to the conclusion that nuclear weaponry might not be sufficient. And she had always thought *she* was stubborn to a fault.

Ha!

"You have to be reasonable about this," she tried again as she shoved a couple of pairs of panties into a backpack, wishing for a second they were made of lead and aimed at the back of his head. "Ash and Drum took a plane back to Ireland, so it's not like you can claim you can't fit on a commercial airline. It's clearly possible."

"It carries too much risk. My way is simpler. We need not worry about the hu—the authorities, nor the arbitrary schedules of corporations. We leave when we want, we arrive when we want. No delays, no hassles, and no chance we will miss this arranged meeting with your contact. It is a much more sensible plan."

"Except for the whole increased chance of death and dismemberment, sure."

He nodded. "Good. Then it is settled."

She bit back a frustrated scream. "It is *not* settled. Baen—" She cut herself off and pressed the heels of her hands against her eyes. The argument was giving her a headache of massive proportions.

Ivy never heard the huge Guardian move, but before she had time to haul in a deep breath and pray for strength, she felt his big hands land on her shoulders and press gently.

"What is wrong?" he demanded in that rough, tumbling-stones voice of his. "You were injured earlier, weren't you? I knew we should have taken you to be examined by a doctor. You could have internal damage. Bleeding, or a brain injury."

She lowered her hands and forced herself not to react to the hot tingling sensation that flooded through her at his lightest touch. She had to be imagining it. Not only was this about the least appropriate time to find herself ensnared in a helpless sexual attraction, but Baen was definitely the least appropriate object for her feelings. Wrong species, wrong temperament, wrong attitude, wrong everything.

Yeah. So I'll just stand here in my wrongness and be wrong and get used to it, she told herself, quoting from one of her favorite old television shows. *Maybe I'll even change my middle name. Ivy Wrong Beckett is much better than Ivy Fitzroy Beckett. It'll make for a snazzy new monogram, too. I can buy embroidered towels . . .*

She took a step back, trying to put some distance between herself and the shockingly warm Guardian. Honestly, it would make things a lot easier if he would just be cold and stony and emotionless like she had expected a Guardian would be. This concerned, hot, sexy, protective-male thing was hell on her hormones.

Hey, maybe that was it. Maybe she could chalk this all up to some exotic hormonal imbalance, and get a doctor's note to prove it: *To whom it may concern—this memo is to certify that my patient, Ivy Wrong Beckett, suffers from a severe, congenital case of Excessive Gargoyle-atropin Hormone Syndrome (or EGHS disease) and cannot be held legally or morally accountable for her own actions. She is not really a giant slut.*

Yeah. That would be awesome.

Unfortunately, for every inch she tried to put between herself and Baen, he seemed determined to take away two. He refused to release her shoulders and drew her to a stop before she could slide out from under his grip.

He never applied too much pressure, never crossed into causing her the tiniest discomfort; he simply refused to surrender his hold.

"I'm fine," she said. Just like she'd said a thousand times since they regrouped in that square while the local fire crew responded to the blaze they had just escaped. "I wasn't hurt, I was only a little rattled and dazed from the auditory episode. I don't need a doctor. Or an overprotective, rock-headed nursemaid."

Baen's eyes narrowed. "Nursemaid? You think me a hovering female? Perhaps drastic action is needed to change your mind."

The Klaxon in her head blared out a warning at the glint in those dark eyes, but somehow she knew it came just a split second too late. Apparently, that was one insult too far for the Guardian.

She tried to backpedal so fast, she could almost hear the chains falling off her mental gears. She opened her mouth to take it all back, but she never got the chance. He pounced like a big cat, and she—God help her—squeaked like a little furry church mouse.

It was humiliating.

It was mind-blowing.

Baen's mouth seized hers as if it were a medieval village, and not the fortified kind either, with walls and moats and actual working defenses. No, she was the laughably vulnerable kind, where there were no men under ninety left to fight off attackers and no one had eaten a decent meal for six months, so they barely had the strength to run and hide.

Oh, who was she kidding? She practically threw him a welcome-home party and crowned him king of her libido. It was downright embarrassing.

Or it would have been, if she hadn't been way too busy enjoying herself to think that hard.

He tasted like fire, or at least like she imagined it tasting, like the burn of alcohol without the sharp sting. Just light and heat and destructive power. He sure as hell destroyed every protest in her head before it could finish forming, leaving her weak-kneed and weak-willed and eager for more of his intoxicating taste.

Her head spun, and she reached out for something to hold on to, clenching her fingers in the smooth fabric of his shirt and leaning into him. It was either that, or fall flat on her ass, and if she fell, she wouldn't be able to reach his lips anymore. Totally unacceptable.

Baen didn't appear to like that idea, either. He finally let go of her shoulders only to wrap those brawny arms around her and pull her snug against his hard body. With the differences in height, he made good use of his altered grip to lift her feet clean off the ground and leave her dangling in midair while he continued to devour her mouth. She felt one arm clamp around her waist to pin her in place while the other moved lower to brace against the curve of her bottom to support her.

And, you know, cop a feel.

That was what finally jump-started her brain cells back into working order, the sensation of that big hand squeezing as it drifted across her ass. Not that she found the sensation unpleasant, but because it took her by surprise. It had been a long time since her last date, let alone the last time she'd gotten this caught up in a simple embrace, and she'd almost forgotten how it felt to have a man's hands on her. Not that any of them had ever made her feel this way. Especially not before the first date.

Ignoring the inner voice in her head whining not to do it, Ivy tore her lips from Baen's and flattened her palms against his chest. She opened her mouth to utter some witty quip, but nothing came out. She was too rattled. He had scrambled her brain like a couple of eggs, and not even a good shake of her head managed to rattle things back into place.

Sheesh, what was *wrong* with her?

Hormones, her brain said.

Overthinking, her hormones countered.

Ride him like a rented pony! her libido shouted.

Ivy ignored the last suggestion and clenched her thighs together to stifle further comment from that quarter. Last time she had checked, her genitalia had not registered to vote.

She cleared her throat to make sure it still worked in theory, then tried again to speak. "Um, maybe you should put me down?"

Instead of the protest she had half expected, Baen merely loosened his grip enough to let her slide to her feet. Slowly. With a lot of interesting friction that told her more than she had really needed to know about how much the kiss had affected him. Don't get her wrong, she was flattered, but really?

Well, flattered and a tiny bit intimidated. Yowzah.

Ivy pressed against his chest again, and this time he let her put a few inches between them. Wait, that sounded wrong. A few inches of *space* between them. "I'm not sure that was such a good idea."

"I thought it worked out very well," he rumbled, the deep, vibrating sound going right to the part of her that was least likely to behave itself when she ordered it to. "You taste delicious."

"Thanks. Wait! Um, I mean—" She caught herself and felt her entire body spontaneously combust.

Well, okay, not really, but she did blush from the soles of her feet to the part in her hair.

She blew out a breath and stepped resolutely backward, a small part of her brain registering stunned surprise when she didn't trip over anything and ratchet up the level of humiliation another notch. "What I meant was that you shouldn't say things like that. It's not appropriate. We need to stay focused on the mission at hand, not let ourselves get distracted by . . . um . . . things. If you really think that I'm somehow your Warden, then that means we're working together, and I have a strict rule that I never get involved with coworkers. Period."

Baen just watched her with his eyes gone black and burning and the corners of his mouth tilted up in that wholly male expression of self-satisfaction known far and wide as a smirk. He *smirked* at her, and the bastard had the nerve to look sexy while he did it.

Jerk.

When he remained silent and crossed those thickly muscled arms across his ripped chest, Ivy tore her gaze from all those tempting grooves and bulges and turned her back on him. Maybe if she couldn't see him, this ridiculous awareness of him would finally fade.

The traitorous flesh between her thighs told her not to get her hopes up.

"Good. I'm glad you agree," she said, not waiting to hear whether he did or not. "It will keep things simpler, and I'm sure we'll all be a lot happier in the long run. I'll go online and see if I can get us a last-minute flight this evening, and then I'm going to study that book on magic that Drum left me. He said there are a couple of simple defensive spells in there that I should be able to pick up in a couple of hours of practice. After this afternoon, I have a feeling I might need them."

She kept her back to him and marched toward the door to her bedroom and the laptop she had left there. She did not run away. No, sir. At best, some haters might want to call it a strategic retreat, but there was no running involved. Not even a jog.

Okay, maybe a race-walk, but that was it.

Honest.

Behind her, Baen chuckled, the sound rusty from long disuse but full of self-satisfaction. Full of *smirk*. She closed the door behind her with a sharp click, then leaned back against the cool panel and closed her eyes. Her nipples remained drawn into hard peaks of arousal, just to taunt her.

Men sucked.

Apparently, even the mythological ones.

Baen remained in the sitting room of the comfortable flat after Ivy fled, satisfaction filling him. She might have run from him this time, but that kiss had told him some very important things. First, that he affected his little human in much the same way that she affected him. He had felt the heat in her response as she returned his kiss, had felt her nipples draw into tight beads of arousal as they pressed up against his chest. He had felt her shudder when his tongue stroked across hers and plumbed the depths of her sweet mouth. She wanted him as badly as he wanted her. That was good.

Secondly, and most importantly, it had told him that there was a chance he had found not just a new Warden to help him fight back the threat posed by the Darkness; he might have found his own destined mate.

The possibility made his heart and mind race.

While there had been little time to spend with Ash and her Warden, the pair had shared a few significant pieces of news regarding the others of his kind. All five of the Guardians to wake in this time had found themselves paired with a Warden of the opposite sex, an individual who seemed to fulfill all the traits told about in the legend of the Guardians and the Maidens.

All except for Drum, of course, but if he proved to be

the exception, that only made sense, because Ash formed the biggest exception Baen could ever imagine. Never before in the long history of their kind had a female Guardian been summoned, which was why it had so shocked Baen to hear her claim him as her brother. He felt ashamed now that he had reacted so badly to the news and had treated her with such disrespect, but surprise had rendered him temporarily unable to think. It had never occurred to him that her existence might be possible, but clearly it was, which made Drum's place at her side more than possible as well; it made it necessary.

That old story the Guardians held so dear and passed on among themselves from summoning to summoning meant much more than most who heard it first assumed. Listeners often tried to dismiss it as romantic fantasy, a syrupy little love story with scant consequence in the harsh world of endless conflict that made up the existence of the Guardians, but it was much more than that.

It was true that the story gave hope to Baen's brethren that they might one day escape the endless cycle of sleeping and fighting that defined their existence by finding a mate, but it did something even more important. Baen believed that it showed them the true path to defeating the Seven in battle. After all, according to the legend, the maidens who woke that first generation of Guardians after they ignored the summons from the Guild had given the warriors purpose and added strength. They had joined them in the battle, stood by their sides and aided in the defeat of the Darkness, a defeat that might not have happened without them.

Baen knew his ideas were radical ones. The Guild had long maintained that the taking of mates weakened the side of the Light because it took experienced and battle-tested Guardians out of the fight, forcing the summoning of new, untried replacements. That argument failed to hold water in Baen's mind. He had once been newly summoned, and he knew very well that each Guardian came into existence in the human world with all the skills and memories of those who served before him. There was no learning curve for a new Guardian. He appeared fully armed, fully trained, and ready to fight, as deadly as the brother he had replaced.

It made him wonder what the Guild hoped to achieve by maintaining their stance of disapproval and discouragement.

Power, his inner voice whispered. It's always about power.

Baen could find no way to argue with that. To a Guardian, the human quest for power would always remain a mystery. Easily recognized as the species' begetting sin, the humans' thirst for power seemed behind all the great conflicts in their history. Certainly, it was behind the plans of the Order of Eternal Darkness and those who followed their masters, for the Darkness itself was always greedy for power. Perhaps that came from the knowledge that the most important power in the universe was the one thing the Darkness would never have—the Power of Creation. Only the Light could bring forth new life; the Darkness could only corrupt, seize, and destroy.

Now he was getting philosophical, Baen admitted to himself with some amusement. It seemed that his little female inspired deep thoughts as well as deep feelings. Part of him urged him to go after her, to corner her in the small room where she had shut herself away and seduce her into admitting her feelings for him.

He stifled the urge with difficulty. If his instincts were right, and Ivy could be his mate, the one destined to change the course of his existence, then he would gain nothing from pushing her. Nothing but an angry, spitting cat of a female. His human had an independent streak.

And, he recalled, a fairly impressive skill with her little consecrated knife. He would do well to step back and give her a little time to see her own feelings more clearly. So that was what he would do. For the moment.

After all, in a few short hours, he would get the chance to distract her for the three hours or so that it took him to fly her from London to Paris. Clasped in his arms high up in the night sky, she wouldn't have the chance to run from him.

Baen could hardly wait.

Chapter Eleven

Baen could hardly believe she had forced him into that metal tube and made him contort himself to fit into the tiny, cramped seat for a miserable trip he could have accomplished faster and much more comfortably all on his own. After all, he had wings, didn't he? If the Light had meant him to ride in unstable bits of human machinery, he would have been summoned without them.

"Would you stop pouting already?" Ivy smirked at him as she led the way through the crowds at the small Beauvais airport north of Paris. They had arrived on the very last flight of the evening, so the terminal was emptying out quickly. "We got here safely, didn't we?"

Baen muttered something that she didn't quite catch. Luckily. "I could have taken us straight to the city," he added in a louder voice.

"Not while I have a breath in my body, pal." She hitched her small satchel higher onto her shoulder and picked up her pace. "Hurry up. I want to make sure we get a cab before they all disappear for the night."

He trailed her toward the airport exit, feeling a little too much like a faithful pet for his liking. He honestly had not believed Ivy would manage to find them a flight on the same day they needed to leave. For some reason he had understood this to be difficult to accomplish in the human world, so he had been anticipating the pleasure of holding her as he transported them between the two cities.

Instead, she had managed the impossible, or nearly so. While unable to book them directly into one of the major Paris airports, she had gotten them close. Beauvais was only about fifty miles from the capital.

"Where will we take this cab?" he asked grudgingly as he followed her out into the chilly evening. "It seems a long trip to ask of a hired driver."

"Well, we are not taking it into Paris." She snorted. "I'd need to mortgage Uncle George's house to pay that fare. We'll go into the nearest town and find a hotel or something, then we can take a train into the city in the morning. We'll still get to our meeting in plenty of time."

He grunted. She didn't seem to require a further response. After all, the human clearly had everything under control. It made him itchy.

Baen was unaccustomed to the quandary in which he found himself. In all of his existence, he had woken to the heat of battle. Never before had he experienced a situation that forced him to face such long periods of inactivity. It left him feeling superfluous and almost useless. Give him an enemy to slay, and he would do it; ask him to entertain himself during a day of waiting and mechanical travel and he grew frustrated enough to scream.

Outside the airport terminal, a short line of taxis had queued up to the curb, waiting to ferry arriving travelers to their destinations. Ivy made a beeline for an empty vehicle and the driver opened his door and climbed out.

"Bonsoir," he said politely, though the boredom in his voice was obvious. *"Avez-vous besoin d'aide avec vos bagages?"*

Ivy flashed the driver a smile, and quickly the man drew himself up straight and puffed out his chest. His gaze traveled over her petite form with obvious appreciation and he started to hurry around his car as if he wanted very badly to help her with something else.

Baen flashed him a smile full of teeth and empty of goodwill. *"Non."* To make himself plain, he reached out to rest his palm against the small of Ivy's back and guide her close to his side. *"Ce n'est pas nécessaire."*

For a second it looked as if the driver would push his luck, but then he tore his gaze off Ivy's sweet curves and caught a glimpse of Baen's expression. Quickly he raised his hands and took a step backward. *"D'accord, d'accord. Euh, où allez-vous ce soir?"*

Ivy looked between them, her brow furrowed. She hadn't mentioned whether she spoke French, or how well, but at least she didn't interrupt to demand a translation. Baen would prefer to handle this driver on his own.

"À la ville," he said. *"Nous cherchons un hôtel ou une auberge pour passer la nuit."* Into town. We're looking for a hotel for the night.

"Bon. Je vais vous y emmener."

Having agreed to the fare, the driver made as if to open the rear door of his cab for Ivy, but a low sound from Baen had him thinking better of it. He scurried back around instead and climbed back behind the wheel while Ivy got in and scooted across the seat to allow Baen to follow.

"What was that all about?" Ivy asked softly, leaning close under the pretense of settling her satchel onto the floor at her feet.

"Do you speak French?" Baen asked just as quietly.

"Like a learning-disabled three-year-old."

He took that to mean she wasn't fluent. "It was nothing.

I merely asked him to take us to a place where we could find accommodations for the night."

Ivy didn't look entirely satisfied by the answer, but something must have convinced her to let it go, because she lapsed into silence beside him and turned her attention to the window. The sun had set just as they landed, so there wasn't much to see beyond the twinkling cluster of lights in the distance that he assumed indicated the location of the nearby town. Still, it was enough to keep Ivy's attention, allowing Baen to turn his back to the driver.

A young man, probably in his mid-twenties, he had cocoa-colored skin and an accent that indicated he'd been born not in France itself but likely one of its former colonies in the northern part of Africa. His smooth, even features probably made him attractive to most human females, Baen conceded reluctantly, but if he wanted to keep those dark eyes of his in his head, he needed to stop using his mirror to steal covetous glances at Ivy as he drove.

Not that Baen couldn't understand the impulse to stare at her. He spent enough time fighting against it, but that didn't mean he liked it when another man followed suit.

Even in another of her disguises, his Warden looked good enough to eat. He hated her wig, of course, even though this one suited her better than the blond thing she had sported when he had first set eyes on her. This one looked as sleek and dark as mink, falling straight to her nape in back but angling down as it moved forward so that the hair in front curved under the smooth angle of her jaw at the sides and fell in a heavy fringe to her eyebrows at the center. The color made her skin look impossibly pale and milky so that the freckles dusting her skin appeared like nothing so much as a sweet sprinkling of cinnamon sugar atop a bowl of rich cream.

Oh, how he wanted a taste.

Swallowing against the sudden watering of his mouth, he glanced back at the road visible through the windshield of the taxi and frowned. Was he imagining things, or did the road they had just turned onto appear to run in the opposite direction of the small town whose lights he had spotted a few minutes ago?

He shifted his glance to the driver's profile and scowled. *"Où allez-vous?"* He demanded to know where they were going.

The driver glanced in the rearview mirror. *"Calmez-vous, Gardien. Vous ne voudriez pas faire peur à la jolie fille."*

Relax and don't scare the girl?

Baen stiffened. In the dim light of the dashboard, he could suddenly see that the eyes that stared back at him in the reflective glass no longer appeared soft and brown but now blazed with a dark and sickly red glow.

Shit. How had the Darkness found them again? Especially so soon and when they hadn't even known their own travel arrangements until a few hours ago?

Now was not the time to stop and ask questions, though. Now was the time for action.

Without warning, Baen jackknifed in his seat, one arm reaching back to seize Ivy around the waist, the other reaching out to wrench at the handle to open the car door. A snapping sound registered in his ear a split second before his fingers jerked at the little metal grip. The small lever snapped off in his hand, and the locked door didn't budge. The driver laughed darkly and punched the gas pedal, sending the car into a fast, forceful acceleration that had Ivy looking around frantically, her eyes wide and startled.

"What's going on?" she cried out, her fingers curling around Baen's arm as he gripped her waist.

"Hold on," he ordered, not bothering with explanations. Those could come later. Right now he needed to move. Quickly.

Pivoting on his seat, Baen pulled up his knees, then slammed both feet hard against the locked car door on the side opposite the hinge. Even in his human form, he still possessed near Guardian-level strength and the lock gave way with a shriek of protesting metal. The door swung wide, so wide that it snapped the hinges as well, and crashed backward to leave a giant dent in the front passenger door before falling away to clatter on the pavement behind the speeding car. The possessed driver shouted a foul oath, jerking the steering wheel hard so that the force of gravity tossed Ivy and Baen to the opposite side of the rear seat, away from their escape route.

It would take more than that to stop a determined Guardian. Securing his grip on Ivy with a firm squeeze, Baen gathered himself and launched them both through the opening left by the missing door. As soon as he felt his hips clear the vehicle, he launched his shift and got in one good beat of his wings, which allowed him just enough control of their momentum to turn their bodies and take the impact of their rough landing on himself.

To her credit, Ivy didn't waste her breath screaming, but the force of the jolt did tear one short, sharp cry from her lips. Her fingers had dug into him the moment he set him moving, and she continued to cling while he climbed to his feet and glanced around to orient himself.

The squeal of brakes and rubber on asphalt accompanied a bright red pulse of brake lights. The car screeched to a stop and the driver's door opened with such force that it repeated the fate of the rear door, snapped hinges and disarticulation included. It thumped to the ground even as the demonic driver raced toward Baen and Ivy across the open field where they had landed.

Baen set his female aside and met the charge with a bellow of rage. The demon's actions could have killed the fragile human, and Baen intended to make clear the penalty for endangering Ivy's life. It would be fast and brutal and bloody and would serve as a warning to any who came after that the woman was under his protection. To hurt her was to beg for death.

A death Baen would grant only too gladly.

The demon met him with a swipe of the claws that burst forth from the fingers of its human host. Like the creature Baen had fought off in the alley to save Ivy the previous night, this servant of the Darkness had no regard for the broken body it would leave behind; it craved only death and destruction. Baen was only too happy to deliver, but he would choose what was destroyed in this battle, not the demon.

Back in his natural form, Baen felt the power of the Light fill him. This was what he had been created to do—to fight against the Darkness hand to hand and claw to claw. To protect. To defend. To defeat.

To be honest, one minor demon offered no great challenge to him, and it made Baen suspicious. Why would the Darkness bother to reveal itself when it had only one human under its thrall? If it had located him and Ivy upon their arrival in France, wouldn't it have proved a better strategy to simply note their whereabouts, leave them at a hotel, and then return with a greater force? Baen might be powerful and fierce, but he was only one Guardian. If faced with sufficient numbers of the enemy he could be defeated, or at least distracted long enough so that they could get to Ivy. Kill his Warden, and the Darkness would accomplish two goals with one blow—they would further weaken the Guild according to their long-term plan, and they could weaken Baen considerably by removing his support and his mate all in one deft strike.

By contrast, this clumsy attack by one possessed human mere minutes after their arrival in France had little chance of success and only served to put Baen and Ivy on their guard. What exactly did that accomplish for the enemy?

Even with these thoughts to distract him, it took Baen mere moments to dispatch the demon. He didn't even bother to summon his bardiche, simply using his claws to tear into the vulnerable human flesh and his strength to snap the neck of the host, rendering the demon powerless. It fled its useless shell in a rusty black cloud of pollution before dispersing into the atmosphere. Baen hadn't destroyed it, but he had sent it back to the plane of its origin, and for the moment that would have to do. At least Ivy would be safe for a time.

He turned to find her gazing at the driver's destroyed body with a vaguely gray cast to her skin. Hurrying to her side, he tugged her close and felt her tremble against him. "Are you all right?" he asked. "Are you hurt? Did the fall from the car injure you in any way?"

She shook her head, but her gaze remained locked on the corpse. "No, I'm fine. I'm just a little . . . um . . . I'm fine," she repeated. "I'm fine."

Baen wondered if she was simply answering his question, or trying to convince herself of something she did not quite believe. He shifted to block her view of the fallen man and waited until she dragged her gaze up to meet his. She looked a little dazed and a lot worried, but he decided she would be fine with a little time and distance.

He urged her away from the road and the car that still idled in the center, lights pointing into the hedge that bordered the pavement. They appeared to be in a quiet area, still close enough to the airport for few humans to be likely to wander here, especially after it had closed for the night. Still, he had the feeling they should not linger. Better to get them to the nearest town, or even to Paris, where they could better blend into the crowds.

Yes, he thought. Right now, the more humans surrounding them, the harder it would be for the Order to isolate them and attack. Not that the *nocturnis* ever cared about avoiding collateral damage, but searching for a needle in a haystack always presented more of a challenge than searching for it on a blank sheet of paper.

Decision made, Baen scooped Ivy into his arms and cradled her tightly against him. One thrust of his powerful legs launched them into the dark sky and on toward Paris. When Ivy barely uttered a word of protest, he pressed his lips together with grim determination. If she didn't fight him about being carried through the air, then she must be even more shaken than he had believed. Time to get her to safety. Once they were secure for the night, they would have the chance to determine what this latest attack had to tell them about the Order's next move.

Whatever it was, he had a feeling that countering it would require more than simple brute force.

Ivy wasn't certain whether she fell asleep or just passed out for the duration of the short trip from Beauvais to the center of Paris. Frankly, it didn't really matter. So long as she didn't have to watch the hard, hard ground flashing before her eyes like a portent of her own painful death, she was fine with it.

Had Ivy mentioned that she *really* didn't like unsupported heights? Or falling from them? Or, worst of all, *landing* after falling from them? The whole chain of events just made her twitchy.

Either way, she felt just as glad not to remember any of that journey. When she woke to the soft jolt of Baen's landing, she opened her eyes, relieved to find herself standing on solid ground. Sort of. Judging by the top of a chimney stack a few feet away and the view overlooking a cozy neighborhood in one of Paris's central arrondisements, Baen had once again chosen to use a rooftop as his own personal helipad. Or Guardi-pad. Whatever.

Deciding it would be pointless and disconcerting to ask him about the flight, she settled instead for, "What time is it?"

The Guardian shrugged. "Most likely two hours or so before midnight. Not late. The trip from Beauvais was not far."

He said it with the unconcern of someone who didn't have to worry about the consequences of being dropped from a height of a couple thousand feet. Winged bastard.

Patting her satchel to reassure herself it was still there, Ivy reached into the pocket of her jeans and pulled out her cell phone, relieved to find it present and working. "Okay, well, first thing we need is to find a place to stay. After that, we can figure out everything else. Personally, I would kill for a cup of coffee right about now, but we should be able to get that in a hotel room." She pulled up her Internet app and started searching for accommodations.

A few seconds later, she found herself scowling and muttering at the glowing screen.

"What is the trouble?"

She shook her head and scrolled down the page. "Nothing. It's just that I'm not finding any place to stay in this neighborhood that has more than one room available. Apparently this is a really residential section, so it's all little B and Bs or rooming houses, no major hotels. Damn it."

"We do not require a second room."

"Excuse me?" Ivy looked up and shot him a level

glance. "I do not sleep with men I've only known for twenty-four hours."

He didn't even bother to hide his dismissive expression. "I have recently woken from a sleep that lasted more than three hundred years. I will not require rest for some time. You may sleep undisturbed."

She eyed him suspiciously, the voice in her head grumbling. Those were pretty big words for a man who'd kissed the snot out of her a few hours ago. Had he suddenly lost interest in her? Was it from carrying her pudgy ass all the way from Beauvais?

Oh, get a grip! she scolded herself. There she went again, talking crazy to herself. She was not here to try to catch the Guardian's interest, so it didn't matter if he thought she was fat or thin or the next best thing to sex on two legs. They had a purely professional relationship and nothing else.

Except for when he tried to devour her whole, like a bowl of ice cream on a hot summer day. That hadn't felt too professional. It had felt delicious.

Down, girl. She tried to wrestle her libido into submission and scoured the listings on her phone to at least find a room that offered two beds. A girl could never be too careful, after all.

She skimmed through the listings, checked the reviews, then shrugged and clicked the button to book the room. After all, they would only be there for a few hours; it didn't need to be the George V. It just needed a door, a lock, and a bathroom.

And two separate beds. Everything else was window dressing.

"Okay." She checked the map on her phone, oriented herself, then shoved her phone back in her pocket. "Five blocks that way. Any ideas on how we get down from here?"

That turned out to be easy. Baen had chosen his landing spot carefully, locating a building of no more than four stories with an exterior fire stair extending up to the top floor. With a little help from him, Ivy found herself lowered to the top landing and quickly led the way down the metal structure to the street.

She didn't even pause at the bottom, wanting to put space between them and the building. Baen might have the ability to move as silently as a shadow even once he shifted to a human appearance, but her mortal feet had clanged hard against a couple of those steps. If any of the building's residents panicked and called the police to report prowlers, she didn't want to find herself in the nearest police station, or trying to explain to the local *gendarmes* what she had been doing at that address.

She kept an eye out during the short walk to the small B and B, but within twenty minutes, they had been welcomed by a beautifully apathetic manager and shown to a small room under the eaves of a seventeenth-century town house on a quiet side street. The moment the door closed behind their host, Ivy plopped herself onto the end of the closest of the twin beds and let out a groan of exhaustion. Apparently, even the last eight months of work as an operator on the Wardens' Underground Railroad hadn't been enough to prepare her for the previous twenty-four hours.

But then again, she wasn't sure anything could have.

While she sat and tried to get her bearings, Baen prowled around the small space, poking into everything, then pushed aside the lacy curtains to peer out the multipaned window. He said nothing, so Ivy finally gave him a verbal poke.

"Any sign of the boogeyman?"

He grunted, a sound she took to mean that he heard

and understood her sarcasm but refused to respond to it. Instead, he merely said, "We should be safe enough here for a few hours. I will keep watch while you rest."

Ivy frowned. "Do you really think that's necessary?"

"We have been attacked three times in the space of a single day." He let the curtain fall and focused his hard gaze back on her. "I find it difficult to ascribe such events to random bad luck."

The man—er, Guardian—had a point.

To be honest, Ivy had been trying hard not to think about that. The chaos of the attacks themselves, combined with the appearance of Ash and Drum and all the other things that seemed to have happened in rapid-fire succession, had made it easy to simply react and set thinking aside for another time. It looked like that time had finally arrived.

"Yeah, I guess that is kind of weird," she acknowledged. "The first time was easy to explain, and I guess since Martin turned out to be on the Dark Side, that one can go down to him, but this last one? The cabdriver? That one caught me off guard."

"Why do you believe the first attack is so easily explained?"

The question took Ivy by surprise. "Well, that's something I'm always aware is a possibility when I'm transporting a Warden out of England. We all know the Order is after them, so we need to stay on our toes and be prepared for an attack at any time. I mean, clearly they don't want us getting the Wardens to safety. That completely blows their plans."

She paused as a thought occurred to her.

"Which, if you think about it, actually points to Asile *not* being one of them. Why try to stop Wardens from reaching him if he was just going to let the Order kill them anyway?"

"Any number of reasons. To maintain a certain appearance of uninvolvement? To prevent closer scrutiny? As a kind of perverse game? I can conceive of many possible explanations."

"Wow, that makes me feel better."

This time, he ignored her sarcasm. "In any event, I am not certain that I agree the first of the attacks can be so easily explained. Did you not keep your identity and your purpose a secret? And did you not take precautions against being discovered or followed during your movements?"

"Of course I did."

"Well, then? How did the demons find you?"

Ivy's mind raced. She didn't like the implications of his questions. "Maybe that's down to Martin, too. After all, we think now that he's been working for the *nocturnis* all along."

Baen lifted one shoulder. "This may be true."

"But you don't think so."

"I do not. Martin's involvement with the Order still does not explain the third attack, and nothing explains the persistence of so many attacks in such a short amount of time."

"So what's your theory, then?"

He fixed her with his gaze and she watched as his eyes went from dark and human to black and burning and something else entirely. "It has occurred to me that the only element common to all three incidents is you, Ivy Beckett."

The statement sent her reeling. Threw her for a loop. Knocked her upside the head. Did all sorts of metaphorical things that all amounted to shocking and scaring the shit out of her. What the hell was he trying to say?

"Are you trying to tell me you think that *I'm* working with the Order, too?" she demanded, outrage propelling her to her feet.

Baen's startled expression told her he had never intended for her to draw that conclusion from his statements. "Of course not." He dropped his arms from their position folded over his chest and his stance noticeably softened. "No, Ivy. I know that you would never aid the Darkness. I did not mean for you to think I even suspected such a thing. I do not."

"Well, then?"

He stepped forward to grasp her gently by the arms, his huge hands careful of their strength. "I am not wary of you, little human. I am wary *for* you."

"What do you mean?"

He hesitated, his palms absently stroking back and forth across her upper arms until she felt gooseflesh rise on her skin. Even that simple, comforting contact made her tingle. She couldn't explain her reactions to the enormous supernatural protector, but she was beginning to be able to predict them. He was quickly becoming her own personal kryptonite.

"I have come to suspect that the *nocturnis* are watching you, little one," he finally told her, his tone making his reluctance to do so obvious. "I believe they have been for some time, and I believe they perceive you as a threat that must be . . . dealt with."

"Me?" She laughed incredulously. "That's ridiculous. The Order knows they have five Guardians out there to deal with—six, now, with you—not to mention the Wardens that go with them. And you think they'd be worried about one little human whose greatest contribution to the fight against the Darkness is as a glorified volunteer travel agent? Are you high?"

He glanced at the floor with obvious confusion. "I am on the same level you are."

"It's an expression, rockhead. It means you're clearly out of your mind. I am absolutely no threat to the *nocturnis*.

I'm not a Warden—" She held up a hand to cut off his protest. "I have no magical abilities, let alone training, and my supposed 'talent' is about as useful as a bikini at the South Pole. What the hell could they possibly hope to gain by coming after me?"

"I do not know, but we cannot dismiss the possibility given the evidence at hand."

"The 'evidence' being that I got lucky enough to be nearly killed three times since last night." She scowled at him.

He glared right back. "The Order might be indiscriminately violent and evil, but they always have a plan. They would not come for you so many times unless they had something to gain by it."

"I'm N-27 on their BeelzeBINGO cards?"

His fingers suddenly tightened their grip on her. "You should not make jokes about your safety."

"Well, what the hell else am I supposed to do? Curl up in a ball and sob? That doesn't help anyone, and all it does is make my face splotchy and my eyes swollen. No, thanks."

Baen looked like he wanted to shake her to see if some sense would settle back into place, but even in that moment, she knew he would never do anything to hurt her. She didn't know where that utter confidence came from, but it was there. She trusted the Guardian more than she had ever trusted anyone in her life. He might drive her crazy, but he would die before he let anyone hurt her, even himself.

"You make me insane," he growled at her, staring down with his expression hard and his eyes blazing. "You scatter my thoughts and test the very bounds of my self-control. Why do you affect me this way?"

Suddenly, the urge to continue bickering with him slid away. She found herself trapped in the flames that flickered behind his dark eyes, caught up in the intensity of his regard. All at once, she no longer believed he was angry with her. This was not the gaze of an angry man. This man hungered for her.

The bottom dropped out of her stomach, and Ivy felt her heart begin to race like a thoroughbred just released from a starting gate—that giant leap from a standstill to a blazing gallop. Her breathing stuttered, her throat tightening until not even air could pass through. She went suddenly cold, then hot, her skin contracting and then flushing until her nipples stood at attention and it felt like her panties might burst into flames.

And all that happened even before his head began to dip toward her.

When it did, her brain shut down.

His mouth didn't settle on hers; it seized, conquered, and pillaged. A sharp nip had her lips parting on a cry, and he swept inside to claim and explore. She felt like he'd planted a flag on her, but for some insane reason she didn't even care. To hell with independence and being a modern woman—that had never made her feel like this.

Once the initial shock of the kiss wore off, Ivy found herself back in control of her own limbs, and she celebrated that return to voluntary movement by wrapping her arms around Baen's shoulders and trying to climb him like a maple tree. He offered not a sound of protest and instead reached down to cup her ass in his hands and help by lifting her against him. She immediately hooked her legs around his hips and clung like a lemur.

A horny lemur.

He didn't even grunt at taking her weight, like it didn't even register with him. He just kept feasting on her, and damned if Ivy didn't nibble right back. Their tongues tangled in the hottest kiss she had ever experienced, but all it seemed to do was stoke the fire inside her to another level. Plug her into something, and she felt pretty confident she could heat half of a major metropolitan area through the worst blizzard ever recorded. And that was without counting the heat she could feel pumping off her partner in this crazy experiment.

Baen pressed against her, his hands kneading her bottom in a way that turned her knees to jelly and made her thighs quiver. In their current position, her hips cradled him, making her keenly aware of the hard bulge behind the zipper of his jeans. It pressed up against her most sensitive flesh, and she couldn't suppress the urge to rock against it until her clit throbbed in time to her heartbeat.

With a low rumble that vibrated in his chest and made her think of hungry predators, he took two steps forward and lowered her to the narrow single bed, pinning her to the soft mattress. She arched up against him, the feel of weight pressing into her making every nerve ending in her body come alive.

She wanted to howl with relief when he stroked his hand over her, but too soon the fabric of her clothing muffled the sensation. Never in her life had she wished harder for real magical abilities so that she could be rid of the pesky material with a quick snap of her fingers.

Baen took care of the problem.

Sliding his mouth from hers, he trailed kisses across her jaw and down her throat, nipping and laving the skin as he went. As soon as he reached the collar of her shirt, he made a frustrated sound and his hands came up to grip the fabric and rip it from her. Buttons pinged against hard surfaces, and the hissing sound of tearing cloth filled her head. Part of her said she should be angry at him for destroying her clothes, but that part got a quick beat-down from the other ninety-nine percent of her that didn't care how they got naked, as long as it happened fast.

She reached out to help, shrugging out of her top and fumbling with the clasp of her bra. Too impatient to wait, Baen shifted a fingertip to reveal a handy, razor-sharp claw, and sliced through the fabric. Her breasts spilled into his hands, and he lifted them to his mouth. His tongue dragged over one stiff peak, rasping the sensitive skin until she moaned and clenched her fingers in his short, dark hair.

When he closed his lips around her and began to suck, her hips bucked up off the bed. It felt like a direct line had formed between nipple and clit, one pulsing in time with the other.

He pressed his weight into her, grinding his pelvis against her and giving her a taste of the pressure she needed. But the barrier of their jeans was driving her crazy. She needed to feel skin on skin, heat against heat. She needed him inside her, damn it.

She moved her hands down to yank at his shirt, dragging the hem from inside his waistband and yanking the fabric up over the top of his head. Unhappily, he let her nipple pop free and finished the job for her. He ripped the shirt off and tossed it aside, his eyes never leaving her beaded flesh.

Before he could dive back to work, she managed to flick open the button on his jeans and tug at his zipper. She couldn't get it all the way down, though, not with the way his erection pressed against it, stretching the fabric to its limits.

Shoving at his shoulders, Ivy made her priorities clear. "Naked. Now."

He looked for a second like he wanted to argue, but the logic of her demand must have sunk in. He had himself stripped and ready to go in seconds and reached out to help her wriggle out of her own jeans, as well.

When the clothes lay discarded and forgotten on the

floor of the hotel room, Baen eased back into place above her, his bare skin rasping over hers and sending her nerve endings into overdrive.

Dear God, the things he did to her.

Ivy had never felt so aroused, so frantic or needy, in her entire life. She hadn't even known this was possible. Every inch of her felt transformed into an erogenous zone. She rubbed the soles of her feet along his calves and felt her pussy clench. Her wrists rubbed against the back of his shoulders and tingled where they made contact. Even her scalp felt tight and sensitized, so that when he tangled one big hand in her hair, the tugging sensation made her whimper.

She burned for him.

The phrase suddenly made sense in a way she had never imagined. Her body felt overheated, her skin tight. When his lips brushed against her, she shivered as if rubbed with an ice cube, or consumed by fever. She could feel her skin grow damp with perspiration and could see the sheen of it on him as well.

They really were hot for each other.

The thought almost made her giggle, but the sound caught in her throat when Baen shifted above her and began to slide his lips down her chest and over her quivering belly. Every one of her muscles from the waist down clenched in anticipation. The long strokes of his hands petting her from neck to knees did little to relax her. They just wound her tighter until she wondered if it was possible for a human being to snap like an overstretched rubber band.

Not the most romantic of notions, but she felt that tense and drawn.

She tried to yank him back up. Maybe another kiss would distract him enough to make him abandon the foreplay. She didn't need it. All she needed was to feel

Baen above her, around her, inside her. All she needed was him.

"Please."

Her fingers clenched so tight around his shoulders she worried her nails might actually draw blood. He didn't even seem to notice. He just shook his head, his lips still so close to her skin that they brushed against the top of her mound with every small movement.

"Soon," was all he would tell her.

Soon would end up being too late if he gave her a heart attack. The possibility looked increasingly likely.

One last frantic attempt to pull him toward her only earned her a burning glance and a new form of torture. He grabbed her wrists and transferred them to one of his big hands, cuffing them in place against her stomach. Then he wedged her thighs open with his broad muscled shoulders and looked down at the core of her like a starving man surveying his first meal in weeks.

Ivy turned the color of poppies and began to shake like a leaf in a storm. She squeezed her eyes shut, unable to look at him looking at her.

She'd had her share of sexual encounters in her lifetime, but nothing—*nothing*—had ever felt this intimate. Nothing had ever even approached it. She felt absolutely vulnerable, naked in a way that had nothing to do with her lack of clothing. Yet at the same time, she had never felt so safe or so cared for. The dichotomy of it was enough to make her dizzy.

Or maybe that was just the mix of arousal and anticipation racing through her veins.

With her lids clenched shut she couldn't see the way Baen's eyes had gone completely inhuman, the whites hidden entirely behind flame-backed blackness, but she remembered her last glimpse of them. They'd been fixed on the puffy pink lips of her sex, on the moisture making them shine, and they had affected her as deeply as a physical touch.

But that didn't mean that if he kept staring instead of stroking, she wouldn't rip his wings off and use them to beat him unconscious.

A slow, quiet shift of air registered in her hearing, and it took her jumbled senses a moment to process it as a deep inhalation. He was drawing in her scent like she was warm apple pie, or bread fresh from the oven. Like she smelled delicious.

A puff of air from the subsequent exhale danced across her skin, making her jump. Once again that rumbling sound came to her, full of satisfaction and anticipation. This time, she could even feel it, and her thighs pressed against him in an involuntary embrace.

Unable to survive another moment of waiting, Ivy opened her mouth to encourage him again, but the only sound that emerged was a strangled shriek. Finally, mercifully, he had done with teasing and he lowered his head to press his mouth fully against her sex.

That's when the world ended, or the sun exploded, or her mind shattered into a billion unidentifiable pieces. Something like that. He began to destroy her with hard strokes and teasing flicks and stinging nips to the very heart of her.

She couldn't think, couldn't speak, couldn't catch her breath. She couldn't even brace herself against the torment, because there was no way to anticipate what he would do next. One moment his lips closed around her clit and sucked hard until she nearly came, but as soon as she began to quiver and lift into the sensation, he would back off and nip at her labia, then soothe the sharp sting with a stroke of his wicked tongue.

Her heels pressed into his back and her wrists twisted

in her frantic attempts to get free, but he held her ruthlessly in place. Honestly, she had no idea where she thought she was going to go, but the sensations he lavished on her were so intense, she didn't think she could stand them.

He controlled her as easily as a fractious kitten, his grip implacable but always gentle. Her head filled with a dull, hoarse sawing sound, and it took ages for her to realize it was the sound of her own harsh breathing as she struggled for air in the face of the overwhelming pleasure. He was going to kill her.

She felt his shoulders roll as he shifted, then a heavy pressure at her entrance. At first, she felt a wave of relief that he was finally giving up and fucking her, but a long hard draw on her clit put paid to that idea. It also pushed her to the brink of a screaming orgasm. Then she felt something hard slide into her channel and realized it was his finger, long and thick and blunt, and curved just enough to scrape against the spongy spot on the wall of her pussy.

He might as well have lit a firecracker inside her.

She screamed and shattered, the direct stimulation to her G-spot combined with the continued pressure to her clit enough to shoot her into the stratosphere. She had never come so hard or so fast or so damned loudly in her life. What had he done to her?

Whatever it was, he clearly wasn't finished. He lifted his head from between her legs and sent her a look so hot and so filled with intense male satisfaction that it barely registered that her eyes had flown open when she came. That didn't mean she could focus on anything—he'd blinded her with pure ecstasy—but it was interesting to note.

"Again," Baen growled, and Ivy shook her head.

"No. Please. I can't."

"Yes you can, little one. Give me your pleasure. Again."

His finger began to pump inside her, scraping against her quivering inner walls with every stroke. She felt herself beginning to go under, but she fought against it. Right up until the moment he withdrew only to return with two fingers, filling and stretching her while his thumb brushed over her sensitive clit with clever strokes.

Shit. He so didn't play fair.

Ivy's head fell back against the pillow and her heels slid to the side to dig hard into the fluffy mattress. She needed to brace against something, because every stroke of his fingers sent her flying further away from reality. She wasn't a multiorgasmic kind of girl, but Baen didn't seem to care. The look on his face told her he'd make her come again if it killed him. Or her. Or poor, innocent passersby.

Damn it, she was not going down without a fight, and she had no intention of going down alone.

She saw him watching her, and she caught his gaze with her own, letting him see the need filling her. She arched her hips into his touch, no longer looking to escape, but mimicking the way she would move if it were his cock inside her instead of just his fingers. She undulated like a belly dancer, parting her lips to free the breathless little moans and whimpers that she had previously struggled to swallow. Let him see exactly what he was doing to her, and how much fun it would be if he let her do it right back to him.

Her strategy worked. She saw the first crack appear in his stony armor when he shifted his weight to the side, no longer pinning her lower body in place with the weight of his. Her writhing against his cock must be starting to make a real impression. That only made her more determined.

Wriggling and panting, she pressed her thigh against his length and made sure to rub skin against skin every time she moved. A muttered curse sent a wave of giddy triumph through her, but it didn't last long. Fingers still working hard between her legs, Baen brought his mouth back into the battle, leaning forward to capture her nipple between his teeth before sucking it deep into his mouth.

Cheater. Unless he gave her back the use of her hands, that was so not fair.

She opened her mouth to protest, but found herself choking on a gasp as the clever, sneaky man pressed his thumb hard against her clit and simultaneously teased her entrance with the tip of a third finger. Just the thought of stretching to accommodate another digit had her sheath clenching hard and the pressure of that against his rough stroking sent her dissolving into another hard orgasm.

This time, he didn't wait for her to beg for anything.

Thank the little baby Jesus.

His fingers slid from her still quivering pussy to grip her hard at the hip, pinning her in place. She blinked up at him, barely able to focus but easily hypnotized by the burning depths of his gaze. He held her there for a breathless eternity, his weight pinning her to the bed, before he finally

Finally

Entered her with a deep, heavy thrust.

Her body stretched around his invading length, the sting she had imagined setting every inch of her on fire. Nothing had ever made her feel so full, so challenged, so perfect. So incredibly, impossibly complete.

She hissed and squeezed him between her thighs. He braced his palm beside her head and began to move back, as if afraid he had hurt her. She would hurt *him* if he so much as tried to leave her now.

"Are you all right?" he asked, his voice tight and gruff.

"I'm dying," she groaned, bucking her hips hard against his. "Now fuck me."

He took her at her word.

Lowering his head and bracing his knees, he began to power into her, thrusting forcefully in and out of her tight heat. Every stroke felt like being plugged into an electrical outlet, and to her shock, Ivy felt her arousal building again.

It almost scared her. After coming twice, harder than she had thought possible, she had ached to feel Baen inside her, but she had never expected to come again. She'd figured no way, she was done. Apparently her Guardian and her libido had other ideas.

She redoubled her efforts to free her wrists from his grip, and this time he relented, using the opportunity to hook his arm under her shoulder to better pin her in place. Ivy almost sobbed with relief, finally able to touch him, to stroke her hands over the shifting, rippling muscles of his back as he moved like a great machine above her.

"Baen." She whimpered his name, everything inside her tightening as he stroked deep and hard within her.

"Come for me," he ordered. "Again. Come on my cock."

His formal manner of speech had deserted him, but the blunt, graphic words only made Ivy more frantic. Her nails bit into his flesh and she tilted her hips, searching for the perfect angle, the perfect pressure to send her sailing over the edge. But Baen was the one who found it. With a grunt, he released her hip and grabbed the back of her knee, pressing her leg back against her chest and opening her even wider. Another thrust drove him deeper inside her and pressed his pelvis hard against her, providing just the right pressure to her swollen clit.

She came again, silently this time. She didn't have the

breath to scream. Every inch of her body seemed to clench tighter than a fist, the climax almost painful in its intensity. It rolled over her like a tsunami, fast and brutal and quickly retreating back to the sea.

Vaguely, she became aware of Baen's last quick, hard movements, of his body going still and taut above her, of the roar that broke from him as he poured himself into her. All she could do was hang on and clutch at him bonelessly as he collapsed on top of her.

After that, she could barely even breathe.

Literally. The Guardian weighed a ton. It felt as if he were still made of solid stone.

Ivy pushed weakly at his shoulders, and eventually, he grunted and shifted far enough to the side to allow her lungs to reinflate. Honestly, they were the only part of herself she could be certain still worked. Everything else felt as limp and useless as wilted flowers, including her brain.

Ah, what the hell, she decided, as she felt exhaustion wash over her. She'd gotten this far without using her brain. What harm would a few more hours do?

Keeping that thought in mind, she closed her eyes and let her body sink fully into the soft, duvet-covered mattress. The fleeting thought occurred that she should probably be sleeping under said duvet rather than on top, but with the huge hunk of man next to her pumping out heat like a forest fire, she figured she wasn't likely to catch cold.

Now, if only she could figure out how to catch 'smart' instead of letting her brain turn off whenever he looked at her . . .

She drifted off, determined to figure it all out tomorrow. After all, chances were she'd have more mistakes to add to her list before she even sat down to breakfast.

She was just lucky like that.

Chapter Twelve

A sharp, well-placed kick to the stomach woke Baen from a sound sleep, which turned out to be the first surprise. After all the time he'd spent locked in his stone form, he hadn't expected to need so much as a catnap for a very long time, and yet clearly, that hadn't been the case. The second surprise came with the discovery that the kick had come from the shockingly small and delicate foot attached to the leg of his sleeping mate.

Ivy had just booted him in the breadbasket, and by the looks of it, she didn't even realize it had happened.

She lay on the narrow bed in much the same position as she had fallen asleep, flat on her back, her head turned to the side and her legs parted. Baen should know; he'd spent the last couple of hours dozing between them, and he'd never felt more comfortable or content in all the centuries of his existence. As far as he was concerned, the decision had been made and Fate had spoken. Ivy was his, and he would spend all the nights of his future in exactly that same place.

Though hopefully, next time she wouldn't kick him.

He frowned down at her sleeping form, wondering what had prompted her to kick him. While he had seen her wield a knife against the demons in that London alley, the last thing he would call his redheaded little female was violent. She might have a temper, but from everything he had witnessed so far, she was more likely to attack with a sharp comment than a sharp object.

Besides, they had both been asleep a minute ago. As difficult as he knew she found him at times, he doubted he had managed to piss her off while unconscious. Even he wasn't that bad. Was he?

Ivy turned her head against the pillow, her brows furrowing above her shuttered eyelids. Was she having some sort of nightmare? he wondered. Should he try to wake her?

He debated with himself, but while she continued to frown in her sleep, his mate did not cry out or move about restlessly. She simply lay there, breathing evenly and looking . . . worried. Perhaps she simply dreamed about something puzzling or confusing. She had been through so much the previous night and day. Did he really want to disturb her rest without more evidence that it might be necessary?

Before Baen could make a decision, Ivy made it for him. Her eyes fluttered open and she struggled into a sitting position, blinking a few times until her gaze focused on him. She looked at him blankly for a moment before recognition appeared to dawn.

"Baen?"

He wrapped an arm around her and cuddled her against his cheek. "Are you all right, little one? You looked as if you might be having an unpleasant dream."

She shook her head, accepting his embrace, seemingly unaware of her nudity. Baen, on the other hand, was highly aware of it. Her sweet pink nipples were warm and soft and he wanted to draw one into his mouth and tease it until it beaded up into a firm little raspberry.

"I wasn't dreaming at all," she said. "I was listening."

Her words almost slipped past him, but something managed to poke through and activate the reasoning centers in his brain instead of just the animal ones. He forced his gaze away from her breasts and met hers.

"What did you hear?" he asked.

"I'm not entirely sure. It was confusing," she said. "There were a lot of voices, and I didn't know any of them, which always makes it harder to guess at context. Hearing people I know comes through clearer for me. But I thought I heard someone mention our names."

"Ours? Yours and mine?"

"Yes."

He digested that. "Was it the other Guardians? Or do you think it was the Order?"

"I don't know. It really was a lot like eavesdropping this time, like listening to a conversation from the other side of a wall. Usually, I feel like I'm right there in the same room as whatever I hear. This time, I probably missed a lot of nuance and inflection, from tone of voice and that kind of thing." She rubbed her face, looking tired. "Hell, I must have. I'm pretty sure I missed entire words and phrases here and there. It was really weird."

Baen considered that and what it could mean. Ivy had been fairly reluctant to discuss her talent, so he wasn't certain he really understood how it worked. That made identifying differences between this experience and the ones in her past more of a challenge.

"What was your impression of what you heard?" he asked.

She looked confused. "What do you mean?"

"When you think about the conversation, did it make you anxious, as if you were listening to a vitriolic argument? Did you feel afraid, as if it posed some sort of danger to you? What impression did it leave when you woke up?"

That made her pause and think. He let her mull it over, stroking her arm with soothing motions while he waited.

"Confused, I guess?" she finally ventured, still sounding puzzled over it. "I definitely wasn't afraid. After yesterday, I'm not real likely to forget how terror feels. And I don't feel like anyone was yelling or anything, which might make me think I was overhearing a fight. But I definitely wasn't relaxed. Somehow whatever they were talking about made me feel like it was stuff I needed to know about. Like it was important somehow."

"And do you remember any of what was said?"

"No, and that's weird, too. Usually I have a really clear memory of what I heard, but not about this." She shivered and automatically leaned closer to Baen's heat. He tried not to focus on the thrill that gave him. "Maybe it wasn't an episode at all. Maybe I was just having a really weird dream with no memorable visual components."

Somehow, Baen doubted it. He didn't know if it was possible for humans to dream without accompanying visions. He'd never heard of anything like that. But regardless of what was possible, Ivy's first instinct had been to tell him it wasn't a dream, and he believed her. She had a rare gift, but she'd been living with it for her entire life; she would know when it was active.

"No," he said. "I do not think it was a dream. I asked you that the instant you woke, and you dismissed the idea. Your subconscious knows the difference, even when you doubt it."

"I guess."

Ivy shivered again and wrapped her arms around herself, seeming to notice for the first time that she had been sitting up in bed talking to him while completely naked. He certainly hadn't minded, but as soon as Ivy realized it, a beguiling flush started across her chest and climbed up until it disappeared into her hairline. It made him want to trace the same path with his tongue.

She fumbled beneath her for the duvet, tugging at the corner only to find it pinned beneath them and completely unable to cover her up. Baen had no intention of moving. He let a faint smile touch his lips and shifted his hand from its comforting caress of her upper arm to a much more intimate stroking over the outer curve of her breast. She remained warm from sleep and from the heat of her bashful blush, and the softness of her skin, the sweet curve of her figure, made his mouth water for another taste of her.

"So, um, I guess it's pretty late," she said, glancing quickly at the darkness outside the hotel room window. "We, uh, we should probably try to get some more sleep. You know, big day tomorrow."

"Hm. I am not tired." He leaned down to nibble the curve of her collarbone, teeth and tongue tracing the delicate sweep beneath a layer of milky skin. The dusting of freckles really did taste almost like cinnamon to him, combining with her natural citrus scent to make him think of pomanders and Yuletide celebrations and long, lazy nights in front of roaring fires.

Once their battle was won and the Darkness had been defeated, he would like to lay his mate down before a fire. He would watch as soft fur tickled her bare skin and the flames gilded it to a rosy gold. Then he would block out the fire and keep her warm in a much more intimate, much more satisfying manner.

Yes, he could hardly wait.

In fact, perhaps he should sneak in a little practice right now, just so he could make certain everything would be perfect. As perfect as the feel of her warm, wet pussy clenching around his shaft. The need to feel that again nearly knocked him off the bed. Never in his existence had he felt such hunger, and only his mate could satisfy it.

"Baen."

Her small palms pressed against his shoulders, but she didn't seem to be exerting much effort in trying to push him away. In fact, the way her fingers opened and closed over his bare skin felt like the kneading motions of a happy little kitten.

"Baen," she repeated, sounding more breathless than the last time. "I don't know if this is such a good idea . . ."

How could it possibly be a bad one? Ivy was his mate. He had suspected it from the first kiss, and knew for certain the instant he slipped inside her. This female had been made for him, created by the Light to complement him and to save him from an eternity trapped in the stone of his own natural form.

And by the same token, he had been made for her. He existed to guard and protect her, to defend her against the Darkness and to keep her safe from all harm. What could possibly be wrong about that?

Wrapping one arm around her back, he cuddled his reluctant mate against his chest and used his free hand to cup the round weight of her breast, brushing his thumb in feather strokes over the tip. Instantly, her areola drew tight, pulling her skin into all those fascinating little crinkles and making the nipple poke out into his palm.

He felt her melting into his touch, felt her muscles softening and allowing her weight to relax into him. It only made him hungrier to feel more.

"Baen, I mean it."

She tried again to protest, but she couldn't even lift her head from his shoulder where it had fallen when he'd begun to fondle her breast. She gazed up at him with those wide gray eyes gone hazy and unfocused and she looked so sweet and innocent and tempting that he wanted to devour her in three quick bites.

"We shouldn't do this. It's going to make everything complicated."

"Nothing is simpler," he reassured her, then cut off any possibility of further protest by the simple expedient of kissing her breathless.

She gave up, gave in to the magnetic pull between them, and let herself dissolve into the kiss. He felt it in the way she seemed to pour over him like warmed quicksilver, infinitely malleable and yet impossible to truly grasp.

She met each stroke of his tongue with one of her own, and instead of pushing him away, she began to press herself closer. Shifting onto her knees, she rose up to even out the difference in their heights. Then, still not content, she swung one leg across his to settle onto his hips with the grace of a well-trained knight mounting up for battle.

Baen had every intention of winning this war.

He grasped her hips and pulled her even closer, pressing his erection into the soft heat between her thighs. He could not bite back the growl of pleasure as he felt himself grow slick from her moisture. The proof that she wanted him just as badly as he wanted her made him feel more triumphant than his greatest victory as a warrior. It was all he could do not to throw his head back and issue his battle cry.

But that would have meant ending their kiss, and nothing was worth that.

He gloried in the feel of her slim arms twining themselves about him, cradling him to her as her fingers sifted through his hair and her nails teased light scratches across his scalp. It felt as if electricity danced on the tips of her fingers, igniting every single nerve he possessed, one by one.

Holding her tightly against him, he reclined back against the pillows and pulled her along until her torso lay draped across his like a living blanket. With her full breasts and soft skin, though, she felt better than any blanket ever woven.

When she shifted, clamping her thighs against his hips and pushing herself up on her hands, he tried to protest, but she broke the kiss and hushed him.

"This time it's my turn to drive you crazy," she told him, and his arguments died under the power of her wicked smile.

Fighting to remain still, he gave up any hope of relaxing, and told himself she would have to be content that he merely restrained himself. If he lasted ten minutes without flipping them over and pinning her beneath him, it would be a bloody miracle.

Then she gave her hips a sensual twist and he decided five would require some form of divine intervention.

Her back arched, thrusting her breasts forward so that his hands were reaching for them before he even realized it. He cupped and cuddled the soft weights, savoring the smooth silk of her skin against his rough palms. After the hard frantic pace of their first joining, he felt the urge to treat her with more care and delicacy. She was so tiny compared to him, so fragile, that he should be trying to rein in his strength and treat her like something too important to bruise or break.

As if sensing his thoughts, her gaze narrowed and her hands came up over his, pressing them more firmly against her. She encouraged him to squeeze and knead as she ground their hips together in a way that felt far from delicate.

"Don't hold back on me now," she said, her gray eyes

gone dark and smoky. "I'm a big girl, Baen. I can take whatever you dish out."

His mind might hesitate, but his cock urged him to take her at her word. It just urged him to take her.

But Ivy seemed determined to be the one doing the taking. Raising herself over him, she reached between their bodies to grip his erection in those slender fingers and guide him to her entrance.

"Here," she whispered, her lips curving in an expression of naughty challenge. "Let me show you."

And she impaled herself on him with one smooth stroke.

Baen bit out a curse. Her body closed around him like a wet furnace, squeezing hard enough to have his balls immediately drawing up tight. If he didn't get ahold of himself, he would be spilling inside of her before he managed a single thrust. She deserved so much better than that. She deserved to feel every bit of the pleasure she was lavishing on him.

Remembering the way her whole body had quivered when he played with her nipples, he shifted his grip on her breasts to take the little peaks between fingers and thumbs. His nails scraped over the tight buds, and he felt her reaction in the way her pussy quivered around him. Fascinated by the instant connection between those two erogenous zones, he pinched the flushed tips lightly, then gradually increased the pressure until she moaned and her pussy tightened, milking his cock like a fist.

A groan of his own escaped. She felt like heaven, and he was quickly becoming addicted to the sensations.

She began to move above him, rocking her hips in a way that stroked both of them along all their most sensitive nerve endings. The pressure ground her clit against his hips, but it soon became obvious that wasn't enough for her. Her breathing changed to panting and she braced her hands against his chest as she began to lift and lower her hips, riding him with intense focus.

Baen grasped her hips and moved with her, thrusting up to meet her downward thrusts, trying to get as deep inside her as possible. He wanted her to feel him all the way to her center, all the way to her heart. He wanted to embed himself inside her until there was no way she could fail to recognize that Fate had created them for each other.

He wanted to claim her, to mark her from the inside out, and then he wanted her to mark him, though a part of him suspected that had already happened. He already felt as if his own stony heart belonged to her. She held it in that pale, delicate hand, and he could only hope she wouldn't toss it aside like an unwanted toy.

Baen might be immune to magic and toughened to the blows of his enemies, but this little human possessed the power to destroy him with a single gesture. The knowledge of it humbled him and made him determined to please her so thoroughly, she would never wish to be parted from him.

He could hear her arousal and pleasure growing in the shortening of her breaths, in the little whimpers and moans that began to fall, seemingly unconsciously, from her parted lips. He could feel it in the tightening grip of her pussy, in the way her nails began to dig into his skin as her fingers clenched instinctively. Her movements grew increasingly irregular, her rhythm dissolving beneath the clawing need to climax.

Baen could help with that. Bringing her to ecstasy would hasten his own pleasure, but that wasn't his goal. He wanted to see her come apart, to watch her face as she came on his cock, to feel the spasms of her cunt and to know that he had brought her to that point. He needed to know that he was the source of her pleasure. Only then would he be able to enjoy his own.

One hand continued to grip her hip, assisting her movements as they grew increasingly frantic and erratic. The other he shifted to slide between them, finding the place where they were joined. He indulged himself for a moment, tracing the way her body stretched taut around him, then dragged his fingers back up to find the swollen bud of her clitoris.

Her hips jerked at the first contact, and her head fell forward. Her shoulders bowed and her breathing sawed in and out of her chest. Her bright hair tumbled forward, the ends tickling his chest. The sensation enthralled him, but the long tresses threw her face into shadow and hid her expression from him. That was unacceptable. Releasing her hip, he used his free hand to gather the strands into a tail at her nape. The grip also allowed him to gently tug her chin back up so he could stare at her beautiful face as she fought and strained for her climax.

By the Light, she was perfect.

"Ivy," he murmured. His voice was rough, much rougher than he intended, but her eyes flew open at the sound, and he found himself lost in their swirling gray mists. She appeared unable to focus, all her attention turned inward, and his heart swelled with arrogant pride at the knowledge that he had caused this, that he was the one who brought her to the trembling edge of orgasm.

Now, he wanted to throw her over that edge.

"Come for me, little Ivy." He dragged his fingers over her clit and felt her jerk against him. Scissoring the digits, he pinned the swollen bud between them and began to squeeze as he rubbed back and forth. "Let me feel you."

She keened and tried to move away from the added stimulation, so sensitive to his touch that she instinctively tried to escape even as her body drove them both toward the crisis point. Baen tightened his fist in her hair and stroked harder, deeper.

"Come," he growled.

She broke apart not with a scream, but with a shrill strangled shriek that escaped from a throat closed tight by clenching muscles. Every inch of her tightened down until he felt like he'd been caught in a vise, her pussy gripping his cock with startling strength as it clenched and spasmed with her orgasm.

It was too much.

He came with a muffled roar, exploding inside of her even as she shook and shivered above him. The orgasm seemed to last for hours, both of them caught in its savage grip. He felt as if he'd been caught in the jaws of a great cat who shook its head to toss its prey about in a display of predatory triumph.

When he finally regained his senses, he felt Ivy sprawled across his chest in a boneless heap, her pussy still quivering around his spent cock. She felt limp and damp and flushed, and he wrapped his arms around her, wanting nothing more than to stay exactly like this for eternity.

He would indulge himself, too, at least until morning.

Extending his senses, he realized they had torn the bed apart in their passion. Nothing remained on it except for their exhausted bodies and the fitted sheet that still clung valiantly to two corners of the narrow mattress.

Unwilling to let his mate become cold, he reached out with one hand and fumbled around until he felt the brush of fabric. Tugging, he managed to drag the crumpled duvet from the floor and flick it up to drape over Ivy's pale, glistening skin. Now, when she dried from her exertions, she wouldn't find herself chilled.

Satisfied, Baen resumed his grip on his sleeping mate

and closed his eyes. He didn't need to rest, but he intended to savor every second of having Ivy's naked skin pressed against him. He had a feeling that the struggle against the Darkness was about to become very serious, and the memory of this moment would lend him strength he would need to defeat his enemy and to keep his female safe from all harm.

Nothing would touch her for as long as he lived.

Nothing, of course, but him.

Chapter Thirteen

Ivy drummed her fingers against the flap of her satchel and scanned the crowd milling around the Napoleon courtyard outside the Musée du Louvre. Baen stood at her side keeping his own watch. According to the last time she had checked her phone, it was six o'clock in the evening. The museum was closing its doors, sending throngs of visitors into the chilly air and making it that much harder to pick out an individual who might be wearing blue and sporting a yellow flower in his lapel.

Baen had already made it clear that he disapproved of this meeting spot Asile had chosen. While it was at least a large open area (the one thing he had grudgingly accepted as adequate for her protection) there were too many entrances and exits, too many areas where someone could conceal himself from view, and while the pyramid in the center might be made of glass, its metal framework and huge size still provided an impediment to his ability to see someone coming at them.

She had listened to him list his grievances, and understood his points, but none of them made much difference. Asile had set the meeting, not Ivy, so they would just have to deal.

Clenching her fingers to keep them from pulling out her phone so she could check the time *again,* she contented herself with grousing. "I hate waiting around. It gives me frickin' hives."

Immediately, the Guardian reached out to touch her, as if checking her skin for redness and bumps. Given that she had bundled up against the cold, the only bare patch he could find was on her neck. The caress of his callused fingers there had her toes curling in her boots. This was so not the time for him to be getting her all hot and bothered, not that he seemed to have to exert much effort for that.

Ivy had been trying hard all day not to think about last night, or about waking up this morning cuddled against Baen like a very happy kitten. He might have given her the most amazing night and the most intense orgasms of her life in the attic room of that little *auberge,* but that didn't change anything between them. They still belonged to two different species, she still didn't believe she was really a Warden, and Baen was still an immortal warrior destined to turn back to stone as soon as the Darkness was defeated.

Assuming any of them lived through the upcoming battle.

Baen squeezed her shoulder. "I told you we need not do this. It is a bad place for a meeting. Too much here cannot be controlled or accounted for. We can leave and send another message, choosing our own time and space."

"And go through this all over again?" She snorted. "No, thanks."

He grunted and dropped his hand to focus back on the crowd of people filling the courtyard. Personally, Ivy couldn't spot anyone who looked like her contact. Plenty of people wore blue, but so far she hadn't seen anyone sporting a fresh flower in his lapel, which she supposed made sense at this time of year. It wasn't exactly daffodil season in Paris.

Then she felt Baen stiffen beside her and she looked up to see his gaze focused intently on something specific. She followed his glance and found herself watching a wholly unexpected form weaving its way toward them.

Asile had indeed worn blue in the form of a long, slim wool coat in a color just a shade too bright to be called navy. Instead of a boutonniere, a yellow daisy had been pinned to the band adorning a very feminine trilby hat perched on the head of a very feminine Frenchwoman. She approached Ivy and Baen cautiously but without hesitation, as if she had no question that they were the pair she had arranged to meet.

"Bonjour," she said, her voice rich but quiet in the busy square. *"Je vois que le lierre anglais c'est aussi jolie qu'on a entendu."*

Ivy's high school French utterly failed her when faced with the woman's quick speech. She caught "I see" and "English" but everything else rushed by her in a blur of lyric syllables. She looked at Baen to see how much better he was doing.

"English ivy is lovely," he said, his subtle emphasis seeming to offer an agreement to words originally spoken in French, "but it looks best when it can remain shielded from the harsher elements."

The woman lifted an elegantly arched eyebrow and pursed her lips. "I had expected one of the Guardians to speak French, not to merely understand it."

"And I had expected someone associated with the Guild not to insult one who had offered them so much past assistance by doing whatever was necessary to make herself understood to *everyone* she addressed."

Ivy heard the warning in Baen's words and saw from his expression that he still didn't trust this meeting, let alone the person who had showed up as their contact. He glared down at the other woman as if expecting her to pull out an Uzi and blow them both away.

Although Ivy suspected that bullets would just bounce off the stubborn Guardian's thick hide, no matter which skin he currently wore.

She hurried to cut through the tension. "If you're Asile, then I'm pleased to meet you. I've wanted to for a long time, although I hoped it wouldn't be because of . . . all this."

The woman's mouth curved, her deep red lipstick making the expression easy to read even in the dimming light. "Your Guardian is right. I should not have been so rude, Warden. Certainly not to one of my own, and one who has done so much to help us. You may call me Rose. I am Rose Houbranche, and I am both relieved and worried to have you here in Paris at last."

Ivy reached out and automatically shook the hand that was offered, taking a moment to get a good look at the contact she had been in touch with all these months. Rose looked nothing like she had expected.

Well, since she had expected a man, that was an understatement. But even so, the Frenchwoman still took her by surprise. Rose stood around average in height, her slim figure difficult to evaluate under her wool coat, but appearing average as well. She blended well with her surroundings, but in an entirely different way from Ivy. Unlike the American-cum-English Warden, Rose maintained the unmistakably chic air of her countrywomen while sporting a distinctive style of her own. She wore little makeup aside from the bright lipstick, but with her carefully curled dark hair, her fitted skirt that fell all the way to the top curve of her calf, and her thick-heeled T-strapped pumps, she looked a little like a forties movie star.

Ivy could picture her as the heroine of a classic thriller, or a heroine of the French Resistance, risking her life to oppose the oppressive rule of Nazi fascism. It made the much more casual and athletic look to which Ivy had resorted feel scruffy and frumpy in comparison. Her boots made running from the bad guys easy, but they certainly didn't show off her legs like Rose's two-toned heels. Who the hell managed to look chic and elegant while fighting the forces of Darkness? It wasn't natural.

Still, Ivy forced herself not to sulk like a jealous teen. Pouting and scowling weren't going to help her feel any prettier. "How did you know it was us?" she asked instead. "You walked over here without hesitating at all, while I was still trying to pick out colors in the crowd."

Rose hesitated for a moment, then replaced her hands in her coat pockets and gave a very Gallic shrug. "It is what I do. My talent. I see things."

Ivy heard the way the word "see" sounded just a little different when Rose said it and tried to figure out what the other woman meant by it. "You 'see' things," she repeated, mulling over the statement. "As in, you have 'the Sight'? Are you precognitive?"

The woman glanced discreetly around them, but no one stood close enough to overhear. Not as long as none of them started shouting. Ivy glanced up at Baen, just in case.

"No," Rose said. "I don't see the future, I merely see the things around me as they really are, instead of what they pretend to be. For instance, when I look at your Guardian, I can see his true form behind his human disguise. It is not difficult to locate a two-plus-meter-tall, winged *gargouille* in a crowd of humans."

No, Ivy didn't imagine it would be. Still, she wondered how such an ability would work with regular people.

As if overhearing her thoughts, Rose continued.

"When I look at you, Warden, I can see that you are most definitely on the side of the Light. I see the strength and determination in you, as well as the fear. Trust me, the fear is natural. It would be unwise not to be afraid of the Darkness and its servants. It will keep you alert to danger and ready to act." She turned to scan the crowd. "I can also see that most of these are ordinary people, mostly good at the core, but each with his or her own issues to face, whether it be pride or lust or greed or anger. Most humans do not turn to Darkness without being pushed there."

"By the Order?" Ivy asked.

"Or something worse."

Ivy nodded, even though she wasn't entirely certain she understood. What she did know was that it must be really exhausting to be in Rose's head at times. She didn't envy the other woman's talent. "You should really call me Ivy. I'm not used to the whole Warden idea, no matter how many times Baen tries to tell me it's true."

"You have doubts?" When she nodded, Rose looked surprised. "You shouldn't. It is clear you are linked to your Guardian, but even without this, I knew even before we met what you were. If I hadn't, you would not have been sending me Wardens for all these months. Times are too dangerous to bring in anyone who is not already part of the Guild."

"That's the thing, though," Ivy protested. "I'm not a Guild member."

"You should be, and you would be if it had not been on the verge of collapse for so many years."

Apparently, that revelation was too much for Baen to let slip. He butted into the conversation like a bull spotting a red cape. "What do you mean?" he demanded. "What is this talk of problems in the Guild?"

Rose shook her head. "Not here. We have already lingered too long. You will come with me to the safe house, and then I will be able to tell you more."

"No." Baen refused, reaching out to grab her coat when the Frenchwoman turned to leave. "My Warden goes nowhere until I am certain of her safety. You might think you can see who and what we are, but how can we be sure you are exactly what you claim to be?"

"Baen," Ivy murmured, shocked by his display of distrust. Everything Rose was saying seemed perfectly reasonable to her. Nothing had tripped any of her warning signals. Aside from being a woman, Asile had turned out to be much like Ivy had expected. So, why was Baen so suspicious?

Rose did not try to free herself from the Guardian's grip. She simply looked up at him and spread her hands out before her. "You can see everything you need to, if you take the time to look, Guardian. It is in your nature to know who works for the Light and who carries the Darkness inside them. Look at me and judge for yourself whether I mean you or your Warden any harm."

There was a tense moment of silence as the huge man and the petite woman stared into each other's eyes. Ivy could only watch and reassure herself that Baen intended only to keep her safe. There was no reason to think he might feel anything other than suspicion or uncertainty about the beautiful Rose. The niggle of jealousy in her stomach was as unnecessary as it was unexpected.

Besides, there was nothing between her and the Guardian. Not really. Sure, they'd had sex, but there wasn't a relationship or anything like that in place. They had been two adults with a mutual attraction who had faced a great deal of stress and danger together. Sex had been a release valve for some of that tension and fear. That was all.

And if she had to repeat that to herself three or four

times like a mantra, it was nobody's bloody business but hers, understand?

The tension crackled around the three of them for several long seconds while Baen took stock of the stranger who met his gaze calmly and evenly. Rose seemed to take the scrutiny in stride, whereas Ivy would likely have spit in the face of anyone who treated her like the enemy right off the bat. Score another point for perfection in the French column.

Finally, Baen released Rose's coat and gave a short nod. "You do not appear tainted, at least. We will follow you to this safe house, but remember that I will allow no harm to come to my Warden, and I will remove any threat to any other servant of the Light I meet."

"I would expect nothing less," the woman replied, her tone dry and her lips curving. "I have a car. Will you agree to ride with me, or would you prefer to fly?"

Ivy didn't care how Baen answered, there was no way she was letting him haul her back into the sky like a mouse caught by a falcon. The next time he tried it, he'd find her knee in his throat by way of his balls. If God had meant for her to fly outside of an airplane, he'd have given her wings of her own.

She saw him hesitate long enough for her kneecap to get twitchy, but in the end a glance around had him scowling in reluctant agreement. "Paris is too large a city in this age for it to be safe to fly. We might too easily be seen. We will go with you."

The "but know I'm watching you, punk" part of his statement remained unsaid, but Ivy was pretty sure everyone got the point.

Rose led the way toward the Place du Carrousel, then down the central path toward the Avenue du Général Lemonnier. A trickle of other figures moved in the same direction, and the reason became clear when Ivy spotted signs for parking in that direction.

The trio did not chat as they reached the entrance to the underground garage. No matter the uneasy truce among them, no one could call them friends, or even casual acquaintances. Walking beside Ivy, Baen tensed and went on high alert as they entered the confined space. "Where are we going?"

"I said to my car," Rose replied calmly, pulling a ring of keys from her coat pocket. "Don't worry, I am only on the second level. We will be out of here quickly."

Baen's grunt indicated he still didn't like having to follow this stranger into what amounted to an enormous modern dungeon. He really didn't want to cut their contact much slack.

Rose rolled her eyes. "If you still do not trust me, Guardian, you and your Warden may wait by the exit gate, but you will have to be quick to enter my vehicle. The parking hosts here dislike anyone who slows down their queues."

He nodded stiffly. "I would prefer that."

"Then look for a silver Renault with myself behind the wheel." She drew something from her pocket and held it out to him. "You should wear this."

Ivy saw a chain of silver coiled beside a small oval amulet with an engraved picture of some sort. It looked like the kind of saint's medallion many Catholics wore, like a Saint Christopher's medal for protection of travelers. Baen, she noticed, eyed it suspiciously.

"What is that?"

Rose heaved a sigh. "It is a talisman. It carries a spell to conceal magic from curious eyes. I wear it whenever I have to move among large crowds in case the *nocturnis* lurk among them. However, at the moment, your power serves as a larger beacon than mine. A Guardian is something even the lowliest pawn of the Order could hardly miss, unless you take this to help you blend in. I know you do not trust me, Guardian, but you can see this is made of pure silver. No one corrupt enough to intend you real harm would allow it anywhere near her bare skin. Now, take it."

Baen reluctantly let her drop the amulet in his hand, but he didn't put it on. Seeming satisfied, Rose turned on her heel. "I will return in a moment. Remember, a silver Renault Clio."

Ivy watched the woman descend into the garage and urged Baen to walk toward the ramp where cars exited from the parking area. When they found a spot to wait, she looked up at his dark expression and nudged him. "You really should relax," she said. "I think she seems fine. I don't get any of the icky vibes off her I usually do around the *nocturnis*. What's making you so suspicious?"

He didn't reply, just shook his head and kept his eyes on their surroundings. Quite the conversationalist he was today. Practically the only times he had spoken to her since she woke up to find him already up and dressed and pacing their small hotel room had been to issue orders or to offer the briefest possible replies to her questions. If she had thought their encounters the night before had meant something to him, she'd have been feeling seriously hurt by now.

Good thing she knew better. If he had already forgotten about the hottest sex in the history of everything, then they were on the same page. She certainly wasn't thinking about it.

No, sir. Not even a little.

And that was a good thing, because not thinking about sex or Baen or sex with Baen meant that she wasn't at all taken by surprise when a tiny silver bullet of a car peeled around the last corner before the parking garage's exit and plowed straight through the gate arm blocking the driveway. The passenger door of the vehicle popped open and Rose appeared in the gap leaning over and shouting frantically.

"Entrez! Vite! Vite! Ils nous ont trouvés!"

Even Ivy understood that much. *Get in! Quick! Hurry! They've found us!*

She didn't give Baen time to protest or think up a reason why this was a trap, she flew to the car, pushed the passenger seat forward and squeezed herself into the hatchback's tiny backseat. "Come on! Let's go!"

Cursing in a dead language, Baen followed, clearly not pleased but just as clearly unwilling to let Ivy go anywhere without him.

To be honest, she wasn't entirely certain how he managed to shoehorn himself into the front passenger seat of the minuscule subcompact that Rose drove, but as soon as he had both feet inside, the Frenchwoman punched the gas and sent the car careening onto the busy street. Baen managed to haul the door shut and brace his hand against the dash as an alarm sounded behind them and a man in a rumpled uniform jumped out of the attendant's box waving his arms, shouting for them to stop, and yelling for the police. Rose didn't even glance backward.

But Ivy did. She turned sideways along the backseat to see a larger, dark-colored SUV follow them out of the garage at somewhere approaching the speed of light. At least, that's what it seemed like, especially as she found herself tossed back and forth across the rear of the car.

Lord have mercy, but Rose Houbranche drove through the busy streets of Paris like she was trying to qualify for Nascar. Ivy fumbled around for a seat belt and managed to strap herself in just in time to get nearly choked when the car took a corner on two wheels (and she only assumed they managed to keep that many on the ground because she didn't die right then and there).

Baen roared out a command to be careful, and Rose shouted back in a stream of words that Ivy was positive Madame Plude had never included in her high school curriculum. The loud voices combined with the squealing of rubber on pavement, the revving engines, and the blare of sirens to leave Ivy almost deaf. She'd never been so disoriented in her life, and it didn't help that every time Rose jerked the wheel to cut around some poor unsuspecting Parisian driver, Ivy's stomach leaped into her throat and threatened to finish the jump right into her lap. Because covering herself in her own vomit was just what would make this situation even better.

"What in the name of the Light is going on?" Baen managed to make himself heard over the chaos, which was good, because Ivy wanted to know the same thing. "If you want to kill us, you could choose a quicker method."

"Ça suffit, Gardien!" Rose snapped. "I try to save you and your Warden, not to mention myself. The *nocturnis* waited in the garage. Without the charm I gave to you, they spotted me *immédiatement.* I drive like this because we must put them off our trail, because we cannot risk them discovering the location of our safe house. Too many lives will be in danger. Now, you will be quiet while I try to keep us all alive."

Ivy dug her fingers into the car's upholstery and tried to pretend she was in a movie, something with Matt Damon or the Marvel Avengers. If she thought of herself as a spy or a superhero—you know, the kind of person who survived a high-speed crash and climbed from the wreckage to walk calmly but determinedly into the sunset—

then maybe she wouldn't picture herself ending up a bloody smear on the French pavement.

Hey, a girl was entitled to her fantasies.

She glanced out the rear window again. Her heart raced when she saw the SUV had dropped back several car lengths, the bigger vehicle finding itself at a clear disadvantage once Rose had turned off the main avenues onto the much narrower yet still crowded streets leading away from the hubs of tourist activities.

"They're falling back. We might be able to lose them."

"Let us hope."

Rose took another corner too quickly, sending Ivy's head knocking into the car window and making her grunt. Damn, that had hurt.

Baen glanced back at her, looking angry enough to breathe fire. Could Guardians breathe fire? Ivy had no idea, but she figured if anyone could manage, it would be Baen.

"Are you all right, little one?" he demanded. "Are you hurt?"

She reached up to touch the point of impact and winced when her fingertips brushed a quickly forming knot. Fortunately, though, when she pulled them away, they came away clean. At least she wasn't bleeding. Maybe there really was a bright side. "I'm fine. It's just a bump."

One that took another hit as the car screeched around another corner.

"Be careful!" Baen bellowed, turning a furious glare on their driver. "If you have caused Ivy serious injury, I will rip you apart, Warden or no."

"*Calmez-vous.* She said it's just a bump. Isn't that better than falling into the hands of the Order?"

Ivy cupped her head carefully and looked behind

them again. Rose had pulled back onto a larger road and there was no sign left of the dark SUV. "Hey, I think we lost them."

Finally stepping on the brake, Rose slowed the car to a reasonable (read: *sane*) rate of speed and merged with the flow of traffic. "I think so, too, but if you would continue to watch, it would be a great help."

"No problem." It would give her something to think about besides her quickly brewing headache. Damn, that glass was hard.

"I think it is time you answered some more questions." Baen managed to keep from shouting now that they were back to moving like normal people and not members of the Grand Prix racing circuit, but that didn't mean he sounded any happier than he had at his loudest. "We might not have reached your safe house, but I think we can be certain that we will not be overheard in here. Correct?"

Rose shrugged and glanced in her mirrors as she changed lanes to follow the road away from the center of the city. "As certain as we can be anywhere, I suppose."

"Good." The Guardian paused and drew a slow breath. When he spoke again, his gravelly voice vibrated with carefully controlled anger. "Tell me exactly what happened back there. How could the Order have known where to find us? Unless you led them to the meeting that *you* arranged."

Ivy couldn't see Rose's face, but she saw the way the other woman's shoulders tensed and her fingers tightened on the steering wheel.

"I took every precaution against discovery," the Frenchwoman said, "but no, I cannot be absolutely certain it was enough. The *nocturnis* keep the city under close watch these days. If anyone with any magic catches their attention, they make certain to investigate. It is why it has become so important—and so difficult—to keep them away from the safe house. We maintain the secrecy of that location at all costs."

"This safe house. It is where the surviving Wardens have been gathered?"

"Yes."

"Is that the wisest decision? If the Order has been hunting down members of the Guild, perhaps they would be better off divided into small groups."

"We tried that." Rose's tone was flat and hard. "We lost three clusters that way. Almost two dozen Wardens. Smaller groups might be easier to hide, but if they are discovered, they become too vulnerable. The smallest mistake can lead the Order to a hiding spot, and at that point, they concentrate all their resources on it until we are wiped out. We found it wiser to stick together and concentrate on concealing one location rather than many. Strength in numbers, is that correct? Especially now that the *nocturnis* are summoning stronger and stronger play-things. They have killed so many of us that hunting down those who survive had become a game to them."

"Maybe they should just download *Angry Birds Star Wars* or *Hitman* on their iPhones like everyone else," Ivy muttered.

"If only, *n'est-ce pas*?" Rose snorted. "Unfortunately, they seem determined to play with us instead."

Baen pressed on. "If all the Guild's survivors are gath-ered together now, should they not have come up with a way to put a stop to such attacks against them? All of that knowledge and magic in one place should make you strong enough for that."

The woman scoffed. "I see you still have much to learn about the current situation, Guardian. What makes you think we have enough survivors to do more than simply keep ourselves concealed? And why should you expect that the strongest and best-trained members of the Guild were not the first ones singled out by the *nocturnis* for extermination? We have been left with mostly apprentices, the unskilled, or the poorly trained." She glanced in the rearview mirror. "What about you, Ivy? Did you notice that any of the Wardens you sent here had magic to spare?"

Ivy thought about that. By the time she had lured them out of hiding, most of the Wardens she had met had been too afraid to light a birthday candle with magic, let alone handle any major spellwork. Not that she blamed them. They had all lived in fear for their lives and had known that using their talents was the surest way to draw attention from the very forces they had gone underground to escape.

"Not really. I mean, I didn't exactly sit down for long, heartfelt conversations with any of them. We never had that kind of time. But they all seemed essentially the same—members of the Guild, but with no particular official position beyond that."

Rose nodded. "Exactly. I have tried to encourage the few well-trained Wardens among us to lead the others in looking for ways to fight, but it is a slow process, and the need to maintain secrecy only adds to the burden." She paused and drew in a deep breath before blowing it out in a quick, heavy exhalation. "There are just so few of us left."

"How many?"

Rose looked away from the road just long enough to catch Baen's gaze. From her position in the backseat, Ivy could see the strain and sadness in the other woman's profile.

"At the safe house? Sixty-two. Including myself, and now Ivy, as well."

That made Ivy go cold. Sixty-two Wardens survived?

Out of a Guild membership Uncle George had once numbered over two thousand? How was that possible? Even padding the number with the others that Ash and Drum had told them about yesterday, that meant that less than five percent of all the Wardens on Earth had survived the massacres and the assassinations organized by the Order of Eternal Darkness.

God help them.

Silence descended oppressively on the car. Ivy was still trying to wrap her head around the concept of the near annihilation of an organization that had previously stood strong across millennia. Rose seemed tense and depressed, as if she expected her passengers to blame her for the extent of the carnage, and Baen brooded and seethed in his corner, his fists clenching and unclenching in his lap as he struggled to digest the situation into which he had woken.

Talk about a nasty shock. If Ivy were him, she would have wondered if she'd gotten everything backward and she'd actually fallen back asleep into her worst nightmare.

Eventually, Rose shifted restlessly and said, "What do you think now? Would you like to return to the city and take the next flight back to London?"

Ivy almost laughed. "Considering what happened before we left, I'm wondering if Antarctica is nice this time of year."

"No."

Baen pressed his palms flat against the fabric of his jeans and shook his head. He had his gaze fixed on the road ahead of them, the sea of darkness illuminated only by their headlights and the succession of streetlights lining the roadway. It was as if he could see their enemy gathering its army out there, and he refused to show them weakness.

Ivy hated to break it to him, but if they had killed

ninety-five percent of the Wardens in the world, she was pretty sure the Order knew how weak they were. They were probably yukking it up right that very moment.

"No, it is important that we know the truth," he continued. "An honest assessment of our resources is the first step to developing a strategy for victory."

Rose shuddered, her breath catching on a sob, and Ivy found herself shocked to see a huge crack appear in the other woman's chic, tough façade. Her shoulders slumped and her grip on the steering wheel turned white-knuckled. "*Merci Dieu*. Then you will stand and fight with us?"

Baen turned his offended expression on their driver. "I am a Guardian. Of course I will fight against the Darkness. It is my purpose and my duty. I will not abandon my honor in the face of any odds."

"Je m'excuse, Gardien," she murmured. "Of course you would not. This has simply been a very difficult time. We have been afraid that we would not find you, and our chances against the Seven, even with all of the Guardians risen, are still not good. It is . . . stressful."

Ivy figured that was an understatement. Then she reviewed the other woman's words and frowned. "Wait, what do you mean? All the Guardian aren't risen yet. You know that, right?"

Rose glanced back in the mirror. "You were isolated in England, but I can tell you that other Guardians have been waking for a long time now. Most are in North America, but now that you are here, I hope to convince them to join us as soon as possible."

"Then you do know about the others."

Confusion made Ivy feel a twinge of the same distrust Baen had displayed when they first met this woman. Why had she not mentioned her awareness of the other Guardians before now? Why had she not said anything when Ivy had first alerted her to Baen's existence? Yes, they had to be circumspect over e-mail. Those communications were too easy to hack, but an oblique reference would have been appropriate, wouldn't it?

Ivy shifted until she could see part of Rose's face in the rearview mirror. "If you've known that five other Guardians were awake before Baen, then you also know they've been searching for the others and for surviving Wardens, but you haven't contacted them, because they've never heard of you. What gives?"

"Gives?" Rose frowned, then shook her head. "If you mean to ask me for an explanation, it was not the right time. Yes, I saw the overtures the others put out on the Internet, but to contact them too early would only have placed everyone in even greater danger than they already faced. I had to wait."

"For what?"

"Until all the pieces were in place."

Baen glowered at the woman. "What is that supposed to mean?" he snarled, the tip of a fang peeking out to betray his emotions.

Rose turned the car off the road and onto a narrow, unpaved lane. Ivy sat up straighter, suddenly feeling very uneasy. They had driven for forty minutes or so by now, and as long as they had stayed on well-marked asphalt, Ivy hadn't thought much of it. Now, she realized they had traveled into the countryside where there were few lights and no other vehicles in sight. Had Baen been right to distrust the stranger who claimed to be on their side?

"Where are we?" Ivy demanded, looking around to see hedgerows growing up on either side of the car, effectively cutting them off from the rest of the world.

Rose didn't slow the car, just continued to guide it into the darkness. "Which question would you like me to answer first? The one about what is going on, or the one about where we are going?"

"You will answer both." Quick as a striking snake, Baen wrapped his hand around the Frenchwoman's throat and leaned forward to growl menacingly. "Now."

Rose barely flinched at the feel of that huge hand threatening to snap her neck with a single motion. Man, but that woman had balls, Ivy thought. She didn't think she could remain so calm in the same circumstances.

Following a curve in the lane, the woman guided the small car out from between the hedges and into an open area dotted with light from the windows of a sprawling old manor house. The lane had been a private drive, and the tall rows of trees and shrubs a barrier concealing the building from the nearby roads.

"In that case, I can tell you that we are going here," Rose said, turning off the ignition, but keeping her hands in sight on the wheel. "This is the safe house. Just where I told you I would take you."

"And the reason for your hiding from my brothers?" Bean prompted, still not releasing her.

"As I said, I needed to wait until everything was in place, until the last of the Guardians had risen. Before then, it was too dangerous to bring them all together in one place. Think of the target that would have presented to the Order."

"But Baen is only the sixth Guardian to wake," Ivy pointed out, not understanding the other woman's thinking. "There's still one out there, only no one has been able to locate him."

Rose stared into the mirror, right into Ivy's gaze, and her lips took on the smallest curve. "I have."

Chapter Fourteen

As bombshells went, Rose had lobbed a good one. Ivy had to fight back the urge to throw herself to the ground and cover her head with her arms, as though she'd been transported into an episode of a World War II miniseries. It was only the thought of the awkward stares that kept her glued to her seat.

Rose didn't suffer the same inertia. She calmly reached up, pulled Baen's hand away from her throat, and climbed out of the car. She got halfway up the path to the manor's front door before Ivy managed to scramble after her. Baen, of course, had followed immediately.

"Explain yourself," the Guardian had ordered, glaring down at the slim elegant figure who had paused beneath a large, square portico that shielded the building's entrance from the elements. A nearby sconce offered low-level illumination to the scene, and Ivy took advantage in order to search for clues to the other woman's game in the shifting of her expressions.

She agreed now that Rose was playing with them. It seemed as if every time she opened her mouth, she revealed some other tidbit of information she had previously kept hidden. Why did she not just come clean and

share all the information she had? Isn't that what someone who was really on their side would do?

"Can't we go inside first?" Rose asked, not appearing
at all intimidated by the scowling hulk of a warrior who
pinned her with an angry, flame-touched gaze. "It might
not be late on the clock, but it has been a somewhat . . .
eventful evening, no?"

Ivy sidled closer to Baen and crossed her arms over
her chest. Even she was becoming impatient with her
contact's elusive behavior. "No, I don't think we can go
inside. Not until you tell us what you mean so we can
decide exactly what it is we're walking into. First you
lead the Order to our meeting in Paris, then you whisk
us out to the middle of nowhere where we only have your
word that we're walking into a Guild safe house rather
than some sort of trap, and now you tell us that you've
been hiding information about the Guardians from us,
and from the rest of them, as well? Uh-uh. I'm done following you around, sister. Start talking."

Baen made a low sound of agreement and shifted to
place himself between Rose and the entrance to the
house. His meaning was clear—either she explained herself, or she would be going nowhere.

"*Merde.* Fine, I will explain outside, where it is dark
and cold, instead of in the nice, warm house, where there
is coffee and brandy and probably a fire burning in the
hearth. I'm sure it will satisfy your very English need to
be as uncomfortable as possible at all times."

Ivy flashed a tight, fake smile. "I'm American.
Couldn't you tell as soon as you heard me?"

"I had hopes, considering what Puritans you people
can be. You're even worse in some ways."

"I like to think we're just more persistent. So, spill."

Beside her, Baen did his best impression of an immovable object. Considering how he spent most of his time, his effort was convincing.

Rose took a deep breath and pressed her lips together in a tight, red line. She seemed to be gathering herself before she spoke. "The war with the Darkness has been raging for far longer than anyone realizes, since before the first isolated strikes against the Guild."

"How much longer? What kind of time frame are we talking about?"

"Years. We estimate five or six, at this point. But perhaps as many as ten."

Baen cursed.

Ivy chewed on the revelation. She wanted to find it surprising. After all, her uncle and cousin had died less than a year ago, and before that, neither of them had given any indication that they were in serious danger. Not that they spoke that often about Guild business, but impending death was something families shared with each other, for practical reasons if nothing else. So there had been nothing to tip her off that the battle had started any earlier than nine months ago, when she'd had her episode in her nice warm bed in New York.

Nothing logical, anyway. Her instincts, however, assured her that Rose spoke the truth. The Order had achieved too many victories for this to have begun so recently.

"At first, they confined themselves to guerilla tactics," the woman continued. "Small strikes, quickly executed, random and unpredictable. They weakened the Guild, but not significantly enough to cause panic. Especially since, by that time, we think that they had already managed to infiltrate the Guild's hierarchy and place a spy in the organization."

"So, you were right," Ivy said, looking up at Baen. He

didn't appear all that pleased to have his theories confirmed by outside sources, but then, it wasn't exactly good news, was it? She turned back to Rose. "Do you know who it was? Have you identified him?"

"Yes, for all the good it does us. He died in the destruction of the Guild headquarters. For him, it was a suicide mission. The *nocturnis* accomplished their goals, and left us nothing useful to learn from, since there was no one left to question once the fires burned out."

Baen shifted impatiently. "This is interesting information, but if all you plan to do is paint us a background canvas, you continue to waste our time. I want to know where my seventh brother is and why he has not joined us."

"Yes, I think that is something we would all like to know."

A loud air disturbance, almost like a parachute unfurling, sounded only a few feet away, and a rush of chilly wind through the portico had the three figures gathered there turning to peer into the darkness of the manor's front garden. From it, four shapes emerged, two very large, and the others rather small. The large ones sported huge wings they slowly furled as they approached.

"Where is our remaining brother, female?" the first Guardian demanded, his expression one of menace and determination. He would have his questions answered or he would extract vengeance from the uncooperative. "Why have you hidden him from us?"

A woman with long, curly dark hair and a shoulder bag the size of a Central American nation stepped forward and placed a hand on the creature's arm. "Hey, tone it down a notch, big guy. Let's give diplomacy a try at least, before we break out the rubber hoses."

"We are diplomatic," the second Guardian grumbled.

He was shorter than the first, but broader, and looked as if he ate bowls of shredded steel in the mornings instead of shredded wheat. "We asked the female to return our brother to us instead of killing her and finding him ourselves. That is very diplomatic."

Beside him, a tiny woman wearing layered T-shirts—the topmost of which read I'M HERE BECAUSE YOU BROKE SOMETHING—snorted. "Right. You're a regular United Nations, you're just with the Committee on Random Acts of Violence. I get it now."

For about thirty seconds, Rose looked stunned, as if someone had just showed her what was hidden behind door number three and it turned out to be the check for one million dollars instead of the year's supply of turtle wax. Then she seemed to gather herself together with determined motions. She inclined her head and spoke with genuine reverence.

"Guardians," she said, her eyes on the ground at the newcomers' feet. "Welcome to Maison Formidable. You are most sincerely welcome. We have all prayed to the Light that this day would come soon, and that I have been able to witness it brings me great pleasure."

Baen looked from the Frenchwoman to his brothers with a scowl. "Why is it that she has spent the last three hours either ignoring my requests for information or treating me like a nuisance, yet when you two appear, you're greeted like conquering heroes?"

The first who had spoken quirked a smile. "If the boot fits . . ." he drawled.

The girl in the T-shirt (because she looked so young, Ivy wondered uneasily whether she was legal to drink in the U.S.) snorted. "It's a Guardian's innate modesty I admire the most, Wynnie, what about you?"

The taller woman with a decidedly bohemian air nodded and pursed her lips in an obvious attempt to keep from grinning. "Humility, that's what it is. An honest desire to do good for good's sake and stay well out of the spotlight of those who would offer praise."

"Quiet, you," the shorter Guardian growled, but his expression gave evidence of his amusement and affection for the woman, not irritation at her teasing.

Ivy's head spun. She couldn't really decide if it was from information overload, recurrent emotional shock, the adrenaline that was finally beginning to ebb from her overstressed system, or the fact that she hadn't eaten since that ham and butter sandwich she purchased from a street vendor for lunch. The cause didn't really matter, though. What mattered was that she had just run out of the energy required to stand in the driveway of the unfamiliar manor house and tease, debate, question, or interrogate anyone.

Closing her eyes briefly, she leaned against Baen like a stupid little weakling and spoke his name softly.

Immediately, he turned his attention to her and bent down to hear her speaking. "What is it, little one?"

"I'm too tired to do this out here. Can't we just all go inside and tear each other new ones while sitting down? I'm fine with the tearing, I just need a chair and maybe a croissant if I'm going to participate. Is that possible?"

Without even bothering to answer, Baen scooped her up in his arms and gave a shrill whistle. The babbling crowd instantly went quiet, curious gazes and wide eyes all turning in his direction.

"We will finish this inside," he declared, not waiting to see if any planned to object. It wouldn't do them any good if they did. Ivy hadn't known the Guardian long, but she knew he didn't accept no when he wanted the answer to be yes. "It grows late, and the cold air is not healthy for the humans. While we have much to discuss, everything that needs to be said can be said indoors as easily as outside of them."

Ivy didn't offer so much as a token resistance. She was cold and tired and very, very confused. And frankly, if they were all gathered together to discuss the impending destruction of the world, she'd rather do it perched on a sofa and cradling a mug of hot cocoa.

Seriously, if the Light wanted her on its side so bad, it could make with the chocolate. Surely that wasn't too much to ask.

The manor house's blue salon really wasn't very blue at all. The walls had been painted more of a dove gray, with acres of surrounding woodwork from wainscoting to crown moldings painted a pale, glossy cream. Bits of gilding on mirrors and picture frames lent hints of burnished gold, and the furniture's warm cherry and mahogany framing leaned toward shades of auburn. Only a small percentage of upholstery and the elegant drapes that fell heavily from the tall windows showed traces of blue.

But then, as Ivy had always expected, rich people were kind of weird.

Rose explained that the house had belonged to a distant relative of a Guild member, someone distant enough not to be of interest to the Order but sympathetic enough to the Guild to offer the space to the Wardens in their time of need. Which was a convoluted way of saying that Rose herself wasn't actually rich. Ivy figured she had to take her word for it, but the other woman looked far from out of place in the elegant surroundings. It couldn't all be just because she was French, could it?

No one else looked quite so at home. The Guardians all stood, Baen beside Ivy's chair, Knox behind the sofa

Wynn (the bohemian brunette) had perched on, and Dag leaning against the mantel a few short steps away from Kylie. Actually, despite her T-shirt, worn jeans, and battered high-top sneakers, the computer genius appeared the most comfortable of them, aside from Rose. Even the two other Wardens who had joined them seemed somehow out of place among the opulent décor.

After Baen's metaphorical storming of the castle, the rest of the groups gathered outside had trooped in through the ornate double doors to be greeted by a small bearded gentleman with thick glasses and a head so shiny it reflected enough light to count as an additional lamp in the manor's front hall. He had jumped when he saw the Guardians pour through the entry, even though they had all assumed their human shapes (wings were never a good idea in confined spaces). Only Rose hurrying to his side had prevented a full-blown panic attack.

She had introduced him as Aldous and dragged him along as she led the group to the salon where they all now gathered. He had generously and eagerly offered to be the one to go fetch the second Warden Rose had wanted them to meet, but she had used a text message instead. Ivy guessed it was to keep Aldous from bolting as soon as he disappeared from view. Somehow he seemed nervous about being surrounded by three giant Guardians and their unfamiliar (if significantly smaller) personal Wardens.

Go figure.

Rose's summons had been answered almost instantly, and after introducing a slim, dark man in his thirties as Thiago, the Frenchwoman had offered them all coffee or brandy. It was all very civilized and annoyingly unhurried, but at least Ivy got her hot chocolate.

Score.

"Perfect. Now that we have all become such close

friends, can you begin explaining yourself, female? And finish the tale this time."

Hm, maybe she should have offered Baen some of her cocoa, Ivy mused. It might have sweetened his disposition.

His voice rumbled with menace as he continued. "I am particularly interested in the part where you explain why you claim to have located the last remaining Guardian."

"Say what, now?" Kylie cocked her head and opened her eyes superwide.

The rest of the room erupted into chaos. That was the only way to describe three Guardians shouting angry accusations, while two Wardens peppered the air with questions, and a lanky Spaniard had to speak soothingly to a babbling German to keep the other man from running away to hide in a cupboard. Rose leaped to her feet and tried in vain to quiet them all down.

Ivy just sipped her cocoa and tried not to picture a big, gooey cinnamon roll to go with it. Darn it, she really was getting hungry.

"Everyone, calm down." Rose held up her hands, as if that were going to impress anyone.

Or maybe a piece of cake, Ivy mused. Cake went with everything, right?

"Please, I will explain, but you should all sit and be quiet so that you can hear me." Rose tried the reasonable approach, which Ivy could have told her wasn't going to work. Not with this crew.

Ooh, she knew what she wanted! A burger. A nice, juicy burger, loaded with cheese, on a toasted brioche bun. Ivy almost drooled at the thought.

Finally, Rose caught on to the audience, hiked up her skirt, and scrambled atop an antique table that was probably worth more than her little Renault.

"Taisez-vous!"

The woman looked almost surprised when everyone did indeed shut up. They stared at her in shock until Kylie broke the silence with an amused snort.

"I'm going to have to remember that trick," the petite hacker said, grinning at her Guardian. "Next time I can't get your attention, I'll jump up on a table and scream till you shut up and listen to me."

"I always listen to you," the burly Guardian grumbled, but his eyes had crinkled with amusement.

"I apologize for my behavior, but I needed you all to pay attention," Rose said, smoothing her skirt back down her legs. Those legs themselves might just have helped with that goal. Even the women in the room had to admit they were pretty spectacular.

The tight-fitting, high-waisted garment Rose wore combined with her pin-striped, tie-necked blouse and glossy, wavy hair to give her a definite forties-chic vibe without making her look like she was wearing a costume. Ivy envied her the ability to pull it off, but not the effort it probably took to achieve.

"This is a complicated story, one I would like to tell only once." Rose accepted Thiago's help to descend back to the floor, but she kept her attention on her audience. "It is true that I know the location of the final Guardian, but first I must tell you all everything that has led us to this point, because we have come to a crucial moment. We are all in terrible danger of falling to the Darkness, and we may have only one chance to save ourselves and the rest of humanity from certain destruction."

Kylie looked around at the others with raised eyebrows. "Am I the only one who feels like this just became a Wachowski brothers' production?"

"Hush," Wynne scolded. "Let her talk."

Knox jerked his chin. "Say what you must, female.

The quicker you tell your tale, the quicker you tell us where to find our brother."

Beside Ivy, Baen grunted his agreement.

It turned out to be a hell of a tale.

Rose repeated what she'd already told Ivy and Baen, about the Order's early strikes against the Guild and the gradual winnowing down of their numbers.

Wynn nodded through most of it. "We pieced a lot of that together, thanks to Ella. She's a research wizard. But it doesn't explain why your groups here never responded to anything we've put out to try to reach other survivors. You must have known we were looking for people like you."

"Yes," Rose acknowledged, "but we discussed it and we felt it was important to wait before we revealed ourselves."

"Why? We could have helped you. Or we could have funneled survivors your way, like Ivy's been doing."

"We have—no, *I* have followed your actions with great interest," the Frenchwoman said. "I have seen the media reports of the incidents in your area, and those of us skilled with computers have kept abreast of the tidbits you have sprinkled around the Deep Web. I know that each time a new Guardian has woken, you have all gathered together to meet him."

"Exactly. We help each other. We would have helped you, too."

Rose shook her head. "You have put yourselves in danger. Each time more of you gather in a single place, you present a bigger target to the Order. You did not even seem deterred by the knowledge that the Seven had begun to break free of their prisons. The minute you heard the rumors, you should have done everything you could to conceal your existence from them. And instead, I read about the so-called riots in Boston. You all gathered in one place and faced one of the Seven in a human disguise. You were lucky none of you was destroyed!"

"You call it luck; I call it skill and superior strategy. How well has 'concealing your existence' worked for you guys?" Kylie asked pointedly.

Rose frowned. "We are still here."

"But you said you had lost three groups early on after you went into hiding, so that's still not a hundred percent safe, is it?"

"It is safer than setting out a beacon that invites *nocturnis* to your doorstep."

"I like to think of us as the Darkness Motel," Kylie quipped. "Evil steps in, but it don't step out."

Wynn spoke up before Rose could reply. "Uh, I think we're getting a little off track here. You said your survivors here didn't want to reveal yourselves too soon. What exactly were you waiting for?"

The second man Rose had introduced to the group leaned forward from his seat beside her to address them for the first time. "Before all of this began, I joined the Guild as a teenager apprenticed to my great-uncle Francisco," Thiago said. He spoke perfect English with a light accent that painted his words with shades of Spain. "Tio Kiko specialized in magical history and lore. He was fascinated by the tales of the founders of the Guild and the very earliest of our kind. He spent his days and nights buried in dusty old books, learning about and even practicing some of the older spells he found recorded in the archives, things no one else had bothered with for centuries. Even millennia."

"How is that relevant?" Knox asked gruffly.

"Those of us at the Maison have developed a theory," Rose said. "We have seen what has happened when small groups of us have tried to take on the Order these days, now that they have freed several of their Masters. Even when there are survivors, such as yourselves, no one has yet managed to stop the *nocturnis* from accomplishing their goals."

"Freeing the Seven and then destroying the world."

Ivy shot Thiago a sour look. He really needed to say it out loud? She was pretty sure everyone in this room knew where they stood at the moment.

"There were four Guardians in Boston, no?" Rose asked. She didn't wait for an answer. "Four! And still the Demon escaped, strengthened by the deaths there and in Dublin. No one might like to admit it, but if we continue on as we are, fighting as we have been fighting, we have no chance against the Darkness, not once the last of the Seven has been released."

Kylie grimaced. "I really hope this isn't where you guys just say, 'Sorry, it's hopeless. Nice knowing you. We have some lovely parting gifts in the back.' I'm not ready to check out yet. No offense."

"No, but this is where Thiago and his uncle's work with the Guild's lore becomes relevant, as you requested."

The Spaniard nodded. "Rose is correct that we cannot win this war with what amounts to conventional weaponry. You will excuse the crude metaphor, but what we require is a nuclear option."

"I really hope you don't mean that literally, because I'm pretty sure the IAEA monitors Craigslist for sales involving yellow cake uranium," Kylie said, shaking her head.

Thiago smiled. "No, not literally. I don't think even a nuclear weapon could destroy the Seven."

"Can anything?" Wynn asked. "Not that I'm the expert, but I thought the Seven couldn't be destroyed at all. Ever. That was why they were split up and imprisoned separately the last time they tried this."

"Exactly, but what do we really know about the last time this happened?"

The witch tilted her head, her brow furrowing. "The last time all Seven Demons were free? They tried to unite in order to give form to the Darkness. The Guild summoned the first Guardians, who defeated them and banished them to other planes, where they were imprisoned until today. That's the story we've all heard. Are you saying it's not true?"

"I am only saying that it is not very complete. Exactly *how* were those Guardians able to defeat the Seven? It was, after all, a very long time before America invented the nuclear bomb."

Ivy set aside her empty cup. "You know, that's a really good point. How did it happen?"

Thiago grinned and snapped his fingers. "Magic."

Rose stepped in. "Thiago has a sense of drama, but I believe he is correct. The last time the Darkness posed this great a threat to our world was not the first time the Guardians appeared; it was the first time they refused to answer the summons of the Wardens."

"The Guardians and the Maidens," Wynn said, her voice taking on a tone of wonder. "You're talking about the time from that legend, aren't you? That was when it took seven women of power to summon the Guardians back."

"Yes," Thiago said. "But my uncle and I believe that the Maidens in the story did not just stop at awakening their Guardians. A few versions of the story say they fought beside them, and you all know how Wardens fight—not with swords and shields, but with magic."

Okay, now Ivy felt really lost. "The Guardians and the Maidens? Is that some kind of Grimms' fairy tale, because I don't remember a Disney version hitting the big screen."

Wynn and Kylie looked at Ivy, at each other, at Baen, and then back at their own Guardians. The three warriors chose that moment to look *particularly* stone-faced.

The witch opened her mouth, coughed, and squirmed a little in her seat. "Has Baen not told you about this yet?"

Okay, Ivy had thought Wynn seemed like a sweet person, but she was about to change that *w* in her personal description to a *b* if the woman didn't spill. "Would I be asking if he had?"

"Right. Okay." Wynn glanced back and forth between Baen and Ivy until Ivy was ready to throw her cup at the other woman's face. Luckily for everyone, Wynn gave in and started talking. "Um, it's a legend from the days of the first Guardians. According to the story, after they were originally summoned and had defeated the Darkness, the Wardens used magic to lock the Guardians in their stone forms so that they would be ready the next time they were needed. And that's what they did each time the Darkness threatened—they summoned the Guardians, then put them to sleep as stone statues. It worked out well for the Guild, because, well, it was convenient."

"But for the Guardians, it sucked the big one," Kylie broke in. "I mean, can you imagine being trapped in a big hunk of rock and only let out when someone needed you to do their killing for them? Those early Wardens treated the Guardians worse than dogs. *Shtunks.*"

Had the internationally known computer genius and programming guru just cursed out a group of long-dead members of the Guild in Yiddish? Had Ivy heard that right? Because as a native New Yorker, she usually recognized the Yiddish when someone started flinging it. Everyone else seemed to take it in stride.

"Which is why, eventually, the Guardians stopped answering when they were summoned," Wynn said, picking up the threads of the story. "The Guild performed the spells and called the Guardians, but they refused to wake. They had grown tired of fighting for a cause that wasn't theirs."

"And of being treated like *drek*."

"After all, they were not human, and the time they spent battling the Darkness never allowed them to grow close to the people they were protecting. Then, as soon as they won, they were sent back to sleep. They had no connection to the human world, so they stopped caring whether or not it was destroyed by the Darkness."

Yeah, that made sense, Ivy thought. She wondered how she would feel if she was put in that position, of having to risk her life to defend something she didn't even understand, let alone really care for. That wasn't the role of a Guardian; it was the role of a mercenary, but unlike mercenaries, those first Guardians weren't even getting paid. They had literally been fighting for nothing, not freedom, not their own people, not even a paycheck. No wonder they had finally decided the Guild could go screw itself. Ivy would have done the same thing, and probably a lot sooner.

Wynn continued. "But the Darkness wasn't going anywhere, and without the Guardians, humanity was in danger of being destroyed, so a woman came forward. She wasn't a member of the Guild, but she was a woman of power. In other words, she had talent and the ability to use magic. So she should have been in the Guild, if they weren't such sexist jerks."

Knox reached down to squeeze his Warden's shoulder. "Wynn," he said in his deep, gravelly voice, but it was a tender sound, more amused than censorious.

"Sorry." The witch blushed a little. "I might still have some . . . issues around that. Anyway, the woman came to the Guardians, knelt at the feet of one of the statues and prayed. She told it about her family and her friends, about the best qualities of humanity. She begged the Guardian to wake and to fight for them, to help her save her people from the Darkness. And he did. She gave him a reason to return to this plane, and more women of power followed her example. Each of the seven Guardians was woken by one of the Maidens, as they became known, and when the Darkness was defeated, the Guardians refused to return to sleep. They claimed the Maidens as their mates, and struck a bargain with the Guild. Once a Guardian found a mate, he would retire from battle and another Guardian would be summoned to take his place. The former Guardian would remain among the humans, giving up his immortality and his ability to shift back to his natural shape, but gaining a mate and the chance to experience a full life."

Huh, it almost did sound like a Disney story, Ivy decided.

"But the 'Maiden' title is just a word," Kylie threw in, her grin turning cheeky. "You know, we're not *literally* maidens. As if."

Ivy's eyes widened. She'd thought she was just listening to a story. She hadn't been searching for subtextual implications. "Wait a second. Are you saying it's more than just a legend? Do you really think that you're the reason the Guardians are awake again?"

Wynn and Kylie nodded, but, you know, Ivy figured they probably both drank the same flavor of Kool-Aid. When Rose nodded as well, Ivy shook her head. "Um, okay, you guys need to have another think about that, because what you're doing is implying that I'm one of these . . . these . . . Maiden people, too, and I am *really* sure that I'm not. I'm not a woman of power. You're like the millionth people I've had to tell in the last forty-eight hours, but I have no magical power, I wouldn't know how to cast a spell if you tied it to a fishing line, and what other people keep calling my 'talent' is a useless waste of time and energy."

She paused to draw a deep breath and stamp down a wave of panic. It laughed and took on tsunamilike proportions. "And I am definitely not anyone's idea of a mate. Period."

That's when Baen snarled something in that dead language of his and Ivy tripped over her own feet to fall kicking and screaming down the rabbit hole.

Chapter Fifteen

The real problem with Wonderland, Ivy quickly decided, is that while nothing—absolutely *nothing*—made any sense, everything still looked exactly the same. It just wasn't fair.

And neither was having three Guardians and five Wardens all ganging up on her to insist that *she* was the one who wasn't thinking logically. All she needed was a hatter, a dormouse, and a white rabbit. But even without them, she was ready to stand up and shout "Eat me!" at the top of her damned lungs.

And yet, here came Baen, ignoring the rest of them chattering away in the background. He stepped forward to kneel in front of her chair, blocking most of the room from her sight. Ivy drew her knees to her chest and shrank back into the cushion, because damn it, she didn't even know who to trust anymore. Baen was a Guardian, which meant he had to know that stupid legend. Did he believe in it, too? Did he think they were some sort of fated pair of mates, like characters from a sci-fi television show? Had he thought that all along? Because as far as Ivy was concerned, that was the kind of thing it was important to share with the girl you were fucking. Preferably before the fucking started, when she might still be thinking clearly.

Or, you know, at all.

"Little one," he murmured, his voice quiet, just for the two of them. He seemed to understand that she curled in on herself because now wasn't the time for a snuggle, so he didn't reach for her. Instead, he braced his hands on the arms of her chair and simply fixed her with that dark, burning stare. "There is no need for fear. I would never do anything to harm you. Do you not know that?"

Ivy scoffed. "Turns out there's a whole lot of things I don't know, doesn't it, Baen? After all, I didn't know about this story you all seem to have memorized. And I sure as hell didn't know there was a possibility you were looking at me like some sort of bloody magical mail-order bride. What the hell is up with that?"

His mouth tightened a little at the corners, but his gaze remained calm and level on hers. "I told you as soon as we met that you were my Warden, Ivy. I knew that if I had not been summoned awake by a member of the Guild, the only other explanation had to be you."

"You told me I was your Warden, sure, and that was hard enough to believe, but I'm pretty damned certain the words 'fated,' 'legend,' 'maiden,' and frickin' 'mate' never passed your secretive, stony lips, buddy."

"We have not exactly been blessed with an abundance of peaceful moments together, little one. Or did you want me to shout it at you while I fought the *ukobahk*? Or maybe during the car chase earlier tonight? After all, Rose was driving, so I did not have to worry about my actions causing us to crash."

She narrowed her eyes and curled her lip at him. She might not have fangs, but she could damn well still snarl with the best of them. "Don't pull that 'we were in danger' crap with me. Were we in danger last night when you were pounding me into the mattress? Or what about for all those hours before we met Rose this evening? You couldn't find thirty seconds during one of those times to mention, 'Hey, Ivy, by the way, I think you're my destined mate. Just FYI?' "

"You believe this is only taking thirty seconds?"

Her palm itched to smack him like a volleyball, but she resisted. Barely. Mostly because right then, she didn't want to touch him. At all.

He must have read her fury in her expression, because he sighed and bowed his head a little. She could see the tension in his shoulders and neck, and she hoped his head was killing him. It would serve him right.

"I apologize," he said. "That was unfair of me. I understand that you are upset, and you have the right to feel that way."

"Gee, how magnanimous of you to grant me permission to feel my feelings. You're just a big ol' softy, aren't you?"

His eye twitched at that one, but at least he wasn't dumb enough to point out that she had resorted to sarcasm. Apparently, he wanted to keep his balls intact and unflattened.

"I am willing to accept the blame for the shock you are feeling." He spoke slowly and evenly with a degree of control that made it clear he had to work at it. "It must be a challenge to take in news of this kind without warning, but please do not think that any of what has happened was ever intended to hurt you, *amare*."

Ivy didn't know what that meant, but she recognized it as a pet name. As long as it didn't translate as "little one," she might be able to let it slide.

Her stomach felt all twisted and uncertain, and she really didn't know what to think anymore. Part of her got what Baen was trying to tell her. They *had* been kind of preoccupied pretty much since the first moment they met. Even when they hadn't been in the middle of running for their lives—or being driven for them—they had still needed to be careful and wary and watchful for the next thing that would jump out from behind a corner to attack them. So, yes, finding a time to drop this kind of news probably hadn't been *(a)* easy, or *(b)* at the top of his to-do list, but that didn't make it any easier to take.

It wasn't the sort of thing a girl wanted to hear when she was trying harder than she had ever expected to not have her head torn off by a bunch of angry demons and demon worshippers. And it certainly wasn't the sort of thing she expected to hear after an acquaintance of approximately two days. Or, even worse, after ten minutes, if Baen was serious about having figured it out right from the start. Who fell in love with someone after ten minutes? People might talk about love at first sight, but that was a bigger fairy tale than the one Wynn had just told her. It simply didn't happen.

Of course, Ivy realized, a chill spreading through her, Baen had never said anything about love. There had been plenty of talk about destiny and fate and even more talk about this just being the way things were, but no one had even brought up the subject of emotions. She didn't know if that realization made things better or worse.

On the one hand, it took some of the pressure off. If Baen wasn't proclaiming his undying love for her, then she didn't need to sort out the snarled mess of her own emotions any time soon, and thanks to the bloody Light for that. At this point, Ivy didn't think she even wanted to know how she was feeling, especially as it pertained to the behemoth currently kneeling at her feet. So, no L-word meant no hurry in deciding how she felt about him in return, and that was a huge relief.

But on the other hand, what did it mean that he could

call her his mate and assume that she was meant to free him from the eternal cycle of being trapped in his stony cage, and yet have no special feelings for her whatsoever? Was that really any better? The idea that he might want to stay with her out of some notion that the rules required him to, actually made her a little queasy. It sounded too much like some kind of medieval marriage of convenience, and what girl in her right mind would agree to that kind of nightmare? It certainly would not be Ivy.

And that brought her full circle, right back to the point where she felt overwhelmed and confused and exhausted and somehow terrified of something way scarier than the end of the world as she knew it, even if she couldn't quite decide what that was.

Ivy dragged her eyes away from Baen's and looked around just to give herself time to clear her head. To her horror, she found every other occupant of the room watching her and the man at her feet as if they were performing a scene from a newly discovered Shakespearean drama. Like she needed that kind of pressure.

But it did give her the impetus to decide that whatever the hell was going on at the moment, it could keep going on for a few more hours until she felt damned good and ready to deal with it. Whatever was happening between her and Baen wasn't going to kill them or anyone else. Therefore, it could be tabled for later discussion.

Of course, that didn't mean she was going to let him off the hook until then. She wasn't an idiot.

She pursed her lips. "Do you honestly think the idea that upsetting me was an accident makes it all right?"

He shook his head. "Of course not, but I could not stand it if you thought me capable of causing you deliberate harm, either physically or emotionally. I would never hurt you, and I would destroy any other who even made the attempt."

Okay, at some point she would need to tell him that while protectiveness could be sexy, threatening other people with murder and/or mayhem really was not.

"All right," she said after a moment. "I'll take your word for it. You didn't mean to hurt me, but that doesn't mean I'm suddenly okay with all this, because I'm not. We're going to need to talk about things a lot more before I can even wrap my head around them, let alone figure out how I feel about everything."

She stretched out her legs, and Baen immediately sprang to his feet to help her stand. "Anything you say, *amare*. I will answer every question you want to ask, and I will hide nothing from you. I swear it."

"You'd better not."

Ivy turned to the group and reached for some tattered semblance of dignity. "Rose, I don't know if you intended to put us all up for the night, but I'm exhausted. Is there any chance you have a room available for crashing?"

"Mais oui." The dark-haired woman rose from her perch on a settee almost as elegant as herself. "Come, I will show you."

"Thanks."

Ivy fell into step behind her hostess, only to jerk to a stop when Baen moved to follow. "Uh, and where do you think you're going, big guy?"

The Guardian blinked down at her, opened his mouth, then caught himself. He clearly had second thoughts about what he had been about to say. "I—you—it—"

She folded her arms across her chest. "Take your time. I can wait."

His jaw closed with a snap, flexed a few times, then opened to allow for a very cautious second attempt. "This has been a very dangerous time for you, *amare*," he finally managed. "I wish to see you safe and well protected at all times."

"That's very nice of you," she acknowledged, conscious of Rose standing beside her and fighting a smile. "I appreciate the concern, but we're in a house full of Wardens. A *safe house*. And now there are two other Guardians here besides you. I think the chances of me staying safe in another room are pretty high, don't you?"

"But . . ." He trailed off. His expression told Ivy he had a thousand things to say but had wisely figured out that none of them would gain him anything other than a knee to the crotch. He deflated, his shoulders sagging and his expression turning down into what on any other person in the universe Ivy would have sworn was a pout.

She smiled. "Good night, Baen."

He grumbled in return. "Good night, *amare*. Sleep well."

"Oh, I will," she said, and with that she spun on her heel and gestured for Rose to lead her out of the room. A small wave to the company and they disappeared behind a set of closed doors.

It felt good to win that round. Now they would just have to see what happened when the bell rang to start the next one.

Chapter Sixteen

Baen watched the parlor doors close behind his mate and their hostess and tried to figure out exactly what had just happened. They had gone from discussing the current threat from the Order, to reviewing the history of the Guardians, to a few tense moments when he had been certain Ivy was about to either tear out his throat or remove his testicles with her cocoa spoon. And then she had somehow used his own apology against him and turned it into a way to wriggle out of any further discussion.

So now here he was, standing like an idiot in the center of a room that wouldn't have looked out of place in a private wing at Versailles, wondering how he'd gotten there. What in the name of the Light had that tiny, red-headed woman done to him?

Behind him, his brothers broke into hearty chuckles. He rounded on them with a challenging scowl. "You have things you wish to say to me, *fratres*?"

The one called Knox held up a palm and grinned. "Only that we feel your pain, brother. Welcome to the world of human mates. Do not worry. You will learn the native language here. Eventually."

His Warden reached out from her chair to smack his leg. "Watch it, big guy. Are you trying to imply that anything Ivy just said to him was unreasonable?"

"Yeah, because I thought she went pretty easy on him," Kylie said. "No name calling, no physical violence. I was impressed by her restraint."

"Anyone with a firm grasp on the situation and the good fortune not to have their thinking clouded by testosterone would be." Wynn shot the Guardians a pointed look and pushed out of her chair. "In fact, I think we should go congratulate her, Koyote. We wouldn't want her to start doubting herself now."

The tiny woman bounced out of her seat and made a sweeping gesture toward the door. "Absolutely not. You're right. After you, Pooh Bear."

Their Guardians said not a word and just watched them leave the room with resigned expressions. Once the door closed behind them, Knox turned back to Baen and sighed. "Do you see what we mean?"

"Are they always like that? All of them?"

"All of them," Dag said with feeling. Baen could hear it in his deep, gravelly voice. "Just wait until Kees and Spar get here. They will back us up. Human females are . . ." He broke off and frowned, as if unable to find the correct word.

"They're exhausting," Knox finished. "More so than a three-day battle without food or drink."

"And more dangerous."

Knox nodded and stepped around to drop into the chair his Warden had just vacated. "Exactly. Take your eyes off them for a moment, and they will find trouble. Or it will find them. They seem to have some sort of magnetic pull toward potential disaster. Just wait. You'll see soon enough."

"I think I already have," Baen muttered. "I woke barely

two days ago to the sight of Ivy trapped in an alley, surrounded by three minor demons, and armed with nothing more than a small silver knife. And since then, no
matter where I have taken her or how careful I have
been, we have been attacked three more times. Three! In
just forty-eight hours. I can hardly believe it is possible."

"Only where a human female is concerned."

Baen did not find Dag's qualification comforting.
"How are we supposed to keep them safe if they are
under such constant siege? Ivy seems unable to obey my
commands without arguing. She must always question
why, or offer her own ideas on tactics. I exist for the purpose of keeping humans safe, and yet it is as if she questions my ability to protect her."

He slumped down onto the ornate sofa, feeling an instant of relief that it did not immediately collapse beneath
his weight. Even though his gaze had fixed glumly on the
carpet at his feet, he saw out of the corner of his eye when
Dag pushed away from the mantel and took the position
opposite his.

Dag made a face expressing sympathy, disgust, resig-
nation, and shared bafflement, all at once. "Believe me,
brother, we have all been there. We have each stood
where you are standing and wondered how in the Light
it had come to this. There is no controlling these women.
The best you can hope for is . . . discreet management."

"What?"

Knox nodded. "He is right. To attempt to force your
mate to bow to your authority will only result in your failure, her rebellion, and your mutual misery. Trust me, I
know."

"We all do," Dag said. He peered at Baen for a moment. "She is your mate, yes? You did not say—"

Baen glowered at him. "She is mine."

"Good. That will give you a small but crucial advan-

tage," Knox said, leaning forward. "The only certain way
to ensure that these females follow your orders and stay
safe is to make them want to do it. They must feel that
remaining out of harm's way is the best way to contribute to your safety and victory in battle. Her feelings for
you will make her want to keep you safe as well, so if
she knows that worrying for her could distract you at a
dangerous moment, she will be more likely to remain out
of harm's way."

"They think they are humoring us," Dag agreed. "I do
not care how they choose to view it so long as Kylie stays
safe."

Baen shifted uncomfortably. Such tactics might
work for these two, but their Wardens were obviously
committed to them, the strength and intimacy of their
relationships obvious to any who looked at them. He and
his little human were still sailing in an entirely different boat. Hell, he wasn't sure they were even on the
same vessel.

He had to force the confession out through gritted
teeth. "Ivy has not yet accepted our relationship fully.
She does not consider herself my mate."

Dag fixed him with an incredulous stare. "Then
change her mind, brother. And do it quickly."

"What sound advice, *brother*," Baen bit out. "Such an
idea had never occurred to me. Where would I be without your sage counsel?"

Knox held up his hands. "Enough. Dag, need I remind
you of your own early days with Kylie? If I do, you might
remember a few moments when you, too, struggled with
this stage in your relationship. Or maybe I should just tell
Kylie that you seem to think you had her wrapped around
your finger from the very beginning."

The statement sounded innocuous on the surface, but
it clearly registered as a threat to the stocky Guardian.

Dag turned a little pale and quickly backed off without so much as a grumble.

Knox focused his attention back on Baen. "What issue does she have with your mating? Is it merely a matter of speed? Because most human women seem to doubt a bond can be formed on such brief acquaintance. Their people have forgotten the power that Fate holds over us all. If that is the central issue, then Wynn and Kylie might be able to offer her reassurance and guidance."

"That does seem to concern her," Baen admitted. "But she also remains reluctant to admit she is even my Warden, no matter how often I assure her it is true."

"What do you mean? How can she doubt what she *is*?" Dag sounded baffled by the very concept.

"She does not believe she has the ability to use magic, and she feels her talent is useless and too insignificant to qualify her to be a woman of power. She thinks she is not capable of being a Warden, or that she is somehow unworthy of membership in the Guild, and yet her family has been associated for generations."

"What talent does she possess?" Dag asked. "My Kylie once thought her own technology magic was merely the result of training and talent, but Wynn and the others demonstrated to her that it was much more than that. Perhaps they could help with your human as well."

"Ivy is a clairaudient. She hears conversations and events that take place in remote locations," Baen explained. "She does not like to discuss her abilities, but from what little I have been able to gather from her, I think it is largely fueled empathically. Her clearest episodes seem to be linked to emotionally charged situations. Her uncle and her cousin were both Wardens. She said that she heard them die at the hands of the Darkness."

Knox winced. "That would be enough to shake any human. Wynn was forced to see her own brother fall after he had been used as a vessel for the corruption of Uhlthor. It caused her immense pain. And she is proof that coming from a Guild family does not necessarily prepare a human to become a Warden. In fact, it can serve as a barrier for some. My mate did not doubt her abilities, but she did doubt that the Guild would welcome her, or any female, into their ranks."

Dag's expression showed his distaste for that situation. "From what I have seen and heard since waking, her doubt was not unfounded. Something happened to the Guild over the years. I do not know when they began to shun the contributions of talented females, but it is clear that they did and that the decision cost them dearly. Every one of our mates should have received Guild membership and training, and yet few of them even knew the Wardens existed before we came to them."

"Believe me, my mate has plans to deal with that issue as soon as the threat from the Darkness has been eliminated. I pity any survivors of the old guard who attempt to gainsay her."

The pair chuckled, but Baen remained focused on Ivy. "That may be helpful in the future, but right now I am still faced with a mate who doubts herself, as well as the challenge of keeping her safe while I attempt to find a way to cement our relationship."

The others grew serious again and exchanged rueful glances before Knox once more spoke. "This will not please you to hear, but if you wait, your bond with Ivy will sort itself out. You are mates. That is the will of Fate, ordained by the Light. Even if she wished to resist it, no one—not human, not Guardian—can defy Fate. She will have to admit to your connection sooner or later."

Baen bared a fang. "You are correct; I am not pleased. What if she fights so hard that she places herself in danger? Again. I cannot allow my mate to come to harm, but I fear that if I attempt to force her to comply with my orders, even if they are given with only her safety in mind—she will endanger herself to spite me."

The looks on the faces of his brothers told Baen that the scenario he envisioned wasn't that far-fetched. These human women were defiant to the bone.

"There is really only one thing you can do," Knox finally admitted. "You must keep her by your side. If you do not let her out of your sight, your mate cannot walk into danger without you being close enough to defend her."

Baen waited a beat, certain his brother must have something else, some much more valuable piece of advice, to offer. After all, even Baen could have come up with "stick close." It wasn't exactly advanced mathematics.

"That's it?" he demanded. "That is the best counsel you can give me? That's no better than what he said." He poked his finger in Dag's direction.

Dag shrugged. "Do you think either of us have magical insight into the workings of the female mind? We are no different from you, brother. We merely have a few months' head start on you."

"Comforting."

Knox chuckled. "Trust us, Baen. It will work out. You may tear out some of your hair in the meantime, but it *will* be all right in the end. So long as we win victory over the Darkness, everything else will fall into place."

"Of course. No pressure."

Clenching his jaw, Baen rose and strode from the room. Helpful bunch, those brothers of his. Catching the tone of his own thoughts, he cursed. Apparently, his little human's tendency toward sarcasm was contagious. If only she could catch something from him in turn.

Preferably the conviction that the two of them belonged together.

Forever.

Chapter Seventeen

Ivy woke the next morning to a house in chaos and the knowledge that the Guardian she had evaded last night was a hell of a lot sneakier than she had suspected. Somehow he had managed to creep into her bedroom while she slept and crawl into her bed without waking her. Now, he lay pressed up against her back with one arm draped over her waist and a possessive hand cupping her breast.

Refusing to think about why she felt so comfortable with this man that she hadn't woken while any of that happened, she reached out to pry herself free from his embrace. As it turned out, Baen was a much lighter sleeper than she.

The instant she shifted, his arm tightened around her and his hand turned from merely possessive to covetous. She felt his breath stirring the fine hairs at the nape of her neck and fought hard to suppress a shiver. The last thing he needed was encouragement.

"Baen, what are you doing in my bed?" she asked, cursing the husky sound of her own voice. It was only because she'd just woken up, but it sounded all sexy and inviting, which were the last things she felt at the moment.

Honest.

He nuzzled her hair. "I am a Guardian. I am guarding you."

The playful note in his voice almost charmed her. Almost. But she fought hard to maintain her strong stance for independence. She wasn't the type of woman to crumble at the slightest temptation. It took at least a moderate level of temptation to sway her.

"Did you forget what I told you last night?" She cleared her throat and tried to make herself sound stern. Who knew that would be so tough? "I think I'm safe enough in a house full of Guardians and Wardens that you can manage to guard me from *off* the bed rather than on it. In fact, I'm pretty sure you could accomplish it from another room entirely."

"But why would I want to?" He pressed warm, teasing kisses to her neck, working his way down to her shoulder. "This is so much more comfortable."

"Baen . . ."

He eased back and carefully rolled her to face him. Ivy sent up a silent prayer of thanks that she was still wearing the T-shirt and panties she'd gone to sleep in. At least she had some armor against him.

"*Amare,* I remember every word that you said to me last night," he told her, his expression serious but softer than she had ever seen it. It woke up a whole kaleidoscope of butterflies in her tummy. "I understand that I hurt you by not explaining everything to you from the beginning, and I regret that more than I can express. I also understand that you are being forced to process an enormous amount of changes to your life, to your world, in a very short time. I wish that I could make this transition easier for you."

Ivy wished he could, too. She could use all the help she could get. But she could hear the sincerity in his words and see the shades of regret and affection on his face. He was being honest with her, and that counted for something. She hadn't decided what yet, but . . . something.

"From now on, I vow that I will always be honest with you. Completely honest," he swore, taking her hand in his and toying with her fingers as if he couldn't decide whether to kiss them or hold them tightly in case she tried to pull free. "I will answer your questions fully and honestly as soon as you ask, and I will try to treat you as my equal, and not as a child I must protect."

And here he had been doing so well. She narrowed her eyes. " 'Try'?"

He huffed out a breath. "Yes, I will try. I cannot change my nature, *amare,* and that nature tells me that you must be kept safe at all costs. You are too precious for me to risk seeing you hurt or, Light forbid it, killed."

Yeah, Ivy didn't much like the sound of that, either. Maybe she could meet him partway on this one.

"All right, I can accept that. And I can promise that I'll try not to take any unnecessary risks." She saw the way he caught the "unnecessary" part, but she kept going. She needed to get this out. "But you also have to give me some time to deal with all of this. I might have known about the Guild and the *nocturnis* and that things had taken a turn for the worse recently, but the rest of this stuff hit me out of nowhere. Everyone else around here might be certain that I'm meant to be a part of the Guild and that I'm really your personal Warden, and that we're somehow—"

Ivy cut herself off. She just couldn't go there, not even in her own head, let alone out loud. She was a long, *long* way from wrapping her head around the concept of fated mates, let alone applying the M-word to her and Baen. Like, light-years.

"Anyway, it's a lot to take in," she finished, feeling—and probably sounding—a bit lame. "I haven't managed it yet, so I'm going to need some time and space while I try to deal. Understand?"

Baen nodded, looking resigned if not precisely happy. "I do understand. I can give you all the time you need, *amare,* but only a certain amount of space. I can agree not to hover over you while others are around to help me keep you safe, but if I believe you are in real danger, there is nothing that can keep me away from you."

She glared at him for a moment, then nodded reluctantly. "Fine. I guess that's not totally unreasonable."

He seemed to relax just a titch. He even managed a small—very small—lopsided smile. "You can take it as proof of my desire to please you, *amare,* because if it were up to me, you would never get far enough away from me that I couldn't do this at any second."

His lips captured hers before she even saw him move.

Sneaky bastard.

Too bad it was hard to tell him off when he was kissing the living daylights out of her. Seriously. She was pretty sure it was leaking out her toes.

He shifted to lean over her, and Ivy sank back into the soft nest of blankets surrounding them. Temptation whispered to her, urging her to give in and pull him fully atop her, to let him press her to the mattress and sink inside her, riding every last doubt from her mind with his huge body and powerful thrusts.

Damn, but that sounded good.

She teetered on the edge for what felt like eternity, simply surrendering herself to his kiss. He had a gift for making her feel cherished and consumed all at once, and the heady combination made her ache for him. They had already had sex once. Well, more than once, to be honest. Would another time really hurt?

Before she could give in, the sound of raised voices joined in the chaos that had originally pulled Ivy from sleep. She tore her mouth from Baen's and frowned at the closed door. "What the heck is going on out there?"

She had barely gotten the question out when "out there" decided it wanted to be in here. The door crashed open to bounce off the side of a tall wardrobe, and a mix of familiar and unfamiliar figures came pouring into the room.

Instinctively, Ivy jerked the covers up over herself. She scanned the crowd, picking out the two couples she had met last night along with Rose, Ash, Drum, and several other people she didn't recognize.

"Bloody hell," she cursed. "Did you people never hear of knocking? What the bugger do you want?"

Kylie plopped down on the corner of the mattress, making the bed bounce, and grinned like a lunatic. "Out of bed, lazybones! The band is getting back together!"

Chapter Eighteen

Twenty minutes later, Ivy sat at the long, gleaming table in the manor's "informal" (which she was pretty sure just meant improbably smaller) dining room, waiting for her blush to subside. It had appeared when the entire population of the world barged into her bedroom to find her canoodling with Baen, and so far it showed no signs of fading.

It should have helped that no one other than her seemed the least bit concerned about what had been interrupted. Should have, but didn't. Ivy just wasn't the sort of girl who got caught in flagrante delicto. At least, it had never happened before Baen. He was turning out to be such a bad influence.

She hoped he didn't think she had missed the subtle hints of encouragement the other Guardians had been giving him since they joined the large group downstairs. They might think they were badass warriors skilled in covert tactics, but when it came to communicating about women, they revealed themselves to be no different from any men, and she wasn't the only one who noticed. The other female Wardens sent her looks of encouragement and solidarity. Ones a heck of a lot less obvious than those exchanged by their mates.

Hmph. Men.

As the last of them settled into their seats, Rose stood at the head of the table and took a deep breath. "I cannot tell you how pleased I am, how enormously relieved, to see you all here in one room. After all this time, I had begun to worry this would never happen, and if it had not, I fear our prospects for the future would not have been worth discussing."

Ivy glanced around. Fourteen chairs surrounded the long board, each one filled with someone who took those words very seriously. All six of the risen Guardians and their Wardens had gathered at Maison Formidable. Ash and Drum had arrived straight from Belfast in the middle of the night, and Kees, Ella, Spar, and Felicity had followed early this morning. Aldous and Thiago had once again joined them at Rose's request. The only piece missing, from what Ivy could tell, was Rose's mysterious seventh Guardian.

"I know from speaking to some of you last night, and the rest of you briefly this morning, that many of you have similar questions," Rose continued. "I know also that some of you have doubts, about why you are here. About me. I do not blame you, but I ask that you bear with me very briefly while I tell you a story, one that I hope will explain everything."

Several of the Guardians shifted restlessly, but their Wardens looked mostly curious, so they settled down again without offering a protest. It struck Ivy how these huge, intimidating warriors seemed to defer to their companions in most situations, though she doubted that would hold true if they scented any real danger. In that case, if Baen's behavior was anything to go by, she figured all bets would be off.

"Already a few of you know me, but I will introduce myself to the others. My name is Rose Houbranche, and for the last two years, I have been working in secret to gather up the survivors of the Order's purge against the Wardens' Guild." She spoke clearly and calmly, but emotion was threaded through every word. There was no mistaking that this story of Rose's was very—deeply— personal.

"I am like most of you. I have never been initiated into the Guild, and I was not given formal training to use my special gift, or to work with magic as the Wardens do. In fact, before I began my work, I had no knowledge of magic at all. I had never heard of a Guardian or a Warden and I thought demons were a relic of the Catholic church's paranoia about sin and damnation. In my world, *nocturnis* and the Order of Eternal Darkness did not exist."

Ivy saw several of the other Wardens at the table nod in clear sympathy with Rose. Ella in particular looked as if she were remembering the moment her eyes were opened, and Fil appeared ready to jump up from her seat and shout "Amen" like a parishioner at a revival meeting. Ivy couldn't blame either of them.

"I remained ignorant of everything about this endless struggle of ours until the night that the headquarters of the Wardens' Guild exploded. That moment changed everything, because I saw it happen."

A murmur swept through the room as those gathered took in this revelation. If it was true, it had to have been one hell of a way to learn the truth. Ivy, and everyone else at the table, immediately wanted to hear the details.

Rose didn't make them wait. She lifted her voice a little so she would be heard until the whispers died down. "My presence that night was purely an accident." Her lips quirked. "Or, at least, one of those things one calls an accident before one truly understands how Fate makes itself known in our lives. I was in a building across from the Guild, ironically enough, trying to extricate myself from a date that had turned out to be a very, very poor choice on my part. The explosion on the other side of the street was powerful enough to shatter the windows in the apartment of the man who was attacking me, and I used that as a distraction to flee from him. I made it down the stairs and out onto the street in time to see something I thought at first must be a hallucination, or a trick of the light and the smoke pouring from the ruins of the Guild. It was an enormous, winged figure soaring up into the dark sky."

Oh, yeah, Ivy thought. That sounded plenty familiar. What was it with the Guardians and their dramatic entrances?

"Perhaps I could have dismissed the sight," Rose continued, "had the creature not rushed back to earth and snatched me from the path of a spell thrown by a lurking *nocturnis*. Not many of them were on the scene, but one who was saw me standing very close to the rubble. Perhaps he thought I had escaped, or perhaps he just did not want to take a chance by leaving a witness to the Order's crime, but that cultist tried to kill me, and it was a Guardian who saved me. The first, I believe, to waken to the call of the growing danger."

For the first time in her life, Ivy got to witness an honest-to-goodness shocked silence. All this time she had thought it was just an expression, but it was as if Rose's confession had knocked the wind out of all those present; or at least all those who hadn't known the woman for more than a few hours.

"Two years."

It was Ella who finally shattered the quiet, even her

naturally soft-spoken voice sounding like a shout in the tense room.

"A Guardian rose two years ago, and never tried to contact the rest of us?" The demure art historian fisted her trembling hands on the table and glared at Rose as if she wanted to jump across the polished wood and strangle the other woman. "Because, trust me, I'd know if you had reached out. I've dedicated every waking moment from the first time I set eyes on a Guardian to finding the rest of them so that we could figure out what the hell the Order was up to and put a fucking stop to it!"

Kees looked almost as surprised as the rest of them to hear his mate use that kind of language. He draped his arm across her shoulders and pulled her against him, his hands stroking as if to soothe. From what Ivy could see, Ella didn't want to be soothed.

"We've all been searching high and low for the other Guardians, for other Wardens, for *anyone* who could help us deal with this nightmare," the irate woman continued. "And you're going to sit there looking like a goddamned ice princess and tell us you were here all along, but you didn't contact us because *you had your reasons*? That's bullshit. Fuck your reasons, and fuck you!"

On the other side of Ella, Felicity reached out to grasp her friend's hand while glaring daggers at Rose. The tough platinum-blonde barely stayed in her seat and most of that had to do with her own Guardian, Spar, pressing a firm hand on her shoulder. Still, he didn't look any happier with the situation than either of the human females.

"Where is our brother, then?" he demanded, pinning Rose with a blazing stare. "Why is he not with us right now explaining for himself why he abandoned his family? What kind of Guardian allows his Warden to make excuses for him?"

Rose laced her fingers together over her stomach, the

only betrayal of her anxiety. Her expression remained cool and serene, the picture of the ice princess Ella had accused her of being. "Ghrem cannot leave his post. It is why all communication with the rest of you has so far come from me. Please believe that I understand you feel betrayed by our actions, but please allow me to explain why we have had no choice."

Wynn pursed her lips, looking no happier than her friends. Oddly, Kylie (the Warden Ivy had pegged as the most outspoken) was the only one not watching Rose with an expression of distrust and anger. The small, usually vibrant hacker appeared intent but neutral in the face of Rose's upsetting tale.

"You can give it a shot," Wynn said, "but I hope you don't have any money riding on us being happy about it."

Beside her, Ivy could hear Baen's snarl of agreement. He had tensed like a coiled spring at hearing the Frenchwoman's story, but he'd remained in his chair. Ivy figured the surprising restraint from all the Guardians had its foundation in their innate sense of honor and the fact that Rose was an unprotected woman. Those two small facts were probably the only things standing between their hostess and whatever the French word was for "body bag."

"Thank you." Rose nodded to Wynn, choosing to accept her words at face value instead of reacting to the sarcasm evident in her tone. "Ghrem took me immediately from the scene of the explosion. There was nothing we could do for anyone inside. They would have died instantly, and the few *nocturnis* fled immediately at the first sound of emergency sirens. They had no desire to face the police or firefighters who rushed to the scene. *Sales lâches.*"

She spat out the French insult, and Ivy didn't have to

speak the language to understand the woman's contempt for the Order's thugs. The meaning came through loud and clear.

"Also, I admit that I did not cooperate easily with my Guardian," Rose admitted, color staining her cheeks. "I panicked when he snatched me up, and I fought to escape him even as he took to the skies. I don't know what I was thinking, or if I was thinking at all. I could have caused him to drop me, but I was terrified, and I had no idea who—or even what—he was. At least, not until he found a safe place to land and forced me to listen to him. To his crazy story."

She shook her head. "I felt certain one of us had to be insane, *n'est-ce pas*? Either I had lost my mind and conjured up this strange beast with wings and claws like a devil, or his tale of an ancient association of evil cultists sworn to serve the embodiment of evil . . . One of these things had to be the result of madness. Nothing else made sense. It took Ghrem hours to convince me of the truth of his words and then for him to calm me enough to accept them. To accept that he had recognized me as his Warden, and that he had been woken from his sleeping spell in order to save me so that we could discover the Darkness's latest threat and put a stop to it."

Once again, everyone around the table seemed uncomfortably familiar with the scenario Rose described. Every one of the Wardens appeared to be recalling a situation where they had found themselves in Rose's shoes. It was the first step in perhaps allowing them to understand the reasons for her long years of secrecy.

Perhaps. No one looked very happy yet, but then, Rose wasn't finished with her tale.

"Perhaps if we had been able to regroup, to step back and make plans calmly, we would have been able to reach out to you all and gather you here with us sooner," she said, "but we were not allowed to make that choice. That *nocturni* who had attempted to kill me had seen Ghrem rise, and he escaped to report this back to his masters. They came after us immediately."

Her voice trembled as if she were reliving that experience, and based on her own recent trials Ivy felt inclined to sympathy. She understood fear and panic and the chaos of being chased and attacked by people who wanted you dead.

Boy, did she understand it.

"We barely escaped." Rose shuddered, though she made an obvious attempt to control the visceral response. "Ghrem killed several of our attackers, but I had no magical skills, so I was nothing more than a liability for him. In the end, he had to turn and run in order to keep me alive. I do not think he has forgiven himself to this day for what he considers an act of cowardice. He will not listen no matter how many times I remind him that I would be dead had he made a different choice."

Ivy could feel the impatience beginning to build in the room. Rose's story might be heartfelt and affecting, but she still hadn't told them what they really wanted to know—why had they stayed hidden so long, and where was Ghrem now?

Ash voiced their concerns. "And perhaps if you had made a different choice, we would have come to you sooner and helped you to put down the Order before their cause advanced this far. Did you think of that?"

To Ivy's shock, Rose reacted to the accusation by smiling.

"Believe me, Guardian, I have thought of little else." She bowed her head for a moment, then gathered herself to continue. "I will spare you the details of the time we spent constantly running from the Order and their minions. Eventually, frustration with our elusiveness made the *nocturnis* turn their attention back to their strategy to wipe out the Guild. If they neutralized the Wardens, they believed the rest of the Guardians would remain asleep and the greatest force for the opposition would no longer be a threat. That was bad enough, but we quickly learned that they had an even more dangerous plan. They began to work on freeing the Seven."

"We know that," Fil said. "They succeeded, too. At least four times."

Rose turned her head and met the blonde's gaze. "Six. All but one walk free even as we speak. Only Belgreth-nakkar remains imprisoned."

The Guardians erupted, knocking over chairs and shouting expletives, demanding explanations and details so that they could go after the Demons immediately. No one could accuse them of not being passionate about their work, Ivy conceded, but as she exchanged glances with the other Wardens, she thought the women might all be thinking the same thing—that the big, bad warriors needed to take a deep breath and realize that sound tactics always emerged victorious over blind rage.

If the galumphs didn't chill out and start thinking instead of simply reacting, they were going to get themselves—and every other being on the face of the planet—killed. Personally, Ivy had other plans for her future.

Unfortunately, the Guardians were on a roll. They stomped around, shouting and gesticulating, several of them spontaneously shifting hands into claws or starting to sprout wings before they got themselves back under control. It was crazy, and it was so loud that they couldn't hear any of their Wardens' urgings to calm down and plant their asses back in their chairs.

Finally, Drum made a sour face, climbed up onto the table, put his fingers to his lips, and gave a whistle so loud and shrill that silence immediately descended. Except for the distant howling of a dog coming from outside the manor.

Seriously, it had been *that* loud.

When Ivy shot Drum a look that conveyed how impressed she was, he shrugged and slid back into his chair. "My pub gets a wee bit rowdy now and then. Sometimes, I need to get the customers' attention."

"Thank you, Warden." Rose nodded to him and made shooing motions to urge the Guardians back to their seats. They ignored her, of course, but at least they kept quiet. "No one is more disturbed by this situation than Ghrem and I—"

"Then where the bloody hell is he?" Baen demanded. "No more secrets or evasions. Where is our brother?"

"He is in the between, personally guarding the entrance to the Seed of Darkness's prison."

Baen sucked in a breath and actually backed up a step. Several of the other Guardians looked as if they'd just been clocked upside the head with cricket bats, and Wynn the witch looked as if she wanted to throw up. She pressed her fingers against her lips and opened her eyes so wide that Ivy wanted to find her a bucket, stat. Whatever Rose had just said had knocked most of the room for a loop, but Ivy had no idea what it meant.

She supposed the only way to find out was to ask. "Um, would someone care to explain what the hell that means? You know, for us slow kids. I thought the prisons holding the Seven Demons were supposed to be on some other plane, and I'm not a physicist or anything, but I'm having a hard time wrapping my head around the idea of other dimensions having doors. Unless it's like the scare factory in *Monsters, Inc.*, and that movie was just way ahead of its time."

"The door isn't literal," Rose said. "And you are correct that the prisons do not exist on this plane. The power of the Seven is too much to be contained by any force that operates in our reality. In order to imprison it, they must be banished to other realms entirely. The between is . . ." The woman paused and made a face, as if confused as to how to define it. "It is what is between our realm and all the others," she finished.

Lamely.

"Wow, that's so helpful. Really clears things up."

"It's a pretty abstract concept, Ivy. It's not exactly easy to explain," Wynn said, moving her fingers away from her mouth to reach out for her Guardian. He returned immediately to her side and grasped her hands in his. "The between isn't tangible. From a lot of perspectives, it doesn't really exist. It's like standing in a doorway between two rooms. For that moment you're not in one room or the other, you're on the threshold, which is another space entirely."

Ivy tried to picture that and felt a headache coming on. "You're right. It's not easy to explain, because I still don't get it."

"You don't really have to. All you have to understand is that things aren't meant to linger in the between, just like they aren't meant to linger in doorways. To do either has the potential to cause all sorts of trouble. It's incredibly, unbelievably dangerous, and if Ghrem is really there, then he's taking a major risk."

Rose nodded. "Believe me, he knows. As do I. We have searched again and again for another way to ensure the Order cannot free the last of their Masters, but this has been the only thing that has kept the Seed of Darkness contained. You all know what will happen if all of the Seven make it into our realm at once. They will be united, and the Darkness will descend upon our world."

"Which I think we can all agree would be totally

ferkakta," Kylie piped up from the other end of the table. She had dragged Dag back to his chair, and he in turn had tugged his tiny mate into his lap. She addressed them all from her perch there like a queen from her throne (a deranged queen from a throne prone to glaring at anyone who looked at her cross-eyed, but still). "The thing is, Rosie-posy, that I think the reason you *did* finally get us all together in one place is not because of how dire the situation is now; it's because you and your pals Baldy and Hunky over there have a plan."

Kylie waved a hand in the direction of Aldous and Thiago, who had sat through the entire morning silent and watchful. Thiago smiled at the hacker, and Dag didn't just glare, he bared his fangs and snarled a warning at the handsome Spaniard. Apparently he wasn't thrilled that his mate referred to the other man as "hunky."

"So." Kylie ignored her mate and raised an eyebrow in Rose's direction. "Care to share with the rest of the class?"

A grin split Rose's face, transforming her features from cool and elegant to vibrant and gorgeous. "I'd love to," she purred, and Ivy actually leaned forward in her seat.

She *had* to hear this.

Chapter Nineteen

Okay, so maybe Ivy hadn't needed to hear Rose's plan quite so badly. Was it too late to take back her enthusiasm? Because to be honest, her original reaction had been predicated on the idea that any idea developed by a genuine Warden with two years to plan and prepare would be a sound one. After all, Rose had experience, legitimate talent, and a house full of Guild members to help her devise the surest, safest, and most effective way to stand against the Darkness and neutralize their threat for good.

Yet with all that going for her, the Frenchwoman had come up with a strategy best described as "Rub ourselves with raw liver, jump into the lion's den, and then hope for the best."

Really? As in, *Are you fucking kidding me*?

But no, Rose had assured them, she was completely serious. Thiago had been able to re-create the spell that the Wardens had used when they stood beside the first Guardians and banished the Seven Demons of the Darkness from the human plane, imprisoning them apart from this world and from each other.

Ivy would be the first to admit that Thiago's work represented an amazing achievement, one for which he should be congratulated and offered the thanks of the Guild, if not the entire human world. Unfortunately, he and Rose both now claimed that in order to repeat the casting of said spell, they would have to first gather all six escaped Demons into one place and face them directly, performing the ritual in the presence of the evil itself.

And that's pretty much when it stopped sounding like such a good idea.

Baen had been among the first to question the strategy. Loudly.

He hadn't been wild about the idea of gathering six of the Seven together—in one spot, he had shouted—and then allowing the Wardens, including his mate—*HIS MATE* (that one was more like a bellow)—to get close enough to them to cast a spell directly on the embodiments of the Eternal Darkness.

How could they possibly have come up with a worse idea? Baen had demanded. Then he had replied to his own question before anyone else had the chance and declared that the answer was, they couldn't. It was physically and theoretically impossible to even entertain an idea with such intrinsic badness as that one, the Guardian had declared, and his brothers (and sister) had agreed with him. The entire plan was predicated on risking the lives of the Wardens, and as such, none of their mates were willing to allow it.

Looking back, Ivy figured it was the repeated use of the word "allow," accompanied by the word "not," that sparked the melee that had followed.

Being a group of highly intelligent and rather independent-minded individuals, none of the Wardens responded well to being forbidden from anything by their mates. More than one voice rose several decibels, and at one particularly memorable moment, a decorative silver memento box was snatched off a table and flung with great force and no little accuracy at the head of a particularly stubborn Guardian. He ducked, but Kylie's gesture still seemed to have made its point—the relationship between a Guardian and a Warden was a partnership, and everyone needed to remember that.

While Ivy appreciated the sentiment, and agreed with it in principle, she wasn't so certain she objected to Baen's position. After all, he was only trying to stop her from doing something her gut told her was roughly equivalent to standing in the middle of some train tracks and asking politely that the locomotive barreling toward her consider not turning her into human-flavored jelly. Could she really blame him for that?

And there was the other million-dollar question of the moment: not just, could she really blame Baen for trying to protect his mate, but did she believe that's what she was? Did they really have that kind of connection?

Did she want them to?

Ivy looked out over the gardens from her position on a small terrace at the side of the manor house, and grimaced. It had been a week since they had arrived and almost as long since the meeting at which Rose and Thiago had revealed their plan, and Ivy had gotten no closer to answering that fundamental question. How *did* she feel about her giant, overprotective, and occasionally overbearing new friend?

You know, aside from bloody confused.

She couldn't deny the connection between them, no matter how much easier doing so would have made her life. It was just there, a kind of invisible cord stretching between them no matter where they went or what they were doing. She felt it just as strongly when they were at opposite ends of the grounds—she learning to work magic from the other Wardens while he sparred with his siblings to keep their skills honed and their bodies occupied—as she did when they lay next to each other in her bed at night.

And that, she admitted, wasn't exactly helping her to clear her head. Her brain told her that if she wanted to make a real decision about where she and Baen stood, she ought to stop jumping his bones every chance she got. The trouble was, that was easier said than done. Or not done, as the case may be, because when they got together, there always seemed to be an awful lot of doing going on.

Physically, Ivy couldn't resist him. He'd become this powerful drug, and no matter how she told herself after each encounter that it would be the last, the minute she laid eyes on him again, she wanted him. No, she *needed* him, like a junkie needed a fix, and that frightened her.

Just not enough.

Not enough to stay away from him, at any rate. Every night, she climbed into bed beside him, and then ended up climbing *him* like her own personal Everest. Either that, or he climbed in with her, and she welcomed him with open arms, not to mention open thighs. She felt kind of like a slut afterward, but in the moment, all she felt was hunger and heat and something frighteningly like . . . affection.

Ivy leaned against the balustrade separating the terrace from the grounds and dug her fingers into the cold stone. You'd think the sensation would ground her, but oh no, it just made her think about Baen, about the way his skin felt when he carried her through the air in his winged form, such a contrast to the smooth heat of his human shape. Both of them enthralled her, which only gave her another reason to worry.

She had never felt this way before, not about anyone. She was twenty-seven, for pity's sake, and she lived in the modern world. She'd had crushes and boyfriends, lovers and even one relationship she had thought of for a while as the One. She'd thought she'd been in love. Hell, she'd thought she had run the gamut, from infatuation to genuine affection to hormone-inspired madness to real love, and none of them had prepared her for the way she felt around Baen.

Cue waves of terror.

How was it that this man who wasn't even a man could make her feel things she had never experienced before? And, even more than that, how did she trust that any of it was real? With all this talk of Fate and magic and mates and destiny, how could she know that what she felt came from her, from her own heart and her own mind, and not from some cosmic force using her like a Barbie doll to act out its own grand plan. Maybe on her own, she would have chosen to settle down with Ken, but instead, the universe had scooped her up, paired her with G.I. Joe, and forced these feelings on her for some unfathomable reason of its own.

The idea terrified her, and her way of looking at it might be a bit silly, but was it really outside the realm of possibility? If she really was "fated" to be with Baen, then where did that leave room for free will and the autonomy she needed to develop feelings for him (or for anyone else) naturally? Wasn't she supposed to have a choice in determining her soul mate? The way Baen described their relationship, she wasn't so sure.

The uncertainty made her want to run. The way she felt when she was with Baen made her want to stay.

Bloody hell.

She blew out a breath, watching it steam up in the crisp evening air. One of these days, she was going to discover who had stood over her crib in the hospital nursery and blessed her with an interesting life. When she did, the bugger was getting a good swift kick right in the babymaker.

The jerk.

When it came right down to it, all her confusion stemmed from the dichotomy of the way she felt when she was with Baen compared to the way she felt when she was on her own, like this, with time to think. So really, you could say that thinking was her enemy; it only made her doubt herself, while Baen just made her feel good.

Really, really good.

It would make her life so much easier if she could shift all the blame for her situation onto his shoulders. After all, they were more than broad enough to bear the burden. If she told herself often enough that Baen's presence distracted her, that his touch clouded her mind, and that sex with him completely cut her off from reality, maybe she could start viewing all those as bad things, instead of as the bright moments in a present full of fear and anxiety and the possibility of doom hanging over the world. Make Baen the villain, and let herself off the hook.

Kind of hard to do, though, now that she'd seen the real villains. Having looked into the faces of demons and *nocturnis,* the intrinsic and uncompromising honor and goodness of the Guardians couldn't be denied, not even for the sake of Ivy's sanity. Which left her right back where she'd started—enthralled, terrified, and having no idea what to do with the giant, sexy creature who occupied her bed and seemed determined to convince her to let him stay there forever.

"You've got a look about you that says you could go one of two ways." A voice interrupted her brooding, and she glanced to her right to see Michael Drummond stroll to a stop against a neighboring piece of terrace railing. "Either you really need a friend to talk to, or you have a grapefruit spoon in your pocket and plans to use it on the next set of bollocks that get within striking distance. I'm hoping it's the former, but if not, I'm hoping my longer legs will provide the advantage of speed in getting away."

His words and wry smile startled a snort of laughter from her. "Yeah, I'll let you know when I decide. How's that sound?"

"Fair enough." Drum leaned a hip against the balustrade and looked from her to the scenery spread out beyond the small, flagstoned patio. "The views here aren't bad. For France, anyway."

Ivy glanced at him. "Not that you could possibly be biased about scenery, or anything."

"I'll admit we've a vista or two back home worth noting." He grinned. "Have you been to Ireland?"

"Once. I spent some time touring the south. Cork, Kerry, Waterford. It was beautiful."

"It is that."

Silence descended, not an uncomfortable one, but one that felt too heavy to be empty. Still, she had enough to keep her mind busy without pressing the friendly Irishman to state his business.

Ivy had gotten to know all the Wardens a little in the past week, and she'd come to like Drum. He was a nice guy, mostly low-key and good-natured, with a quick smile and a laid-back, somewhat dry sense of humor. She found him an interesting contrast to his Guardian, Ash, the only female Guardian ever summoned. Where her Warden came across as mellow and kind, Ash seemed much more intense, serious, and almost brooding. They didn't seem like a good match, and yet they fit together like two pieces of a puzzle, tab A into slot B. Perfect.

She wasn't naïve enough to believe it had really been that easy for them. It was never that easy for anyone, let alone couples who had to cross a species barrier in addition to all the normal ones. But that didn't keep a small part of her from feeling a twinge or two of envy. Maybe it hadn't been quite as hard for Ash and Drum as it was turning out to be for Ivy and Baen.

"You know, you've been doing very well with your lessons. I had a bit of a mental block when I first started, but then I had to do a few things in the heat of the moment before I ever got a real lesson, so I can admit I was a bit impatient with starting over from the beginning."

Ivy shrugged. "It's all still a little surreal for me. I never even wondered what it would be like to be able to do this stuff. Not because I didn't believe in it, but because . . . I don't know. Maybe because I figured that if I could have, I would have by now. I feel a little bit like an adult having to sit down with the kindergarteners. You know, squeezed into one of those tiny chairs with my knees pressed all the way up to my chin."

"Oh, you mean a Kylie-sized chair."

She chuckled. "Something like that."

Drum turned around, leaning back against the railing now and focusing on Ivy. "You're doing fine. I think we all felt like that in the beginning, but you're picking things up fast. Not that you have much choice, given the situation."

"Yeah, nothing like the specter of certain death hanging over your head to make a girl study hard."

"And when it comes to the big spell, we've all started from even ground. No one's tried to work anything like that before, and you're holding your own with the rest of us. We can't ask any more than that, can we?"

"Sure you could. You'd just be doomed to disappointment."

"No one is disappointed in you, Ivy girl." He laid a reassuring hand on her shoulder and squeezed.

She blew out a breath and stared hard into the distance. "Baen is," she admitted quietly.

"Ah." Drum folded his arms back across his chest and gave her a knowing look. "I thought that might be the real reason behind those frowns of yours."

Was she really that obvious? she wondered for a second, then gave in and admitted the truth. Yeah, she probably had been.

"I have no idea what I'm doing with him." She shook her head. "He keeps telling me all this stuff about Fate and destiny and how we're partners and how much we mean to each other and part of me really wants him to be right. But the rest of me thinks he's just clinically insane."

Drum chuckled. "Yes, I remember that stage. Believe me. It wasn't all that many months ago. Have you gotten to the point where you think everything will just be fine if you move to a different continent and leave no forwarding address?"

"I hear Greenland is highly overlooked in terms of quality-of-life issues."

"I was thinking Australia, personally, but after a lifetime of Irish weather, I was looking for sunshine and beaches. You know it's perfectly natural to feel that way, don't you? Think about it. Think about what's happened in your life in the last week or two and compare that with all the . . . what? Twenty-four years? That went before it."

"Twenty-seven. It's not just the suddenness, though. I honestly don't think that's what I'm hung up on. Not really." She hesitated, unsure whether to keep going. Drum was easy to talk to, but was she really ready to admit to him what had her so tied up in knots? Just because he was with a Guardian didn't mean he would get it. Besides, if she had this talk with anyone, shouldn't it be with Baen?

Not that she'd been doing much talking with him. Every time they got a few minutes alone to themselves, they ended up naked and sweaty. It wasn't conducive to soul-searching, or to meaningful heart-to-heart discussions.

There were too many other body parts pressing against each other.

"Let me guess. Destiny?" Drum asked, then grinned and launched into an impression of Gene Wilder's character in *Young Frankenstein*. " 'Destiny! Destiny! No escaping death for me!' "

Ivy laughed. She couldn't help herself. The moment perfectly summed up her inner conflict, while pointing out the inherent ridiculousness of her reaction to it. "Yeah, something like that. You do a mean Frederick Frankenstein, by the way."

Drum pretended confusion. "Who? That was me, when I first met Ash."

Ivy imagined him repeating the scene in front of the tough, serious Guardian and laughed again. She could just imagine the female's expression. "Right."

"Well, nearly, in any event," he said. "I didn't take very well to the news. Not to any of it, really. I'd grown up in a family where a little gift wasn't a great surprise to anyone. I have a knack for finding things that have gotten lost, for instance, and my baby sister can see what hasn't happened yet, as I told you. Those things I had known all my life, and I had no trouble believing in that kind of magic. But the rest of this? Stone statues that spring to life in the middle of the night? Real, tangible demons and crazy cultists who worship evil in ways the chat shows couldn't even fathom? No, none of that made sense in my pretty little world. I didn't like it at all, and I wanted it to get the hell out of my pub and never come back."

He gestured to himself and the house and his smile

turned wry again. "You can see how that all worked out for me, in the end."

"Well, Ash doesn't strike me as the kind to take no for an answer."

He raised an eyebrow. "But Baen does?"

"Touché." Ivy wrapped her arms around her torso, wishing she'd put on a heavier jacket now that the sun had fully set. "No, Baen is pretty determined to make me see things from his perspective. I'm just . . . having a hard time with this idea he has that it's all been predetermined."

"Because if it's just Fate that's thrown you together, how would you know whether either of you had genuine feelings for each other, and you're not just ending up stuck with each other because some big mouth in the heavens up there said you had to."

Her head jerked up and her gaze flew to his face. How had he summed up all her angst so perfectly in just a few words?

"Because I wondered exactly the same thing, love." He answered her unspoken question with a grin. "Trust me. No one in this world has a more complicated relationship with the notion of Fate than an Irishman. They mix the stuff into our baby bottles. Everyone where I come from believes in Fate, whether they call it that or destiny or the hand of God. We Irish are a fatalistic bunch. But that doesn't mean I was ready to surrender the most important decision in my life to some outside force. I intended to choose the woman I loved, thank you very much, after much searching and careful deliberation."

"So what happened?"

"I met Ash, didn't I?"

"And you just gave up on having it be your own idea?"

"Oh, not quite. There may have been some kicking

and screaming and bare-knuckled punches thrown at Fate's ugly mug before it was all said and done."

"May have been? Do not lie to the poor human, Michael. You fought like a tiger and sobbed like a little girl before you finally manned up and accepted the inevitable." Ash joined them in the dim light cast on the terrace from the sitting room beyond. "To be honest, I was embarrassed for him. He lost all sense of dignity for a time."

Grabbing his mate around the shoulders, Drum hauled her against his chest and growled a playful threat. "I don't recall you giving in gracefully there, my stony love, so let's be careful where we cast the blame, shall we?"

Ash pretended a cool indifference, but Ivy didn't miss the way she leaned into her mate's embrace, fitting against him as if she belonged there. "I merely report on events as I recall them, and I recall you pouting like a child deprived of sweets."

Drum lowered his head to nuzzle his mate's cheek and murmured, "Then you'll just have to give me a taste of honey to keep me happy, won't you?"

Ivy looked away and pretended she hadn't heard that. With any luck, it was too dark out here to see her blush.

Ash hushed Drum and spoke to Ivy. "The point that I believe is important to remember, is that most of us resist Fate in the beginning. It is the natural response of any animal to fight against a restraining hand, and humans remain animals like any other in this regard. Fighting Fate is not a bad thing. In fact, I believe that Fate wants us to struggle against it, for if we accept it too quickly, it can see that we may lack the strength for what it has planned."

Ivy didn't think anyone could accuse her of giving in too quickly here. Especially not Baen.

"What is important," Ash continued, "is to recognize

that if Fate insists on guiding us along a certain path even after we resist, it is not because it wishes to trap us, but because it knows that the place it guides us toward is the place we will best be able to become our true selves. In other words, Fate does not wish to be humanity's puppet master, only our treasure map."

She offered Ivy a smile, hooked her arm around her mate's waist and guided him back toward the house. Watching them go, Ivy mulled over the Guardian's words. If Fate wasn't trying to force Ivy into a relationship with Baen, but merely offering her an opportunity that would inevitably give her much more than it cost her, then what was she really fighting against? Fate? Baen?

Or herself?

Ivy had disappeared from the house that evening before dinner, and it had cost Baen every ounce of self-control he possessed not to hunt her down like a wily fox. She had been behaving erratically toward him since they had arrived at the manor, warm and affectionate one moment, running away to avoid him the next. He had told himself that she needed time to adjust to the idea of being his mate, but his self had started to grumble back and insist that she'd had plenty of time, and now it was their job to demonstrate all the benefits of accepting their relationship. Most of which, if his inner voice was to be believed, had to do with nudity. Lots and lots of nudity.

As it turned out, his inner voice belonged to an insatiable pervert.

It had to be insatiable, because the one place where Ivy had not tried to run from him over the last week had been in the bed they shared every night. All he had to do was touch her, and she turned to him, sweet and eager and pliant in his hands. She gave as good as she got, too, lavishing him with pleasure on a few memorable occasions that had made him fear the other members of the household would respond to his roars to see who had died or been killed. Luckily, the others seemed to know to stay away. Either that, or the manor bedrooms had some of the finest soundproofing ever installed in a private home.

Yet despite all the time he spent in his mate's sweet arms and sweeter body, he never seemed to get enough of her. He had only to think her name or hear her voice and smell the scent of sweet oranges, and he wanted her again. For a male who prided himself on his honor and self-control, it was turning into something of an embarrassment. Even more so because of the teasing to which his brothers liked to subject him.

They went at it again, subtly over dinner in the presence of their mates, and then with less restraint in the smoking room, which they commandeered for themselves most nights. Not because any of them smoked, but because no one in the house did, either, so it afforded them quiet, privacy, and an environment with heavy, masculine furniture they did not have to worry about breaking every time they took their seats.

Instead of smoking, most of the Guardians spent their evenings honing weapons, reading through books and pages their Wardens had passed on to them, and taking advantage of the novel experience of having so many of them gathered together in one place. Even the eldest of them had only rarely spent time together in the past, and most of that had taken place on the field of battle, where opportunities for conversation appeared sparingly. Sharing a common archive of memory and knowledge was one thing, but being able to actually speak to each other freely and openly made for a refreshing change.

Most of the time. Baen found it less of a delight when

the others of his kind used it against him. Especially when they did it with such open glee.

"Given up on your little female for the night?" Knox asked, throwing the evening's opening salvo. "Or did she chase you off with that satchel of hers? She wields a mighty weapon, considering it is made of canvas and leather."

Most of the others chuckled while Baen glowered at them all from his comfortable leather chair. It had been days since Ivy had struck out at him with her bag, hitting him square in the side of the head when he had pushed her too far on the subject of their mating. He had thought they were alone when he had pursued the subject, but apparently one of his brothers had been lurking nearby, and they had yet to let him forget the incident.

"Leave him alone," Ash scolded. She perched in the corner of a heavy sofa with her legs curled up tailor fashion and her lap full of hardware. "Or perhaps you'd like me to share what I know of your own courtship? A little birdie told me it wasn't all smooth sailing between you and your witch, brother."

Knox's smile morphed into a frown, one with a distinctly petulant air about it. "A little birdie named Kylie, I presume. That one certainly likes to share a story or two, doesn't she?"

Dag passed behind Knox's seat and smacked his brother across the back of the head. "Watch your tone when you speak of my mate. Even when you might be speaking the truth."

Another chuckle rippled through the room, and Knox joined in. None of them had been able to completely escape the group's teasing, but that didn't stop Baen from feeling he'd been a particularly popular target. Of course, there was the slightest chance his nerves being on edge made him a tad oversensitive of late, but he preferred to discount that notion.

"Don't listen to these beasts, Baen." Ash ran a soft cloth over her weapons, polishing surfaces that already gleamed. "They might be our brothers, but they have little notion of how to deal with women, especially human women. That any of them have managed to win, let alone keep a mate, is a testimony to the forgiving nature of their better halves, not any credit to themselves."

Kees hooted. "As if you had such an easy time yourself, sister. I heard that the path between you and your Drum did not run entirely smooth."

The female Guardian refused to take the bait. "I had two barriers to surmount in my case. Not only was my mate human, but he had the mind of a man, as well. That made my job twice as hard as any of you, because I had to overcome the limitations of masculine thinking."

Boos and hisses and good-natured grumbling greeted her words, and a few balled-up pieces of paper and decorative pillows were immediately lobbed in her direction. Ash merely ducked, dodged, and smiled as she continued her polishing. "I rest my case. Males always try to reduce complex issues to one of two things—fighting or fucking. Females require slightly more advanced tactics before they can be won."

Baen snorted, speaking before he could think better of it. "Neither of those seem to be a problem for my little mate and me. We seem to spend any time I can engineer for us to be together doing one or the other. Or both."

Spar snickered. "Trust us, brother. We've heard."

Ash snatched up one of the pillows that had landed beside her and landed a solid blow to the angelic-looking Guardian's smirking face. "Say something like that in front of the human, and you'll earn more than a pillow to the face, Spar, and from more than me, I would wager. Have some respect."

Baen shifted uncomfortably. While he found enchanting the way his mate's cheeks flushed rosy red when she felt angry or embarrassed, he would not want his friends to be the cause of such emotions. Nor would he want her to add that to the long list of grievances she must have against him by now.

"Yes, remember what Dag said to Knox," he finally grumbled. "Watch your mouth when you speak of my mate."

"But that is your whole trouble, isn't it?" Dag pressed, dropping onto the far end of the sofa opposite Ash. "The little redheaded female has not admitted that she is your mate, has she?"

Baen answered with a narrow-eyed glare.

"Easy, brother. That was not my attempt to goad you, merely to clarify the situation. We all understand this part of the wooing process, and we all remember how it felt to be there. Knowing your mate stands before you and having her refuse to acknowledge your claim is maddening. We know."

"Then I would think you would all be able to offer me useful advice, instead of poking fun and teasing me at every given opportunity."

"Oh, but the poking is so much more fun," Spar quipped.

"Frankly, I did not think you would appreciate my advice." Kees grunted. "I would not have, when I was in your position."

"What is it?"

"Patience." Kees smiled when Baen made a sound of disgust. "You see? You do not appreciate it. I was right."

"In more ways than one," Knox said. "You were right that your advice is not appreciated, but it is correct. There is nothing else to be done with females like ours. They might look small and delicate, but they are fierce in their own right, and there is nothing a male can do to hasten their acceptance of their fates. You must let them come to realize the truth on their own."

Frustration gathered in Baen's chest, threatening to either strangle him or make him roar. Neither would accomplish anything more than a brief release of tension, though, so he fought back the emotion and focused on his brothers. "And what if she never stops fighting? My mate is stubborn."

"No, she is afraid." Ash threw down her cloth and shot Baen a look of disgust. "You need to pay more attention, Guardian, and listen to what your mate tells you."

"Listen? I always listen!" Baen protested. "She barely speaks to me!"

"She says enough. She says that she is uncertain, and yet your response is not to offer reassurance, it is to tell her that her uncertainty is unfounded because Fate brought you together."

"Because it did."

The female Warden rolled her eyes. "And what does that matter to a human's heart? They don't know the power of Fate, brother, not like we do. They do not trust it. They build their lives on the concept of free will, that they can all choose their own destinies. And then you appear before her, telling her that none of it was true and she must give up her entire belief system and throw herself in your arms like a mindless hussy? Tell me, would you really want that from your mate?"

Baen stilled and focused on her words. He had never looked at the situation in those terms before, and he found them unsettling. Of course he did not want Ivy to abandon her personal beliefs for him, nor did he want a mate who meekly accepted his word without question, who went along with whatever circumstances arose in her life just because someone—even him—told her it was destined. He wanted his mate to think and reason and act independently, and Ivy did, which were among the reasons he found his little redhead so appealing.

Spar leaned over Knox's shoulder and pointed. "Look, you can see the light beginning to dawn. Does anyone have one of those intelligent phone devices? We could get a picture."

A second pillow hit Spar square in the face.

Ash hadn't even bothered to look when she threw that one. Her gaze remained on Baen. "You need to show your mate that while Fate might have brought you together, you still want her to choose to be with you. Ivy needs to have good reason to do so."

"And before you start planning to impress her with your strength and ability to keep her safe from harm," Kees broke in, "allow me to save you some trouble. Humans have no difficulty understanding that we are stronger and faster and can protect them from harm. They appreciate it, but only to a point. Your mate doesn't need to be reminded of that. What human females value is when we reveal our emotions to them. Do that, and your Ivy will stop struggling against her fate."

Baen felt shock, then panic. "Guardians do not feel emotion."

The five other figures in the room broke into raucous laughter. Spar actually wiped tears of mirth from his eyes. "Oh, brother, you cannot still believe that old nonsense, can you?"

Ash rolled her eyes. "Everything that lives, feels. Magic or no magic, emotion is the fuel of the living mind. Of course we feel. The only ones who said otherwise were the founders of the Guild, and remember, these were the same humans who trapped us in stone and wanted to leave us there like hibernating guard dogs who would only be let loose at *their* whim. By telling us we did not feel, they kept those leashes short. But they lied."

"All you need to do is think of your mate, and you will know the truth," Dag said. "Your *feelings* for her are clear to anyone who sees you together, and anyone who bothers to watch your face whenever you set eyes on her. You feel plenty, Baen. All you need to do is acknowledge it."

Kees nodded. "And then share it with your mate."

Baen must have looked as shocked as he felt, because Knox chuckled and hastened to reassure him. "Be comforted to know that all your brothers—and your sister," he corrected himself when Ash cleared her throat. "All your siblings before you have gone through this same experience. We have all come to feel deeply for our humans, and by sharing those feelings have claimed the mates we were destined to have. They have made us better men—er, better Guardians—and your Ivy will do the same for you."

Chapter Twenty

To her surprise, Ivy opened the door to the bedroom Rose had shown her to that first night, and found the space empty. For the past week, every time she had managed to slip away from her six-and-a-half-foot shadow before bed, she had found him already here, waiting for her, showing no intention of leaving, no matter what she might order him to do. Any time she protested, Baen would just kiss her until she forgot all about maintaining distance and not complicating matters with sex. Or really, her own name. When that giant Guardian touched her, Ivy could not think at all.

She could only feel.

So where was he tonight? And for goodness' sake, why did she feel such a wave of disappointment at the idea that all her previous attempts at pushing him away might have finally had the (ostensibly) desired effect? She should be whipping out the pompoms and doing her happy dance, not feeling the hot press of tears behind her eyes.

Well, maybe she could at least blame that last part on PMS? Hormones were always a good excuse. Right?

Sniffling and calling herself ten kinds of idiot (idiot

with cheese, diet idiot, idiot with chocolate sauce, et cetera, et cetera), Ivy padded into the en suite bathroom and washed up in preparation for bed. She'd had a little time to think since that conversation with Drum and Ash on the terrace before dinner. Even though there were people everywhere in the manor, they had all seemed to be operating according to some shared understanding that Ivy should be left alone. Even after dinner when it had been expected that she join the other Wardens in the blue salon, the conversation had flowed around her, including her without demanding much in the way of responses from her.

Maybe Drum had tipped the others off? She couldn't see him gossiping or directly reporting what they had talked about to anyone else, but he was such a nice man that she could see him warning the others that she had a lot on her mind, and maybe they should give her some space.

She'd gotten that, and her mind had put it to use almost without asking permission. Or, in other words, she'd spent the remainder of her night brooding about what to do about herself, her Guardian, and all the conflicted feelings currently twisting up inside her.

There hadn't been all that much else to choose from. In the past week, Ivy had learned that life at the manor moved in time with the traditions of the French countryside. While they might be less than forty miles from Paris in the geographical sense, in all other ways Maison Formidable occupied a world apart from the capital. The Wardens who had sought refuge here had come from all over the world, and yet they seemed to have embraced the slow pace and unhurried lifestyle of the local population. Only, you know, with magic, instead of farming.

That meant that days were spent learning how to cast spells and catching up on the history of the Guild, while the Guardians smashed at each other with sharp and/or heavy objects. Evenings, on the other hand, revolved around conversation and games, rather than television or painting the town. Ivy had heard rumors that the manor did have a satellite dish and several accompanying TVs, but hadn't spotted one since her arrival. Instead, she'd spent time reading and talking and studying.

And studiously avoiding the very being she had expected to find waiting for her in the bedroom. Now that he had failed to show after she'd spent the entire evening searching her soul to discover how she really felt about him, Ivy couldn't help but feel a little miffed. How dare he give up on her just as she had maybe, almost, sort of, half decided that she didn't want him to?

Ivy finished brushing her teeth, rinsed out her mouth, and made a face at herself in the mirror. She at least had enough self-awareness to realize how ridiculous she sounded, even inside her own head. But that didn't change the feelings behind her thoughts.

Hours of quiet reflection had told her that it was entirely possible she had feelings for Baen that had nothing at all to do with Fate or destiny or anything in the universe other than the fact that he made her heart race and her knees go weak. If she admitted that to herself, then she also had to admit that if he had been any other man on the face of the earth, she'd have been chasing him across the manor grounds, not leaving it the other way around. She didn't like to think of herself as a bigot, but what was really stopping her from doing exactly that? Other than the fact that he was a Guardian and she was human.

Who cared? Not a single other couple around them had let that put a stop to their relationships, so why should Ivy?

Turning off the bathroom light, she crossed back to

the bed, climbed under the downy duvet and clicked off the bedside lamp. As she settled herself in a nest of fluffy pillows, she allowed herself to admit the answer.

Fear.

Fear had held her paralyzed since the first moment she laid eyes on Baen in that dark, narrow alley, and if she didn't start fighting back, fear might rob her of her greatest chance at happiness. So what if destiny had brought them together? Most people would kill for the sure knowledge that they had met their soul mate. They wouldn't be pouting and whining over it like she had.

Maybe it was time to embrace the idea that while Fate might have conspired to present Ivy with certain opportunities over the last several days, it was up to her to seize them and make the most of them. That was a choice Ivy could make, and after several hours of introspection, she had.

She wanted Baen.

The question then became, did he still want her?

She didn't hear him approach, but then she never did. What she did feel was the way the mattress dipped when he settled his heavy weight on the edge beside Ivy's hip. Her gaze flew through the dark to settle on his face, barely visible in the unlit room. She didn't need to see him, though. She felt his eyes on her, that reassuring warmth she had come to take for granted over the past week.

He sat in silence for a long time, and it fascinated her to see the way his gaze caught fire as he watched her. She saw the first spark leap in the dark black pools and watched as it ignited a tiny flame that then burned brighter and brighter the longer he looked at her. For the first time it really struck her that *she* was the reason his eyes burned, and it made her stomach turn slow somersaults in nervous excitement.

"I was starting to think you'd found somewhere more comfortable to sleep," she whispered after a moment. The words came out so quietly, she could barely hear them herself.

Baen shook his head. "There is nowhere else. Not for me."

Her heart leaped, but her brain cautioned her not to read too much into the words. Maybe he meant that the house was crowded and he couldn't find an empty room. Or that he felt too duty-bound as her Guardian to leave her vulnerable to attack while she slept. His words could have any number of explanations, and she was afraid to interpret them in case she drew the wrong conclusion.

When silence stretched between them, she felt her nerves stretch as well until she couldn't bear the tension. "Baen—"

He pressed a finger to her lips. "No. I need to speak with you, *to* you, and I must tell you before we go any further. Before you distract me once again."

Ivy wanted to protest that she wasn't the only one providing a distraction over the past week. He should know by now what happened when he flashed those rippling muscles of his and paraded around the room half naked, with his jeans hanging low off his Adonis belt. Every time she saw those grooves carved into the sides of his hips, she wanted to trace the lines with her teeth and tongue. And he called *her* a distraction.

His finger slid from her mouth to her cheek, cupping it in a tender caress. "For all of the long years that I have lived in your world, I have believed certain things to be true," he began. He spoke slowly and quietly, as if he himself needed to understand as much as he wanted her to do so. "I believed that I existed for only one reason—to fight against the Darkness. I believed that being trapped in sleep for centuries upon centuries had purpose and honor, because my brothers and I were told this by those who summoned us. I believed that as a Guardian, the only emotions I could feel were those that swept through me in the heat of battle—rage, fury, hatred for my enemy, triumph and pride when I emerged victorious."

Ivy listened and felt her heart contract. What an empty existence he described, cold and gray and in the end futile. His battles against the Darkness kept humans like her safe, but his life of eternal sleep punctuated by nothing but brief moments of danger and bloodshed sounded to her as if they'd been designed to create an army of serial killers. With nothing of hope or love to soften their experiences, the endless rounds of conflict and pain should have warped the Guardians into monsters. The fact that they remained stalwart and honorable, dedicated to the service of the Light, only demonstrated their essential goodness. And contrasted it with the frankly evil actions of the generations of Wardens who had kept them imprisoned.

She reached up and laid her hand over Baen's, squeezing in acknowledgment and silent encouragement.

"All of that I believed, *amare,* and to me it seemed like graven truth that I should be separate from the world I defended, that I should form no attachments to it, since it would pass by me as I slept. To have developed feelings for humans who would grow old and die while I slumbered would have driven me mad. It seemed wiser and safer to allow things to continue on as I believed they had always done."

His thumb stroked across her bottom lip and the corner of his mouth lifted in a tiny smile. "And then you appeared, and all of the universe tumbled into its *proper* alignment."

Her heart skipped and shuddered into a much faster

beat, racing ahead while Ivy stared into those burning eyes and tried to contain the rush of excitement and hope that welled inside her.

"I looked at you," Baen continued. "I looked, and I saw the true purpose of my existence laid out before me. You were the thing I had been summoned to defend, and to protect the rest of your kind was only a happy accident. You were the Light I could never let fall to the Darkness, the Light that guided me through all the long years of waking and sleeping. You were the reason for the heart that beat within me, the reason I could feel anything other than the bleak, numb emptiness of endless solitude."

Ivy's throat tightened until she couldn't have said anything if her life had depended on it. All she could do was look into his gaze and hope he could see the words reflected in hers.

"Ivy. *Amare.* My perfect little human." He leaned down and brushed his lips gently over hers, more of a caress than a kiss, infinitely tender and full of reverence. "I know that your own world has turned upside down in the days since you met me, and I know that you have been overwhelmed with new knowledge and new rules, with magic and legends and talk of Fate and your responsibilities as a Warden. I know all that, but I want you to believe that none of it is as important as what I have to say to you."

Baen reached out with his other hand to hold her face cradled between his palms. He leaned in until he hovered only inches away, until all she could see was the fire in his dark eyes.

Until all she could see was *him*.

"Ivy Beckett, of the red hair and the smoky eyes," he murmured, his lips smiling but his voice deep and serious. "Ivy of the quick tongue and the tender heart, know that whatever you decide, whatever path you choose to

tread, guided by Fate or your own bright mind, I am
yours. I shall always be yours, to embrace or to cast aside
as you wish. For as long as I draw breath in this realm, I
shall protect and defend you, walk beside you or behind
you and support you in all things."

Forget not being able to talk. When Ivy heard those
words, she forgot how to breathe. Her chest seized up and
her heart felt as if a fist had wrapped around it and
squeezed. Her vision began to blur, and it took a moment
for her to realize that it was from the tears that had welled
up in her eyes. Tears of happiness, or gratitude, or too
much emotion in too small a body.

Tears of love.

And Baen wasn't even finished. He had saved the best
for last.

"I love you, *amare*."

He said it simply and softly and with so much conviction, it might as well have been etched in stone like the
Ten Commandments. There was no question of doubting
him. His words were Truth, and they were for her alone.

She didn't know how to contain the emotions welling
inside her. She had a feeling they would spill over at any
moment.

"I love you. I will love you always, and whether you
grow to return my feelings or you send me away from
you, I will not cease to love you for as long as there is
Light in the universe. Because you are my Light, and
everything aside from you fades into insignificance."

"Baen."

She breathed his name, blinking away the tears only
to find more welling up to take their place. She stroked
her hands up his arms to curl her fingers around his broad
shoulders. She needed to hang on to something, and she
needed to prove to herself that he was real, that she hadn't

imagined this entire scene, hadn't conjured it up from a wishful heart.

"Baen. You terrify me," she admitted, hating the look of hurt that crossed his face, but needing to get the words out. "Not because of what you are, but because of what you make me feel. I didn't think this was possible. I didn't think that there was any such thing as one perfect partner for everyone. I didn't believe in true love or soul mates or happily ever after. And I certainly didn't believe that someone could swoop into my life out of thin air and wind up being the only thing in the world that I couldn't live without."

She reached up to brush her knuckles over his raspy jaw and struggled to find the words to admit to both of them what her heart had already assured her was true.

"That's why I keep running away from you," she admitted, ashamed of how she'd been treating him, blowing hot and cold, shunning him one moment, and melting into his embrace the next. "That fear. I've been so afraid, I haven't even been able to admit to myself how scared I really was. Until tonight." She took a deep breath. "Tonight I realized that the only thing that scares me more than what you make me feel, is the idea of losing you because I was too afraid to hold on."

He started to protest, but she shook her head and hushed him. She needed for him to hear this, and she needed to say it aloud. "No, it's the truth. You don't deserve to be treated the way I've treated you, and I don't deserve to live my whole life with the fear that whatever I love is going to be taken away from me. We both deserve better than that."

Her mouth quirked in a trembling smile. "Besides, I don't have to grow to love you, Baen. If I didn't love you already, I wouldn't be so bloody terrified of losing you."

"Amare." His thumbs rubbed the tears from her cheek, his mouth descending to kiss her watery eyes. "You could never lose me, little one. There is no place under the Light where you could go that I would not follow. No, I am afraid you are stuck with me. I will follow you into the heart of Darkness, if I have to."

Ivy laughed. The sound came out a little gurgly because of those tears she still couldn't stop, and a little giddy because of all the joy welling up inside her. But hey, those weren't necessarily bad things, right? Baen didn't seem to mind.

"You know, if I didn't totally get where you were coming from, that would sound a little stalkerish," she teased, pulling him down to kiss him through her wide grin.

"Stalkerish?" He frowned. "What is that?"

She chuckled. "I'll explain later. Right now, I feel like celebrating. C'mere."

Baen offered not a word of protest. In fact, he seized control of the kiss she pressed on him, devouring her mouth with unchecked fervor. And here Ivy had thought him passionate before. Apparently, the big Guardian had been holding back on her.

Well, not anymore. He made that clear when he crawled onto the bed on top of her, caging her in with his huge, muscular body. He made her feel small and vulnerable in the most exciting way, because she knew he was strong enough to overpower her and yet too respectful and tender to try.

Unless she asked him to, very, very nicely.

At the moment, she didn't have that option. He had captured her mouth and showed no signs of yielding the territory. He nipped at her lips, stroked with his tongue, and basically drove her crazier and crazier with each breathless minute that passed. Hmm, she had a sneaking suspicion that two could play at that game.

She surrendered to the kiss, responding to his demands with eager participation, but as busy as her lips were, her hands hated to miss all the fun. They glided down Baen's sides to the waistband of his jeans, tracing the path of the denim to the button closure in front. A few quick tugs had it popping free, and a few more brought his zipper hissing down.

His erection spilled into her hands, already full and hard and leaking drops of fluid from the tip. She curled her fingers around the shaft and brushed her thumb across the head, rubbing his own moisture back into his heated skin. He groaned into her mouth, a fierce, guttural sound that only made her more determined to shatter his control.

She tightened her fingers, squeezing his cock, and began pumping his length in slow, firm strokes. His groans turned to a low, rumbling growl that vibrated against her chest and made her press her legs together against the tingling arousal at her core. The fact that she could affect him this way enthralled her. To have all his power at her mercy made her head spin and her sex grow slick and eager. She wanted him inside her, but she was having too much fun teasing him to rush things.

Too bad Baen seemed to be in a bit of a hurry.

He gripped the neck of her tank top in two huge fists and tore it to shreds without even bothering to break their kiss. A second later, her panties suffered the same fate, scraps of lace and cotton fluttering to the floor like confetti. She might have cared if she hadn't been too busy shuddering at the press of his skin against hers as he settled his body over her and pressed her into the mattress. Trapped between a rock and a soft place, Ivy couldn't think of a single location she'd rather be.

She used her free hand to push his jeans down over his hips, refusing to release her grip on his cock. The soft skin over the hard length fascinated her, and the way he hissed and grunted every time she stroked him only fueled her arousal. With his trousers loosened, she wrapped her legs around his bare hips and used her feet to push the annoying fabric completely out of the way.

She couldn't bear to have anything between them any longer, and Baen seemed to share her sentiment. He kicked the garment to the floor and settled heavily between her thighs, rocking against her until she could feel the backs of her own fingers pressing into her wetness.

Enough of that.

Giving up on her teasing, she guided him to her entrance, pressing up against him and begging him to enter her. Lifting his head, Baen broke the kiss and held her gaze and he began to drive himself within her. *"Te amo, amica mea."*

Ivy wrapped herself around him, arms and legs clinging, feeling his muscles shift and flex as he joined their bodies together. Her pussy stretched and ached and welcomed him. Having him inside her made her feel complete in a way she hadn't known was possible before now. She arched beneath him, wanting nothing more than to draw him closer. If she could have pulled him inside her skin, she'd have done it just to feel him even closer against her heart.

Baen dropped his head and took her mouth again. She felt dizzy and breathless and higher than a kite. She felt like her heart could burst and her lungs could seize and it wouldn't matter, because they shared one heart and one breath and that was all they needed to survive.

Each other.

He began to move inside her, sliding deep only to draw back over and over, every motion a rough caress to her inner nerve endings. She began to tremble as the tension built inside her. She felt it like a knot of fire and pressure behind her pelvis, and the only way to assuage it was to move with him, to take him deep and cling tight against every attempt to withdraw. She fought a losing battle, but it didn't matter, because they would both be able to claim this victory.

"Baen!" She shouted his name as he shifted his weight, bumping the head of his cock against a bundle of nerves that sent firecrackers exploding behind her closed eyelids. Her body clenched hard around his and he growled something unintelligible before repeating the movement again and again.

She shattered, body bowing off the mattress only to be slammed down again with the force of Baen's final thrusts. All she could do was cling to him while the world fell away and her consciousness burst into millions of tiny fragments that danced off into the ether like the sparks from a popping bonfire.

Vaguely, she felt Baen go rigid as he surrendered to his own climax. She just held on while he emptied himself with shuddering groans, then collapsed atop her on a long, grunting sigh.

The sound made her smile, at least inside her head. She couldn't feel a damn thing, so she had no idea whether her lips moved or not. It didn't matter. That had been worth some paralysis and possible permanent sensory damage. It had been worth everything.

Love was, after all.

Chapter Twenty-one

She wasn't certain what she heard first, the chanting or the screaming. In the end, it didn't matter. They both came to her with unsettling clarity, and they both meant the same things—pain, death, evil.

Ivy struggled against the experience, but her "gift" had her firmly in its grasp, and it had no intention of letting go.

The voices chanted in a language she didn't recognize. She couldn't even be certain it was a language, because she couldn't distinguish any words at all. It sounded as if someone had built a coded speech out of nails on chalkboards, microphone feedback, and the sound of breaking bones. It made the hair on her neck— hell, the hair everywhere—stand on end and sent her stomach pitching and rolling in her abdomen. It was, she realized, what the Darkness sounded like.

She didn't need a translation. Whatever was being said had only one purpose, to cause pain and terror as it built a giant cone of Dark energy at the center of the assembled nocturnis.

Once Ivy realized that, her mind switched its focus to the screams, and those she recognized easily. Martin.

It didn't matter that she hadn't spent more than a few hours in his presence, didn't matter that she'd never heard anyone scream like that, full of so much terror and agony that they no longer sounded human. It didn't even matter that he had been a traitor to the Guild and all the people she had worked so hard to save. None of that mattered, because no living creature ever deserved to suffer the way Martin was suffering.

"No! Master, please! I have served you faithfully! Nooooo!"

The chanting never ceased, never so much as hiccupped, but a low hissing voice began to slither underneath it. It made Ivy freeze and the urge to run, to run far, far away, filled her, but she couldn't move. Her body was trapped by the power of her "vision," and she couldn't move a muscle.

"And you continue to serve us," the voice mocked. "Your blood serves us as it stains these stones your forefathers laid down. Your pain and your terror serve us as they echo under the seat of our enemy. Your soul will serve us when we rip it from your body and feast in the presence of their impotent Light."

More screams, terrible screams, and sobbing. Even in her paralyzed state, Ivy had to fight to swallow the bile that rose in her throat. She knew those sounds would haunt her for years to come.

"Scream, human," the voice ordered, glee underlining its viperous tone. "Scream and beg and feed our power. Help us draw the Guardian to the home of his wretched kind that his blood may free our final Brother! Scream!"

Ivy had no words for the sounds that came next. She didn't want words, not for the horrible, wet rending sound, nor for the inhuman shriek of agony that followed it.

Nor for the outraged bellow that echoed inside her head as she sat bolt upright in the pitch-black bedroom, the pale sheets sliding away from her sweaty skin.

"Ghrem!"

Beside her, Baen jackknifed into a sitting position and reached for her. "*Amare!* Ivy, what is the matter?"

"The others." She clutched at him with fingers that shook so hard, she almost couldn't make them grip, no matter how badly she needed to cling to his strength. "Get the others. I just heard something. Something bad. We need to hurry."

The Guardian wasted no time asking questions. Whether he heard the truth in her words or read the terror and panic on her face, it didn't matter. He immediately left the bed and grabbed some clothes, bundling her into an oversized T-shirt and a pair of sweats, moving her arms and legs like a doll to get her dressed. He spared another two seconds to yank on his own discarded jeans before scooping her up into his arms and shouldering his way out of their bedroom.

He strode down the hallway lined with bedroom doors and bellowed loud enough to wake the dead. "Kees! Ash! Dag! Everyone wake! Spar! Knox! To arms!"

The huge old house began to thump and rattle as bodies tumbled from beds and doors flew open. Huge, broad-shouldered men and rumpled women began to appear, looking alarmed but alert.

"What has happened?"

"What is it? What is going on?"

"Yo, where's the fire, Hudson?"

Rose stepped out of her room, tying the belt of an old-fashioned smoking jacket she wore as a robe. "Baen, what is this about?"

"Ivy heard something. Something significant. She says we all need to hear it."

The woman looked from Baen to Ivy, who lay curled against his chest, shivering and traumatized. She tried to show with her eyes how important this was, because she couldn't speak. Her teeth were chattering too hard. She felt as if she stood naked on a glacier during a blizzard. Never in her life had she felt chilled like this, like her bones had been constructed of ice and were freezing her from the inside out.

Rose must have sensed something, because she gave a brisk nod and waved for everyone to head toward the stairs. "We will meet in the blue room. You go down. I will make certain everyone is awake and get them to assemble. Go on now. And if someone wishes to make coffee, that would be appreciated."

It took another ten minutes to get everyone together. Ivy spent it in Baen's lap. He had claimed a well-padded love seat, settling her atop his thighs and wrapping her in the soft chenille blanket Fil found draped over a chair in the corner. Ella had rushed off to make coffee and dragged Wynn along with her, so by the time the stragglers appeared and chose seats of their own, the two women were passing out cups of the strong brew.

Baen doctored a mug with cream and sugar and helped it to her lips. She sipped gratefully, still shaking too hard to hold anything for herself. She supposed it must be shock putting her in this state, but it didn't much matter what she called it.

Hell, it didn't much matter what she felt. What mattered was what she had heard and what it revealed about their enemy.

"Ivy," Rose prodded gently. "Can you tell us what you heard? What has put you in such a panic?"

It took another mouthful of coffee, several deep breaths, and the tightening of Baen's arms around her before Ivy could manage to speak. And even then, she sounded like Katharine Hepburn with the worst of her tremors.

"I heard the Order. A ritual, I think," she said, leaning heavily against Baen's chest and grateful for his warmth. "I never see anything, so all I can tell you is what I heard."

Rose nodded and made a gesture of encouragement.

"There was chanting, from a lot of voices. Dozens, at least. So many. They used a language I've never heard before. At least, I'm assuming it was a language. It sounded more like . . . chaos." The memory made her shudder. "It had a definite rhythm, and it kept getting faster and faster, like they were building up to something."

"Oh, I do not like the sound of that," Fil murmured from the sofa opposite.

The Warden had no idea.

Ivy continued. "I also heard screaming. A person screaming," she clarified. She looked up at Baen, then her gaze searched out Ash and Drum, the only others who shared the connection. "It was Martin. I'm sure of it."

Ash cursed. Drum didn't look much happier.

"Martin?" Rose frowned. "That was the Warden you were meant to send here, no? The one who betrayed you to the *nocturnis*."

"Yes. They apparently decided to return the favor. They were—" Ivy broke off. She had to swallow hard against the bile that rose at the memory. "They tortured him. To raise power, I think. That was the purpose of the ritual. They tortured him and then they killed him."

"Human sacrifice?" Wynn looked sickened, but not surprised. "That would certainly raise a good bit of energy, and not a drop of it untainted."

Knox squeezed his Warden's hand. "What did they need so much power for?"

Ivy shifted uncomfortably. She knew what she had heard, and she knew what her instincts told her, but she couldn't be certain what the others would think when she told them. Would they believe her, or would they decide she had too little evidence to support her assertions?

Baen gave her a gentle cuddle and nodded when she met his gaze. His support and encouragement made her shove aside her doubts and just pour it out. Until she did, no one would take action; they would have no reason to.

"I think they used it to pull Ghrem out of the between. A voice said something that implied it, and just before I came out of it, I thought I heard him shout. One of those Guardian roars." She met Rose's shocked gaze and tried to convey both sorrow and sincerity. "Like I said, I couldn't see him or anything else, but I'm certain that was what happened."

"But why?" Rose asked, sounding confused and frightened and verging on panic. "Why should they pull him into our realm again? They were safer while he was busy in the between."

Ivy braced herself to deliver the news she really, really wished she didn't have to pass along. "That voice I heard said something. About that. It said his blood would free their final brother."

"Mon Dieu! Non!"

The quiet French plea was drowned under an explosion of rage and denial. The Guardians looked ready to charge the gates of hell, and the Wardens looked horrified.

Ivy searched out Wynn's gaze. The witch hadn't been a Warden the longest, but she'd been using magic her whole life, and she understood how it worked better than any of the rest. She could work it better than any of them, too.

"Do you think that could be possible?" Ivy asked her. "Could the Order believe that using a Guardian as a sacrifice could finally break down the strongest prison and let the last Demon go free? Would they even try it?"

"They would try *anything,*" Wynn replied. "They've killed teenagers, crippled the Guild, and destroyed entire villages to get this far. If they could get their hands on a Guardian, they would absolutely try to sacrifice him to raise the power needed to open the last prison. No question."

"But would it work?" Drum asked.

"I am very, very afraid that it might," the witch said grimly.

"But I thought you guys were immortal," Kylie said. "I mean, I know that doesn't mean invulnerable, but I've seen you get hacked at with weapons, blasted with spells, even attacked by minor demons. It would have to take a special kind of weapon for the Order to think they even had a chance of taking one of you out."

"And even if they had something like that, how do they think they're going to control one of you?" Ella asked. "I've seen the odds some of you guys have taken on. You plow through *nocturnis* like they're toy soldiers. Pulling Ghrem out of the between is one thing, but once they got ahold of him, it's not like he wouldn't be fighting his way out of there like a scene from an old Errol Flynn movie."

It wasn't the sheer number of voices that she recalled from her episode that Ivy thought of, it was the gleeful way the hissing voice had spoken of its plans. She offered the others an apologetic look. "I don't think this was some kind of 'seize the moment and see what happens' thing. This was planned, carefully planned, well before tonight. If they had time to think about it, I'm pretty sure they had time to come up with a way to keep a single Guardian contained."

"There are spells they could use." The timid voice came from the corner of the room, sounding almost apologetic for being there. Aldous pushed his glasses up his nose and seemed to shrink a little when the others turned their focus on him. "Guardians are immune to magic, but when certain material barriers are magically reinforced, the reinforcement becomes intrinsic to the material itself, and therefore can serve to contain even a creature as strong as a Guardian. Or, so the sources claim."

"And a weapon could be manufactured," Thiago added.

The two Wardens had been Rose's support system while her Guardian was absent and had helped to develop the plan to defeat the Darkness, so it was clear the French-woman valued their opinion. She had invited them to join tonight's meeting. Considering that they were also training the other Wardens in the house to fight with magic in the face of the Order, it made sense that she should keep up to date with the threat they all faced.

"What kind of weapon?"

Thiago shrugged. "The Seven are the natural enemies of the Guardians, therefore they have been adapted to inflict harm. If one of the Demons were to sacrifice a claw, perhaps, or a tooth, it could be fashioned into a blade as effective against a Guardian as one of steel is against an ordinary man."

Oh, now that was good news, Ivy thought. She clung a little tighter to Baen and tried not to think about what the Order had planned. She already knew too much for her own comfort.

"Then what Ivy heard is possible?" Rose demanded.

"I am afraid so." Aldous nodded.

Rose fell silent for a moment. Her chin dipped toward

her chest, and she clasped her hands together in front of her as if in prayer. She drew several deep breaths before she looked back up at the Guardians and Wardens gathered around her, and her eyes glinted with fury and determination as she spoke.

"If that is the case, then we have no choice," she said. "We will not leave one of our own in the hands of the filthy *nocturnis*. We will rescue Ghrem, and we will put a stop to the rise of the Darkness. *N'est-ce pas?*"

Her words might be polite, but Ivy heard the steel and fire behind them. She certainly wasn't going to be the one to gainsay the mate of a threatened Guardian. Especially not one she had seen hurl fireballs the size of Volkswagens during their magical training sessions.

So, that just left one thing to do. In order to save the missing Guardian before he ended up sacrificed to the Darkness, they first had to find him.

Had anyone been listening when Ivy said she didn't *see* anything in her visions? She hadn't the faintest clue where the Order was hiding their captive. For all she knew, he was tied up in the underwater lair of a villain out of a bad James Bond movie.

Ghrem could be anywhere in the world right now. Now ask her again how they were going to find him?

The room full of people asked Ivy where to find the Order's hiding place, the location where they kept Ghrem while they waited to spill his blood. It was the one advantage they had at the moment, that the *nocturnis* would not likely carry out the sacrificial ritual immediately. According to Aldous, they would wait for the next night when the moon went dark and the earth passed through the shadow of an ominous astrological object called a dark star. A thing of legend and cultic fascination, it provided what the little German called the perfect atmosphere for the raising of Dark energy. A great deal of such power would be necessary to rewrite the Seven.

Unfortunately, that meant they had only hours to locate Ghrem and bring down the Seven before it was too late. At the apex of the new moon, Aldous predicted, the priests of the Order would perform their ritual, kill Ghrem, and release Belgrethnakkar, bringing the Seven back together at last. The Guardians and the Wardens could not afford to let that happen.

Baen understood all that. He felt the same compulsion to destroy his enemy and rescue his fallen brother, but it didn't make it any easier to deal with the way the others threw questions at his mate in rapid succession. They peppered her with demands, asking her to provide information she clearly didn't think she had, and as she sat in his lap, shaking and retreating from the relentless barrage, he grew angrier and angrier with his friends.

"Enough!" he barked when he saw the way Ivy's eyes had begun to glisten with moisture. He knew how badly they all wanted to find Ghrem, but he would not have his mate reduced to tears to accomplish it. "You give her no room to breathe, let alone to search her mind for your answers. If you cannot behave responsibly, you can all keep your mouths shut."

Ivy sagged against him, her gratitude obvious as silence descended on the tense group. "I'm sorry," she said, her voice tight. "I wish I could tell you where he is, but I didn't see it. I didn't see anything. I never do. That's why I told you I don't have a talent worth mentioning. You'd get as much out of some well-planned eavesdropping as you get out of me. Believe me, I want to find him as badly as you do. After what they did to Martin . . ."

She lapsed into silence, shuddering. The expression of pain she wore and the way she bit hard into her lower lip showed how much the memory of what she'd heard haunted her. Baen could not resist gathering her close and rocking her with comforting motions.

"Hush, *amare*," he murmured. "Never say your talent is useless. Without you, we would not know what the Order has planned for us. You have given us a chance to stop them before it is too late. That is not only worth mentioning, it is invaluable."

Rose agreed. "Baen is right, Ivy. We should apologize for the way we just treated you. Our worry and the pressure of time is our only excuse, but it is a poor one. You have already done us all a great favor."

Ivy scoffed. "By showing you what you have to look forward to? I wouldn't exactly call that a favor, myself."

"Stop, little one," Baen ordered. "Push aside your doubts and your worries and focus on me. Can you do that? I want to try something."

She turned those gray eyes on him and frowned, but she was already nodding her agreement. "Try what?"

"Seeing things is not the only way to gather information. I think if only one of us asks the questions, you might be able to recall something from what you heard to give us some clues. Will you try for me?"

The corner of her mouth kicked up. "I'd try anything for you."

He felt his heart swell and had to force himself to focus. "Thank you, *amare*. Now, close your eyes and listen to my voice. Can you try to remember the first thing you heard earlier? Was it the chanting?"

Ivy leaned back against his arm and let her eyelids drift shut. He saw the way she shifted her attention inward with a small frown that drew a tiny crease between her brows. He ignored the way it made him want to trace the soft skin with his fingertip.

"The chanting and the screaming," she said, her mouth tightening. "I heard both at the same time."

"What did it sound like? Not what they said, but the environment. Could you hear anything in the background? Traffic outside, planes overhead, mechanical noises of any kind."

Her frown deepened as she concentrated on her memories. After a moment, she slowly shook her head. "None of that. It sounded . . . cut off. Isolated. Like it was separate from everything. Secret. The voices drowned everything else out. Except for the screams."

"Good girl. What about acoustical qualities? Was there an echo? A reverberation, like in a cavern or a concert hall?"

"No echo." She paused. "And not exactly a reverberation. Oh, hell, this is so not my field of expertise." Her eyes popped open, and she stared unhappily at him. "I don't know acoustics, Baen. All I know are words, but I do remember what the voice said to Martin, and a few of its phrases struck me as odd. Tell me if you feel the same."

Baen listened as Ivy did her best to re-create the threats and taunts of the hissing voice that had spoken to the doomed Martin. He stiffened to hear the way the voice spoke of "stones your forefathers laid" and the "seat of the enemy." The wording gave him an uneasy feeling.

Apparently, he wasn't the only one. As soon as Ivy mentioned the idea of feeding on Martin's soul "in the presence of the Light," Aldous jumped to his feet and cried out as if he'd just been goosed with a cattle prod.

"It can't be!" The German gasped. "They could not have desecrated our most sacred rooms that way. Light forbid it."

"What are you talking about?" Ivy demanded. "Did that crap mean something to you? Because if it did, you need to tell us. Now."

Aldous wrung his hands and looked like someone had

just kicked his puppy. His voice shook when he tried to answer her question. "You are very certain you heard those particular words? 'In the presence of the Light'?"

"I'm positive."

The little man whimpered and looked at Rose. "I fear that the Order has befouled our very home, *Fräulein*. The stones laid by our forefathers are the stones of the Guild headquarters in Paris. And calling it the seat of their enemy only confirms this. The *nocturnis* have gathered at our stronghold in order to destroy us! They mock us with bringing Darkness to the heart of a place that was built to serve the Light."

Ella pounced on that possibility. "That can't be right. The headquarters was completely destroyed in the attack two years ago. Rose, you said you were there, and I know you've been to the site since then. Is there enough of the building left to hold rituals in, let alone to hide a captive Guardian?"

"You don't understand," Aldous continued before Rose could respond. "They are not *in* the building; they are beneath it. The first Wardens used magic to dig a stronghold under the site of the headquarters and built a series of rooms deep under the ground. They were meant to be used as a refuge in the case of a direct attack by the Order, and in the early years of the Guild, it was said that the Inner Council used them for important rituals. Those rooms were the site where the Guardian summonings used to take place, and they say that the central room featured a mural inlaid with magic and precious stones. It was supposed to depict the servants of the Light and to have been created by one of the Maidens. The work itself was known as *The Light*, and if the Order is within its presence, then they are in that room!"

Baen turned to Rose. "Could these underground rooms have survived the blast? Is it possible that the *nocturnis* returned there after they destroyed the building and have been orchestrating their evil from under our very noses?"

"The site was fenced off for safety reasons, so I have not walked through it, but I saw no signs that the foundation was compromised." The Frenchwoman looked pained. "I think it is very possible a secret cellar might have remained intact. If the area giving access to it also survived, or was suitable for excavation . . ." She shrugged. "*Oui*. It might be the case."

Curses in a number of different languages exploded into the room. Kylie's Yiddish and Fil's Lithuanian added color to the mostly dead languages the Guardians seemed to prefer. Baen certainly found himself giving his Latin a workout.

"I guess that means we're going to Paris," Wynn said calmly, but with steel underlying her tone. "It doesn't matter if they're using our space, or even if they've decorated every single wall with smeared blood and severed heads. We know where they are, so we go after them. We're not leaving Ghrem in their hands, and we're not letting the Darkness win. Am I right?"

"You're right." Drum agreed. "Though I do hope you're wrong about the severed heads."

The Wardens shared a brief smile, but what pleased Baen was seeing how every head in the room nodded in agreement. Guardians and Wardens all appeared united in their determination to strike back at the Darkness and banish it from this world permanently.

Thiago stepped forward, his dark features set in lines of resolve. "I have showed every Warden here the spell we will need to defeat the Demons and return them to their prisons. I had hoped we would have more time to practice together, but you all know what you must do. I am confident you will do it well."

"Wait. Is that all the spell is going to do?" Dag

demanded. "It only sends the Demons back to the same places from which they already escaped? How does that help us? They have proven those prisons will not hold them forever. What happens the next time they begin entertaining ambitions?"

"The problem did not lie with the prisons themselves," Thiago said. "It was the fault of the Guild. They grew complacent in the millennia since the Darkness was banished. They forgot that even the strongest wards need to be maintained. They failed to renew the energy in the magic that sealed the prisons. Believe me, the new Guild will not be so lax."

Baen was glad to hear it. He only intended to fight this battle once.

He also saw the way the Wardens greeted Thiago's declaration. It had a proprietary ring, as if the Spaniard expected to have a definite say in the reconstruction of the Wardens' Guild. Based on the strength of the other Wardens in the room, Baen was betting the man would face some stiff competition when it came to deciding who would run things in the future. If they were lucky, it would create a better and stronger organization for all of them.

"So that's the plan, then?" Kylie asked, rising to her feet and bouncing up and down on her toes. The tiny human rarely kept still. Even while she was seated, one foot beat a rapid rhythm against the air in front of the settee. "We storm the castle—er, basement—we wave our magic hands, and we bippity-boppity-boo the Demons into the Detention Dimension?"

Baen blinked. Sometimes it took him a few minutes to translate Kylie's irreverent and slang-laden speech into English he could understand. This was one of those times.

After he'd digested the question, he nodded cautiously. "Yes, I believe that is the plan."

"Hm. And what about the whole bunch of chanters Ivy here heard doing that ritual? I mean, we've all gotten our feet wet with fighting off *nocturnis* when we've had to, but it sounds like when we go in there, we're gonna be seriously outnumbered. Not to mention that we Wardens are going to be distracted while casting the big spell. How are we supposed to do that while we have a battalion of pissed-off whack jobs trying to turn us into latkes?"

Thiago interjected. "We will bring the other Wardens, the ones who have sheltered here. I will gather volunteers. I am certain most of them will wish to join the fight. They will handle the *nocturnis* while the seven Wardens bound to Guardians cast the spell."

"Most of them, huh?" Kylie pursed her lips and turned to face Rose. "In that case, I think you're going to need a bigger car."

Chapter Twenty-two

They did need a larger car—actually, several vans—but only because the Guardians could safely carry no more than one or two Wardens at a time for the short flight back to Paris. Ivy volunteered to drive, but Baen would have none of it. The big galoot refused to let her out of his sight for a minute, let alone most of an hour.

Which was why when she got to the French capital late the following evening, she needed a moment on solid land to remember how to work her legs again. She didn't care what Baen said. She was *not* going to get used to that kind of flying. Not ever. She wanted a seat, a flight attendant, and a little rolling cart of free soda. Jumbo airliner, watch her come.

The *nocturnis*, on the other hand, were welcome to look in an entirely different direction. Move it along, she thought as she stuck close to Baen's side. Nothing to see here.

They had landed on a (another) rooftop in a maneuver with which Ivy was becoming uncomfortably (and reluctantly) familiar. This one gave them a view of the rubble-strewn lot that was all that remained of the former Guild headquarters. The other six Guardians occupied similar positions on the surrounding streets. For the moment, they waited and watched, timing the moment when they would make their appearance as party crashers at the Order's little soiree.

Providing, of course, that the waiting didn't kill her, Ivy reflected sourly. Patience had never numbered among her virtues, and she already felt as if she'd been waiting for the signal to move forward since they had hammered out their plan in the wee hours of the morning.

No one had left the blue room until after sunrise, the group using the hours in between to discuss exactly how they would get into the Guild's secret basement. Now that they suspected the place was crawling with *nocturnis* and whatever inhuman minions they had decided to conjure up that day, it seemed wise not to just burst in with guns blazing. Chances were, a full frontal assault was exactly what the Order would be expecting.

Luckily, their little Rebel Alliance had two advantages working in their favor. First, Aldous had actually visited the hidden rooms once, at least the ones closest to the entrance, and as a certifiable Guild geek, he had researched the rumors and the few known facts about them. All that had enabled the German to draw up a reasonably accurate floor plan of the space. So at least they knew they wouldn't get lost, or waste all their time trying to fight their way through to a glorified storage room. Because that would just be awkward.

Their second advantage was Drum. Although he had spent a lot of years like Ivy, ignoring his gift or dismissing it as having little value, he had recently learned its true strategic importance. Drum could locate things. He could focus on an object or a person and track them down using the magic of his talent, basically homing in on them as if they wore a GPS tracking device. According to Ash, he was more reliable than a bloodhound and only snored half as loud.

Drum had shot his mate a look that promised retribution, but then accepted an article of clothing Rose said had belonged to Ghrem and had used it to focus on the missing Guardian. Several tense moments later, the Irish publican had been able to confirm that Ghrem was indeed in Paris, he was definitely someplace underground, and he was absolutely being guarded by a heavy force of cultists.

It hadn't exactly been good news, but it had let them know what they were walking into and that at least they were looking in the right place. As reconnaissance went, you couldn't beat that.

Of course, just because everyone knew where they were going and what to do once they got there didn't mean they could just rush in yelling "Banzai!" (Or, as Kylie had suggested, "Bonsai! Little trees!") No, they had to be smart about this, and that meant working according to a multistage plan.

Part one had involved the logistics of simply getting everyone to Paris from Maison Formidable. Rose's little Renault carried four, maximum, and it helped if all of those individuals had small frames and close relationships. The manor boasted a spacious estate car and a compact van, which helped, but they had still been forced to call in favors from friends, relatives, and trusted neighbors in order to transport thirty-seven volunteers to the field of battle. Or in this case, a safe house in a neighboring *arrondissement*. Arrivals had been staggered throughout the day, so that by early evening, the Guardians had been the last of the pieces to settle into place.

Cue the waiting. All. The. Waiting.

While Ivy tried to keep her muscles from atrophying

on that rooftop, several skilled Wardens were busy down below implementing phase two. Using magic to conceal their presence, those volunteers were searching the ruins for the concealed entrance to the basement. They would also use the opportunity to clear out any traps the Order might have laid and to dispatch any *nocturni* guards left aboveground.

The third stage of the plan was the most dangerous, and Ivy had been both surprised and touched when she had witnessed half a dozen Wardens in hiding step forward as volunteers. Their job would be to descend into the secret rooms ahead of the others and form a clear path for the Guardians and the rest of the Wardens.

According to Aldous, the rooms beneath the Guild's headquarters had been arranged along a central axis. The stairs opened into an entry chamber from which two short halls led to medium-sized rooms to the left and the right. From those, another set of short halls led to two more rooms, before the final set of matching corridors converged into a large anteroom capable of holding a hundred *nocturnis*. Beyond that lay the final chamber, a vast, high-ceilinged space with plenty of room for a Guardian to spread his wings.

This was the Guild's ritual room, and the one bearing the mural known as *The Light*. It was where the Order would be gathered and where Ghrem was being held.

It was also the space in which six of the most powerful and corrupt creatures of the Darkness would be gathered, each one capable of destroying cities all on its own. It was where Ivy and the six other Wardens would have to cast a spell that hadn't been performed since the days of the Roman Empire, with nothing standing between them and death but the Guardians who had sworn to protect them.

But, you know, no pressure.

Part of Ivy wanted to buckle under the pressure of her own fear, to just race in, metaphorical and magical guns blazing, and get this whole thing over with. Baen and his siblings had no doubt about their ability to fight through any resistance the cult might put up, but to do so would only alert the *nocturnis* and other things deeper inside the chambers to their presence. They needed the element of surprise to pull off their plan, or to at least keep Ghrem alive long enough to be rescued.

After the way was clear, the remainder of their little army would file inside, splitting themselves between the two paths to the main chamber. They guessed there would be guards gathered in the anteroom, but hopefully the Wardens' tactic of coming at them from both sides would help to foment confusion in their ranks.

Once the battle began there, the Demons and the high priests of the Order would know what was coming, and they would be prepared to fight. The bulk of the Wardens would remain to do battle in the antechamber, while the Guardians, the seven Wardens, and the most powerful of the remaining volunteers would head straight into the ritual chamber where the real war would be waged.

Ivy, Ella, Fil, Wynn, Kylie, Drum, and Rose would take up their positions and begin casting the spell to bind the Darkness. Thiago, Aldous, and a few other hand-picked Guild members would set up in a defensive formation around them and keep them safe from the priests and any other minor or moderate threats, while the Guardians would keep the Demons from killing them all.

That was the plan anyway, but Ivy had heard that battle plans rarely lasted beyond the first shot fired. She only hoped that if this one went to hell, it at least took the Demons with it.

She sat at Baen's feet and tried not to brood over what

could go wrong for what felt like hours. Finally, just when she was pushing away an image of her own blood being used to paint moustaches on all the figures in the famous mural down there, Baen shifted.

"That is the signal," he murmured, bending low so she could hear his quiet words. "Now they will move below. It will not be much longer now."

Pushing to her feet, Ivy shook her arms and legs to get the blood flowing again and tried to stay out of sight. "Not long" wasn't an exact measurement of time, and she had discovered recently that Guardians had a very different concept of time than humans, anyway. She figured it had something to do with being immortal, but what seemed to feel like a minute or two to Baen felt more like ice ages to her. She needed to be ready when he said go, but she also needed not to be spotted before it was their turn to move.

Once again, she found herself waiting, shivering in the cold night air. She estimated it must be near midnight by now, but even in this quiet neighborhood, lights still shone and an occasional pedestrian or vehicle passed by on the nearby cross streets. The clever magic users among the volunteers had thought ahead and placed a spell on this block to turn away anyone who might otherwise pass by. Nothing dangerous, they had assured Ivy, just a strong compulsion that they really, really wanted to be someplace else in a hurry. So far, it seemed to be working.

An eternity later, Baen rose from his crouch. "That is the main group heading below. Get ready."

Why he bothered with the warning, she would never understand. She barely had time to register his words before he was scooping her up and throwing them off the side of the building. She clenched her teeth so hard to contain her instinctive scream that she had to tell herself to get her butt to the dentist as soon as this was all over. If she lived through it, she was going to need some serious repair work to counteract all that grinding.

They had barely touched down before Baen was hustling her though a yawning opening in the dirt, halfway concealed by part of a collapsed wall. Ivy eased in warily and down the stone stairs into darkness.

It wasn't completely pitch-black, but a few seconds were required for her eyes to adjust enough to realize that. Once they had, she could make out a faint glow coming from two different areas at opposite sides of the entry chamber's rear wall. While this room remained unlit, those glows promised some form of lighting deeper in the warren of rooms. She swallowed a tight ball of relief. A person didn't have to be afraid of the dark to not like the idea of a demon using it to sneak up behind her.

Baen didn't let her linger in the entrance. He urged her forward, steering her toward the right-hand glow with a hand against her back.

"We go this way," he murmured in a tone lower than a whisper. Even with him bending close, she had to strain to hear him. "I will go in front. Stay close to me, and keep your guard up. If we are attacked, get down and keep yourself safe. Understand?"

Ivy gave a sharp nod, which seemed to be all he was waiting for. Baen stepped forward and eased through the doorway while more and more of their allies streamed into the entrance chamber behind them. Call her a coward, but Ivy found the backup reassuring. For now, at least.

They passed through the first short corridor, the dim glow growing brighter as they moved. It provided the perfect way for their eyes to adjust so that they weren't blinded when they stepped into the first of the two middle rooms, which was lit by a series of torches lining the walls.

When they entered, they found Ash and Drum waiting for them.

"The first group is waiting in the next chamber," Ash said, using the same low voice as Baen. Ivy found herself reading the Guardian's lips as much as listening to her words. "Once we join them, we'll all converge on the anteroom. Let the volunteers do the fighting. Our jobs are to get through to the ritual chamber and keep the Wardens safe long enough to cast their spell. Through and through, understand?"

"I'll be right behind you." Drum grinned. "Probably ducking and using your wing as a shield."

Good idea, Ivy thought. Since about four of her could fit behind either of Baen's broad wings, she figured he probably wouldn't even notice she was back there.

Baen nodded at the female Guardian. "On your count, Ash."

"Good. Let's go."

They moved through the room into the next corridor. Ivy tried not to notice the motionless bodies slumped along the walls, or the way the volunteer Wardens had begun stacking them out of the way like cordwood.

She also tried not to notice that there were a lot fewer of them than they had expected. Somehow, she didn't find that at all reassuring. Instead of convincing her that the enemy had fewer numbers than her "vision" had led her to believe, she had the sinking feeling that it only meant they hadn't yet reached the real center of resistance.

Ivy found herself clenching her fists as they walked so that she wouldn't reach out and grab onto the edge of Baen's furled wing or the back of his kiltlike garment. She refused to be a hindrance in case he needed to move swiftly to fight. And besides, she reminded herself, she had confidence that nothing on earth could get through

him to get to her. If she also counted the Wardens filing
down the hall behind her with Fil and Spar hot on their
heels, she didn't even have to watch her own back. She
was as safe as it was possible to be in the circumstances.

Really, she just had to stop thinking about those circumstances.

The groups paused again briefly in the second chamber. By now, their numbers had swelled to a good couple
of dozen bodies, which seemed to fill the confined space.
The first wave of volunteer Wardens had been waiting for
them here, and Ivy was happy to see that no one was
missing and none looked seriously injured. Whatever resistance they had encountered up to this point had been
minimal.

Once again, that failed to reassure her.

Joining the dozen first Wardens' unit, Ash, Drum, Ivy,
and Baen all pushed into the space, with Spar and Felicity edged in at the rear. No one spoke this time, all too
aware of the anteroom awaiting them at the end of one
last short hall. Instead, Ash used hand signals to remind
everyone of the formation they were to use—Wardens
first to clear the path, with the Guardians and their mates
at the rear ready to plow straight through to the ritual
chamber.

Ivy drew in a deep breath and held it for a moment.
Her stomach overflowed with butterflies, and she swore
she could feel her heart racing double time in her chest.
She pressed a hand to her sternum and forced the air back
out of her lungs.

You're a Warden now, she reminded herself, *and even
Wynn said you can throw a pretty mean sonic blast with
magic if you need to. But Baen will be there to protect
you, the volunteers will have your back, and all you have
to do is cast one little spell. You've got this.*

One spell that would hopefully save the world and change the course of the future. No big.

A series of nods responded to Ash's signals, and the group shifted as each member moved into place. At another gesture from the female Guardian, they all faced the final corridor and moved quietly forward.

The quiet didn't last long. The moment the first Warden stepped into the antechamber, all hell, Hades, Tartarus, and Niflheim broke loose. If Pandora's box had sat on a nearby shelf, Ivy felt pretty sure that would have cracked open, too.

Dozens of *nocturnis* swarmed around the chamber. As soon as the Wardens appeared, they shrieked in outrage and began throwing magic like spitballs. Ivy thought she saw more than one cast a summoning circle to conjure up some demonic assistance, but she didn't have time to look more closely. Baen, Ash, and Spar were already hustling her and the other mates through the crowd of bodies, sending anything that got too close flying into the nearest wall. Thiago had his handpicked volunteers following closely in their wake.

They ran though the entrance into the ritual chamber, hurling themselves into peril at a dead sprint. What greeted them there turned Ivy's blood to pure ice.

The seven robed priests were bad enough. With their heavy black garments and deep hoods drawn up to conceal their faces, they looked like extras from an occult horror movie. Complete with the wet stains that glistened along their sleeves. Oddly enough, though, the *nocturnis* barely registered in comparison to the other six figures gathered in the defiled sanctuary.

They used to be people, Ivy thought. She guessed. What else could they be? They wore human shapes and human faces and human bodies, wore them like clothing.

Humanity hung off of them like cheap, off-the-rack suits that no one had bothered to tailor. Not even along the hems and cuffs. The bodies of people, of human beings, made ill-fitting costumes on whatever lay beneath.

Ivy prayed—quickly, silently, and fervently—that she never had to see the true nature of that evil. She had enough material already to fuel her nightmares for the rest of her life, and the excitement had barely begun.

There was a moment of brittle silence. Shock hadn't caused it. No one in the room looked surprised to see anyone else. No, this had more to do with the way two groups of predators faced off before a fight to the death, assessing each other's strengths and weaknesses, looking for the tender, unarmored vulnerability that would bring down a foe with one swift strike.

Please God and the Light, let the good guys be the ones to make that strike.

A battle cry shook the walls and ceilings of stone, and the Guardians surged forward like the tidal bore of an oncoming tsunami. The inhuman figures leaped to meet them, and the battle for humanity commenced in the underground heart of the Wardens' Guild.

"Quickly!" Thiago pushed the groups of mates and Wardens toward a clear space in front of the infamous mural. The curved walls of the alcove in which it had been painted formed the guide for part of a large circle. "Get to your places! We must hurry!"

Ivy darted to the wall, planting herself at the center of the huge artwork, not daring to waste a moment to examine it. She had the impression of rich color and brightness that almost glowed before she turned her back to it to face the rest of the chamber.

The other Wardens filed in around the space, arranging themselves according to Thiago's instructions. Each mate stood at a designated point like seven spokes in a wheel, but in reality they were forming the seven points of a star, a septagram. The rest of the group staggered themselves outside the star to form a magic circle of protection while the spell was cast.

They had reviewed this a dozen times in preparation for this moment, but their practice sessions hadn't included what would happen when Rose caught sight of the raised stone table at the other end of the room. No one could have prepared the woman for the sight of the bloody form bound to its surface.

"Ghrem!" Rose shrieked and flung herself forward. She would have immediately raced to his side, uncaring of the spell, the Demons, or anything else on the face of the earth, but Thiago stepped into her path and stopped her.

It took three of them. Three Wardens grabbed hold of the desperate Frenchwoman and restrained her while she fought like an enraged lioness to go to her mate's side.

"Rose, stop!" Thiago shouted at her, shaking her roughly to get her attention. "Rose! The others will get to Ghrem, I promise, but you have another duty. You have to cast this spell. If you do not, we all die, Ghrem included. The *world* will die, Rose, and all your mate's valor will have been in vain. *Is that what you want?*"

Ivy's heart ached as she watched the other woman go from fighting dervish to sobbing heap the moment the words penetrated her shell of fear and desperation. Ivy imagined herself in Rose's place, and knew she would have behaved no differently. If faced with the choice of saving the world or saving Baen, she would have hesitated, because what use was the world to her now without her mate? Only the knowledge of what Baen himself would have urged her to do could have forced Ivy to remember her responsibilities. It was the only thing that could sway Rose.

Unfortunately, the delay gave the *nocturni* priests an opportunity to strike. Two of them split off from the others and rushed the group of Wardens, flinging blasts of sickly, rust-colored magic at their targets. Ivy noticed right away that the women were the ones the priests focused on, and she moved instinctively to defend herself.

Stretching her arms out in front of her, she pressed her palms forward and breathed the words Wynn had taught her. *"Tontru alradi!"*

A wave of concussive force shot outward and blasted the approaching figures off their feet. It also knocked two unsuspecting Wardens into the wall of the chamber. The witch had been right—Ivy really needed to work on her focus.

Thiago shoved Rose back into her place with a squeeze of encouragement and then raced to urge the fallen Wardens back on their feet. "Hurry!"

Ivy felt adrenaline flooding into her veins, the urgency of the moment almost overwhelming her ability to concentrate. She deliberately kept her eyes off Baen and the other Guardians locked in furious battle with the human-hosted demons, because she knew that if she watched, her fear for her mate would make doing her job impossible, the same way it had threatened to derail Rose.

Instead, she watched Aldous sneaking around the edge of the room toward the altar table to free Ghrem. The small, studious man had prepared for his task by cramming information related to methods that could be used to imprison a Guardian, so if anyone had a chance to free the bound behemoth, it was Aldous. Ivy just prayed he could manage it before the priests spotted him.

She glanced in their direction and found herself shocked to see them paying no apparent attention to the melee taking place just a few feet away. Nor did they seem concerned with what the Wardens had gathered before the mural to do. In fact, they looked like they were beginning another one of their foul chants, their hands pressed together and their focus turned toward the empty space at the center of their group.

Realization hit her like a sledgehammer to the forebrain. She knew exactly what was going on over there, and it was really, really, *so. Not. Good.*

"They're completing their summoning!" she cried, uncaring whether or not she interrupted the circle of Wardens around her as they constructed a magical barrier against further attack. "They must be using the energy of our attack and the battle for fuel. They're trying to free number Seven!"

Thiago spun toward the group, then turned back to their circle, his face grim. "Then we'll just have to work faster than they do. Get ready."

Right, because it was supereasy to concentrate on casting an unfamiliar magic spell while your mate was fighting Demons, war was waging in the background, and the forces of Darkness were attempting to free the creature that would cause the end of the world faster than you could save it. Sure, no problem at all.

A horrible shriek made Ivy jump. Her gaze flew toward the writhing, clashing maelstrom of battle between the Guardians and Demons in time to see Knox's double-bladed weapon slice the head off an unfortunate creature that had probably once been a lawyer, or a banker, or some unsuspecting mid-level executive. The fleshy skull fell to the floor, cracking against the stone like a ripe melon just before the body crumpled after it.

Unfortunately, the death of its human host meant little more than inconvenience to the Demon inside it. It poured out of the neck stump like a stream of black tar before

taking shape from the corrupt ooze. It slithered and shim-
mied and bent itself into unnatural shapes and angles
before settling into a form that burned itself into Ivy's
retinas.

Short and squat, it achieved its appearance not by lacking height, but by being so huge that its wideness gave the
appearance of stunted stature. Its upper limbs hung all
out of proportion to the rest of it, dragging on the ground
behind it so that its claws pointed up into the air like the
spikes of an iron fence. Its head, long and narrow like a
bleached cow skull dipped in crude oil, looked entirely
out of place perched atop its broad shoulders with no hint
of a neck in evidence. Probably to better support the
weight of the enormous ram's horns that curled alongside
the spaces where a human's ears would have been.

Ivy didn't see any ears, but then she didn't look too
closely. Just glimpsing the Demon's true shape made her
stomach lurch and her throat close and panic threaten to
overwhelm her. Tearing her gaze away, she reminded
herself what the others had told her. The fear didn't come
from her; it was generated by the Demon itself, a powerful magic it used to intimidate and paralyze its foes. If
she refused to give in to it, its power would eventually
weaken.

She hoped it weakened fast.

All at once, the Wardens' circle snapped into place
with a force and presence that Ivy could feel. It felt like
a giant bubble had just enveloped her and the other
Guardians' mates, like a wall of cotton muffling the impact of the sights and sounds outside the magical enclo-
sure. The sensation reminded her of the way it felt after
an airplane took off, when her ears finally popped as the
altitude leveled off, only in reverse. Instead of sounds becoming clearer, they had been dampened, and she and
the six people around her were left simultaneously pro-

tected and isolated, cut off from the chaos that roiled around them.

"Well, what do you say, guys?" Kylie piped up, bouncing on her toes. "Wanna save the world?"

The hacker's irrepressible confidence and boundless energy radiated off her in waves even larger than usual, and Ivy noted with surprise that it seemed to bounce off the interior of the circle. It ricocheted around them, gradually amping up the energy of the circle and filling the space with a commodity they could all use a lot more of—hope.

Squaring her shoulders, Ivy met the brunette's sparkling gaze and nodded decisively. "Yeah, that sounds like a plan. You guys ready?"

Agreement flowed around the space.

"Let's do it."

"We got this."

"Maidens to the rescue?"

Drum grumbled. "I'm really beginning to hate that legend, you understand."

The women laughed.

"Hey," Fil said, "I'm not all that happy with the inherent misogyny of the label either, and I've learned to live with it."

"You have the advantage of breasts."

The platinum-blonde glanced down at her chest. "You may have a point."

Laughter buoyed their spirits and strengthened Ivy's resolve. Judging by the way the others adjusted their posture and drew back their shoulders, she guessed it had affected them the same way.

Rose remained quiet and drawn, but even she lifted her chin as she raised a hand and pointed her palm toward Ella, who stood at the five o'clock position relative to the first Warden. "Are we ready, *mes amis*?"

The resounding "yes" almost made her smile.

Speaking the first words of the ancient spell, Rose directed a stream of pure, pale energy from her palm to Ella's. "By the Light and the power of Life and Birth, I bind the Darkness from human earth."

Chapter Twenty-three

Baen felt the change in the atmosphere immediately, and knew the Wardens had begun their casting. Now, it was up to him and his brothers to contain the Demons within this chamber until the ancient spell bound them once more to their remote prisons.

Easier said than done.

Guardians had been created to defend the world from the Seven, but a very long time had passed since the Demons had been set free on earth. They seemed determined to enjoy their moment, fighting like the cornered animals they were to regain access to the billions of human souls on which they could feed.

It didn't help that not even a Guardian's summoned weapon could kill one. Baen could hack and slash and stab and spear, his bardiche singing through the air and striking true with every attack, but the creatures made of Darkness could not be slain. Like the Light itself, Darkness was part of the fabric of the universe and could never be either created or destroyed. It could only be contained, which was why his mate and her comrades had to succeed with the spell they were attempting to cast.

While the Guardians could not kill the Demons, the

human hosts those creatures occupied possessed no such claims on immortality. The warriors cleaved through those easily, leaving the empty husks to fall to the chamber floor. Frankly, it was a mercy to the poor bastards. Their souls had long since been consumed by the evil possessing them, so there was no humanity left to mourn. Better to free the bodies from the indignity of what the Demons had made them do, and allow the memory of the people they had been to fill the hearts of those who had known them.

As each disguise fell away, the true shapes of the Demons of Darkness emerged to face off against the Guardians. Hothgunal emerged first, forming from the black, putrid slime that flowed from the body Knox beheaded. Then Uhlthor and Shaab-na, the one a vision of a devil, part animal and part humanoid, and the other an insectlike nightmare with chitinous armor and multilensed eyes that glowed with the dirty coals of corruption.

Dohlzhrek burst forth from the body Ash felled, splitting it like an overripe fruit and launching itself toward the ceiling with an earsplitting shriek. The Unquiet beat wings like rags stitched across bony frames, its vulturelike appearance only matched by the smell of decayed flesh that clung to it in a foul cloud of stench. Then Nazgahchuhl slithered forth, its giant, serpentine form hissing across the stones every time it moved.

When the last body fell and Tloth emerged like a black-lacquered collection of blades bound to a central core of armored sentience, Baen shifted his grip on his bardiche and bared his fangs. These sideshow monsters would not be allowed to unite under his watch, and he would prove it.

He roared out a challenge and unfurled his wings, beating the air with one heavy stroke, enough to launch him into the path of the hovering Dohlzhrek. The shaft of his weapon swung hard, the blade biting into the vulture's leg and raising its shriek another decibel. The sound of pain and rage only fueled Baen's battle frenzy, and he lashed out again. And again.

The Demon struck back, darting forward to swipe at the Guardian with the serrated edge of its wicked beak. As he spun out of the way, Baen's gaze swept over the hooded figures of the Order priests, and it didn't take more than that brief glimpse to understand what they were up to.

"The priests!" he shouted to alert his brethren. "They complete the summoning."

"But Ghrem!" Kees bellowed back, just in time for them to watch the final Demon-blooded chain fall away from their final brother's limbs.

Baen held his breath. The Guardian had lain so still beneath those chains that he feared they might have arrived too late to save him. The fact that the priests had moved to complete the summoning ritual without returning to the altar on which he lay only added to that worry.

But now, as the last binding withdrew, it was as if a spell had been lifted, and Baen supposed that it had. Ghrem's eyes flew open and the huge warrior leaped to his feet atop the stone surface. Throwing back his head, he let loose a battle cry that reverberated through every inch of the Guild's underground stronghold, and then he launched himself into the fray.

He could have been Spar's dark twin with black-feathered wings and features like a fallen angel. He stood tall with lean, powerful muscles and claws not just on his fingertips, but emerging like hidden blades from his wrists as well. He used them like a set of deadly stilettos, calling no other weapon to his hand. Ghrem fought as one nearly vanquished but now reinvigorated by the taste of freedom.

The priests' chanting grew louder, the frenzy of their magic raising their voices and increasing the speed of their rhythm until the hideous words of their Dark language ran together in an endless screeching cacophony. The urgency of their summoning was obvious, and as the pressure in the room began to build, Baen felt the first taste of fear that it might succeed. That Belgrethnakkar might be freed and the Darkness united over them all.

From across the room, a blindingly bright blue-white light began to fill the space, fighting with the oppressive energy raised by the Order to claim the space in the ritual chamber. Even as he turned to see, Baen witnessed the passing of power between Drum and his Ivy, the stream of energy hitting her outstretched palm and making her gasp at the impact.

"We seal this world from evil's grasp, its power confined, its Dark outcast."

His mate took in the energy, her red head tipped back as she adjusted to the power filling her, and a second later she refocused. Her chin came down, her spine straightened, and she looked back at the Wardens surrounding her, her gray eyes literally glowing with the Light inside her.

"Baen!"

The warning shout from Dag made him duck just in time to avoid one of Tloth's blades in his heart. Cursing himself for becoming distracted, he parried the next blow and hooked the enemy's spear with his bardiche, tearing it away and throwing it aside. The Demon howled as if a limb had been removed, which it had, managing to make the sound in the absence of anything resembling vocal chords, or even a mouth.

"Guardians!"

The next shout came from a human, from Aldous, who cowered behind the now empty altar, his arms covering his head as he tried to make himself as small as possible. And Baen could see why.

In the center of the gathered *nocturni* priests, the fabric of reality had begun to thin, the precursor to a tear between the planes. Once the rift opened, the last of the Seven would be able to step through, and the Darkness would be united again.

They had to stop it.

Baen rushed the Demon standing between him and the Order's mages, sending the creature flying toward one of his brothers. Trusting the other Guardian to cover his back, he launched himself toward the priests.

BAEN! NO!

Ivy's voice yanked him to a stop, shocking him for more than one reason. First, because it cut through the rage and urgency he felt to stop the priests before they could unleash the Cursed One, the final component of the Darkness; and second, because at the same time he heard it, his mate was speaking other words entirely.

Startled, he glanced her way to be certain. She met his gaze, her own eyes pleading with him to listen to her even as she performed her part of the complex spell the Wardens were casting. She had absorbed the energy sent to her by Drum, who had taken it from Kylie, who had received it in her turn after Wynn and Fil and Ella. The magic had passed through each Warden, amplifying as they all added their own power to the mix. And now Ivy focused and sent the stream on back to Rose, completing the circuit and closing the form of the seven-pointed star.

"By the Law of Light, bound art thee!"

Confused and desperate, Baen turned back toward the priests. He didn't know what Ivy was trying to tell him, but he couldn't allow the last Demon to escape from its prison. That was what they had all been fighting against this whole time. It was what this war was all about. He had to stop it, and hopefully they would all live long enough for Ivy to explain to him what that pleading glance had meant.

"Baen! Guardian, stop!" Thiago leaped in front of him and tried to shove him aside like an American football tackle. "You have to let it come! The Seventh must be released!"

The words nearly sent Baen reeling, hitting him harder than the puny human's physical assault. He could see a pinprick disruption in the air where reality had stretched thin, and he knew he had only seconds left to stop Belgrethnakkar from stepping into the human world.

"Traitor!" he snarled, attempting to thrust the Spaniard aside. "Get out of my way!"

But Thiago clung like a limpet, a barnacle on the Guardian's tree-trunk leg. "No! You don't understand, but I was afraid of this. The spell won't work unless they're all on the same plane. If the Seventh does not come through now, the other six cannot be banished! I swear, it is truth. *¡Para la Luz, lo juro!*"

Baen, please.

And it wasn't the begging Thiago who made Baen hesitate. It was the voice of his mate whispering again inside his head.

That hesitation was all it took. The fabric of reality tore with a sharp hiss and a shape with no recognizable form oozed through onto the mortal plane.

It was not meant for human eyes to see, nor the human mind to understand. Even a Guardian could look on it and not comprehend its true contaminating pestilence. It writhed like a ball of snakes, and roiled like thick, sentient fog. It moved with odd jerking motions, like a horror-film zombie, and left behind it a putrid blight that sizzled against the stone floor like acid. It was black and sickly green, like a gangrenous wound, and rusty brown like old, dried blood.

It was made of Darkness, and where it traveled, Darkness followed.

Around him, the other Demons shrieked and howled with triumph. They abandoned their battle against the Guardians and tried to converge on the Cursed form of Belgrethnakkar, but the Guardians refused to let them off so easily. They renewed their attacks, desperate to stave off the moment when all Seven pieces of the Darkness would unite and the world itself would fall into night.

Of course, that would only happen if the Wardens allowed it.

"Bound! Banished! Reviled! Dispelled! Banned from this plane and forever compelled!"

Rose shouted the words, her voice rising above all the chaos of the Demons and the commotion of battle, echoing off the ceiling and walls of the underground chamber. The power she received from Ivy lit her up like a beacon and the completed star flared with a magical light so bright, that Baen had to look away from the blinding glow.

"As we have willed, so mote it be!"

In unison, each of the seven mated Wardens stomped a foot down on the stone floor beneath them and reality cracked again, but this time, it cracked in seven distinct places, one above each of the Seven Demons of the Darkness. The cracks exploded with pure white lights brighter than a thousand stars. Baen flung his arm across his eyes to shield them, but he could hear a noise like an eagle's cry at the volume of a jet engine for an instant.

Then.

Silence.

Ivy passed out.

It wasn't very heroic, or even dignified, but apparently that was what happened when she performed a world-saving spell on approximately two hours of sleep and an empty stomach. She fainted. So, sue her.

She wasn't out long; at least, she didn't think she was. She came to lying on the stone floor of the Guild's underground ritual chamber with her hair tangled and sweaty, her eyes burning and stinging, and her cheek tingling. That last bit, though, was easily explained. It was where a familiar hand kept lightly patting her in an attempt to wake her up.

Well, to Baen, it was probably patting. To Ivy, it felt like a series of tiny, stinging slaps.

"Ow," she complained, her voice a hoarse rasp. "I call this mate abuse."

"Ivy?"

He sounded half panicked, so she summoned the energy to force her eyes open and peer up at him. Her poor Guardian had gone pale as marble, his normally deep gray skin bleached by worry.

"Are you all right?" he demanded, running his hands all over her, as if checking for broken bones or . . . she didn't even know. Bullet holes? What exactly did he think had just happened?

"I will be once you stop prodding me." She tried to push herself into a sitting position, wincing when every single muscle in her body protested. Loudly. Who knew spell casting could provide the kind of full-body workout that called for a hot tub and a massage after?

He helped her into the new position, but adjusted it by swinging her up into his lap. "You terrified me, *amare*. I turned to find you after the binding, and you were lying on the floor in a heap. I thought you were hurt."

"I'm fine," she reassured him, trying to peer over his shoulder to look around the room. She saw no more disgusting inhuman creatures lurking in the shadows, only Guardians and Wardens and enough blood and carnage to make her wrinkle her nose in distaste. "Does this mean the spell worked?"

Baen grunted. "It worked, but it knocked half of you unconscious and made the other half vomit as if they'd eaten bad shellfish."

Ivy winced. "Yeah, I'd rather not have to do that again, if it's all the same to you."

"You will not have to."

The deep voice came from a lot farther above her head than Baen's familiar rumble. Ivy looked up and up and finally craned her neck to get a glimpse of the one Guardian she had not met. "Huh, you must be Ghrem, right?"

The huge warrior smiled. He had beautiful chiseled features, like some kind of male model. You know, the kind made out of stone and with wings and fangs and stuff. At his side, Rose leaned against him, looking tiny and exhausted and fragile. She wore a smile broad enough to light half of Paris.

"You are correct, Ivy," Ghrem said. "And I owe you thanks for what you helped my Rose do here tonight. You and the other Wardens saved an enormous number of lives—mine, your own, and the rest of the world's among them."

"Oh, it was nothing." Ivy tried waving away his words and nearly smacked herself in the face. She snorted. "Sorry, I guess I'm a little punch-drunk."

"Un petit peu." Rose smirked.

"No apologies. You wielded a great deal of power tonight. It will have drained you. You must rest and replenish your strength. Thiago and Aldous are arranging to transport everyone back to the manor house. They should have vehicles here shortly."

Baen shook his head. "I can fly us there easily."

Ivy thumped him. "I could have died tonight, and now you're threatening to kill me? How is that right?"

Ghrem chuckled. "I take it your little mate does not like to fly, brother?"

"Flying is fine," Ivy protested. "It's why God invented airplanes. Aerial kidnapping without safety equipment conforming to FAA regulations is another thing entirely."

"Fine." Baen huffed. "You had a difficult night. We will ride in the van."

"Thank you." Ivy smiled and brushed her lips over his cheek. "I did have a difficult night. I suppose I should say it was nothing, but like I said before, that was one spell I don't want to have to repeat."

"You will never have to," Ghrem assured her. "I meant that. Thiago tells us that the binding on the Demons can be kept intact provided a smaller, much smaller, spell is cast once each decade to shore up the defenses. If the Guild had performed the proper maintenance over the past centuries, the experiences we have all shared would never have happened."

"See? This is why I insist on maintaining all my own equipment." Kylie's voice carried through the room ahead of her. She strolled toward them with her protective Guardian hovering over her. "Never trust someone else to do a job when you know you should be doing it yourself. It only leads to grief."

"Or an uncomfortable brush with Armageddon," Wynn added.

She and Knox had followed, and Ivy could see the other Guardians and their mates gathering around the spot where Baen still sat on the floor, cradling her in his lap. Somehow, having that many powerful beings staring down at her made her a little uncomfortable. Especially now that she'd seen firsthand what they all could do when motivated.

She scrambled to her feet but allowed herself to lean against her mate when he joined her. Her gaze flitted around the lopsided circle of Guardians and Wardens. "So, I guess we kinda saved the world, huh? What do you suppose we do for an encore?"

Chuckles greeted her, but Kylie was the only one who took the question seriously. "I don't know about the rest of you, but I could really go for tacos. What do you say, Rose? Do you have any decent Mexican places in Paris?"

The woman blinked in surprise. "Er, I am not certain. Perhaps you would settle for something else?"

"No snails," the hacker warned.

"*Pas du tout.* Not at this hour. I was thinking . . . pizza? We can bring some back to the manor with us and save everyone from having to cook."

Kylie pursed her lips and nodded. "I could do pizza. With champagne. After all, when in France, right?"

Baen smiled. "I would say that we definitely have something to celebrate. Wouldn't you?" He leaned down to brush a kiss across his mate's lips.

Ivy quirked a brow. "Good triumphs over evil?"

The Guardian glanced around them. Ivy followed his gaze, realizing what he was really seeing—a group of warriors and humans who had begun as strangers and now become friends.

No, more than that. Family.

Seven matched pairs, male to female, Guardian to Warden, heart to heart. Stone figures brought to life, then given a free future by the mates who loved them. Now that she considered it, Ivy figured that made for a pretty good story.

"Good triumphed," Baen agreed, smiling at their

family before turning back to meet Ivy's smiling gaze. "But more importantly, love conquered all."

Her smile turned into a grin, and she stretched up into his kiss.

"Oh, yeah," she murmured against her mate's lips. "I'll drink to that."

Read on for an excerpt from
Christine Warren's next book

BABY, I'M HOWLING FOR YOU

Coming soon from St. Martin's Paperbacks

"Hey, wait a second!"

Renny had bitten her tongue through the entire phone conversation, but now she wanted answers. How was it possible that she had collapsed onto the property of a man who knew her stalker? Talk about "of all the gin joints." The world couldn't possibly be that small, could it?

Mick ignored her, and she frowned. She scrambled from the SUV, reached out, and grabbed his arm before he could walk away. "Mick, wait—"

She didn't get out another word.

The moment her hand touched his skin, he went off like a nuclear warhead. At least, she felt as if she'd been hit by one. The wolf reversed their grips, seizing her by the wrist she'd held out to him and jerking her toward him. She crashed into his body and felt the impact like his muscles had turned to concrete. He was hard all over.

All over.

His mouth slammed down on hers, all heat and hunger and barely controlled fury. She wasn't entirely sure what he was mad at, whether it was she or Geoffrey who had earned his wrath, but when the taste of him sank into her, she no longer cared.

Coffee and pine and thick, powerful musk combined on her tongue. The flavor was so rich, it made her head spin. Seriously. If he hadn't had her wrapped up against him by then, she would have toppled over. Her legs went weak and threatened to buckle, and still he kissed her like he wanted to devour her whole.

For the first few seconds, shock kept her frozen. She couldn't do anything but let him kiss her. Not that she suffered from it, of course. In the back of her mind, her wolf had thrown back its head, howled for joy, and promptly thrown itself over to wriggle around on its back like a golden retriever begging for belly rubs. Their mate was kissing them!

Then the initial surprise wore off, and Renny did the only thing she possibly could. She grabbed on and kissed him back with every ounce of passion in her soul. If this turned out to be a momentary aberration, and he went back to trying to ignore her existence the way he had the night before, she intended to enjoy every single toe-curling second of it while it lasted.

Judging by the way her belly clenched, her insides melted, and her pussy dampened, her body was totally on board. As far as it was concerned, she could just lie down on the asphalt and let her mate have her. Road rash and passing vehicles be damned. This was the kiss she'd been waiting for all her life.

If any last thread of doubt had existed in her about whether Mick was really her mate, the kiss burned it up like the fuse on a stick of dynamite. He feasted on her mouth, his tongue mating with hers like he wanted to taste every inch of her from the inside out. The feeling was mutual. She felt herself drowning in the essence of him, and her body began to ache with the need to feel him inside her, above her, behind her, touching her everywhere, in every way, all at once.

Fuck reality. She would defy the laws of physics if she had to, but Renny needed him. Now.

And then he yanked himself away from her as violently as he'd pulled her to him. One minute, she was drowning in pleasure, and the next she was just drowning. Or at least, that's what it felt like, because at some point during that kiss, she had forgotten how to breathe.

She stood there, mouth open, lungs straining, and Mick just clenched his jaw and turned away. "Let's go."

Go?

A voice inside Renny's head laughed a little. No, scratch that. It giggled a bit hysterically. She couldn't feel her arms or legs, couldn't get oxygen to her brain, and he wanted her to master the art of independent locomotion? Was he high?

He was not, she realized, as sanity slowly began to leak back into her body. Her lungs expanded in a gasp, and she staggered for a second before she could catch herself. She'd been the one who'd gotten high, and it turned out that the alpha wolf was her drug of choice.